Critics STARK COUNTY
LIBRARY PROGRAM

"A delici...
Regency ...

Because of you

"Cathy Maxwell brings both a luscious sense of humor and a special poignancy to her romances that allow readers to laugh and cry simultaneously."

—*Romantic Times*

Falling in Love Again

"Cathy Maxwell has a flair for writing charming, witty, funny and sexy Regency romances that delight the mind and fill the heart with joy."

—*Romantic Times*

D0035599

When Dreams Come True

"Reaffirming all the sheer pleasure and joy that is part of love, as well as the magic that is an integral part of romance, Cathy Maxwell lifts readers' spirits and gifts them with a radiant read."

—*Romantic Times*

More Praise for Cathy Maxwell

"An author who understands the human heart and whose stories touch our souls."

—*Romantic Times*

"She keeps getting better and better."

—*Affaire de Coeur*

Applause for
LIZ CARLYLE

"Sensual and spellbinding . . . Liz Carlyle weaves passion and intrigue with a master's touch."

—Karen Robards, bestselling author of *To Trust a Stranger*

"A treat! Romance fans will want to read this one and remember Liz Carlyle's name!"
—Linda Howard, bestselling author of *Open Season*

"Carlyle delivers great suspense and several sensual love scenes."
—*Publishers Weekly*

Beauty Like the Night

"Enthralling . . . Liz Carlyle captures the essence of the era and the passion of lost love found."
—*Romantic Times*

My False Heart

"Watch this new star rise on the horizon."
—*Romantic Times*

Books by Liz Carlyle

A Woman of Virtue
Beauty Like the Night
A Woman Scorned
My False Heart
Tea for Two: Hunting Season

CATHY MAXWELL

Tea for Two

Two novellas

LIZ CARLYLE

POCKET STAR BOOKS

NEW YORK   LONDON   TORONTO   SYDNEY   SINGAPORE

This book is a work of fiction. Names, characters, places and incidents are products of the authors' imagination or are used fictitiously. Any resemblance to actual events or locales or persons, living or dead, is entirely coincidental.

An *Original* Publication of POCKET BOOKS

A Pocket Star Book published by
POCKET BOOKS, a division of Simon & Schuster, Inc.
1230 Avenue of the Americas, New York, NY 10020

In a Moonlit Garden copyright © 2002 by Catherine Maxwell
Hunting Season copyright © 2002 by S. T. Woodhouse

ISBN: 0-7434-4581-3

First Pocket Books printing May 2002

10 9 8 7 6 5 4 3 2 1

POCKET STAR BOOKS and colophon are registered trademarks of Simon & Schuster, Inc.

For information regarding special discounts for bulk purchases, please contact Simon & Schuster Special Sales at 1-800-456-6798 or business@simonandschuster.com

Front cover illustration by Lisa Litwack

Printed in the U.S.A.

Contents

In a Moonlit Garden

❧❧

Cathy Maxwell

for Vern and Aavon Powers

Chapter One

Our hero is issued a challenge for Love

Colonel Michael Sanson didn't understand women.

He certainly didn't understand himself when it came to them . . . or rather to one in particular—Ivy.

She was his Ideal. His Helen of Troy. His Cleopatra. His damn, bloody Delilah.

Five years ago, when she had been fresh from the schoolroom and he just turned one and twenty, they'd fallen in love. Of course, as the fifth son of an earl, he'd had little to offer her—a point her father, Sir William Lewin, had made clear to him. Michael hadn't been afraid to prove his mettle. He'd purchased his colors in the military and had distinguished himself on the front lines of Barrosa and Vittoria. There'd been hardships but he'd been determined. While other officers had held back, he'd charged forward and had been promoted and honored for his valor.

Now, he had returned, a war hero and a man of substance—and he'd not once had a private moment alone with Ivy.

She hadn't had time. Instead of the shy ingenue he'd left behind, she was now considered the Incomparable, the Toast of the Season. Men lined up at her door, wealthy, titled men who could offer her everything in the world.

Worse, Michael wasn't certain how well she remembered the fervent promises of love they had once shared. She seemed completely different from the woman he had left behind. She knew how to keep him coyly at bay while offering enough of a hint of the girl he'd fallen in love with to keep him dancing to her tune.

However, his patience was growing short and he understood tactical strategy.

He'd forced himself to ignore her at Lady Radcliff's rout. He'd wondered if she'd noticed he wasn't among the crowd of her many admirers. She had. The next day, he received a request from her for a private audience and, congratulating himself, he was on her doorstep in a trice dressed in his most dashing uniform of deep blue cloth and gold braid.

The butler escorted him into the formal sitting room where Ivy waited, looking more beautiful than any woman on earth had a right to. Blond, elegant, poised. She rose at his entrance. The air in the room was filled with the lily fragrance of her perfume, and he felt a moment of triumph.

"You are angry with me," she said. Was it his imagination or did she appear as if she'd been crying?

Immediately, Michael was at her side. She was willowy tall with china blue eyes and a straight, aristocratic nose. "I'm not angry," he said. "But I fear your interest may have waned."

She shook her head in surprise. "Oh, no, not ever."

Her vow was music to his ears. He took her hand. "Truly, Ivy? Do you still love me?"

She smiled, a benevolent goddess able to bestow on him his most cherished wish. "I have never forgotten you." She lowered her eyes, her dark lashes sweeping down upon her cheeks, the expression both demure and seductive. "Do you not love me . . . just a little?"

He stepped closer. "I worship you."

She hedged away a step. "But how would I know? Last night at Lady Radcliff's party you barely spoke to me."

Michael wanted to pull her into his arms and demonstrate his passion with a kiss, and yet he held back. She'd always been reserved. "I would talk to your father this minute if you would say the word."

"Say *what* word?" Sir William's voice boomed from the doorway of the room. Ivy hurried to her father's side.

"Nothing—" she started, but Michael decided to seize the moment.

"I wish to ask for your daughter's hand in marriage," he said.

Sir William frowned and closed the door to the room. Michael catered to him because he was Ivy's father and for no other reason. The man fancied himself a radical and a scientist and always had schemes for new inventions on his mind that he hoped would make him rich. Once, he was very successful in devising an oar lock for the navy and earned a knighthood for his brilliance—but he'd not had a great idea since. He also had an irritating habit of stroking his chin as if he sported a beard. The gesture was usually a sign he was formulating some sort of scheme. He stroked his chin now as he repeated, "You wish to marry her, you say?"

Michael did not hesitate to answer. "It is my one desire."

Ivy colored prettily, but did not speak. Her father strolled into the room where Michael stood and walked around him, his beady eyes assessing. Michael straightened his shoulders and met the man's gaze. Sir William stopped. "How much do you want her?" he asked, his voice low.

Michael frowned at such an indelicate discussion in front of Ivy. "If you are asking about a dowry, I'm making no demands. I can support her in fine fashion. I've done very well for myself under Wellington."

Sir William laughed softly. "I am aware that you have done well for yourself, Colonel, and that you have made several wise investments. There is much about you to be admired. However, what I want to know is what would you be willing to do for the honor of my daughter's hand?"

The odd phrasing of his question brought up Michael's guard. "I'm not certain I understand your meaning, sir. If you are questioning my devotion, let me assure you I remain as steadfast in my commitment to Ivy as I was before I left for the war."

"Ah, yes, commitment," Sir William echoed with a funny little hum in his voice. He paused and looked to his daughter. "My dear, would you please ask Norell to send in some refreshments for our guest and give us a moment alone."

"Yes, Papa," Ivy replied, her relief apparent at being given a reprieve from the conversation. She dutifully hurried from the room, shutting the door behind her.

Michael sensed there was something odd going on. Nor did he trust Sir William's smile. "What do you want?"

Sir William laughed. "I admire directness, Colonel. Please sit down."

"Perhaps you should tell me what you wish first."

"A favor—nothing more, nothing less. And in the end, if all goes well, I may grant your request for my daughter's hand."

Michael sat.

Taking the chair next to his, Sir William said good-naturedly, "Don't appear so uneasy, sir. I want you to marry my daughter."

"But . . . ?" he prodded.

Sir William gave a worried sigh and dropped his gaze to his hands in his lap. "But I have a small problem I was hoping you could resolve for me. You see, I have been robbed and I need to have my goods returned to me."

"If you've been robbed, call the magistrate."

Sir William shook his head. "The case is too delicate for a public hearing."

"Then hire a Bow Street Runner."

Sir William rested his elbow on the chair arm and stroked his chin for a moment before saying, "I may have made a mistake. I'd thought you wished to marry my daughter and could help me, you know, as a family member would. Ah, well, I can see I may have made an error in judgment."

He started to rise. Michael leaned forward. "What do you want me to do?"

"Not very much," Sir William said, sitting back down. "I have been on the verge of an important discovery utilizing the properties of a substance called rubber."

"The stuff of a child's ball?"

"The same. However, it could have vast and important uses. My idea was to use it to make fabric waterproof. Imagine the implications. But I am in danger of having all my careful work stolen from me. I need someone resourceful like yourself to fetch a copy of the formula from the pirates who would claim my work as theirs. It will call for a bit of subterfuge."

Michael lifted an eyebrow. "Subterfuge?"

"A disguise. The Royal Society is a very touchy group. I would not want my name connected with the formula's disappearance. I believe you can understand my actions could be misconstrued by those eager to discredit me."

Something was not right. Michael was not surprised Sir William was puffed up over his own consequence. Every ounce of common sense Michael possessed warned him to get up and leave.

As if seeing the direction of Michael's thoughts, Sir William said, "A young viscount has been calling on Ivy. Good man. Excellent background, five thousand a year. You may know him, Thorpeton? My daughter could do no better."

"But she promised herself to me," Michael said.

"Years ago, Colonel. And what is the promise of a young girl without her father's consent?" he asked rhetorically. "Absence does not always make the heart grow fonder. My daughter is as practical as she is vain. She would like to be a viscountess. However, a word from me could make the difference."

Michael drew back. "Am I being blackmailed?"

"Blackmail? No. Consider this more a quest, like Jason in search of the Golden Fleece."

"Golden Fleece?"

Sir William leaned forward. "Make no mistake about this, Colonel, the formula could be worth a fortune . . . for both of us."

At that moment, there was a light knock at the door and Ivy entered without waiting for a summons. Michael came to his feet. She closed the door and looked to her father. "Will Michael help us, Papa?"

"He has not said."

Her gaze flew to Michael and he sensed for the first time that she really saw him since he'd returned from the Continent. "You must help us. There is no one else we can ask."

She was so beautiful. He could not bear the thought of her going to another man. Not after he had sacrificed for her over all these years. He'd grown up in a large, gregarious but ambitious family where, as the youngest, he was often an afterthought. Ivy's attention had made him feel special and given his life purpose.

"If I do as you ask," he said carefully, his eyes on Ivy but his words directed to her father, "will you consent to our marriage?"

"Absolutely," Sir William replied. "With a healthy dowry and my blessings. Why, you could be married within the fortnight if you are quick about the matter. I'd even purchase the special license."

Ivy looked away, becoming color staining her cheeks. She was as soft and submissive as a houri. He had the urge to protect her, even as he suspected he was being manipulated.

"What do you want me to do?" he asked.

Sir William smiled. "I need you to go to Wye, a small village on the river Avon. Geoffrey Kenyon lives there, an inferior scientist who makes his living off the backs of other people's work. He has a formula that I suspect is mine."

Michael tore his gaze away from Ivy. "How did he get the formula in the first place?"

His expression bitter, Sir William said, "Through a mutual friend, one whom I trusted. He sent it to Kenyon claiming my work as his own and refuses to discuss the matter with me. His credit is better with the Royal Society and he knows it would be his word against mine."

"Why don't you just write the formula down again?"

Sir William threw his hands up. "Does every housewife remember her recipe for cake? I wrote it down, but misplaced the scrap of paper. I'd have to start over again."

Ivy took a step forward and placed her hand on Michael's arm. "Please, help my father."

Michael felt a bit dizzy when she stood so close, especially when her breasts brushed his shoulder. And there was his family, none of whom was as wild about Ivy as he. He did not want to lose her so they could say I told you so. "What will I have to do?"

"How do you feel about pretending to be a tea merchant?" Sir William responded.

"A tea merchant? A peddler?" Michael almost spit out the words. "I'd rather be a rat catcher."

"A peddler is the perfect disguise," Sir William said. "I've been thinking on this. As a tea merchant you can go all over the countryside without anyone being the wiser. I've even thought of a name for you.

Donaldson. Michael Donaldson. Very nondescript."

"I'd rather walk up to Kenyon's door and demand the formula back."

Sir William came to his feet with a frustrated sound. "He won't give it to you—and he might even destroy it rather than face its loss or the public humiliation. If he does, we all lose. No, you must steal the formula and a tea merchant is a very good disguise."

Michael did not trust him, not at all. Then, he thought of the sacrifices he'd already made for Ivy—of the hardships, the battles, the witnessing of the deaths of good men. He was ready for home and hearth.

Compared to what he'd already done to win her, peddling tea would be easy.

He swung his gaze to Sir William. "I'll retrieve your formula. But, while I'm gone, you must keep her safe—for me."

Sir William did not mistake his meaning. He understood Michael expected him to keep the other suitors at bay. "Consider it done," he said. "When you return with my formula we shall have a wedding that will leave all London talking. Is that not right, daughter?"

Ivy's face had gone pale but she nodded her head. Michael wanted a moment alone with her. He wanted to hear the promise from *her* lips. But it was not to be. Sir William took over, refining his scheme and embellishing it.

The next morning, Michael exchanged his uniform for an ill-fitting coat and valise containing an assortment of East Indian teas for sale to the discriminating country housewife. He set off for Wye and the strangest adventure of his life.

Chapter Two

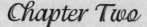

Miss Kenyon's Need for a Dark Stranger

Jocelyn Kenyon charged into her dearest friend Lucy Lettman's kitchen the moment Lucy answered the knock on her kitchen door. Without waiting for a greeting, Jocelyn declared, "This is the worst day of my life and Uncle Geoffrey is completely oblivious."

She yanked at the ribbons of her bonnet, her fingers shaking so hard she couldn't untie the knot. Exasperated, she quit the struggle and pulled a heavy vellum envelope addressed to herself and her uncle out of the pocket of her dress . "Did you receive one of these?" It was an invitation from Lord Vaughn to attend a ball in honor of his daughter Elfreda's betrothal to Thomas Burkhardt.

Lucy closed the door before admitting, "Yes, I did. I'm afraid, dear, one was sent to everyone in Wye. Lord Vaughn is determined to make this the social event of the parish."

"That means I *must* be there," Jocelyn whispered and felt her knees go wobbly. She walked down the hall of Lucy's house and into the comfortable sitting room where a cheery fire blazed in the hearth, but she could not feel its warmth. Everything inside of her was cold with the certainty of complete humiliation.

Lucy put her arm around Jocelyn's shoulders. "Jocelyn, we all understand—"

"Yes, I know." She stepped out of her friend's comforting embrace and slipped her finger between the ribbons. This time, the knot gave way gracefully. She pulled her bonnet off her head, for once not caring about the springiness of her curls. "Everyone *understands*, and everyone *pities* me. For the past six months it's been 'poor Jocelyn, what shall she do?' Don't pretend it hasn't been, Lucy. I know people have been discussing me over their teacups. Of course, the gossip was worse in the beginning when Thomas started paying marked attention to Lady Elfreda, but once he'd jilted me—" She broke off, afraid she might give way to tears and she'd already shed too many.

Thomas had been the love of her life. He'd been by her side since the day she'd first met him sixteen years ago. She'd been eight; he was ten. Her parents had died and she'd been shipped off to Wye to live with an uncle she'd never met. Thomas's friendship had eased the transition. He'd made her feel accepted and she'd idolized him. Around the parish, it had been a foregone conclusion they would marry . . . someday. Neither one of them had been in a hurry.

But then Elfreda had returned after years spent in London and had started taking part in the parish social circles. She was everything Jocelyn wasn't—tall, blond, sophisticated, *wealthy*. She'd stolen Thomas's heart as easily as a child throws a ball.

The whole parish had been a little surprised Lord

Vaughn had approved of the match, but then Elfreda wasn't his oldest daughter. She was the middle of seven and he liked Thomas, a farmer with his own land. He'd even sent Thomas to London to get what he'd called "Town bronze" and now Thomas was back and the betrothal would be announced.

"What am I going to do, Lucy? Everyone will notice if I'm not there. And if I do go to the ball, it'll break my heart to see him and Elfreda together."

Lucy hugged her tightly. "You must make the best of it, Joss. You must hang on to your pride and not let him see how much he has hurt you."

"I don't know if I can." She stuffed the invitation back into her pocket and tossed her bonnet into a straight backed chair before walking over to the window. Folding her arms, she leaned against the sill, looking outside but not truly registering the flowering lilac in Lucy's small garden or the farmer out on the road who drove his oxen toward the village.

Wye was as picturesque a spot as any in England. Its streets and paths were nestled among rolling green hills dotted with fat sheep and along the curving banks of the Avon. Some poet had once described the village as "a piece of heaven on earth." Jocelyn agreed with the assessment. This was her home.

"It was easier when Thomas was away," she said quietly. "I could pretend nothing had changed. Now, I hear they will be living at her father's estate. I'll see him every day for the rest of my life."

She faced her friend. "It's not right that Lady Elfreda shows up after years away and *steals* him from me. He was mine."

"He *was*," Lucy reiterated sadly. "Joss, you are going to have to live with this. I know you can't see beyond this moment, but someday there will be someone else in your life."

"Not like Thomas."

"No, better."

Now, Lucy was wishing on stars. Jocelyn rolled her eyes. "Who? Billy Fletcher?" Billy was the miller's son and the only eligible bachelor of her age available. A more pompous, lazy man could not be found. He had bad breath and overlarge ears. She pushed away from the window. "I'm four and twenty and I have no dowry. If someone doesn't marry me for love then I shall not be married at all. And Thomas loved me," she said with conviction. "I don't know what spell Lady Elfreda cast over him, but *he loved me*."

Lucy sat on the edge of the rocker by the hearth. She placed her hands together as if in prayer and said, "We all thought he did. However, Joss, he left you. How much could he love you to have been so fickle?"

Here was a touchy question and not one Jocelyn wanted to explore too deeply . . . because it didn't cast Thomas in a very good light. "It's Lady Elfreda's fault," she insisted. "One day, he will wake up and realize how unhappy he is. I only hope it's not too late. And I just wish there was *something* I could do to let him know how deeply he has hurt me."

"Like make him jealous?"

There was a good suggestion. "Yes, and why not?" Jocelyn stirred with interest. This idea had merit and would earn her a bit of her own back. She walked the perimeter of the room, working out the details in her mind. "If I could find a more handsome and taller man than Thomas, then I would have no difficulty attending the ball. Can you not picture the scene now, Lucy? I enter the ballroom on the arm of a man, one who is not Billy Fletcher, and conversation stops. Why, the whole parish would be struck mute with curiosity." She straightened, poised, acting out the part. "All eyes are on me and this handsome gentleman, who has appeared out of nowhere and apparently has swept me off my feet."

"Oh, this is good," Lucy said, leaning back in the rocker to enjoy the story.

"Ummmhmmm," Jocelyn agreed, involved in her scene. "Thomas won't notice us at first. He'll be too busy talking to Elfreda, but he shall hear the quiet—"

"You can't hear quiet—"

"Shhh," Jocelyn returned. "He senses something is different in the air."

"Better."

"I think so, too." Jocelyn directed her hand to point out where Thomas is standing. "He looks up, puzzled. Lady Elfreda is still talking—like she always is. She likes hearing words come out of her mouth. But he isn't attending. Instead, he slowly turns toward the door where I am standing. I'm wearing my yellow muslin with the embroidery around the trim."

"That's my favorite dress on you."

"I like it, too. And so does Thomas." She smiled, liking this dream. "At first, Thomas will be riveted by my beauty." She smiled to herself over that one.

"You *are* beautiful," Lucy insisted.

Jocelyn lifted one of her dark unruly curls and

snorted. "Yes, I have beaux lining up to write poems to my shoe size."

"Joss—!" Lucy started to protest, but Jocelyn didn't want to argue. She wanted to dream.

"Anyway, Thomas is riveted and then his gaze shifts." She snapped her head comically to demonstrate. Lucy laughed as Jocelyn knew she would. "He notices I am not alone. I have my handsome, broad-shouldered escort beside me. A dark stranger with smoldering looks and sensual lips."

"Sensual lips? Good for you," Lucy said.

"Yes, good for me . . . because Thomas is overcome with jealousy. He's *green* with jealousy." Jocelyn paused dramatically and then said softly, "And *crippled* by remorse because he thinks he has lost me." She could see his expression in her mind and sighed . . . and then, to her horror, tears threatened because it was never to be.

Lucy came to her feet. "Joss, please don't cry. And come down from the clouds. Thomas doesn't deserve you. The banns will be posted starting the Sunday after the ball and I say good riddance."

"I wish I could." Jocelyn walked over to the hearth. "Just like I wish I was taller and had blue eyes and straight blond hair. I wish I could make Thomas jealous and then he'd see that marrying Lady Elfreda will be the worst mistake of his life."

"I think you'd best be careful what you wish for." Lucy crossed over and placed her hands on Jocelyn's shoulders. Looking her squarely in the eye, she spoke slowly and distinctly. "I love you like a sister. You are my dearest friend and I would not say this to hurt you, but, Joss, sometimes you refuse to see the world the way it really is. Thomas is with another woman. You must go on with your life. I want you to make him jealous because I want you to start living again. There is someone out there for you. Someone who will love you better."

"No, Lucy, I love him."

Lucy groaned her frustration, throwing her hands up in the air. "Why am I arguing?" She shook her head. "First things first. We need to find a suitable escort for you to Lord Vaughn's ball."

"Not Billy Fletcher," Jocelyn was quick to say.

"No, not Billy Fletcher, but perhaps Kent knows someone." Lucy referred to her husband, Lord Vaughn's land manager and a very good man. "He might know someone outside the parish . . . or there is his cousin Simon—"

"Simon is seventeen."

"Oh, he is, isn't he? He looks older." Lucy made a face. "This isn't very promising."

Jocelyn took pity on her friend. "It's not your fault or your worry. I mean, I won't mind being a spinster. I have Uncle Geoffrey to take care of and maybe I can cultivate a hobby or two and start taking in cats."

"A hobby like what?" Lucy asked, suspicious of Jocelyn's motives.

"Pi-geons," Jocelyn said, breaking the word into two syllables.

A gleam appeared in Lucy's eye. She knew Jocelyn was teasing. "Pigeons?"

"Oh, yes, I shall raise pigeons. Perhaps I'll write an article or two and submit them to my uncle's scientific journals. I shall be the Pigeon Woman of Wye and people will come from far and wide to hear me speak and I'll wear a big rose and gray hat and pontificate like the Clark sisters do for hours and hours."

"I'm almost willing to let you do it to see how it all turns out," Lucy said. "Cats and pigeons! But be serious, Jocelyn. You are still too young to place yourself on the shelf." A knock sounded at the front door. She started out of the room, throwing over her shoulder, "And losing you to another man, one worthy of your affections, will make Thomas good and sorry." She opened the front door.

Jocelyn had to agree. She wouldn't mind seeing Thomas grovel in apologies—

Lucy's swallowed gasp of surprise interrupted her thoughts of a groveling Thomas. Her friend stepped away from the door, her eyes as round as saucers.

Alarmed, Jocelyn moved forward, then stopped midstep when she heard a deep, well-modulated male voice say, "Good afternoon, I'm looking for Mrs. Lettman."

Lucy raised a distracted hand up to her hair. "I'm she," she said. Jocelyn had never seen such a silly female smile on her friend's face. "Please come in."

The man entered, removing his hat as he stepped through the door—and for a second, all Jocelyn, too, could do was gawk.

His tall, broad-shouldered frame filled the narrow vestibule. His hair was thick and wavy and so black it almost appeared blue. His jaw was strong, determined, reinforcing his air of authority.

And he had sensual lips.

"I'm Michael Donaldson, a tea merchant. They told me in the village you had a room to let." He introduced himself as if reciting by rote and Jocelyn had the strange feeling he was decidedly uncomfortable.

"My husband and I do rent out a room on occasion,"

Lucy said. "Please, come in." She motioned him toward the sitting room where Jocelyn stood.

Mr. Donaldson had to duck to come in through the low doorway. But what caught Jocelyn's interest was the grace with which he moved. Here was a man who was all hard muscle, a natural athlete. He would be as at home on a horse as he would on a dance floor. Never in a million years would she have guessed what he did to earn his living.

Then he looked directly at her—and time stopped. He was a handsome man with his square jaw and long nose, but what held her mesmerized were his eyes. They were silver and as bright and full of intelligence as any she'd ever seen. Even the dust of the road, which showed he'd traveled a good distance, could not diminish the presence of those eyes.

Jocelyn was aware she was staring and quickly shut her mouth. Lucy, standing behind him, caught her eye. With a wave of her hands, she mouthed the words "this is the one."

The One. The dark stranger. The man who could make Thomas jealous.

Escape was Jocelyn's first thought. It was one thing to laugh and pretend. It was entirely another to believe such a scheme could be put into effect.

Unfortunately, Mr. Donaldson and Lucy blocked her path.

"Mr. Donaldson, this is my friend, *Miss* Kenyon," Lucy said to Jocelyn's undying mortification.

"Kenyon?" Mr. Donaldson's sharp gaze homed in on her like a beam of light and she sensed he didn't miss any detail.

The time had definitely come to leave. There was something about this man that unsettled her. He was too handsome, too big, too everything. She snatched her bonnet up from the chair. "Well, I must be going—"

"It is a pleasure to meet you," he said, blocking her exit. He offered his hand.

"And I you," Jocelyn murmured, reluctant to take his hand. Something was not right. Jocelyn sensed it. For one, the name Donaldson didn't seem to fit him. It was too common and this man was anything but. And secondly, he stirred something deep within her. It was becoming hard to breathe naturally. She was sensitive to the bay rum in his shaving soap and her heart beat as if she'd run a fast race. She took a step toward the door. "I hope you enjoy your stay in Wye. Now, if you will excuse me—"

Once again he placed himself in her escape route. "Do you drink tea, Miss Kenyon? I could show you some of my wares."

Something about his offering to display his wares set her body on fire . . . a condition not lost on Lucy, who fairly danced with laughter. She came around to saucily hook her arm in Jocelyn's, forcing her to stay. "Tell me, Mr. Donaldson," Lucy said with the easy frankness of a married woman, "how long will you need the room?"

He tore his attention from Jocelyn. "A few days. No more than a week."

He would be here for Lord Vaughn's ball. Jocelyn could almost hear the words ringing in Lucy's matchmaking head. "No," she warned, the sound low.

Lucy ignored her. "Do you dance, sir?"

Jocelyn could have died of embarrassment—and she couldn't slip her arm free without prying off Lucy's hold.

He was startled by the question. Now, *he* was the one to back up. "Is it a requirement to rent the room?"

"Oh no," Lucy answered. "But there is a dance going on this Friday in the parish. Since you will be available . . . well, we can always do with another bachelor."

"My uncle is expecting me to be home," Jocelyn said pointedly. "If you will excuse me?" She attempted to twist her arm free.

Lucy refused to let go. "You will come to dinner tonight, won't you, Jocelyn?" she asked. "And you, Mr. Donaldson, dinner is included in your room rate. We'll make it a happy party!"

"Unfortunately, I won't be there," Jocelyn said, finally managing to pull her arm free. She edged toward the door. "It was a pleasure meeting you, Mr. Donaldson."

And she would have made her escape but for Lucy following her into the vestibule and fiercely whispering in her ear, "You *must* come tonight. Can you not see? The man is gorgeous and he is interested in you."

"He barely noticed me."

"He's staring at you right now," Lucy said—and she was right. He was watching her closely, his head tilted as if trying to hear what they were saying. "Dinner. Tonight," Lucy ordered and did not wait for a yes or no. Instead, she swept Jocelyn out the door and returned to her new boarder.

Jocelyn stood on the front step, lost in indecision. She could hear Lucy trill her welcome to the tea peddler. The very *handsome* tea peddler. "Oh, dear," she muttered and, putting on her bonnet, went on her way, knowing she had no choice but to return for dinner.

*   *   *

From the sitting room's front window, Michael watched Miss Kenyon turn at the end of the walk and head in the direction of her home.

How fortunate for him to have stumbled upon a link to Geoffrey Kenyon so quickly. Especially such a fetching link.

Funny, but he'd been so devoted to Ivy he'd not really noticed many other women—but he'd been instantly attracted to Miss Kenyon and he wasn't certain why.

She was pretty enough, with her lively brown curls and clear dark eyes, but what had caught his interest was the air about her, a vivacity, an earnestness for living. Funny, he'd never noticed such a thing in anyone before, but he definitely felt its presence with Miss Kenyon.

She hadn't believed his story. She wasn't one to hide her thoughts, and she had doubts about him, he'd seen it in her eyes. Her friend Mrs. Lettman had upset her and he wondered why.

His question was answered when Mrs. Lettman said, "I have an offer to make, sir, one I hope you won't think me too bold for suggesting."

Michael turned from the window. Her smile was open and friendly and he found himself liking her. In fact, everything about the village of Wye impressed him. It was like coming home. A man tired of war could make a good life in such a place.

"What kind of offer?" he asked.

"I'm willing to waive the charge for your room for the week if you will escort my friend Miss Kenyon to the ball this coming Friday night."

She then proceeded to tell him the whole story of an unfaithful lover and a scheme to make the lad jealous.

Chapter Three

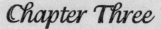

A Faithless Lover Receives a Taste of His Own

*T*homas Burkhardt was a man who should have been completely happy.

After all, his betrothal to Lady Elfreda was quite an accomplishment. She was beautiful with a substantial dowry and her father was the most generous of men. The lads down at the local pub, the Rooster's Den, all envied him and even the squire treated him with new respect.

Furthermore, his mother—not always the easiest woman to satisfy—was very, very pleased.

The only person who wasn't completely certain about this marriage was himself.

Yes, Elfreda was lovely, and she was kind and good. But she was also a little dim.

There, he'd finally admitted it to himself. In the beginning, he'd been so flattered by her marked attention, he had overlooked the fact that she didn't always catch the humor in his jokes or know anything about farming, horses, or hunting—his three main interests.

She was so lovely, he'd dismissed his suspicions that she was usually a bit confused in conversations about anything other than fashion and hairstyles . . . and she wasn't really very practical. For a while, he'd felt protective of her. However, three weeks in London with her family had opened his eyes and almost driven him up a wall.

Short of himself, little interested Elfreda. He didn't mind being the whole sum and focus of her attention, but it grew tiresome. She rarely let him out of her sight—this trip out for a ride being an unusual exception—and he didn't fit into her social circle in London. Not at all.

So he was caught in a dilemma. If he backed out of this betrothal, even before it was announced, well, the matter could get sticky. And there would be the problem of hurting Elfreda, whom he genuinely cared for. But over the past weeks away from Wye, he'd realized she wasn't Jocelyn. The good people of Wye might not forgive him a second jilting.

Lord Vaughn certainly wouldn't.

As if his mind had conjured her, Jocelyn appeared at the edge of the field where Thomas sat on his horse. She was obviously taking the shortcut on her way home from Lucy's, as she had hundreds of times before. They had met here often over the years.

She'd removed her bonnet, which she swung by its ribbons. The afternoon sun caught the shine in her tangle of curls that no amount of brushing could tame. Her cheeks glowed with good health and brought out the sparkle in her eyes. She batted the head of a weed that had grown overtall and then jumped over a dry rivulet formed by rain in the field.

He knew the moment she caught sight of him waiting for her in the line of trees outlining the border of his land from her uncle's. Her step slowed, then halted. He nudged his horse forward. The animal was a gift from Lord Vaughn, a beautiful gelding of which Thomas had grown very fond. As he drew closer, he couldn't help but notice Jocelyn wasn't wearing gloves.

Elfreda never went anywhere without gloves.

He reined in the gelding a few feet from where she stood. Their gazes met and he spoke first, "Hello, Jocelyn."

She pressed her lips together, refusing to speak. *Damn*, he'd hoped she wasn't going to be like this, that her heart had softened toward him. Instead, tears pooled in her eyes and she looked away.

For the first time, he realized how deeply he had hurt her. He'd been so caught up in the excitement of having a lord's daughter single him out, he hadn't been as kind as he should have been to Jocelyn. He'd even convinced himself that they could still be friends. Now, he wasn't so certain.

Then, with the pluck he had expected of her, she hardened her gaze and met his. "Hello, Thomas." She started to walk right by him, her head high. He noticed she didn't "float" when she walked, like Elfreda did. No, hers was the good honest pace of a real person. He pushed his horse to fall into step beside her.

But what did he have to say? Once, conversation had always been easy between them. Now, he felt awkward.

And then the right words flew out of his mouth without conscious thought and he understood why he'd come here this day, this moment. "I'm sorry if I hurt you."

She stopped. Her nose twitched with expectancy.

"It was never my intent," he said.

She nodded. She knew. Then in a voice that was barely a whisper she said, "I thought you loved me."

Oh God. Words choked in his throat.

What was worse was seeing the disappointment in her eyes when he didn't speak. But then, what could he say?

Her chin came up. "I'll manage without you, Thomas. Don't feel guilty on my account. I will see you at the ball."

"Perhaps we can have a dance," he suggested, knowing it was a terrible idea. Elfreda would be distraught if he paid attention to any other woman.

She pulled the gaily colored ribbons of her bonnet through her fingers. "I don't know. You've been gone some time, down in London and all. Things have changed."

"In what way?" Wye had appeared the same upon his return as when he'd left.

"I, too, have found someone else. He will be escorting my uncle and me to the ball."

If Jocelyn had hit him over the head with an axe handle he could not have been more surprised. She had a suitor? Another man had taken his place?

Thomas couldn't speak. He was too shocked that she'd actually found someone else. Or that he'd been back five days and no one had told him Jocelyn had a caller, not even the lads at the Rooster's Den.

She smiled, a gleam of triumph in her eyes, revealing she knew exactly what he was thinking. "I shall see you Friday night." She practically sang the words to him, before turning and marching toward the trees and out of sight.

Stunned, Thomas sat for a long time until his fancy new gelding shifted his weight and let him know it was time to either travel on or get off his back.

Setting his heels to the horse, one question consumed Thomas's imagination: who was Jocelyn's new suitor?

He knew he wouldn't rest until he found out.

Chapter Four

The Die Is Cast

Once out of Thomas's sight, Jocelyn lifted her skirts and ran home.

She'd done it!

She'd given him a bit of his own back and the expression on his face had been priceless.

She reached her uncle's house, a brick manor set well back from the road. Running inside, she slammed the door and holding her bonnet in one hand, she fell against it, pressing her other hand against her stomach.

What had she done?

Her initial triumph faded as she realized she'd backed herself into a corner, all for the price of pride. Now she had no choice but to bring Mr. Donaldson up to scratch. He *had* to escort her Friday night or she'd be thoroughly humiliated.

Fear rattled her nerves . . . but there was also a sense of anticipation. Lucy was a well-known schemer, especially when it came to matters of the heart. More than one couple in Wye owed their marriage to her matchmaking abilities. Chances are she'd already made arrangements.

"Josie, is that you?" Her uncle Geoffrey came out of his laboratory, a study converted to his scientific needs located in the back of the house. He walked down the hall toward her.

He was a dear, gentle man with a slight build and a bushy head of silver-gray hair always in need of a trim. He paused, concern in his eyes. "You look pale. Has something happened?"

Jocelyn hung her bonnet on a hook by the door. When Uncle Geoffrey worried, he couldn't work and she'd learned long ago how important work was to him. Consequently, she was in the habit of taking care of her own problems. Not that he wouldn't have done anything for her. He would. He just wasn't very effective when it came to dealing with people and their feelings.

"Everything is fine," she quickly assured him. "I ran the distance from the pasture, racing myself."

He wasn't convinced. Searching her face, he said, "I hear young Thomas is back from London."

Jocelyn was surprised. He usually seemed oblivious to the doings around the village. "Yes, he has returned."

Uncle Geoff's gaze narrowed. "He's a fool. You are a fine catch, Josie. He shouldn't have chosen a hothouse *Liliaceae* like Lady Elfreda over a native *Rosaceae* like yourself."

A gardener herself and long used to her uncle's habit of referring to plants by their Latin names, Jocelyn knew he was comparing lilies to roses. "That is the nicest thing you've ever said to me, Uncle Geoff."

He blushed as if he'd said too much. "I know I'm not

the type of parent you should have had. If my brother and his wife had lived you would have gotten much more of what you needed."

She put her arms around him. "You've given me everything I've needed."

"I'm a cranky old man," he corrected. "And I know the reason you didn't marry Thomas years ago is because I got sick. Not to mention the fact, his mother and I never rubbed each other well."

"She is a bit of a dragon."

"She's a snob."

Jocelyn grinned. "At least we haven't blown up the house in a good six months, so she can't drum up support in the village against us." She spoke of a time when her uncle had been experimenting with gunpowder. Jocelyn had become very good at putting out small fires.

He laughed as she knew he would. She changed the subject. "Lucy has asked me to join them for dinner this evening." She hesitated. "There will be a gentleman there they wish to introduce to me." Another pause. "I've met him before—" Which was true. "—Although, I'm certain if you wish to meet him, Lucy would add another setting."

Her uncle visibly shivered in horror. He hated to go out, especially when he was intensely involved in a problem. "I'm sure all will be fine," he said. "Kent can see you home. I'm so close to stabilizing the properties of rubber. Very tricky it is. I've almost gotten it." He took a step back toward his laboratory, his mind already shifting from her concerns to the scientific world.

Jocelyn thought about the invitation in her skirt

pocket. She pulled it out and silently handed it to him. "Please, you must come."

He read the script and nodded. "Of course, of course. Must be there for you." He paused and then added, "Will we have to stay more than an hour?"

"We don't have to do anything we don't want to," she told him grandly, and he took solace from the idea. "Well, must get back. I left four grams of rubber cooling and must measure the temperature."

"And I'd best go dress for Lucy's. I'll slice some of the chicken we had for lunch for your dinner."

He nodded absently. His mind had already returned to his experiments. "I'll see you later?"

"Yes, Uncle," she replied dutifully and watched him walk down the hall. She hadn't known he blamed her not marrying on his sickness. It had been true she had put Thomas off . . . but she did not regret her actions. Uncle Geoff was the only family she had and she loved him with a fierce loyalty. She'd not let anything happen to him.

On that thought, she went upstairs to her bedroom to dress for dinner.

Chapter Five

Elfreda didn't know what she was going to do. Yesterday, Thomas had promised he'd be over for a visit. Instead, she learned from her footman, Thomas had been seen out riding instead.

She knew for what purpose. He had gone in search of Jocelyn Kenyon.

In London, everything had been wonderful between her and Thomas. However, since they had returned to Wye, he'd grown unusually quiet.

Her father told her not to worry. All prospective bridegrooms got cold feet.

But she had to worry. She loved Thomas Burkhardt more than any other thing in the world and she feared she could not keep him.

Elfreda had no illusions about herself. She knew she didn't have much to recommend her beyond her looks. Her sisters were much brighter than she and far more ambitious. All she'd ever wanted, all she'd ever *let* herself want, was Thomas.

If he started drifting away, if he was thinking about Jocelyn, Elfreda didn't know what she was going to do. However, she did know she'd fight to her last breath before she'd lose him—and Jocelyn had better beware.

Chapter Six

☙☙

The Rogue in the Garden

Michael could not believe his good fortune. Mrs. Lettman's scheme played right into his plans.

Of course he would escort Miss Kenyon to the ball. In truth, he sympathized with her plight. He knew the pain of unrequited love. Was he not on this fool's errand to win Ivy's heart? Helping Miss Kenyon to put this Burkhardt's nose out of joint would also pacify Michael's uneasiness over stealing the formula.

There was one wrinkle to Mrs. Lettman's matchmaking scheme and it came from her husband's innate good sense and honesty. Kent had a ruddy face with curling blond hair. Both he and Michael got on well with each other right from the beginning, quickly switching to the informality of using their Christian names. Nor was Kent one to mince words.

"You should stay out of Jocelyn's affairs, especially on this one," Kent told his wife.

"I can't. She is so unhappy."

"I know she is and Burkhardt is a rogue for jilting her, but better the truth than having Michael here pretend to be an admirer."

"He's escorting her to a dance," his wife said with a great show of patience. "Nothing more, nothing less. If Thomas realizes he is truly in love with Jocelyn because of Michael's presence, that is no fault of mine."

Her husband rolled his eyes in patent disbelief. He addressed Michael. "And you think this wise? I'll warn you now, while other women stitch or paint, Lucy matchmakes."

"Very successfully," she added.

Kent grunted a response. "Two couples have married. The other three can't stand the sight of each other."

"Those are good odds," Lucy announced and her husband gave her a pat on the behind, which he didn't think Michael saw, for her impertinence.

Michael liked the playfulness of the couple. They reminded him of his older siblings and their spouses. Even his parents, who were very much in love after almost forty years of marriage, engaged in loving banter. He'd once imagined he and Ivy taking part in the same sort of teasing; however, now he realized the Incomparable she had become lacked the air of earthiness one needed to enjoy this type of closeness.

He pushed aside his reservations over Ivy and answered Kent. "It's a country dance. What harm can come of my escorting her? Miss Kenyon seems a nice person and I wouldn't mind tweaking the nose of the man who hurt her."

"I'd like to give Burkhardt a fist in his face," Kent agreed. "He used to be a good one but now, he's a bit full of himself. And you are right about Jocelyn. She's an angel with a bit of the devil in her."

At the same moment, there was a knock on the door. Miss Kenyon had arrived, coming to the kitchen as friends of long acquaintance were wont to do. She'd changed from the serviceable day dress she'd been wearing that afternoon into a gown of robin's egg blue with a pair of cream gloves and a matching shawl. The dress style was simple and the color suited her. She'd threaded ribbon of the same soft blue through her curls and the effect was lovely.

Michael was startled to realize she used no artifice of any sort—no hairpieces, no cosmetics, no perfumes. Her scent was the freshness of the evening air and when she entered the house it immediately filled with her own special sparkle. He'd never met a woman with such presence.

They sat down to a simple, yet delicious dinner. The Lettman's home was a cozy dwelling—the dining room was really not much more than an alcove—and Michael enjoyed not having the fuss of servants. There was ample room at the table and the conversation and laughter flowed easily among all of them.

Michael had not taken time to go home and visit his family when he'd returned from France for two reasons, the first being his eagerness to see Ivy and claim her hand. The second was that ever since his oldest brother had accused him of arrogance in his pursuit of Ivy, there had been some estrangement. His brother had been the only family member brave enough to suggest Michael was too single-minded on the subject of Ivy. Angered, Michael had left for the army and not looked back. Nor had he made many friends in the military. He'd been too ambitious and, to some, too foolhardy in the risks he took for the sake of advancement.

Now as he found enjoyment in the companionship of new friends, Michael understood a bit of what his brother had been trying to say. Ivy was not a person who valued the genuine warmth of family and friends and this evening was showing Michael how much he did.

At the table, Miss Kenyon sat across from him. Without thinking, his long legs took up most of the space. Once or twice, his boot would accidentally bump the toe of her slipper.

The first time he did it, she moved her foot. The second, she kept her foot where it was, a gleam in her eye issuing a territorial challenge.

Charmed, Michael tapped his foot twice, watching her closely across the table and pleased to see a sign of humor in her eyes. She lifted his toe up with her own, and he pressed down. She pulled her toe back just in time.

A dimple appeared by the corner of her mouth and he couldn't help but smile back.

Lucy stopped her soliloquy on the shortcomings of the vicar. She looked from Miss Kenyon to Michael and back again. "Did I say something funny?"

"No," Miss Kenyon said. "Why would you think so?" She helped herself to more peas.

Their hostess frowned. She looked to Michael but he wasn't going to admit to playing like children under the table. She changed the subject. "Jocelyn, I've explained all to Michael and he wants to escort you to Lord Vaughn's ball."

A most becoming blush stained Miss Kenyon's cheeks. "You know all, Mr. Donaldson?"

"Should I not have?" Lucy asked alarmed, but Miss Kenyon covered her hand with a reassuring one of her own.

"No, it's best." She looked to Michael. "I appreciate your performing this small favor. I'm certain you are very busy selling tea, but it is kind of you to help."

"I'm honored," Michael replied. "And it will be fun."

Again, their gazes met. How straightforward and honest she was.

A pity her uncle was a scoundrel. Of course, he shouldn't talk, considering his own subterfuge.

Her expression changed as she reacted to something she heard Lucy say. Michael was so attuned to her, he noticed instantly. He directed his attention to the table conversation as Kent announced proudly, ". . . the baby will be due by next spring." His wife blushed with pride.

"A baby?" Jocelyn sounded a bit stunned. "Lucy, how wonderful for you, for you both."

Something in her tone didn't ring true to Michael. He murmured his own congratulations and the dinner proceeded well enough from there with the talk moving from the baby to land prices to agricultural laws. Michael noticed Miss Kenyon grew unusually subdued. Her friends didn't notice. They were too wrapped up in their own cocoon of happiness.

At the first opportunity, Miss Kenyon did not surprise him when she excused herself. "I must be going home. The hour grows late."

"I'll walk you home," Kent started, but his wife interrupted.

"I'll go, too, and you also, Michael. I'm certain you wouldn't mind seeing Jocelyn home. Would you, sir?"

"Lucy," Miss Kenyon protested.

"I would be honored to see you home," Michael responded eagerly. This would give him an opportunity to meet Geoffrey Kenyon and scout out the formula without raising anyone's suspicions. These were kind people and the sooner he finished with the formula, the better.

"It's a lovely night for a walk," Lucy said romantically. "Full moon and all." She leveled a speculative look at Michael and Miss Kenyon and he knew she was visualizing them as a match.

Uncomfortable, he forced a smile while silently promising himself he would be very careful to not lead Miss Kenyon on.

There was nothing left to do then but to leave. Miss Kenyon pulled on her gloves and put on her bonnet while Michael picked up his hat. Again, he sensed something was bothering her. However, Lucy and Kent didn't seem to notice anything wrong.

The two couples set out for their walk. The night truly was marvelous. The air was velvety soft and the moon's blue light softened the hard edges.

A good number of villagers were out and about. Lucy and Kent quickly dropped behind to talk to friends. They were also content to hold hands and whisper to each other, leaving Michael and Miss Kenyon to their own devices.

Seeing that they were alone, Miss Kenyon said, "You shouldn't have to see me home. You've already agreed to escort me to the dance. I fear Lucy is becoming carried away. She hates the sight of an unattached bachelor.

You'd best beware." She lengthened her stride, walking with purpose.

"I don't mind," he responded keeping in step beside her. "Besides, it's a good night for a walk."

Miss Kenyon did not slow her step. In fact, she almost acted as if she were attempting to escape him. She nodded here and there to people she knew but did not linger to visit.

Michael found her behavior odd. They'd gone about a fifth of a mile, and were well beyond Lucy and Kent, before he hooked his arm in hers and forced her to stop. "Miss Kenyon, what have I done to offend you?"

She blinked in surprise. "Why nothing, Mr. Donaldson."

"Then why are you trying to outdistance me?"

"I don't mean to be rude. I was just going home," she announced primly. "I have a fast walk."

He shook his head, doubting her word. "Something disturbed you when the Lettmans announced their good news about the baby. What is it?"

She wasn't about to give in easily. "Mr. Donaldson, why should you care?"

"Because I like you, Miss Kenyon."

His honest answer hung in the air for a moment before she knitted her brows together and confessed, "I am afraid what I was thinking does not say much for my character, sir, and it bothers me greatly."

"Let me be the judge of that. Please," he added when she still remained unconvinced. "Sometimes when you share a trouble, it becomes lighter."

"You don't believe that," she answered. "I sense you are very much a loner."

Her accuracy caught him by surprise. "What makes you say that?"

"There is a reserve about you. A wall, if you will, that you allow few people to breach."

Michael shifted his weight, impressed. He didn't deny it. "What gave me away?"

"No one thing in particular. Call it intuition or that I hazarded a lucky guess. You are accustomed to doing things the way you want to do them."

He held up his hand, asking for quarter. "I am. But what of you?" Narrowing his eyes thoughtfully, he said, "I sense you are someone who takes friendships seriously."

"Keen observation there," she mocked him and started walking down the road, albeit at a slower pace.

Her poke at his remark goaded him into trying harder. He ate the distance between them with his longer legs and stepped in front of her. "All right." He took a moment, considering her closely and then said, "You are someone who likes to be thought of as independent, but in truth, you are quite vulnerable. And if I had to name one thing you wanted above anything else it would be . . ." He paused. Here he would have to think harder. Inspiration struck. "I believe what you want most in the world is security or else you wouldn't be so bound to this Thomas Burkhardt when he is about to offer for another woman."

She drew in a sharp breath and took a step back. Seeing her reaction, Michael said, "Wait, I didn't mean to be so personal—"

"No," she said, cutting him off. "I'm not angry, just struck by the truth of your words. I had not realized . . ."

She shook her head. "Did Lucy tell you I was an orphan?"

Now, Michael truly regretted what he'd said. "No, and I am deeply embarrassed."

She placed her hand on his arm. "Please, do not be. If anything, you have done me a service. I mean, I love Thomas." She stated the fact as if reminding herself and then said thoughtfully, "However, I'd not pictured myself as clinging to him. It's not an attractive idea."

"Miss Kenyon, I don't know where my words came from. I am not an insightful person."

She smiled, the dimple appearing again. "No, just a forthright one—a quality I happen to admire," she added quickly as if fearing he thought her critical. "There is no value in delusion, or so I keep telling myself. But I do love Thomas."

Michael wanted to wince. She'd done it again—stating her love like it was a slogan instead of a declaration, but he decided this time to keep his opinion to himself.

Unfortunately, she read his mind. "You don't understand. I'm certain I pushed him away. As to my earlier annoyance over Lucy," she said, smoothly changing the subject, "I fear I'm a bit jealous. You see, Lucy is like a sister to me. In the past, I would have been the first to hear all of Lucy's good news. But tonight, it struck me that her husband is the closest to her now. This afternoon when I saw her, she said nothing to me about the baby. Of course, I was too involved in my own problems, but still . . . one's closest friend should hear first, don't you think?"

"I must side with the husband," Michael admitted.

A flash of annoyance appeared in her eyes. He braced

himself but then she said, "Sometimes honesty is a brutal trait." Her anger evaporated, released on a resigned sigh.

"There is no fun in being left behind," she murmured, and he nodded.

"How would you know?" she challenged as they both began walking, side by side.

Michael was tempted to answer her. To tell her of how lonely he'd felt in London when he'd returned and realized that life had continued on without him. While he'd been off fighting the monster Napoleon, the woman he'd loved, his friends, even his family had gone on peacefully enjoying life. They'd not heard the roar of cannons, seen men torn apart, or feared for their own lives.

Oh, yes, he'd very definitely been an outsider in London. But he couldn't tell her this without revealing his identity.

"They say change is inevitable," he said, a safe noncommittal statement.

Miss Kenyon nodded. "But that doesn't mean I must like it."

Her candor startled a laugh out of him. He took her arm. "Miss Kenyon, I am so glad I've met you. For the past several weeks, I thought *I* was the one out of step with everyone else."

"What do you mean?"

He shrugged. He could not tell her his complete tale, but there were parts . . . and why not? She *should* know. "I'm in love with someone—"

She skidded to a halt. "You are not married, are you?" she said with alarm.

"No, heavens no," he promised and she relaxed

slightly, then asked with curiosity, "Is this other woman in love with you? Or does she cause you uncertainty? Is that why you've agreed so quickly to aid my cause?"

Michael looked up at the night sky. How to explain his love for Ivy? "I think she is in love with me. At one time, she was. I love her."

"Now you sound like me," Miss Kenyon chided softly.

Michael grunted a response and continued. "In truth, when we first pledged our love, we were very young, but knew our own minds. However, over the years, her affections have—" He paused, suddenly realizing he'd been about to confess a fear he'd not even admitted to himself, a fear Ivy no longer loved him. The realization was unsettling. "She loves me," he said almost as if convincing himself. "However, I need to win her once and for all. Unfortunately, I've agreed to do something foolish and perhaps I'm trying to atone for my transgression by helping you."

Miss Kenyon lightly touched his arm, empathy in her eyes. "Love isn't easy, is it?"

He glanced down at her gloved fingers. "No," he agreed.

They started walking again, at an even slower pace this time. Michael found it felt good to broach the topic of his doubts over Ivy with someone. He'd kept all this to himself for too long. "My family has never truly admired her and they can't seem to comprehend my devotion. I've changed my life for her. I've given everything I have to marry her."

"Thomas was the first person who accepted me in Wye. We were both children. My parents had just died and I didn't know my uncle very well. Thomas's friendship meant everything to me." She frowned and added, "Of course, my feelings of being left out are actually jealousy, aren't they? Humbling thought."

"I understand all too well." And he did. Jealousy had eaten him alive in London as he'd watched Ivy flirt with other men. He'd agreed to this fool's errand out of his jealousy. He saw that now.

And it made him uncomfortable.

They walked on a few more steps and then he couldn't stop himself from asking, "You say you love Thomas, but do you truly believe he loves you?"

"He must," Miss Kenyon answered. "We were so close. We could finish each other's sentences and I always knew what he was thinking. Perhaps my uncle is right. If Uncle Geoff hadn't taken ill when he did, then I would have married Thomas and all would be well."

"Or perhaps such constant companionship breeds more familiarity than love?"

She didn't like his observation. "We were in love," she said firmly.

"Were?"

Even in the moonlight he could see her blush over her mistake. *"Are,"* she corrected. "I saw Thomas this afternoon. I told him I had an escort for the ball. He was upset."

Michael shook his head. "If he could so easily promise himself to another, why would you want him back?"

She whirled on him. "Because love means one should forgive. He hurt me, but only out of his own weakness. Some men turn to jelly in the company of a beautiful woman and Lady Elfreda is beautiful. She also comes with a handsome dowry. If I were in Thomas's shoes, I don't know if I wouldn't choose her over me. However, a love of such long-standing as ours must count for something. Loyalty should have a value."

He didn't know anything about Lady Elfreda's beauty, but Miss Kenyon, standing there in the moonlight and vowing her love, appeared radiant in his eyes. And, yes, loyalty should count for something.

"It does," he agreed quietly. "More than you shall ever know."

She blushed again, hearing the admiration in his voice and this, too, charmed him. Unlike other women, she seemed completely oblivious to her own special loveliness. "Well, sadly, we will not be able to solve the problems of love in one night. Especially now that I'm home."

He looked around and saw they'd come to a gate. Geoffrey Kenyon's home. A long path led to the front door of the brick house. There was no welcoming lantern and inside all was dark. "Are you certain someone is home?"

"My uncle rarely goes out," she assured him. She opened the gate. "Thank you for walking me home."

"My pleasure." Michael found he was reluctant to let her go. He offered his hand. "Good night, Miss Kenyon."

"Jocelyn," she corrected. "After sharing such confidences, and since we both seem to be star-crossed lovers, we have become more than simple acquaintances."

She was right, and he felt better for having talked to her. He raised her hand to his lips and gave it a light kiss. "Good night, Jocelyn." He liked the musical sound of her name. "I'm Michael."

"Good night, Michael." She gave the tips of his fingers

a small squeeze. "And thank you for having the imagination to take part in Lucy's scheme. It may work."

"I hope you win your heart's desire," he said, meaning the words.

Her eyes crinkled with pleasure. "And may the woman you love see what a gallant and thoughtful gentleman you are."

Their hands parted, and Michael felt the loss of connection.

Did she?

Her gaze met his, her smile tentative, and then with the grace of a moonlit goddess she turned and hurried up to the door of her house. She gave him one backward glance, a small wave of her hand, and she slipped inside. A second later, he saw the flicker of a candle.

Michael stood for a long, thoughtful moment. He wished Ivy had a touch of Jocelyn's conviction, of her spirit.

Then, he'd be more certain whenever she said she loved him.

He started walking back down the road and came across Kent and Lucy. The three of them returned home but Michael wasn't ready for sleep. His conscience bothered him. He didn't know what impact his stealing the formula would have on Jocelyn's life, but he feared it could not be good. Furthermore, he'd just spent the whole evening with her and hadn't brought up the subject of her uncle once. There was something about Jocelyn that made him forget his mission.

Nor was he good at subterfuge and Michael decided the sooner he caught the goods on Kenyon the better he would feel.

Tonight was as good as any to scout Kenyon's house.

He stole out of the Lettmans' and made his way back toward Jocelyn's home. Leaving the road and cutting through a pasture, he approached the house, checking for any sign of movement. All was quiet. Both Jocelyn and her uncle were obviously asleep.

Satisfied, he traveled to the rear of the house and found himself in a moonlit garden. Even at night, it was a lush and beautiful place. A path of crushed shells gleamed in the darkness and there was the scent of newly budded roses and fertile soil in the air. He could imagine Jocelyn here.

Creeping up to the side of the house, he peeped in some windows. Moonlight through the windows allowed him to see a portion of the rooms. He went from one window to another until he saw a desk covered with papers. There was also a table piled high with glass containers and different instruments he could not define. The rest of the room was as dark as Hades. Even with the windows closed there was the peculiar odor of sulfur and chemicals in the air. This had to be Kenyon's office.

The find made him feel good.

He took a step back, trying to decide what to do next when he heard a footfall behind him. There followed a soft gasp of surprise.

Michael whirled and there stood Jocelyn, still wearing the robin's egg blue dress although she'd taken the ribbons from her hair, which curled down around her shoulders. She'd removed her gloves.

"What are you still doing here, Michael?" she asked.

What the devil was *she* doing wandering around the garden in the dark of the night?

She'd caught him—and he had nothing to say.

The military had taught him the best tactical strategy was always diversion. So Michael did the first and most expedient thing he could think of to take her mind off his damnable snooping.

He swung her around and kissed her.

Chapter Seven

A Full Moon's Lunacy

Jocelyn was shocked. For a second, she couldn't breathe, she couldn't think.

Restless, with a hundred doubts and worries, she'd decided a turn in the garden would ease her mind. She had not expected to find herself waylaid in her own yard, and of all things—kissed by Michael. Why, she'd just been introduced to the man that day!

Even more astounding, she wasn't afraid. She pressed her hands against his shoulders to push him away—except curiosity got the better of her.

Her uncle wasn't the only one willing to experiment. Jocelyn had never been kissed by any man save Thomas and his had been safe pecks on the cheek and not this all-out assault. Besides, this kiss felt right.

For the briefest of moments, she allowed herself to relax in Michael's arms. His body was rock hard and solid, a far cry from what one would expect from a tea merchant.

From him came a slight hesitation, a hint of surprise.

The kiss changed.

It was as if he, too, were a bit curious. For whatever reason, he pressed the advantage, gently urging her lips to part and accept him. The effect was a bit like swallowing a thimbleful of peach liqueur—it went straight to her head and made her pleasantly dizzy.

Their kiss took on a life of its own. Their mouths fit together perfectly. His arms around her waist pulled her closer, and she discovered their mouths weren't the only thing that fit together perfectly!

Then, she felt the brush of his tongue against hers. *What was this?*

He did it again. His hand cupped her cheek and eased her into accepting him. Tentatively, she responded. Their kiss took on a new passion and Jocelyn reveled in the discovery of new sensations. She could have stood here kissing like this for hours—but then, he broke it off.

"Jocelyn?" His voice sounded as if he'd been drugged with laudanum.

"Michael?" She didn't sound more coherent herself.

He removed his hand from where it had been resting on her waist. A rush of cool night air brought her to her senses and she was immediately embarrassed.

She practically jumped out of his arms. "What were you doing?"

Her sharp words sobered him, too. He placed a finger over her lips. "Shhh. Pretend we are lovers."

"We were just doing a remarkable imitation." Her cheeks burned at the memory of how completely she'd given herself over to him.

In the moonlight, she could see the planes of his face, but the expression in his silver eyes was lost in shadow.

His arm returned to her waist, his voice a low hum close to her ear. "Your Thomas is here, lurking beyond the garden. You wanted to make him jealous, didn't you?"

She started to turn to look but his arms pulled her back. "No," he whispered against her hair. "We don't want him to think we know he's there. What better way to make him believe I am a serious suitor than to be caught in the garden together?"

Something was not right. "Why would he be lurking in the garden?"

"I don't know. I've never laid eyes on him."

"Then how do you know it is him?"

Michael pulled back, his mouth flattening into a frown. "Are you always this suspicious?"

"Do you always grab women and kiss them?" she countered.

Before he could answer, there was movement in the overgrown Hebe bushes at the back of the garden.

Jocelyn went still. Thomas *was* there. She could feel his presence. She stepped closer to Michael.

"So you believe me now," he crowed quietly.

"Hmmmm," she murmured, all too aware of his body heat and not really in a rush to move away. Funny, she'd never noticed another man except Thomas. However, here in Michael's arms, she was aware of every nuance, every detail. He smelled spicy warm and very masculine. His hands were large and capable, with long tapered fingers. They were the hands of a man who could handle anything.

She shouldn't be this observant if she were in love with Thomas . . . should she? Even though Michael *was* doing her a favor?

He moved a step closer, the weight of his hand at her waist comfortable and reassuring. The tip of her nose rubbed against the underside of his chin. His beard was already growing in and she couldn't resist nuzzling his skin, intrigued by the prickly smoothness.

This was madness.

Michael had congratulated himself on his quick thinking. He'd spun quite a story out of her need to make her former suitor jealous and he thanked the Lord for the rustling of whatever animal was in the bushes to give credence to his lies—except now he found himself the victim of his own ruse.

Her kiss had almost undone him. It had been a heady mix of innocence and innate sensuality. Jocelyn was not the kind of woman who would hold back. No, she would give all and right now, with her breasts against his chest and his manhood happily ready for duty, his thoughts were anything but gentlemanly.

Then her nose tickled the underside of his chin. He frowned down at her. Her eyes were shiny in the moonlight. "Do you think he's left?" she whispered, snuggling closer.

"I don't know." His heartbeat pounded in his ears. Could she not *feel* his reaction to her?

"We can't stand here all night."

He didn't want to *stand* here all night. He wanted to lift her skirts—

Dear God, what had he gotten himself into? He'd never been a lothario. He'd always had control over his lusts. After all, he'd taken his promise to Ivy seriously.

So why did he hear himself say, "One more kiss and he'll be good and jealous?"

Her eyes widened slightly at the suggestion and then she nodded, her lashes fluttering down as she offered her mouth up to him. Michael felt like a scoundrel taking advantage of her trust, and yet he could not resist.

He brushed his lips against hers. She caught her breath. Against his chest, he felt her nipples tighten. He could picture her breasts in his mind, firm and ripe with dark seductive nipples. He was lost. There was no hesitation as he claimed his next kiss, nor did he hold back. Hot blood raced through his veins and he couldn't have attempted caution if he'd wished. He kissed her soundly and fully and she met him every step of the way.

Her tongue slid along his. Her hands fisted the material of his cheap "peddler" jacket and held on tightly as if she feared being swept away. He slipped his hand down along the indentation of her waist, over the curve of her buttock, pressing her intimately against himself.

A man could lose all sanity with a woman who could kiss like this—

A snore with the resonance of a bear's rumble broke through the stillness of the night.

Michael barely registered the sound but it had an immediate and dramatic effect on Jocelyn. She started, her hands pushing him away. Dazed, he broke the kiss, keeping a protective arm around her. "What is that?"

"My uncle. He often falls asleep in his laboratory and when he is deeply asleep, he snores so loud the roof shakes. I shall have to wake him and urge him to his bed."

Jocelyn pulled his arms from her waist. "I must go

in. It would not be good if he caught us out here."

He nodded, his movements slow. After all, there was no blood in his brain at this moment.

She leaned up to his ear, her body stretching along his, but her words were anything but lover like. "I think Thomas is gone now."

Her question was a bucket of cold water on his passion. Here he was, his arms around the girl . . . and she was thinking of another man. He wanted to roar with frustration.

What was it about him that the women he courted couldn't seem to give him their undivided attention?

The whole reason he had his entire body wrapped around Jocelyn was to prove himself to Ivy, who was probably off somewhere in London flirting with a viscount. Meanwhile, Jocelyn worried over a bumpkin without the wit to know what he had.

"Oh, I am certain he is long gone," Michael answered brusquely, hating even his own lie at this moment.

She nodded and took a step toward the house. "I must go." Impulsively, she reached out and gave his hand a brotherly squeeze. "Thank you. Thank you for all that you are doing. You are a kind man, Michael."

She faded into the shadows and was gone. He heard the door open a crack and shut behind her.

Kind?

He stood alone in the garden moonlight feeling like a bloody fool.

He couldn't' believe how caught up in the moment he'd been. He'd enjoyed her kisses, hell, he was *obsessed* with them. He'd wanted to sink down to the ground with her and make endless, mindless love to her.

And she thought he was merely being *kind?*

Was this how Ivy saw him and why she hadn't been more receptive to him in London? While he thought he was being a gentleman, did she view him as some sort of prig and long for more of the rake? After all, what man wanted to be thought of as *kind?*

Geoffrey Kenyon's resonant snore mocked him.

Michael turned away and walked toward the road. Jocelyn was probably already in bed, dreaming of the man she loved while he'd stood out in the garden ready to howl out of frustration. Especially when he realized he'd been too busy kissing to gain any information on Kenyon or his formula!

He walked fast to burn off pent-up energy, his mind working furiously.

He had to continue to see Jocelyn. After all, she was his entry to her uncle . . . and he would take her to the ball. He'd promised. But that didn't mean he couldn't enjoy the venture—and yes, he had enough pride to want Jocelyn to see him as a potent lover. He was *not* some "kind" man. The characterization left a sour taste in his mouth.

But what if he were too much of a gentleman? What if that was the reason women chose others before him?

The question haunted him long into the night.

From the darkness of her bedroom, which overlooked the garden, Jocelyn peered through the curtains and watched Michael leave. He swatted at a rosebush as if something angered him. She touched her lips. They were still swollen from his bruising kisses and deep within, she felt edgy with need.

What had she done?

The kisses she'd shared with Michael could have set the village afire. They certainly had sparked a flame in her—and she had only met the man today. She'd allowed him to take shocking liberties. If her uncle's snore hadn't reminded her of where she was, who knows what could have happened?

And right there in front of Thomas.

She strained her eyes to see if she could spot Thomas, but she couldn't. Perhaps he had slipped away while she had been busy kissing.

Dropping the curtain back into place, she walked barefoot to her bed and climbed between the sheets, but she didn't go right to sleep. She couldn't. Of course, she should have been sleepless worrying about what Thomas thought of her kissing Michael. Instead, she found herself worrying over her yellow muslin dress.

Before, it had been fine enough to wear to the ball. Now she needed something else. She wanted something new, something special.

Counting on her fingers in the dark, she attempted to estimate how much she could spend on a dress if she economized the household expenses for the next month.

The sum was not impressive.

She told herself she would think of something. After all, Thomas would really notice her in a new frock. However, as she fell asleep, it wasn't Thomas she was thinking about . . . it was Michael and his kisses.

Dear Lord, that man knew how to kiss!

Thomas came out of his hiding place in one of the overgrown Hebe shrubs and shook off the twigs and the leaves. He had come over this evening to talk to Jocelyn and find out who was escorting her to his betrothal ball. He hoped it was Billy Fletcher.

And of course, he'd had to be careful. What if someone saw him at the Kenyons' and reported back to Elfreda?

Her uncle had informed him she was dining with the Lettmans. Thomas should have returned home, but he hadn't. Instead, he'd hidden in the garden waiting for her to return. He'd felt a bit foolish—but he had to see her.

Unfortunately, he was rewarded for his patience when she'd returned from the Lettmans' with a stranger. This man was *not* from Wye. Furthermore, Jocelyn had *never* kissed Thomas the way she'd been kissing him. Nor had they ever had assignations in the garden in the middle of the night.

He covered the ground between her house and his own, his mind troubled. Here he had thought she was brokenhearted . . . and in reality she was involved in a love affair.

The thought brought Thomas to a standstill. Jealousy raged through him.

Yes, she was free to pursue another. After all, he was marrying someone else, *but she hadn't waited very long, had she?* Why, his betrothal hadn't even been announced yet!

He was in a foul mood when he returned home and not ready for his mother's curious questions. Of course, she'd waited up; she always waited up. But he wasn't in the mood to talk.

Chapter Eight

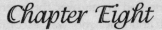

Another Tangle to the Web

$\mathcal{R}$ose Burkhardt loved her son Thomas but knew he needed direction in life. For the past ten years or so, she'd feared he would marry Jocelyn Kenyon. She'd always known he could do much better.

Her conviction had been vindicated when Lady Elfreda had singled out her son. And her choice had made Rose a celebrity in the village.

It was a good match and Lord Vaughn was very generous. Rose was not going to let Jocelyn Kenyon ruin this marriage. Oh, she had no doubt the chit would try if she could. Ever since the orphaned Jocelyn had arrived in Wye she'd latched on to her Thomas. Public sympathy was on Jocelyn's side and over the years Rose couldn't say anything derogatory without appearing churlish. But that didn't stop her from practically doing a jig in the street when Thomas had solved the problem himself by falling in love with Elfreda.

Or was he really in love?

Rose was too aware that there was still time to cry off

and that wherever Thomas had been this late at night, he'd *not* been to Lord Vaughn's.

She could have wagered the milk money her son had been to see Jocelyn and his sullenness did not bode well for his marriage.

After a sleepless night, she came up with a scheme.

The next morning, at a reasonable hour, she went to see Lady Elfreda on the pretense of offering her good silver platter for use on Friday night.

Lady Elfreda was happy to see her. "Thank you so much for your offer. However, I believe everything is in good order."

"Yes, of course it is," Rose said. "I knew it would be. I don't know what I was thinking. I didn't sleep well last night." With a long-suffering sigh, she admitted, "Thomas was out late. I never sleep whenever anyone in my family is out at night. I was the same way about my dear departed husband, bless his soul. Never could shut an eye."

She knew the mention of Thomas's name would command Lady Elfreda's complete attention. "He was out late? He left here early."

"I'm certain he was with friends," Rose offered.

"Yes, he is very popular." However, a small line of worry appeared between Lady Elfreda's brows.

"He is," Rose agreed, waited two beats and then speculated, "Of course, I do know he saw Jocelyn Kenyon yesterday. I don't mean to meddle, my lady, but you must be on guard at all times. There are women who wouldn't hesitate to poach on another's intended."

The color drained from Lady Elfreda's face at the mention of Jocelyn's name. "He saw her?"

"Oh, they are old friends. You have nothing to worry about in that quarter," Rose said, knowing full well Lady Elfreda would do exactly that.

"Yes, you are right," the younger woman murmured.

Then, having decided the proper interval for a call had been observed, and having accomplished her purpose, Rose said her good-byes.

Thomas would not have another chance to dally after Jocelyn. Oh, no, not at all.

Of course, once the betrothal was announced, all would be safe.

Chapter Nine

❧

Wooed in Earnest?

*B*y midmorning, Jocelyn finally reached a decision about her yellow muslin . . . and successfully put the kisses in the garden out of her mind, sort of.

She would take the dress to Mrs. Jeter, the local seamstress, to see if she could freshen it, perhaps fashion a new bodice out of another material or put a flounce hem on the skirt. This way the cost would not be out of the range of Jocelyn's meager funds.

With the relatively new dress and Michael by her side, well, Thomas would have to take notice.

In the calm light of day, she could dismiss the kisses she and Michael had shared. The moonlight had caused both of them to lose their heads a little. There had been no meaning to those kisses other than to put on a good show for Thomas—although she wasn't going to let Michael kiss her again. There was no sense in pressing her luck!

Downstairs, a foul smell made her nose wrinkle and led her to her uncle's laboratory. "You promised you weren't going to burn the rubber anymore," she complained.

"I had to," he threw over his shoulder with frustration. "I can't figure the stuff out. The only way I can manipulate its properties is with heat."

"Open a window," she ordered, and then seeing he wasn't paying attention, she went around and did it herself. For a second, looking over the garden, she paused, remembering last night.

Her garden was her delight. It was an eclectic mixture of shrubs, flowers, and herbs. Some of the plants had come all the way from the Orient. The overgrown Hebe bushes formed the back "wall" and a bench in the center was surrounded by roses, lavender, and germander.

She and Michael had been standing beside this window where morning glories climbed the brick. A sudden heat rushed through her and she had to forcefully put the memory of their meeting from her mind. "I'm going to the dressmaker's."

Uncle Geoff nodded, too involved in his experiment to answer.

Jocelyn put her yellow dress into a basket, tied the wide pink ribbon of her Gypsy straw bonnet beneath her chin, and stepped outside. There was the promise of summer in the air. The day was perfect for an outing with huge, fat clouds drifting across a blue sky. And, as she walked down the steps, she saw Michael waiting for her by the gate.

Her heart kicked up a beat. *Dear Lord, he is handsome.*

He smiled as if reading her thoughts. "How are you this morning?"

"Well. Thank you."

His smile turned lazy, his gaze dropping to her lips. "I was coming to pay a call."

Jocelyn struggled to keep her wits. "I'm sorry. I have an errand to run." She slipped out the gate. "Perhaps later?"

"Where are you going? I'll walk with you," he replied.

She didn't know if that was a wise idea. Her resolve to keep her focus on Thomas was quickly evaporating. "I'm certain you have more important things to do," she persisted. "Like sell tea."

"Oh, that." He frowned, and then brightened as he answered, "I could sell some to you. What is your preference? Indian spice or Earl Grey? Do you like a strong or mild blend?"

"I'm not truly a tea drinker. Perhaps you should ask someone else?"

He dismissed the idea. "I can do that later. Right now, nothing is more important to me than you."

Jocelyn stopped dead in her tracks, uncertain. Gone was the easy friendship of last night and in its place was something more heated. Something more interesting.

He took her basket from her. "Here, let me help." Before she could protest, he started walking toward the center of the village and she had no choice but to follow.

They walked in silence for a moment. Jocelyn found herself in a wondrous panic over the thought he might actually be attracted to her. What did this mean?

And how did she feel about it?

Words failed her. After all, she was in love with Thomas . . . or so she had to remind herself.

On such a fine day, a good number of people were out

and about. A group of girls giggled into their hands over some joke only they knew and neighbors were out sweeping their steps or meeting on the street for a gossip. They eyed Jocelyn and Michael as they walked by and there were more than a few raised eyebrows. The Clark sisters, the village spinsters, couldn't help a soft "Oh my," as they passed and Jocelyn felt a touch of vindication. The sisters had been the first to shake their heads and announce her "on the shelf" when Thomas had jilted her.

"We are causing some comment," Michael observed dryly.

"There are few strangers in Wye."

"And the one stranger there is is walking with you."

Again, he gave her a warm, appreciative smile that set her stomach fluttering. His marked attention, especially in public, made her uncertain. "Your escorting me to the ball is an arrangement between us," she reminded him in a low undervoice. "You don't need to playact for the village."

"Who said I'm playacting?"

Jocelyn turned to him, but any retort died on her lips because when she looked at him, all she could think about were his kisses. Yet, some inner voice warned her to be careful. This was all too quick, too convenient. He had a motive she couldn't quite understand.

Then she remembered that last night he'd confessed he was in love with someone else. She became even more suspicious.

However, before she could question him, the vicar's wife, Mrs. Banks, came out of the butcher's shop, right in front of them. With a hint of surprise, she said, "Hello, Miss Kenyon, how are you?" Her question may have been directed to Jocelyn, but her gaze was on Michael. Her husband the vicar was Uncle's Geoff's closest friend.

Jocelyn grudgingly introduced Michael, and he was quick to charm the woman. Mrs. Banks was obviously impressed. "You sell tea? I drink lots of tea. You must call on me."

"That I shall," he assured her.

"Don't let him forget," she warned Jocelyn.

"I won't."

Mrs. Banks smiled again at Michael. "One would never imagine you a peddler, such polish. Good day, Miss Kenyon, Mr. Donaldson." She turned and went on her way but had gone no more than six steps before the Clark sisters and Mrs. Mayes waylaid her, obviously full of questions.

"She's right," Jocelyn said thoughtfully, moving away from the chattering women. "You do carry yourself well, much like I imagine a soldier would. Have you been in the military?"

Her observation apparently surprised and, to her mind, pleased him. "What makes you suspect that?"

"The straightness of your back and the precision of your movements. You also have this habit of acting as if you should be the one in charge. You don't like following another's lead, do you?"

He laughed. "I do like giving orders. Of course, I was the youngest of five brothers and three sisters. I've had more than my share of being bullied around. If I didn't speak up, I'd be drowned out in the crowd."

That he had such a large family intrigued her. "Where were you raised?"

"Sussex. You can't tell?"

She shook her head. "You have no accent. And I can tell you are well-educated by the way you speak. Mrs. Banks is right. You are not the sort of man I would imagine to be peddling wares over the countryside."

"Peddling is honest work," he countered. "The villages are the backbone of England and I like meeting people."

"Undoubtedly," she answered. "But why would a soldier be marching through them pretending to be a tea merchant?"

Her question had been a stab in the dark and she was surprised to realize she'd hit a mark.

More amazing was that instead of denying her accusation, his lips curved with admiration. "Well done, Jocelyn." He leaned toward her, his voice close to her ear. "And my answer is, perhaps he is looking for a dark-haired beauty with a lively intelligence. The sort of woman a man can't find just anywhere."

His compliment robbed her of speech. She stared, uncertain whether to believe him.

He accentuated his words by bringing her hand up to his lips. Right there, in front of Mrs. Jeter's dress shop and all of Wye.

Jocelyn's heart pounded against her chest. His kiss on her fingers had been a mere brush of the lips and yet she felt the heat of it all the way through her York tan gloves.

She pulled her scrambled wits together. "You didn't answer my question, Michael."

"About why I enjoy being a peddler?" he asked, equivocating.

"No, about what it is you want, and why," she answered, her voice barely a whisper. "I may be naïve, sir, but I am not slow-minded. I sense there is more to you than meets the eye."

His silvery gaze met hers. "Isn't it obvious what I want? I want you."

Jocelyn stared at him, a part of her wanting to believe his words, and another part warning her to be wary.

His lips curved into a lazy smile. "Give ground, Jocelyn," he begged softly. "I want no more than your friendship."

She might have challenged his statement except he changed the subject. Opening the door to Mrs. Jeter's shop, its merry bell announcing their arrival, he said, "Shall we go inside?"

"You would go in with me, too?" she asked, not moving.

"Of course, why not?" he said.

"Well, because there isn't a man in Wye who likes to cool his heels inside Mrs. Jeter's."

He laughed, his straight even teeth flashing in the sun. "I want to be where you are." He held up a hand to ward off her protests. "Please, Jocelyn, don't warn me again that I need not be attentive—" Which was exactly what she'd been about to do. "—Or that I should go sell tea. I'm where I want to be."

And, God help her, she wanted to believe him. Jocelyn had no choice but to enter the shop.

Mrs. Jeter was pleased to see her—and she liked the look of Michael, too. She offered him a glass of cider and a chair by the window while they conducted their business.

The dress shop was a small room with a long counter and several tables stacked high with fabric. One stack was silks, another cambrics, and another muslins, all in various shades and colors. Fitting rooms and a workshop were in the back, separated by a flowered curtain.

Jocelyn was a bit shy about talking over changes to the dress with Mrs. Jeter in front of Michael, but he appeared lost in his own thoughts as he studied the comings and goings on the street outside.

Mrs. Jeter thought she had a piece of green velvet that would make a lovely bodice and hem to the yellow muslin. Jocelyn didn't know how the two fabrics would look together and she was no longer certain she wanted to cut off the embroidered hem.

"I'll bring it out and we'll have a look." The dressmaker went into her back room.

As Jocelyn turned to say something to Michael, she noticed his gaze was riveted to something he saw outside the window. She looked and caught sight of Lord Vaughn's coat of arms on the side of his coach.

Less than a heartbeat later, the welcoming bell over the door tinkled and Lady Elfreda walked in . . . escorted by Thomas.

Chapter Ten

The Yellow Muslin

*F*rom the way Jocelyn tensed, Michael instantly knew this was Thomas and his new love. The three of them froze in a tableau of annoyed recognition and dismayed surprise.

Of course, there had been no mistaking the earl's coach. As the son of an earl, Michael knew what impact the coat of arms on a coach could have on a sleepy village . . . and he sensed Lady Elfreda knew it, too.

He'd come to his feet when she entered the shop and almost had to rub his eyes to see if they were playing tricks. Lady Elfreda was a beauty—and an identical twin to Ivy! On closer inspection, her features were not as fine as Ivy's but there was a definite likeness. They could have been sisters. She had the same glorious blond hair, vibrant blue eyes and she carried herself with the studied grace of the schoolroom, much like a hundred other debutantes.

He found himself unexpectedly thinking he preferred Jocelyn's more animated style than Elfreda's refined gentility.

But the true object of his curiosity was her beloved Thomas. And he was disappointed . . . naturally.

Yes, the man was darkly handsome in a roughhewn manner. Lucy had said he was a farmer and obviously a successful one. He also had those deep blue eyes the ladies all seemed to like, but to Michael's mind he wasn't anything special. He saw nothing about Thomas that should command Jocelyn's loyalty.

Thomas met his frank gaze with a scowl so fierce it took both the women by surprise. Lady Elfreda wrapped her arm possessively around his while Jocelyn moved to stand in front of Michael, who couldn't understand what he'd done to earn the younger man's instant animosity.

Jocelyn looked back over her shoulder. "The kiss," she whispered.

But Michael knew Thomas hadn't actually witnessed the kiss, so his obvious jealousy must stem from his still being in love with Jocelyn.

Michael discovered he didn't like that thought.

Poor Mrs. Jeter walked out of her back room, a piece of green velvet in her hand, and came to a halt. "Oh, my," she murmured, aware of the crosscurrents in the room. She hurried forward and bobbed a curtsey. "Good morning, Lady Elfreda. Your dress is almost ready."

"Thank you," Lady Elfreda said, pointedly giving her back to Jocelyn and Michael.

It was not a wise move. Jocelyn bristled at the slight. Michael took a step to her side. "She's jealous. Be careful."

His warning served to bring out her stubbornness. "Good morning, my lady," she said in a bright, cheery voice. "How are you today?" She studiously ignored Thomas's presence.

Lady Elfreda appeared tempted to cut Jocelyn and yet had enough good manners to not be so unwise. "I am well, Miss Kenyon. And yourself?"

"Very well, thank you. Let me introduce you to Mr. Donaldson. He's a tea merchant who is visiting Wye and is staying with Mr. and Mrs. Lettman. Mr. Donaldson, this is Lady Elfreda and her—" A slight hesitation here. "—Her escort, Mr. Burkhardt. Mr. Donaldson will be escorting my uncle and myself to the ball if that meets with your approval."

Lady Elfreda's reserve instantly thawed. "You wish to bring a guest? Why, by all means, please do." She gifted Michael with a radiant smile. "Welcome to Wye, sir. Have you known Miss Kenyon long?"

"For a very short time, but I must admit I am enjoying my stay and her company." He placed his hand possessively on Jocelyn's elbow and enjoyed watching Burkhardt grind his teeth while pretending bravado.

"A tea peddler?" the farmer said with a smirk and then turned away to laugh quietly under his breath.

Lady Elfreda gave him a cross look and Michael couldn't help but like her. She was no snob and struck him as a good soul, especially when she tactfully changed the subject. "May I try the dress on, Mrs. Jeter?"

The seamstress picked up her cue. "Yes, my lady, this way, please." She started for the back room.

Turning to Burkhardt, Lady Elfreda said, "I shall not be long. Perhaps you have an errand or two to run?"

Burkhardt shook his head and to her dismay said, "I'll

wait. Perhaps I can convince Mr. Donaldson to brew a cup of tea for me."

Michael wasn't about to comment on such a juvenile swipe, knowing both women were smart enough to look down on Burkhardt for being a fool. Instead, he said pleasantly, "I'll be happy to set an appointment to show you my teas."

"Don't bother," Burkhardt countered.

"Thomas," Lady Elfreda started even as Jocelyn stepped between the two men.

"I'll behave," Thomas promised Lady Elfreda, who had no choice but to go in and try on her dress.

Jocelyn moved Michael back over to the corner where he had been sitting. "It's working," she said with an excited whisper. "I've never seen him so jealous. Your kisses did the trick."

"Yes, yes," Michael murmured, frustrated to be a victim again of those blasted kisses. Perhaps *both* women weren't wise enough to see Burkhardt for the buffoon he was. He turned away.

If Jocelyn noticed he was irritated, it didn't seem to bother her. Instead, she fetched the piece of velvet the dressmaker had placed on the counter and held it up to her yellow gown. She stood not more than four feet from Burkhardt.

Michael frowned, an action the farmer caught. The air between them tensed, especially when, with a smile, Burkhardt sidled along the counter toward Jocelyn.

"What are you doing?" he asked. "You aren't going to change your yellow dress? It's my favorite on you."

"Well, all things must change," Jocelyn replied blithely and Michael wanted to shout "Good for you!"

But then Burkhardt took the dress away from her. He deliberately gave Michael his back and leaned forward to talk to Jocelyn in confidence.

Michael had enough.

He didn't like Burkhardt and, to his mind, he'd lost his chance with Jocelyn. He should leave her alone.

In two strides, he cut between them, took Jocelyn's arm and led her back toward the window. "Come, I want to show you something," he said loudly. However, once he had her safe, he murmured, "He's a boor."

"He's jealous," she answered and couldn't have sounded happier. "Your plan last night worked. And I think Lady Elfreda admires you."

"What?" He was so shocked he hadn't bothered to keep his voice down.

"Is something the matter, Jocelyn?" Burkhardt asked.

"No, everything is fine," she said blissfully.

Michael pulled her closer and his actions had nothing to do with his playing a role. "No, everything is *not* fine. You can hatch schemes for yourself but don't go matchmaking for me."

"Oh, I forgot. You already have someone you care for." Was it his imagination or was her comment a bit pointed?

"Yes, I do," he stated flatly and then realized Burkhardt was attempting to eavesdrop. He frowned, bringing Jocelyn closer into the corner with him. "You are the one scheming," he told her. "I'm merely an innocent party."

"I know." She glanced before adding unrepentantly, "I still believe you and Elfreda would make a handsome couple."

"Jocelyn."

"She's wealthy."

"I have my own money."

"Not like she has," she said with certainty.

He grunted an answer, definitely out of sorts. Here he'd been doing everything to charm her and she was trying to toss him to Lady Elfreda.

All this was his own fault. He shouldn't have gotten personally involved with Jocelyn's plight. But then, he understood the lovelorn, or thought he did. He just didn't think this Burkhardt was worthy of her, and perversely, even though it was none of his business, he told her as much, right there in the dress shop with the rascal glowering at his back.

"You don't know him," she answered.

"Have you ever kissed him the way you kissed me last night?"

Her brows came together in indignation. "I've kissed him before."

He raised a suspicious eyebrow. "Like you kissed me last night?"

"Of course."

"You're lying."

"What makes you think that?"

"Because I've had more experience kissing than you have and kisses like those we shared don't come along very often. Jocelyn, take my advice and forget about Burkhardt. He'd bore you to death in a fortnight." The moment he spoke the words, he knew they were true.

But she wasn't going to believe him, not the stubborn and proud Jocelyn. She gave him a cold look. "I've known Thomas all my life. He's the only man I could ever love."

"Except I'm the better kisser," Michael goaded.

Jocelyn rolled her eyes. "I kissed you to make him jealous. I knew he was watching."

"You're lying," he answered with a calmness he was far from feeling.

"No, I'm not." She punctuated this statement with a complacent little smile.

This woman could drive a man to madness. She couldn't have kissed him the way she had last night and not have had *some* attraction for him. Or could she?

He used their close proximity to demonstrate to her she wasn't impervious to him. "I'd like to kiss you again," he said quietly. "Right here. I'd like to lean you back over those bolts of fabrics and kiss you senseless."

Now, he had her attention. He continued, lowering his head so his lips brushed her ear. "And then, I would make love to you, right there on top of those silks. And when I was done, there would be no thought of any man but me in your brain."

Her mouth dropped open. She was shocked by his boldness and yet, her nipples had hardened into tight buds that pressed against the material of her bodice.

Michael smiled. "You are not unaffected by me, no matter what your lying lips may say."

"Jocelyn, is something wrong?" Burkhardt's voice cut into the moment.

She pulled away and Michael let her go. He'd proven his point.

"No, nothing," she said, looking daggers at Michael.

Burkhardt moved forward as if coming to her rescue but Jocelyn ignored him by turning her back and pretending to be interested in the fabrics. When she realized she was examining a silk, her cheeks reddened and Michael knew she had visions of them making love.

Her gaze met his and for a second, the heat her look inspired threatened to set him on fire.

What was he doing? Why couldn't he have left well enough alone? His job was to retrieve a formula, not sort out Jocelyn's love life or become attracted to her himself. Years of careful planning and sacrifice were in danger of being thrown away.

Especially when she returned her attention to the silks, rubbing the fabric between her fingers. Without looking at him, she whispered, "This woman you love must be very lucky."

And he almost confessed all.

Fortunately, Lady Elfreda came out of the back room with Mrs. Jeter preventing his response. "My dress is going to be beautiful," she announced, but her smile turned uncertain as she sensed the tension in the air. She looked to Burkhardt, who glared at Michael, who in turn was focused on Jocelyn. The sparkle in Lady Elfreda's eyes died and Michael laid her unhappiness at Burkhardt's door.

The foolish farmer wanted both of them. The idea made Michael unreasonably angry.

"I believe it is time to leave," Lady Elfreda informed Burkhardt. Her words seemed to remind him of his responsibilities.

"Yes, of course."

"The dress is nice," she told him.

"I'm certain," Burkhardt replied, his attention straying back to Jocelyn.

The corners of Lady Elfreda's mouth tightened. She gave last-minute instructions to the dressmaker, turned on her heel, and left the shop. Burkhardt had to hurry to catch up with her. Michael looked out the window and watched the two of them go down the street toward the church on another errand.

"I don't like him," he announced.

Mrs. Jeter didn't know what to say and Jocelyn pointedly ignored him. Instead, she walked to the counter and continued the discussion about the green velvet bodice that Lady Elfreda's arrival had interrupted.

Michael sat back down in the chair, feeling very much like a schoolboy who had been dismissed by his elders.

What the devil was happening to him? He loved Ivy . . . and yet there was something about Jocelyn that caught his imagination, that provoked him and made him want her to see how much better she was than Burkhardt.

He watched the women compare the velvet against the muslin. He didn't understand why Jocelyn was refashioning the dress save for the possibility that Kenyon was not a wealthy man. Of course, that would be his motive for stealing Sir William's formula.

The two women left him to step into the back room. Michael hoped Jocelyn wasn't going to be much longer.

The bell rang over the shop door. Burkhardt entered and walked directly up to Michael.

"Don't think I'm fooled by you," the young farmer said in a low, heated voice. "You harm Jocelyn and I shall see you tarred, feathered, and maybe worse."

Michael rose. "How can I harm her any more than you already have? I'm not the one who jilted her."

Burkhardt's eyeballs practically popped out of his head, he was so angry. However, before he could say something else, the dressmaker pulled back the curtain. "Did someone come in? Oh, Mr. Burkhardt. Was there something else Lady Elfreda needed?" Jocelyn stood behind her.

Burkhardt recovered his temper quickly. "She thought she left her gloves in here."

"Why, no," the dressmaker said. "She had her gloves on when she left. I distinctly remember her putting them on."

"She must not have noticed," Burkhardt replied stiffly, caught in his lie. He abruptly left the shop without so much as a "good-bye."

A small frown appeared between Jocelyn's eyes. However, she finished her conversation with the dressmaker. "I'll let you know what I decide."

"You'd best hurry, dear," Mrs. Jeter said. "The ball is in two days. I can't work miracles."

"Yes, I know. Thank you." Jocelyn placed the yellow muslin back into her basket. She looked to Michael. "Are you ready to leave?"

He nodded and opened the door for her. Lady Elfreda's coach was gone.

They walked in silence for a bit, heading back in the direction of her uncle's house.

"You didn't do anything about the dress," he observed, prodding her into conversation. He found he did not like a quiet Jocelyn.

"It's fine as it is."

No, it wasn't. He had sisters. He knew enough about balls and women to know she would rather have had a new dress.

"I think our scheme is working," she said. "Thomas came back to the dress shop to see what we were up to, didn't he?"

This was not the subject Michael wanted to discuss; however, he had no choice. "He warned me away from you."

She stopped. "He did?"

"Pleased?" He couldn't help the cynicism in his voice or stop himself from adding again, "I think you can do better."

"So you've told me," she answered briskly. "However, I love him."

"Do you love him, or are you afraid of change?" He wanted to needle her into seeing her precious Thomas in a new light, except for the first time, his words struck a chord within him. Was he not guilty of the same with Ivy?

Jocelyn refused to answer. Head high, she resumed walking. He wished he knew what she was thinking— once she got her back up, she could be tricky. He changed subjects to draw her out.

"Why don't you ask your uncle for a new dress?"

"I like my yellow dress," she insisted.

"Why? Because you've worn it to every dance in memory?"

She stopped and faced him, a flash of fire in her brown eyes. At last, he felt she was truly looking at him. "And what if I have? Oh, pardon me, you are flush in the pocket, Mr. Tea Merchant; money means nothing to you."

"Selling tea isn't a bad living." It was the only thing he could think to say and he sounded stupid.

She shook her head and started walking.

But Michael realized he'd created an opening to ask about his real reason for being in Wye. He came up beside her. "What does your uncle do?"

He's an inventor. A chemist, actually. But he's also a bit of a tinker and a mechanic. He's very good. I mean, scientists from all over England correspond with him."

"What inventions has he created? Anything I would know about?"

She considered for a moment. "He helped one gentleman with what he called the 'trajectory' of a bridge and another he helped to make explosives not flare so quickly in a rocket."

"Rockets? Like what Congreve invented?"

"Absolutely. In fact, Uncle Geoff worked with Congreve. They are great friends."

Michael had seen some of Congreve's rockets fired during battle and they'd been so inaccurate at reaching their target, he had not been impressed. "What is your uncle working on now?"

Jocelyn shifted the basket from her left arm to her right. "Something dull but what could be very practical. He's been playing with rubber."

His voice carefully neutral, he asked, "Like India rubber, the stuff they make balls out of?"

"Yes, but he believes there are many good uses beyond an expensive child's toy if we can imagine a way to mold the material properly."

Here was the heart of what Michael had come in search of. "Uses like what?"

"Well," she said, forgetting her snit and dropping her voice to a confiding level, "he has a formula he believes will allow us to paint the rubber onto cloth so that the material can't be penetrated by water."

"There would be a hundred uses for something like that."

"Absolutely, and if he is successful, the manufacture of such a cloth could be worth a fortune."

"Did he create the formula or is this something he is working on with others?" Michael dared to ask.

Jocelyn shook her head. "Mr. Redding sent it to him. Mr. Redding is another chemist who lives in Dover. He's working with someone else, although I don't know that gentleman's name. Mr. Redding is hoping Uncle Geoff will be successful where they had failed."

Her story was completely different from Sir William's and made him wary. Someone was not being honest and he didn't like the notion it might be Sir William.

"You uncle must not like sharing his discoveries," Michael said.

Jocelyn laughed. "Oh no. He says nothing in the sciences could be achieved by a single mind. They all build one discovery on top of the other. Well, here I am."

Michael was surprised to realize they'd reached the gate of her house. He wasn't ready to let her go yet. He enjoyed her company.

As if reading his mind, she said, "I must go in. I have some letters to prepare for my uncle. I handle most of his correspondence."

So she *would* know if he and Mr. Redding had exchanged letters. "Tell me, have you ever heard of a Sir William Lewin?"

She considered for a moment. "I believe I have. He is an inventor of sorts. His name is on the rolls of the Royal Society. I'm certain Uncle Geoff knows him. Is he a friend of yours?"

"An acquaintance," Michael answered, speaking the truth. After all, how well *did* he know Sir William? He certainly didn't trust him and now suspected the motive for his being sent to Wye.

Of course, Michael's goal had been to win Ivy . . . although he hadn't thought about her very much today.

"You suddenly appear sad," Jocelyn said. She lightly touched his hand. "Why don't you come to dinner this evening and meet my uncle? He can be truly fascinating when he talks about his experiments."

There it was, an open invitation to accomplish what he'd been sent to do. "I'd like that," Michael said, and he wanted the opportunity to judge Kenyon himself. "What time?"

"Half past six? My uncle likes to eat early."

"Thank you," he said. "I'll be there." He held open the gate for her, although he was reluctant to let her go. As she passed him, he caught her fresh scent—air, flowers, and woman. It was more potent than any perfume.

"I'll see you this evening," she said. She started toward the house but then paused. "And, Michael?"

He looked up from closing the gate. "Yes?"

"You do kiss amazingly well." She colored prettily and hurried on her way.

Michael watched her until she went in the door. Thoughtfully, he turned and started walking away.

Something was not right. Either Sir William was not being completely honest with him; or Geoffrey

Kenyon was a scoundrel with a very attractive niece.

Putting his doubts aside, he headed back toward the village. There was one thing he did want to do, something that would assuage his conscience a bit.

He returned to the dressmaker's shop. Mrs. Jeter came out of her back room to greet him.

"I wish to buy a dress," he said.

"For whom?"

"Miss Kenyon."

The dressmaker's brows shot up.

He relied on charm to put her at ease. Leaning close to the dressmaker, he said, "I know it isn't proper, but I believe she needs one to wear to this ball, don't you?"

"After the way Mr. Burkhardt treated her? Absolutely," Mrs. Jeter said.

"I'm treading carefully here," he admitted. "However, I sense her uncle doesn't have the money for many extras."

Mrs. Jeter laughed. "Mr. Kenyon doesn't have a practical head for anything. His niece keeps him going. He always claims someday he shall make a fortune. To my thinking, the only way that man will be wealthy is if he can invent a way to turn lead into gold."

Or rubber into waterproof material.

"I want this dress to be *our* secret, Mrs. Jeter. Can you keep a secret?" He helped her to decide by pulling out his coin purse.

"Oh, yes, I can, sir," she answered.

"Good. Then, help me to design a dress that will make Miss Kenyon shine."

And she did exactly that. Mrs. Jeter really was talented and she knew what material would become Jocelyn best. Of course, he had to pay extra to ensure the dress would be ready for Friday.

"You will deliver it?"

"Personally," she answered.

"And not a word to anyone, not even Miss Kenyon?"

"Absolutely, sir."

He paid her handsomely and left. He didn't know if he was doing right or wrong. Jocelyn thought she wanted her farmer. Michael was certain Burkhardt would bore her in a month and he feared stealing the formula might ruin her uncle.

But whatever happened, she would look her best.

Mrs. Jeter watched the handsome Mr. Donaldson leave her establishment and almost danced with joy. He'd paid her in coin, right up front.

And if Mr. Donaldson was a tea merchant then she was a crown princess. She knew people and he was no peddler. Why, he hadn't even asked her to purchase tea, not once! He should if he wanted to make a living. But then, with a purse that full, he needn't worry about funds.

She wondered what game was being played but was also glad Miss Kenyon finally had a champion. She said as much to the spinster Clark sisters when they came in to choose a new set of feathers for the turbans they planned to wear to the ball.

"He is handsome, isn't he?" the oldest Miss Clark agreed. "No one more handsome in Wye. Pity about Miss Kenyon being jilted by Mr. Burkhardt. Bad form that was."

Mrs. Jeter knew she'd been sworn to secrecy . . . but some secrets were hard to keep.

The dress was one of them.

After all, everyone liked Miss Kenyon, so she had to share the news with the Clark sisters . . . who later told Mrs. Mayes the story . . . who couldn't wait to mention the dress to Mrs. Banks. Mrs. Mayes reasoned the vicar's wife had a responsibility to know *everything* going on in Wye.

And so the story traveled and by midafternoon, everyone knew Mr. Donaldson had purchased a dress for Miss Kenyon.

Some villagers were appalled by the impropriety. Others were titillated. And some were glad the kind Miss Kenyon had found someone new.

But the person most interested in this news was Rose Burkhardt.

She hurried out to the barn where her son was supervising a crew rebuilding hayricks. "You aren't going to believe what I've just heard," she started, and told him about the dress.

He didn't believe her . . . at first.

However, later, when he had time to think, he began to wonder. He thought of Jocelyn in the dress shop with Donaldson, of their closeness and the argument they'd had in the corner of the shop—and his jealousy knew no bounds.

Chapter Eleven

&

An Unsuitable Gift

*J*ocelyn stopped by her uncle's study to let him know she'd returned from shopping and to tell him about Michael. She'd not said anything about the tea merchant and perhaps she should.

Uncle Geoff was dozing on his favorite piece of furniture, a Turkish retiring chair upholstered in well-worn Moroccan leather. It sat in the far corner of the room and he catnapped often when he was working. He claimed sleep helped him to find solutions to difficult problems.

For a second, she watched him snoozing peacefully and thought how lucky she was. He was a dear, caring man with a brilliant mind but a complete lack of practical sense. The two of them had managed quite well together over the years. He'd made her feel safe and protected. Thomas had not been happy when she'd expected him to wait for her while she nursed her uncle to health during his sickness—and yet she would not have done it any other way.

She wondered if Michael's reaction would have been

different. There were also other differences between the two men. Michael was taller, more handsome, and had conversation on something other than himself, hunting, or farming. She also sensed that he was honorable, a true gentleman. Of course, he was promised to another, but would he be paying her such marked attention if his obligation was unbreakable? Unlike Thomas?

For the first time, she thought of Thomas's defection without heartache . . . and felt the stirrings of anger. She would have waited for Thomas. She'd even been willing to put up with his dragon of a mother!

As if aware of her presence, Uncle Geoff woke. Sitting up, he ran his fingers through his already tousled hair. "I closed my eyes for a minute."

"Hmmmhmmm," she agreed with him, knowing better, and sat down on the edge of the chair. "Is the formula working out the way you wish it to?"

"No. Something is not right. Drat it all. I feel I am on the verge of discovering the secret, but it eludes me."

"You'll work it out. You always do." She soothed his hair into a semblance of order and then added thoughtfully, "I've invited a guest for dinner."

Her uncle winced. "I wanted to work. Must I be there?"

"Yes." She hesitated and then added, "I invited a gentleman. Mr. Donaldson. He is going to escort us to Lord Vaughn's ball Wednesday night."

"A ball? Josie, did I say I would attend a ball?"

"Yes, you did. It is Lady Elfreda's betrothal ball to Thomas and I need your support."

He leaned back down, remembering. "But what of this Donaldson? If he is going, why must I?"

"You are going as a chaperon," she replied firmly. "And

you can spare one night. Everyone in the parish will be there. You must be there, too."

"But my work—"

"Will wait." She'd had this argument with him before and she always won. She rose and leaned over to kiss him lightly on the forehead. "I'll be interested in your opinion of Mr. Donaldson."

"My opinion? You've never asked such a thing before." His brows came together. "If you'd asked my opinion of young Burkhardt, I would have given you an earful."

"Did you really not like Thomas?" she asked, surprised.

Uncle Geoff sat up and put his feet on the floor. "He was fine enough, I suppose, if you like a lad whose mother leads him around by the nose. And as I remember, she never liked you very much."

"Well, we can hope she likes Lady Elfreda better." Jocelyn started straightening the stacks of scribbled notes and papers on her uncle's desk.

"I imagine she does." He watched her for a moment and then said, "You aren't very sad, are you, Josie?"

A week ago, she'd been heartbroken. Now, the future didn't look bleak. "I'm recovering," she answered.

"So who is this Donaldson?"

Jocelyn wiped some dust off the edge of her uncle's desk, carefully avoiding the jumble of books stacked one on top of the other with their spines open to particular pages. "He's a tea merchant."

"A what?"

"He sells teas to different establishments, but you can ask him the particulars over dinner. Remember, at a quarter past six, I expect you to wash up and change your neckcloth. The one you are wearing has spots of something on it. And perhaps you might want to change your shirt as well?" she suggested tactfully.

Uncle Geoff frowned. "Damn me, Josie, but you are finally ready to stop sulking over Burkhardt, aren't you?"

"Yes, uncle, I believe I am." She left the room.

The moment Jocelyn disappeared, Geoffrey returned to his experiments. He knew some people thought he tinkered in vain . . . but to him, he was unlocking secrets of the universe. Of course, for once, this endeavor promised to be lucrative. He'd been fortunate Redding had brought him in on it. Now, if only he could devise a way for rubber to not melt in the summer and grow brittle in the winter while being able to apply a coat thin enough on fabric to make it flexible.

He quickly lost himself in the problem and was not pleased when a knock sounded at the window of his study. Geoff looked up and was surprised to see Vicar Banks standing outside in the garden.

He crossed over to the window. The vicar said through the glass, "I must talk to you."

"Go around to the front and come in," Geoff replied reasonably.

"I can't. I don't want Jocelyn to know I'm here."

Now he had Geoff's attention. He opened the window and leaned out. Vicar Banks stood in the soft garden soil. Josie would not be happy to see his boot print in her peony bed. The vicar was a tall, narrow man and Geoff's closest friend in Wye.

"Why are you behaving so secretively?" Geoff asked.

"Because I believe you should know about the rumors my wife overheard."

"Rumors about me?"

"No, about your niece. Geoffrey, there is a tea merchant in the village who has been paying her marked attentions."

"I know. I'm to meet him this evening."

The vicar frowned. "Be wary. You know what they say about peddlers and you will not like this rumor one wit."

Geoff leaned farther out the window. Jocelyn was probably in the kitchen, which was located not too far from his study. The smell of bread and a ham baking filled the air. In a hushed voice, Geoff asked, "What is the rumor?"

Vicar Banks looked left, then right, to make sure they were not overheard before saying, "He is buying her a dress to wear to Lord Vaughn's ball."

"Buying her a dress? That doesn't sound so bad. Josie hasn't had a new frock in ages. She'll be happy to hear the news." He would have turned away to go tell her when the vicar grabbed his arm at the wrist and pulled him back out the window.

"No, Geoff. This is terrible news. Every tongue in the village is wagging. The Clark sisters started the talk and they are vipers. They are wondering what your niece has done to earn such a favor from a gentleman she is not related to."

"Why, she's done nothing. She only just met the man." Punching the air with one finger to accentuate the words, he said, "She is a good, modest girl—"

"Who is spending time with a peddler. I'm warning

you, Geoff, if she were one of my daughters, I'd not let the man close to her."

Geoff ran a hand through his hair. "I don't think Josie would do something disreputable." He hesitated and added, "He's escorting us to the ball. He's to come to dinner tonight to make my acquaintance."

The vicar motioned Geoff to come closer. "They say there was a bit of a scene today in Mrs. Jeter's shop between the tea merchant and Burkhardt. Young Thomas isn't happy. Not one bit."

"He has forfeited his right to say anything," Geoff countered.

"My wife and the other ladies in the parish believe he may still have feelings for your niece."

"Well, he can't have her. I'd rather she take up with this peddler than that fickle warthog."

The vicar spoke earnestly, "Geoff, be careful. I've warned you before, you give Jocelyn too much freedom. With this peddler you are going to have to keep a sharp eye out, and you need to do something to stop the rumors about the dress."

"What do I do?" Geoff asked. He was not good at dealing with people at all. Whenever there was a crisis, Jocelyn handled the matter.

Vicar Banks leaned into the window and took Geoff's arm by the wrist. "Courage, man! This is no time for a faint heart. What I would do if some stranger started sniffing around my daughters is take the man aside—" He held up Geoff's wrist, his grip tightening. "—And warn him that if he did *anything* to hurt my child, he'd wish he was in hell after I finished with him." He gave Geoff's a fierce twist for emphasis.

Geoff stifled his cry of pain lest Josie hear. "In hell," he repeated dutifully, not quite liking the sound of it. He pulled his arm back, rubbing his wrist. "Should I say something to Josie? I mean, she shouldn't wear the dress, should she?"

"Not unless she wants the whole village talking."

"And what if she likes this man? What if he's turned her head with compliments and promises?"

The vicar frowned. "That is a difficult question. Trust God, my friend."

Geoff hated it whenever his friend started referring important questions to God. Geoff had been waiting for years and God hadn't yet given him one straightforward answer and there had been times he'd really needed guidance while raising Josie. Perhaps that was why he preferred science. Answers could be found.

"I must go. Be careful," Vicar Banks said and tiptoed off, pausing to check around the corner of the house before he disappeared around it.

Geoff wished he could climb out the window and follow him. Instead, he bumped his head when Jocelyn said from the doorway, "Uncle, you need to go upstairs to dress for dinner."

Rubbing the spot where he had connected with the window frame, Geoff murmured, "I'm going up now."

"It's almost time for him to be here," she said as he passed.

Him. The bounder. "Right, right," Geoff replied and wished he could barricade himself in his laboratory— but he had to be there for Josie. He'd failed her with Burkhardt and the farmer had broken her heart.

He'd not let the peddler have a chance to hurt her, too.

Chapter Twelve

❦

An Interesting Evening

Michael found he was anxious to have dinner at Kenyon's that evening.

Yes, he'd have an opportunity to learn more about the formula, but he'd also be seeing Jocelyn again. There was something between them. An attraction he didn't want to name and shouldn't be feeling.

He loved Ivy . . . or so he had to remind himself. He rationalized his infatuation with Jocelyn was because he empathized with her. In truth, it was because she was a vibrant, passionate woman. He enjoyed her company and no matter how hard he tried, he could not put their kisses in the garden out of his mind.

He could have had her. He knew it and she had been fortunate he was a gentleman. Another man might have taken advantage of her trust.

However, when he arrived at her house and she opened the door to greet him, lust hit him full force, in a way he'd never experienced before.

Jocelyn was wearing a peach muslin gown. The color

blended with the glow of her skin and Michael could all too well imagine her naked.

The dress's high waist emphasized the full swell of her breasts. He knew her waist was tiny and sensed her legs would be well-proportioned and long. Her wild tangle of curls was again caught up in ribbon. This one was emerald green and its color brought out the red highlights in her dark hair and the warmth of welcome in her brown eyes.

For the space of several heartbeats, they did not speak but stared, happy to see each other again.

She broke the silence. "My uncle is anxious to meet you."

"And I him." He wanted to touch her, to make love to her. Instead, he removed his hat.

"Please come inside," she offered.

He entered. The smells of roasted meat and fresh baked bread greeted him. He was surprised to see the rooms were small and sparsely furnished. There were no servants, no expensive rugs on the floor or paintings on the walls.

There were, however, flowers. Jocelyn's flowers raised by her own hand in her garden. Their color and their fragrance turned the house into a home.

"The sitting room is right here," she said, directing him to a cozy room off the main hall. "My uncle will join us shortly."

A loud voice interrupted her. "Josie, has our guest arrived?" Geoffrey Kenyon stomped down the staircase that ended by the front door. He was dressed for dinner although his neckcloth was slightly askew and his hair ruffled.

"Yes, Uncle. This is Mr. Donaldson—"

"I know who he is," Kenyon said belligerently. He walked right up to Michael and attempted to stare him in the eye . . . which was difficult because Michael was a head and a half taller than he was. "Josie, I think you'd best see to our supper."

"But Uncle—"

"Mr. Donaldson and I need to talk, man to man. Into the sitting room, sir!" He didn't wait for a response but marched that way himself, expecting Michael to follow.

Jocelyn's surprised gaze met Michael's. She shrugged, conveying her puzzlement. Michael's guard went up. Could it be Kenyon knew of his purpose for being in Wye? Was it possible he suspected?

"All will be fine," Michael murmured to her. He had no desire to be unmasked in front of her. "Man talk," he said lightly.

She forced a smile. "Dinner will be served shortly."

Uncle Geoff returned to the door of the sitting room. "We'll be done shortly," he said. "Now, off with you," he told her and waited until she'd gone down the hall. "Mr. Donaldson, this way." He motioned Michael into the sitting room.

Inside, Kenyon didn't waste time but announced, "You, sir, are a scoundrel."

So, he knew. And Michael welcomed the opportunity for plain speaking. "I could say the same of you, sir," he countered.

Kenyon looked taken aback. "Me? We're talking about you!"

"Oh, no. *You* are the one guilty of dishonorable conduct," Michael replied. "Sir William told me all of it."

"Sir William?" Kenyon scratched his head. "Sir William who? What are you talking about? What does this Sir William have to do with the dress you purchased for my niece this afternoon?"

"The dress—?" Michael took a step back, adjusting his thinking. "You know about the dress?"

"Yes, I do, and I wish to know what your intentions were in purchasing it." As if going by rote, Kenyon continued, punctuating the air with his finger. "Jocelyn is a good, decent young woman and we don't want her corrupted by the likes of a traveling peddler. Or this Sir William! Who the devil is he, anyway?"

"Sir William Lewin," Michael said. "Um, a friend who said he knew you."

"Knew me?" Kenyon appeared to search his memory. "I do not recollect the name. What does he have to do with the dress?"

"Nothing," Michael said honestly. "I thought there was a connection between you and he." The deeper he was going into this affair, the more odd it became. Could Sir William have been wrong or was there something more sinister going on?

The thought that he might be being played for a fool did not sit well with Michael. "He is a fellow scientist," he prodded.

"Never heard of him. However, I did hear about you buying my niece a dress. You know such a gift is inappropriate."

Michael didn't deny it. "I asked the dressmaker to keep quiet."

Kenyon gave a bark in laughter. "There are no secrets in Wye. I'd wager the gossips knew who you were the moment you took your first step into the parish. And this dress is a problem. There are many, myself included, who are wondering what your intentions are, Mr. Donaldson, and want you to know Josie is no easy prey."

Here the truth would suffice. "I meant no disrespect. I knew the ball was important to her and, having sisters of my own, I understand how women feel about clothing. I wanted her to have a nice dress to wear, one that would make her feel special."

"And that is the only reason? There is no—" Kenyon eyed him sharply. "No *ulterior* motive?"

Well, there had been the kisses, but Michael wasn't going to bring it up. Instead, he said easily, "None. I met Thomas Burkhardt today, didn't like him, and decided I wanted to help Jocelyn shine."

"Jocelyn, is it?" Kenyon queried. He walked around Michael, looking him up and down with a shrewd eye. "In Wye, when a gentleman buys a young woman an expensive present, it's the same as making a marriage offer."

Michael raised his hands to ward off the suggestion. "Oh, no. I can't, I mean, I would, but I couldn't. And Jocelyn knows my intentions." He lowered his hands, concerned. "I wasn't thinking. I wanted Jocelyn to be happy and I thought she would like the gift."

"Tea peddling brings in a pretty penny, yes?" Kenyon asked.

"Enough," Michael said carefully.

"And you are *not* courting my niece?" Kenyon's belligerence was gone and in its place was a tone of regret.

Michael shook his head. He sat on the back of the

settee, one foot swinging back and forth as he realized his mistake. His decision to buy her a dress had compromised her. "I wasn't thinking. I've made everything worse, haven't I? Everyone knows about the dress and is expecting a declaration."

"Or a dishonorable offer." Her uncle sighed. "Well, I'm glad it isn't the latter. I was afraid I'd have to take you to task and you're much younger and stronger than I, lad."

"I'm sorry." And Michael was. "People will think she has been jilted twice."

Kenyon leaned against the settee beside Michael. "I don't want her to be hurt again."

"Nor do I."

"There must be a way out."

The two men thought hard, each in his own way. After a few moments, her uncle said, "This is all my fault. I could have been a tutor and made a good living. Instead, I seem to fail at everything I do."

"Jocelyn says you are a good inventor."

Modesty stained Kenyon's cheeks. "I have my areas of expertise but I've not yet made a name for myself. Poor Jocelyn, she's wasted her life taking care of me and you're right, Mr. Donaldson, she did deserve a new dress. Especially to wear to that ball in particular." There was a beat of silence and then he asked, "Is it a pretty dress?"

"Yes, it will be," Michael had to admit. "Mrs. Jeter suggested a white muslin with a rose over sheath. She said it would look quite lovely with Jocelyn's coloring."

Kenyon eyed him suspiciously. "You are quite taken with her, aren't you?"

Yes, he was.

The forthrightness of his thought startled Michael. "I admire her," he answered, more to convince himself than Kenyon, "but my attentions are already fixed on another."

"Oh. Pity," her uncle said.

Yes, Michael had to agree. It was a pity. Jocelyn was someone special and unique. Lately, he was having to force himself to remember Ivy—and if she ever heard he was buying another woman a dress—!

Michael had an idea. "We could tell everyone you purchased the dress."

"Me?"

"Why not?" The more Michael thought about it, the better the idea sounded. "We'll say I was your agent because you were . . ." He trailed off, needing a reasonable excuse.

Kenyon had one. "Busy! Here with my experiments." He straightened. "Everyone knows I do not shop. And you shall be a friend of the family. Yes, since we are weaving a story, we can add whatever details we wish." He smiled, liking the scheme. "And everything will be acceptable. Jocelyn shall have her dress although I must pay for it." He frowned as if this were a problem.

"I've already paid the seamstress."

"But I can't let you. I mean, I will pay you back but I'm a bit short of funds. Of course, if this rubber works out, I should come into a substantial amount of cash and when I do, I will repay the debt."

"As you wish," Michael agreed. Kenyon's statement supported Sir William's claim that the formula could be worth a fortune. However, after getting to know Kenyon and his niece, Michael was more and more certain Sir

William might not have been completely honest with him. He did not like being played for a fool.

"Let us go see Jocelyn," her uncle said. "She hates to have dinner waiting. When shall I tell her about the dress?"

"Whenever you wish."

He clapped his hands in anticipation. "She'll be pleased and surprised. Oh, yes, very surprised."

"Then I am happy to be of service, sir," Michael said.

"I like you," Kenyon responded ingenuously. "You may be a peddler, but you are a good man. And you're spoken for, you say? Another woman has your affections?"

"Yes," Michael replied firmly. He had his obligation to Ivy although with each passing day in Wye, it seemed more distant.

"Pity," Kenyon repeated. "Well, come, let us go to the dining room."

Hunched in a cubby in the wall, Jocelyn heard everything that had been said in the sitting room of the drafty old house. She quickly escaped into the dining room before the men left the sitting room. She was deeply touched not only by her uncle's concern; but also by Mr. Donaldson's.

He'd bought a dress for her. The generosity of the gift astounded her. However, his empathy for her feelings was what truly touched her.

By the time the men entered the dining room she was putting glasses of cider on the table. They had no idea she had been eavesdropping.

Her gaze met Michael's. He gave away nothing of what had transpired in the living room and she knew he wouldn't. He was the kind of man who valued confidences and who had just proved through his kindness he was more aware of her than she'd imagined.

And, in the blink of an eye, Jocelyn fell in love. Real love.

She'd thought she'd known what love was. She'd believed she'd experienced it before. After all, she'd known Thomas for years and had only known Michael for the span of two days. But being familiar with someone and being friends was not the same as passionate love . . . and she definitely felt passion for Michael.

What she felt for him was a thunderbolt, a flood of emotions, a maelstrom of conviction . . . and it was a need to be with him and never let him go.

They sat down to dinner. Jocelyn discovered she was aware of every move Michael made. He liked the ham, the peas, and the cider she'd pressed herself last fall. He ate with calm deliberateness and she wanted to feed him every day of his life. She wanted him here, across from her at a table where she would be content to hear the sound of his voice, to marvel at even the slightest gesture, and to bask in the strength of his companionship.

Uncle Geoffrey was very animated, more so than she'd ever seen him. He liked Michael—and his approval made her love all the more wonderful.

Just when supper was about to end, Uncle Geoff cleared his throat and said, "Josie, I have a surprise for you. I've purchased a dress from Mrs. Jeter for you to wear to the ball."

Michael did not give away, by any sign or look, that he was behind the gift. Thomas could never have set aside his own pride long enough to be so generous and Jocelyn fell even deeper in love. "Thank you, Uncle," she murmured, but her gaze was on Michael.

He sensed her regard and looked up. For a long moment, their eyes held. All she could think about was the kisses they had shared, kisses that held the promise of other things . . . and she found herself wondering if he, too, felt this attraction between them. He had to; the very air in the room seemed to vibrate with it.

"You deserve the dress and more," Uncle Geoff started proudly, and then stopped. He looked from one to the other and then whispered, "Oh, dear."

His soft words of worry brought Jocelyn to her senses. "I'm sorry, what were you saying?" she replied, a bit too brightly.

"Nothing of importance," her uncle answered and then became very interested in getting his peas onto his fork.

Michael commented on Jocelyn's flowers and the conversation flowed smoothly again as she discovered he, too, had a love for working the earth. "You sound like a farmer," she teased him.

"I am," he admitted.

"A farmer who likes to sell tea?"

His expression sobered. "I grew up on an estate. It was a good boyhood and I hope to offer the same life to my children someday."

Children, a family, roots. He'd described heaven to someone who was an orphan.

"Perhaps you would like to take a turn in the garden after dinner?" she suggested, offering them a chance to be alone . . . and, yes, possibly to have another kiss.

His silvery eyes met hers and she knew he was thinking the same thing. The tension tightened between them. "I would like that very much," he answered and for a moment, it was as if no one else was in the room with them.

Her uncle interjected. "Actually, I believe we need an early night." He even leaned forward as if to come between her and Michael. Jocelyn wouldn't have been surprised if he'd waved his hand in front of their faces. "Don't you think, Donaldson? Time to turn in?"

Michael couldn't ignore such an obvious hint. He smiled regretfully at Jocelyn and she sighed. "Yes," he agreed, "I don't want to overstay my welcome."

They rose from the table and Jocelyn walked Michael to the door, her uncle trailing behind her, his ears attuned to everything being said. After so many years of careless attention, he'd obviously decided to become a doting chaperon in one night.

"Thank you for dinner," Michael said.

"You're very welcome," Jocelyn answered and offered her hand. Michael took it and kissed the tips of her fingers. For a moment, neither of them could move. She was too lost in the wonder of newly discovered love. She prayed he felt the same.

"Good night, Donaldson," Uncle Geoff said jovially but firmly, opening the door and handing their guest his hat.

Michael had no choice but to take his leave. He did not go without one last lingering look at Jocelyn. It was that look that proved to be her undoing; with her newly discovered love, she didn't think she could bear for even the space of one night to be parted from him.

Once the door closed, she collapsed on one of the stair treads, overcome with the prospect of happiness.

"You like him," Uncle Geoff said, his reservations clear on his face.

"I like him very much. Don't you?" Michael and her uncle had seemed to be getting along, especially when they had conspired over the dress.

Uncle Geoff frowned. "We don't know very much about him. He has a bit too much presence to my way of thinking to be a simple tea merchant."

Jocelyn didn't want to hear doubts, even those she'd expressed to herself. "What else could he be?"

"I don't know," her uncle said.

"I sense he is a gentleman," she ventured.

"Absolutely," Uncle Geoff agreed and then added somberly, "He is promised to another."

Jocelyn had been trying to ignore that fact. Deep in her heart, she wanted to believe all obstacles could be overcome. And Michael never spoke about this other woman. She sensed with a woman's intuition that perhaps he wasn't as firm in his convictions as he had originally thought. Or was her natural optimism encouraging her to believe their love was possible?

For right now, she pushed doubts aside. She just wanted to embrace and enjoy the euphoria of love.

Uncle Geoff sighed, a sign he knew better than to press the issue. Still, he said, "You know I love you, don't you, Josie? Even though I'm somewhat of an absentminded old goat? In my mind, you are my daughter."

"I've always known you loved me, Uncle. And I shall cherish the dress. It is a very special gift."

He smiled, pleased. "You have been a gift in my life."

He lightly touched her head, a gesture he'd often made when she'd been a child. "Well, I'm ready for my bed. I shouldn't have fallen asleep in my chair last night. My back hurts. I plan to straighten it out tonight."

"Go on up. I'll be close behind you."

"Good night."

She quickly cleaned up from dinner, blew out the candles, and followed him up the stairs. She went into her room, but was too excited to sleep, not with Michael on her mind. Instead, she sat on the deep ledge of the window overlooking her garden—and noticed a movement in the shadows of the house.

Jocelyn leaned forward, craning her neck to see just as Michael took a step out into the moonlight and then quickly hid himself again. He stood by her uncle's study windows and a second later, she heard the sound of wood against wood as a window was opened.

Chapter Thirteen

❧

Moonlit Encounter

$\mathcal{M}$ichael had a problem—he still loved Ivy, or so he reminded himself . . . but he couldn't stop thinking about Jocelyn.

Again, tonight, he'd spent time around a table and was reminded of being with his family. What he had tossed aside so callously years ago, now meant something to him. And his parents, his brothers and sisters would all adore Jocelyn if they were ever to meet her.

Nor did Kenyon strike Michael as a thief. The man was very forthcoming about his experiments—even his work with rubber, leaving William's motives suspect.

Michael had always prided himself on his sense of honor. For Ivy's hand, he'd undertaken the most havey-cavey of escapades and he felt he'd compromised not only his reputation but perhaps his heart as well.

There was only one way to discover the truth to this situation, and that was to take a look at the formula for himself. If it were Sir William's, it would be in his flowing script.

Michael decided to break into Kenyon's laboratory.

He wasn't going to make the same mistake he had the night before. This time, he hid in the line of woods bordering the property until he saw all the lights go out in Kenyon's house and he believed they were asleep.

Carefully, he moved through the shadows to the laboratory windows. To his good fortune, he found one that was open a crack. Straining his eyes, he peered into all the corners to make sure Kenyon wasn't asleep in a chair like he'd been the night before. The good-size red leather chair in a corner was empty and there were no bearlike snores to disturb the night.

Michael eased the window up, lifted himself onto the sill, and climbed inside. He started combing through the papers on the desk. He soon began to recognize Kenyon's squiggly writing but the formula could be anywhere. Kenyon was an eccentric thinker and had a habit of sticking notes and papers between the pages of books he had stacked all over his laboratory.

Perhaps the formula was over on the table Kenyon used for work? Michael started leafing through the papers there and was so busy, he didn't hear a footfall until it was too late.

He looked up, suddenly aware he wasn't alone.

Jocelyn stood inside the doorway. Her glorious curls were down around her shoulders and she wore nothing save for a thin cotton nightgown with a shawl thrown over her shoulders. Her feet were bare.

She didn't appear surprised to see him. "This is the

second time I've caught you snooping, Michael. What is it you want?"

He cleared his throat. "This isn't what it seems."

Her shrewd glance took in the open window. "You didn't come in through the door."

"I didn't want to wake you."

"How polite," she returned coldly. "Why are you searching my uncle's laboratory?"

There it was, the dreaded question. A thousand lies leapt his lips . . . but he chose the truth. "I was searching for the formula to adhere rubber to cloth."

She obviously hadn't been expecting that answer. "Why?"

"Jocelyn, please hear me out and I'll tell you everything."

"You're not a tea merchant."

"God, no. I'm a military officer." It felt good to say those words, to be who he was.

She pulled the shawl tighter around her. "And your name is not Donaldson, is it?"

"No." She'd suspected. Her intelligence was keener than he had imagined. "It's Sanson. Michael Sanson." And then, because he wanted her to know, he added, "*Colonel* Michael Sanson."

"Ah," she cooed before adding softly, "and the army sent you here because they are afraid Napoleon had escaped again and could be found in my uncle's laboratory?"

He deserved her sarcasm. "I've reason to believe your uncle stole a formula from another scientist."

Her reaction was immediate. She walked right up to him. "He'd never do such a thing! Who made such a vile accusation?"

"Sir William Lewin."

"The man you asked me about earlier?"

Michael nodded.

"The name means nothing to me."

"Your uncle's path must have crossed his at one time or the other. Otherwise your uncle wouldn't have the formula."

She shook her head. "My uncle would never steal another man's work. He's been asked to *help* others solve problems but he'd never claimed work that wasn't his as his own. This Sir William must be lying. Besides, I know a Mr. Redding requested his help and sent the basics of the formula to him."

Michael seized the opportunity to persuade her. "That's why I'm here. I want to know the truth."

Jocelyn wasn't that gullible. "So you steal into a man's house and expect *him* to prove your unfounded suspicions are wrong?" He knew she was seeing him with new eyes. Gone was the softness and in its place was suspicion and doubt. "There's more to this than is on the surface."

"It is as I told you." He needed her to believe him.

She took a step back. "You want me to trust you," she said quietly, "even though you came to Wye to rob my uncle—"

"Robbery is too strong a word."

She almost laughed, the sound bitter. "Or not strong enough. Because, everything you've done, from letting a room from Lucy and Kent to spending time with me, has been a scheme to gain the formula, hasn't it?"

He did not want her to form this conclusion. "No. Not quite. I mean, I can explain, Jocelyn."

She wasn't in the mood for explanations. "And the kisses last night—! It was a ruse. Thomas probably wasn't even there. You were going to break in then and I discovered you."

"I hadn't intended on kissing you. What happened between us—none of that was planned."

"No, of course not," she agreed brittlely. "I was supposed to be snug in my bed while you rifled my uncle's possessions."

"Jocelyn—"

"I *trusted* you." Her words damned him. "I was starting to fall in—" She broke off, unable to speak the thought . . . but he knew what she had been about to admit. She'd started to fall in love with him, and he felt like the blackest of scoundrels. He'd always done what was right, what was honorable.

Michael stepped forward, coming around the table toward her. He wanted to reassure her, to touch her and make amends. "You *can* trust me. I merely want the truth."

"Get away from me!" She backed toward the door, her eyes angry glints. "You don't have to apologize. You said your affections were spoken for. My gullibility is my problem. However, I must fetch my uncle. He will want the magistrate to see to you."

The magistrate! Michael did not want the authorities involved. He was feeling foolish enough as it was. She started out the door, but he reached out, snagging her arm, drawing her back.

A hand on each arm, he said, "You must listen to me, Jocelyn—"

She kicked him firmly in the shins with her bare

feet and attempted to jerk herself out of his hold.

He grunted, but he was not really hurt. Catching her by the wrist, he prevented her from running from the room. "Jocelyn, please—"

She started to scream. He instantly cut off the sound by placing his hand over her mouth, avoiding her sharp teeth. Kicking shut the laboratory door, he moved the two of them to the leather retiring couch and unceremoniously dropped her onto it. He leaned over to angrily inform her, "I'm not here to hurt you, so stop behaving like a madwoman."

Her answer was to raise her knee and almost unman him. She hit his thigh with bruising force and pulled back, ready to try again. He fell on her, trapping her thrashing legs and holding them in place.

She glared at him, their faces so close together they breathed the same air. He saw the fear and pain of betrayal in her eyes . . . and the desire.

Suddenly, he was aware she wore nothing beneath her nightdress, that the hem was up to her waist, and that they were very alone. Lust as he'd never known it before replaced anger.

"Jocelyn," he said, the musical sound of her name his benediction, his request begging her to understand. Then, slowly, he leaned forward and kissed her.

She could have turned away. She could have rejected him. She didn't.

Instead, she held herself very still, the small frown between her eyes that he'd come to know as concern. It was as if she did not trust herself.

As for himself, he was dangerously close to the point when he would not be able to turn back. From the moment he'd laid eyes on her, he'd wanted her. Her skin was soft and smooth, and the scent of woman filled his senses.

Still, she resisted. He wanted her to understand. He needed her forgiveness. He deepened his kiss, searching for a response.

And he received one.

With a sigh, she gave in. Her lips parted and her arms slid up around his neck. She drew him down to her.

Michael wanted to shout joyful hosannas. He would explain and she would understand now . . . but as their mouths melded together, explanation ceased to be important. And when she lightly stroked him with her tongue, he was lost.

The man who prided himself on control vanished. In his place was a man who had one simple need—Jocelyn. He wanted her with a passion that bordered on the savage.

Perhaps if she had struggled. Perhaps if she'd protested or let him know in word or deed that she wished him to stop, he could have.

But she didn't.

Instead, she became a willing accomplice to her seduction. She offered no protest as he slipped her nightdress down around her shoulders, the shawl having fallen away when she'd first landed in the couch. He cupped her breast, reveling in the firm weight of it. Her nipples were bold and proud . . . perfect. He broke the kiss and took one into his mouth.

Jocelyn cried out his name in surprise and then pleasure. Her hands tugged at his jacket, his neckcloth, his shirt, as if not wanting any barriers between them.

Michael bent her to his will, not hesitating in showing her the joys of lovemaking. And bless her, she offered herself to him with soft sighs and sweet moans of passion and gratitude.

Who cared about science and formulas and petty betrayals when he had such a magnificent, responsive creature in his arms? One that at this moment he'd give his life to possess?

He began unbuttoning his breeches.

Jocelyn no longer recognized herself. Every muscle, every nerve in her body yearned for what only he could give her. She'd never known this edginess or that this need existed inside her. It had lain dormant all this time to be unlocked by his kiss.

She knew what was happening. She understood the functions of the body and she wanted this joining. She couldn't seem to stop herself; it felt too good.

Anticipation hummed through her. She felt him free himself, felt his hardness press against her. Her body glowed with internal heat and a need to be filled.

"Michael," she whispered and instinctively curved herself to receive him.

He needed no further invitation. With one smooth thrust, he broke through the barrier of her maidenhead and buried himself deep inside.

For a beat, neither one of them could move. She'd felt a small tear but nothing uncomfortable. Her body adjusted to the feel of him. Her heart pounded in her chest.

His voice near her ear, he asked, "Are you all right?"

"Is this all? Is it done?"

He laughed, obviously pleased. "No, love, it is only beginning."

He began moving then, long, slow thrusts that filled her being. He was gentle at first with many kisses and soft, sweet words of encouragement. But then his lust began to mount. His movements became more demanding, more in need of her passion.

She moved to accommodate the shock of his thrusts and found her own yearning enjoyment in each new, incredible sensation. Michael knew what she needed. He created a bond between them, one she wanted to have go on forever.

Her blood grew heated. Her body ached for something she could not define. She arched against him, calling his name, fearful and excited at the same time, the intensity building—

The ecstasy caught her by surprise.

One moment she struggled and in the next she'd never been more alive. She hugged Michael tightly, afraid and exalted all at once.

He whispered her name and she heard in his voice the same wonder she felt, the same loss of control. It made her feel powerful. And when he buried himself to the hilt, spilling his seed deep within her, the forceful vibrancy of life passing between, she knew they had become one . . . and she was complete.

Neither moved. They couldn't. They lay intertwined, savoring the closeness. The wild beating of their hearts slowed.

Jocelyn stared up at the ceiling, her arms around Michael, her whole being sparkling with joy. She smoothed her hand over his back. He still wore his jacket, his neckcloth was hopelessly misconstrued, and his breeches were down around his knees. And she was naked save for her nightdress around her waist like a sash.

Michael raised himself up on his elbows and looked down at her, the expression in his eyes unreadable.

"I didn't expect that," he said.

"I didn't know such a thing existed," she admitted.

Her words spurred his conscience. "Dear God, what have I done?" he whispered.

He would have risen, but she tightened her arms around him. "Please, don't. Not this minute. I don't want to think of consequences. I don't want regrets."

The light in his eyes softened, moonlight and shadows outlining the hard, masculine planes of his face. He gathered her in his arms. "You're beautiful."

Jocelyn closed her eyes and smiled with pleasure. "I *feel* beautiful."

Michael nuzzled her neck. "No pain?"

She'd been warned the first time was supposed to be horrid. Even Lucy had confided she'd needed several glasses of wine to relax her before she'd finally succumbed to Kent. "I felt nothing but pleasure."

His lips curved into a smile against her skin. He covered her breast with his hand and her nipple tightened against his palm. "This is madness," he murmured with a soft sigh.

She curled her fingers in his hair. "It's the moonlight."

"Aye, only the moonlight." He kissed the tender skin beneath her jawline and she felt him rouse again, pressing against her.

He didn't ask permission. None was needed. He

entered her, the movement smooth and strong. Gone was the earlier urgency and need. He took his time. His lovemaking was tender and yet more intense.

Jocelyn gave herself over to him. She now knew what to expect and craved the pleasure she knew was coming. Michael whispered encouragement, urging her to fulfillment. And when at last she found it, he joined her on the crest and together they drifted to earth, wrapped in each other's arms.

"Is it always like this?" she said, dazed.

"It's *never* been like this," he answered.

His confession made her proud. This was right between them. She'd not have any regrets. In less than a week, he had revolutionized her world. She'd fallen in love and become a woman.

Michael lifted his head, listening.

In a second, she heard the sound of steps coming down the staircase. "My uncle." Panic froze her, but not Michael.

Swiftly, he rose, pulling her nightdress back up around her shoulders. He grabbed her shawl and threw it around her. She pushed her hem down to her ankles.

Taking her face in her hands, he said, "I will see you tomorrow morning. First thing. We have matters to discuss." He gave her a quick, hard kiss and then he rose, pulling up his breeches as he moved. "I will make everything right," he promised. "You're mine now. Do you understand? *Mine.*"

She nodded, too rattled to think.

"Put your arms through the sleeves of your gown," he ordered, his silver eyes alive with laughter. She scrambled to comply.

The footsteps ended. The handle to the door turned and Michael jumped out the window into the garden in one fluid movement that ended in a soft grunt of pain.

The door opened and her uncle entered, holding a candle.

He didn't notice her at first. Muttering to himself, he walked to his worktable, set down the candle and paused. He stiffened and slowly turned to look directly at her.

She gripped the shawl tightly around her.

"Why, Jocelyn, what are you doing here?"

"The window was open." She offered no more explanation and Uncle Geoff didn't seem to need one.

"So it is," he said. "I must have forgotten to close it when Vicar Banks came by today."

He started for the window. With a hop and a skip, Jocelyn beat him there. "I'll close it," she said, fearing he'd see Michael outside. But when she looked, her lover was gone.

Gone.

He'd said he would be back. First thing in the morning.

Jocelyn tried not to listen to doubts. "Good night, Uncle," she murmured.

His mind was already back to his experiments. She left the room.

Upstairs, she went to her bedroom window and looked out over the garden. She saw no movement, no sign of Michael.

Suddenly, the enormity of what had happened, what had transpired between them, hit her.

"Sanson," she said out loud, recalling his true name

and wishing him here all at the same time. Dear God, what had she done? What if he did not return in the morning?

Jocelyn climbed into her bed, pulling the sheets up over her. He'd meant what he'd said. She had to trust him, to believe. If not, the betrayal would cut her to the bone.

Michael hurriedly righted his clothes as he walked away from the house. He'd barely escaped being caught. Other men bragged about flying out the window of a woman's boudoir before a husband or chaperon walked in—but Michael had never thought to be one of their number.

What had come over him?

He who had always known his own mind was now confused. Jocelyn had cut right through the control on which he'd always prided himself.

Furthermore, theirs had been no ordinary coupling. He'd heard the poets claim the earth could move during lovemaking, but he'd never experienced it—until now. He'd had her twice and even wanted her again. He didn't think he'd ever tire of her.

Of course, now that he'd compromised her, he'd have to marry her—

Michael stopped dead in his tracks, right there in the middle of the road.

He *had* compromised her.

She'd been a virgin—a willing one, but untouched all the same. He must marry her. It was the honorable thing to do.

Marriage. He shifted his weight from one foot to the

other, attempting to change his mental image of the word. He'd always pictured himself with Ivy.

Now, he couldn't remember Ivy's face.

He'd started off on this fool's errand to win her hand and instead, he'd found something else. Something finer, more brilliant, more satisfying.

He'd found Jocelyn.

This was not how he had foreseen his life, but having Jocelyn by his side—in his bed—would not be a bad thing. Not at all.

His moment of panic abated. He had no choice, he told himself. He had to offer marriage.

He even started whistling as he made his way to the Lettmans'. He would talk to Jocelyn in the morning and explain everything. He had no doubt she would accept his offer. What other choice did she have?

Of course, there was the matter of Ivy, but at this moment, on a starry, moonlit night with the music of crickets and bullfrogs in the air, the haughty Ivy seemed a lifetime away.

Instead, in his mind there was only Jocelyn.

And he slept well on his decision. In fact, he slept better than he had in years.

He even *over*slept.

Chapter Fourteen

€2

The Twists of Fate

*J*ocelyn did not sleep well.

She alternated between dreams of being in Michael's arms and fears of being abandoned by him. As an orphan, she'd learned at a young age that love could be irretrievably lost. Thomas's defection had reinforced those deep-seated fears. Now, morning couldn't come soon enough for her to find out if Michael would keep his promises.

She woke early, bathed, dressed and came down-stairs.

Still in robe and nightcap, her uncle was snoring in the leather chair in his laboratory. He'd obviously been up late, which wasn't unusual for him. His worktable was a mess. She knew she'd have to tell him about Michael's snooping. She didn't know how he would take the information, but she would hear Michael out first.

In the kitchen, she put water on to boil. The hour was only half past eight. Michael would not be there for quite some time. Jocelyn made herself a cup of tea hoping to calm her jangled nerves—and yet it served to remind her of Michael's false profession.

She took her teacup out into the garden. The day promised to be sweet and clear. She sat on the wooden bench in the garden's center and watched a spider weave a web across the tips of a lavender shrub.

If she closed her eyes, she could remember the feeling of Michael deep within her and remember the expression of exaltation on his face as they'd discovered passion together. She clasped her hands around her teacup.

He would come.

He'd promised.

"Jocelyn?"

Her heart skipped a beat. She stood, fearing her imagination played a trick on her. A footstep sounded on the flagstone path leading around the house.

"Jocelyn?" There was no mistaking that someone had called her name, but now she recognized the voice. It was Thomas.

He came around the corner of the house and hurried up to her. He did not look good. His eyes were red-rimmed from lack of sleep. He'd shaved but done a poor job of it, as if he'd been in a hurry.

When he saw her, he pulled his flat-brimmed hat off his head and stood for a moment like a penitent, hopeful and earnest.

"Thomas, what is wrong?"

For a moment, words seemed to fail him and then he said, "I love you. I can't marry Elfreda. You are the one I've always wanted."

His words vibrated in the air between them and then

he started laughing, obviously relieved by the confession.

"I love you," he stated again, louder this time and with more conviction. "I was a fool, a blind fool." He started toward her, his arms wide. "I'm sorry for all the hurt I've caused you. I don't know how I could have been so misguided as to take the love we had for each other for granted."

Numb, Jocelyn heard him as if from a great distance. She took a step back, holding him at bay. "But what about Lady Elfreda?"

Thomas's happiness faded a bit; he stopped short. "Well, there is a problem there. I haven't told her my feelings have changed, of course. I don't know what to say. I thought, first I'd talk to you and we could manage a solution. After all, the betrothal hasn't been announced yet."

She was to provide him with a solution? "The ball will be tomorrow night. Everyone in the village is planning to be there. Are you saying you would subject her to public humiliation?"

"Jocelyn, she's never given a fig for your feelings."

Jocelyn nodded. *When had Thomas grown so arrogant—or had he always been this way?* She'd never imagined him to be one to trounce happily on others' feelings.

He continued on, assuming she agreed with him. "Of course, the hard one to break the news to will be Mother." He laughed nervously. "She will be disappointed, perhaps bitterly so. It turns out she's never quite approved of you because of that nonsense of you being an orphan and not having a dowry."

"I know."

"You knew?" He acted surprised. "I didn't until I offered for Elfreda, and, well, Mother let her true feelings be known then."

How could Thomas have been so dense? His mother had always disapproved of Jocelyn. Yes, at one time her animosity had been better hidden than it was now . . . but it had always been there.

Thomas continued boldly. "I shall tell her she must accept you or go to live with her sister in Bath. My house will be your house and she will have no choice."

Now, Jocelyn really felt terrible. Mrs. Burkhardt and her sister could barely abide each other. The gossips still buzzed over the fights they used to have when they were younger and lived under the same roof. "Your mother has never lived anyplace in her life save Wye."

"I've thought this through," he insisted with a dismissive wave. "I'm setting the rules and Mother will do as you say if she wants to stay."

Yes, and she'd simmer with smoldering resentment and probably make her daughter-in-law's life a living hell.

Jocelyn shook her head with disbelief. If he'd come to her Monday last with such an offer, she would have snapped it up.

Now the idea of living the rest of her life with an aggrieved mother-in-law and a man who could jilt *another* girl without one ounce of sensitivity to her feelings left her cold. Thomas was not the man she had thought he was. Maybe he had never been.

And then there was the fact that Jocelyn had given herself to another. Thomas would not be happy with anything less than a virgin bride, because that is what he thought real love was—having a wife as a possession.

Michael would not be that way. She knew it in her heart.

He reached out to her again. Deftly, she sidestepped his arms, placing the bench between them. "What caused you to change your mind?" she asked, curious.

"Several things. I suppose jealousy, most of all." He gave her a boyish grin, one that used to melt her heart into forgiving him anything and now struck her as a bit irritating. "When I heard that the tea peddler was buying you a dress, I almost went wild."

"But he didn't buy the dress," Jocelyn quickly informed him, latching on to the lie Michael and Uncle Geoff had invented. "My uncle did."

"That's not what the Clark sisters are saying and they received the story straight from Mrs. Jeter," he said patronizingly—and that, too, was annoying.

"Yes, but it is what the facts are." Or would be as soon as her uncle went down to Mrs. Jeter's shop and made the arrangements.

For a second, Thomas appeared ready to argue the point, but then changed his mind. "Whatever you say," he agreed pompously. "It doesn't matter anyway. There will be no ball."

"What of the expense Lord Vaughn has gone to on your behalf?"

Thomas's smile held no remorse. "Would you be happier if I married Elfreda, a woman I didn't love?"

"But you were going to do exactly that," Jocelyn said quietly.

He frowned, unaccustomed to self-introspection. Of

course, in the past, she would never have commented on his shortcomings. He had been her stability, her life-line—until he'd left her and her eyes were opened.

She realized that over the past two days she'd discovered she had learned new strengths. Fickleness was not a quality she wanted in a man. Had Lucy not tried to warn her?

Still a part of her, the part that held close to her childhood, had strong feelings for Thomas, feelings that begged to be resolved. She knew of only one way to do it. "Thomas, kiss me."

Her request startled him. "Right now?"

"Yes."

"Jocelyn, it's morning. Why, only a bit past nine. What if your uncle strolls by?"

"Then we tell him the happy news." She set her tea-cup down on the bench, silently daring him.

"A kiss," he muttered and she wondered why he hesitated. Michael would have the deed done by now.

Thomas came to his decision. "Very well. One kiss. Then we must go make our happy announcement." He started to step around the bench but she moved away. She needed a bit of space between them.

He placed his hands on her shoulders. They felt like lead weights. She moved back. "I don't want a peck like what we usually do," she instructed. "I want a *kiss*."

"A kiss," he echoed, then pulled her up into his arms, the bench still between them. His mouth came down over hers, just as Michael's had . . . except Thomas's mouth was closed. He mashed hard lips to hers in an imitation of ardor—and she instantly knew she could not marry him.

Once upon a time, Thomas's kisses had been enough. Now she wanted the passion Michael's kisses inspired.

Thomas pulled back. "There. Good?"

Jocelyn struggled not to wipe her mouth.

"Come along," he said. "Let us go find your uncle." He took her hand, but she didn't follow. Instead, she held her ground, an arm's length between them. "I can't marry you, Thomas. I won't." The moment she spoke the words, her soul felt lighter.

"What?" He half-laughed in disbelief. "Wait. You're angry. You are upset because I had jilted you for Elfreda and now you are paying me back."

"No," Jocelyn said softly, hating to say the words but knowing they must be said. "I can't marry you, Thomas. My affections have shifted."

"But you've always loved me!"

Her mouth went dry. She understood the hurt he was feeling. "I did. I loved you once . . . but you left me and now, I've found someone else."

"The tea peddler?" he demanded, incredulous. "He just arrived in Wye. You know nothing about him."

"I know he is kind." Yes, she did know that.

"What sort of quality is that in a man?" Thomas shot back. "Kindness." He said the word as if it left a bad taste his mouth.

In the face of his mockery, Jocelyn found her equilibrium. "It's a quality I admire," she returned, a touch of steel in her voice, and she felt the stirrings of her temper.

He forced a laugh. "You would turn me down for a peddler's life."

"Yes," she said decisively. "Yes, I would. Good-bye, Thomas. We shall not speak of this conversation again. I shall see you tomorrow night at your ball and will congratulate you when your betrothal is announced."

His response was to kick the bench, sending the teacup flying. "You did all this knowingly. You wanted to see me grovel."

"No, I have never wanted to see you hurt," she flashed back. "Thomas, we were part of each other's childhood. Perhaps if our young love for each other had never been broken, matters would be different. However, *you* are the one who made the choice and you were wise. I see that now. Lady Elfreda adores you. Her family is going to honor you tomorrow night and your marriage will be the talk of the parish." She lightly touched his arm. He jerked it back, but she knew he listened. "The reason you are here today is because before you could face the future, you had to make sure the past was truly behind you."

As the truth of her words sank in, the anger evaporated from his eyes. In its place was sadness. "I did love you, Jocelyn."

"And I loved you . . . however, we outgrew each other."

He nodded and then with a deep breath, placed his hat on his head, setting it at a cocky angle. He smiled and said, "Well, at least Mother will be happy."

Jocelyn couldn't help an answering smile. "She will."

"I never meant to hurt you, Jocelyn."

"I know."

He took a step back. "I shall see you tomorrow evening?"

"I wouldn't miss this ball," she said, and meant the words.

Then, to her surprise, he came over, bent, and gave her a brotherly kiss on the cheek. Without a further word, he left.

Jocelyn watched him leave. This was a bittersweet moment, but an exciting one, too. Her future lay ahead.

The back door opened. Uncle Geoff came out on the step. He was still wearing his robe, slippers, and night-cap.

"Are you all right?" he asked.

"Did you hear any of it?"

"How could I not? You both woke me from a sound sleep with all that prattling about kisses." He paused, then asked, "You do not regret losing him?"

"No."

"And so it is the peddler?"

Jocelyn looked to her uncle and knew she should tell him the truth about Michael—but didn't.

She told herself it was because Michael should be the one to explain all to Uncle Geoff. Of course, the truth was that her faith, her trust in love, had already been shaken by Thomas, a man she'd known most of her life. Michael was a stranger and even admitted he'd made her acquaintance under false pretenses. His true interest had been to get close to Uncle Geoff. And, yet, she told herself his goal had changed, that he truly cared for her.

After all, she'd given him not only her trust, she'd given him her heart. Heat rose in her cheeks as she remembered what had happened.

She prayed she hadn't been played for a fool.

"You don't look well, Josie," Uncle Geoff commented with concern. He came down a step.

She raised her hand to overheated cheeks. "I need to go see Lucy." Enough of waiting. She had to talk to Michael. She had to see his face in the morning light and know his feelings for her were true.

She started past Uncle Geoff to get her hat, gloves, and shawl.

He stopped her, gently touching her arm. "Is it wise?" In his gaze, she could see he knew more than what she'd thought he did.

"I must see him," she murmured, and slipped inside.

Michael's first waking thought was of Jocelyn and the sex.

She had a passion that matched his own. He wanted her in his bed and he wanted to spend hours enjoying her.

Furthermore, now that he'd made the commitment in his mind, marriage to her would be much easier than marriage to Ivy. He was actually surprised at how effortlessly he was able to shift his devotion from a woman he'd worshiped for years to one he'd only known for days.

Ah, but there was something vital and alive about Jocelyn, something Ivy didn't have. Yes, that was it. Fate had intervened and instead of marrying a pampered ice princess, he craved Jocelyn's warmth and vibrancy. He even liked the village of Wye.

This solution would also save him from his ill-advised mission to take the formula from Kenyon. Let Sir William perform his own subterfuge. Michael was glad to be free of the nonsense.

But he was wasting time. He knew Jocelyn would be

anxiously waiting for him. They had much to discuss and he couldn't wait to see the expression on her face when he made his offer of marriage.

He dressed quickly, taking extra time with his shaving, and headed downstairs.

Lucy met him in the vestibule, but instead of her usual cheery good morning, she said quietly, "You have visitors. They are waiting for you in the sitting room."

If it had been Jocelyn, her uncle, or anyone from the village, he sensed she would have said their names. "Who are they?"

"An older man and a young woman. They would not identify themselves because they said they wanted you to be surprised."

The military man in Michael hated surprises. He murmured "thank you." He couldn't imagine who was calling and then wondered if it could be Burkhardt, except Lucy would have said as much.

He crossed the few steps to the sitting room and then stopped in astonishment. Sir William sat on Lucy's couch, holding a cup of coffee in his hand. "Donaldson," he greeted Michael cheerfully. "Are you surprised?"

"Absolutely," Michael answered and then let his gaze drift over to Ivy, who stood by the fireplace looking more beautiful than ever.

She smiled, her expression tentative and he caught himself holding his breath, waiting for the rush of desire he usually felt whenever he saw her.

Chapter Fifteen

❧❧

Miss Kenyon Meets Lady Elfreda's Cousin

Jocelyn knocked on Lucy's kitchen door. There was no answer. Impatient, she turned the handle and went inside. "Lucy?"

Her friend came to the doorway between the hall and the kitchen. She held a finger over her lips, urging Jocelyn to silence, then motioned her to follow.

As they tiptoed toward the sitting room, Lucy said, "Mr. Donaldson has visitors." She led Jocelyn to the edge of the staircase where they could shamelessly eavesdrop without being detected.

Jocelyn leaned around the banister, craning her neck to see inside the sitting room. Michael's back blocked the doorway. "It's a man and woman, a beautiful woman who is so similar in looks to Lady Elfreda, it is uncanny," Lucy told her quietly. "They're obviously quality although they did not give me their names. They know Mr. Donaldson very well."

Turning her attention to what was being said in the sitting room, Jocelyn heard Michael ask, "What are you doing here?" He did not sound pleased.

A hearty male voice answered, "We had an occasion to visit. My brother is holding a betrothal ball in honor of his daughter tomorrow night and invited us. I realized this was a perfect opportunity for you and me to meet without anyone being the wiser."

"What was wrong with London?" Michael asked.

There was a slight hesitation before the gentleman answered, "The walls have ears in London. Here the two of us can talk."

"Good. I have questions for you," Michael said, walking into the room, and Jocelyn caught a glimpse of the man. He was of moderate height with intense eyes, and a receding hairline he attempted to conceal by combing all his hair forward. He wore an overlong velvet jacket as if he were a character in a Chaucer story.

"Such as?" the man asked.

"Geoffrey Kenyon has never heard of you before, Sir William. How can he steal from a man whom he does not know?"

Sir William, the man who had falsely accused her uncle. Jocelyn edged closer toward the door to hear his response. Lucy tried to draw her back, but Jocelyn shook her off.

"Did he tell you that?" Sir William answered lazily. "He's lying."

The accusation stung Jocelyn to the quick. Throwing caution to the wind, she stepped from hiding and charged into the room to confront the man. "My uncle never lies."

Sir William frowned. "Who is this?"

Jocelyn didn't give Michael a chance to answer. "I'm Geoffrey Kenyon's niece and I have worked on his correspondence over the years. I want to know why you wish to claim my uncle and Mr. Redding's research as your own?"

Sir William stood. "You are misguided," he replied stiffly. "I started experimenting with rubber years ago."

"That doesn't mean this particular formula is yours," she answered.

"It means I have some claim to the results," Sir William said.

Michael stepped between them. "Enough. Let us take this to Kenyon and see what he says. It is what you should have done in the beginning, Sir William."

"Yes," Jocelyn agreed. "And I am certain the Royal Society will also want a part in arbitrating this dispute."

"The Royal Society," Sir William said with disgust. "If they had allowed me to present my paper the way they should have, my claim would have been established."

"Either way, we will talk to Kenyon," Michael said.

"And what about *us?*" a melodious female voice said from the other side of the room.

Jocelyn turned toward the sound. She had been so incensed by Sir William's false claims, she'd not noticed the woman standing by the fireplace. For a second, she thought Lady Elfreda was in the room . . . except this woman was more lovely—and more certain of her own beauty.

The woman crossed to Michael and slipped her arm possessively through his. "What about the promises you made to me?" she purred up to him.

"Yes, what about those?" Sir William echoed, the light of a thousand devils in his eyes. "You asked for my daughter's hand in marriage and I offered it to you provided you help return my formula to me. You do know he is here under false pretenses, don't you?" he said to Jocelyn. "The fake name and all that nonsense. A little subterfuge."

"Which was your idea," Michael said in his defense.

"He told me all," Jocelyn managed to croak out . . . and she was glad she knew even as she felt completely betrayed. She stared at their entwined arms and felt dowdy beyond all belief. There was no way she could compete with such a creature, and it wasn't just the woman's looks. She was dressed in the height of fashion. She'd probably paid more for the dress she was wearing than Jocelyn spent for a year's worth of clothing.

Michael attempted to pull away. "Jocelyn, please, I have to explain."

"That we are to be married?" Sir William's daughter asked, cuddling closer. She met Jocelyn's gaze with such a superior, dismissive air it made Jocelyn angry. The woman was laughing at her!

Well, she'd not stand here and take it. "He's told me all," she coolly informed the beauty. "And you are welcome to him." She took a step back toward the door.

Michael followed her, the beauty laughing as she took his hand and held him back. "Please, Jocelyn, we talked about this last night."

"I don't think I understood the depth of your commitment," Jocelyn said. "Or my response would have been different." She slid her gaze to Sir William's daughter. "Very different."

Like the she-cat she was, the beauty agreed, "Yes, we *are* very different."

Jocelyn didn't make another response. Instead, she wrapped herself in her pride, turned on her heel, and left the room, walking out the front door without a backward glance.

Michael swore softly and shook off Ivy's arm. "You've barely given me a moment of your time since I returned to England and now you latch on to me like a leech?"

Her smile hardened. "What's mine I keep."

"She's a bit spoiled that way, lad," Sir William agreed.

"Yours?" Michael almost laughed. "You don't want me, Ivy. Your father put you up to this for his own gain. Well, it worked. Like some lovesick swain I went on some idiotic quest, and now I realize the price for your heart isn't worth the cost."

He looked to Sir William. "I'm going to do what I should have done from the beginning. I'm telling you to take your complaint to the Royal Society or confront Kenyon yourself."

"I need proof," Sir William argued. "I need a copy of Kenyon's formula."

"Knock on his door and ask for it. The man is completely open about his research . . . although he may not trust you. I'm done with the two of you."

He started toward the door but Ivy hurried ahead and put herself in his path. "Wait, Michael, what about me? About us?"

"Us?" he questioned, surprised to see she was genuinely upset.

"You've always been there for me, Michael. You were the first to promise your devotion."

He understood now. She wasn't interested in being

his wife. She never had been. His devotion to her had been a prize, a trophy. "I may have been the first but I'm certain I'm not the last. You will die brokenhearted, Ivy."

"And will your country girl?" she countered petulantly.

"I'm going to make certain she doesn't," he promised, and left in search of Jocelyn.

Chapter Sixteen

ℰℰ

Miss Kenyon's Decision

Michael knew he would find Jocelyn in her garden.

She sat on a bench, watching a fat robin chase a beetle.

He walked across the flagstone path, his booted heels announcing his arrival. She did not look up, even after the robin flew away.

He stopped, uncertain of his welcome. "It's not what you think," he said.

She smiled, not looking at him. "How do you know what I think?"

"I can imagine." A beat. "Jocelyn, I confessed the truth last night and I have never misled you about Ivy."

"Ivy," she repeated. "It's a lovely name."

"Lovely or not, Ivy no longer means anything to me." He waited, expecting a response—a smile, a blink.

There was none.

He knew he was going to have to give more. He

walked the few remaining steps between them and knelt at her feet. "Jocelyn, I loved her once or thought I did. We were both young when we met and I was the youngest of five brothers, all of them more successful and offered more opportunities than I had. She noticed me. She made me feel special and I worshiped her. Can you not understand how it was?"

"You don't need to explain yourself to me, Michael," she said coolly.

She shifted as if preparing to leave. He placed his hand on the bench, his arm blocking her escape. "For Ivy, I made something of myself. I—" He paused. He could not explain the horrors of war, the risks he had taken to line his coffers and gain rank and privilege. Here in the peace of her garden, such things should not be mentioned. Instead, he said, "When I returned from the Continent, she did not have time for me. The pain of rejection and blow to my pride was unbearable. I'd hoped to prove myself again by performing this small task for her father. Jocelyn, I thought I could not live without Ivy and yet, you've made me see differently. Ivy means nothing to me. Not anymore."

Her lips twisted at the irony of their respective situations. The expression in her eyes softened. She lightly brushed her fingers down the side of his jaw and then let her hand drop. "I have no regrets either, much to my embarrassment. Before you came, I was thinking you were a lesson I had to learn. One I should have discovered with Thomas."

He did not like being compared to the farmer. He would have said so, except she continued, "Good-bye, Michael. I know you have unfinished business with my uncle. I'll send him out so the two of you may talk. However, I believe matters between us are settled."

"Jocelyn—"

She pressed her fingers over his lips, stopping words. "It isn't your decision, Michael. But mine."

"You can't just walk away from me. There is something between us, something we shouldn't let go."

"Ah, but there is no *trust* between us. Not any longer. Without trust, nothing else matters."

She was right.

He rocked back, embarrassed by his actions and at a loss as to how to breach the growing chasm between them. "There could be repercussions from last night," he said, unable to let her go. "You will need me."

"Are you suggesting I could be with child?" She shook her head. Her curls moved with their own vitality while the expression in her eyes was distant. "I'm not." She placed her hand on her abdomen. "If I were, I'd know. I'd sense it. So, you truly are free . . . whether you decide to return to Ivy or not."

She stood and, this time, he let her go.

However, she'd only taken four steps when he came to his feet. "Is it because of Ivy . . . or is there some other reason?"

She hesitated, then said succinctly, "I'm sorry, Michael, but you were not a gentleman." She walked into the house.

Her verdict stunned him.

She was right. He'd compromised himself in attempting to please Ivy and he'd lost sight of what was really important.

He'd also lost the woman he loved.

Love. The word reverberated in his mind. From the first moment he'd laid eyes on Jocelyn, he'd been attracted to her, but love?

A bee buzzed happily behind him, making its way from one rose to another, and he knew that last night, his body had understood what his mind had not yet accepted—he'd fallen in love with Jocelyn. Truly, deeply, madly in love.

And now she was gone from him, her trust lost.

He had no choice but to leave and he went where many a young man turns when he wishes to lose himself in sorrow. He went to the pub.

From her bedroom window, Jocelyn watched Michael put on his hat and leave the garden. Only then did she let down the curtain and, throwing herself on her bed, gave in to a good cry.

But she had pride this time. Oh, yes, she'd kept her pride.

Outside his niece's bedroom door, Uncle Geoff helplessly listened to her sobs and they tore at his heart. He'd known how to bandage bumps on the head and help solve a list of sums . . . but how did one heal a broken heart?

He'd thought she was getting over Thomas—a man he'd never really liked—and he'd been pleased with Donaldson. There had been true magic between the young couple.

Whatever had happened, Donaldson was a fool to let Jocelyn go—and he should tell him.

Once the idea took hold, Uncle Geoff could not give it up. The time had come for him to champion Jocelyn's cause. So, he did something he rarely did. He took his hat and headed out the door, fully intent on hunting Donaldson down and giving him a piece of his mind.

Chapter Seventeen

❦

The Rooster's Den

The Rooster's Den was busy at noonday when Michael made his way there.

He chose a chair in a far corner, ordered a local ale, and would have drowned his disappointments—except for the odd sensation that someone was watching him. He looked to his left and saw Burkhardt giving him the evil eye.

Michael raised his tankard and toasted the bastard who appeared already half in his cups.

Burkhardt stood and made his way over on unsteady feet. Several of the pub patrons knew him and called out good-natured jokes about his upcoming betrothal. Burkhardt ignored them. Reaching Michael's table, he practically fell into the chair across from him.

"You've won," he slurred out.

"Won what?" Michael asked.

"Joss. She's yours and I am doomed to unhappiness." Burkhardt placed his arms on the table and slowly lowered his head to rest his chin on top.

"You are soon to be a married man." Michael couldn't resist the jab.

"Joss says I should be happy. She says Elfreda loves me. Maybe she does," he finished. "But I shall miss Joss. Of course, I didn't realize it until you arrived. I thought I had everything in control."

"As did I," Michael agreed and felt a stab of sympathy for his rival. He added, "Lady Elfreda is nothing like her cousin."

"Ivy?" Burkhardt shuddered. "She's a man-eater, that one."

"I wish you'd given me that advice earlier," Michael muttered. *"Years* earlier."

"What?" Burkhardt asked, not even listening, and then lazily shook his head. "Lucky devil, you. Got Joss." His mood shifted. He looked around for the barmaid, a round, buxom woman of about fifty-five. "I need another one, Angie dear. And bring one for my new friend."

Angie gave Michael a frank inspection. "You're the one who has been courting Miss Kenyon," she said in greeting. "Aye, I'll fetch another round for both of you."

"She wouldn't talk to me when I jilted Joss," Thomas confided. "I suppose she has gotten over it." He hiccuped. "S'cuse me." He laid his head back down.

The door opened, spreading rays of daylight into the dark pub and Geoffrey Kenyon walked in, dressed in a bottle-green jacket and starched white neckcloth. His appearance in the pub was enough of a novelty to attract attention. He looked around the room, spied Michael and started heading his way.

"Oh pother," Thomas mumbled. "Joss's uncle. He never liked me."

"He's going to like me even less," Michael answered.

"What?" Thomas repeated again, so caught up in his own worries he hadn't been attending.

"Never mind."

Kenyon came up to the table. "Donaldson, I must talk to you." It was obvious he'd been giving this a great deal of thought and would have his say one way or the other.

"You are welcome to join us," Michael said grandly, "but first I must tell you my name's not Donaldson. It's Sanson. Michael Sanson. *Colonel* Michael Sanson."

Thomas lifted his head and Angie, who had returned, paused as she set their tankards on the table. Nor did she hurry to leave.

"Ah, so that's part of it," Kenyon said, as if piecing matters together in his own mind. He pulled up a chair and sat. "Go on, let's have the rest."

"It isn't flattering," Michael said, surprised the man wasn't more suspicious. Instead he seemed ready to hear a bedtime tale.

"Schemes never are," Kenyon said. "I mean, Jocelyn schemed to make Burkhardt jealous and you know that didn't work."

"It worked very well," Burkhardt mumbled. "I'm out of my mind."

Angie hit him with her tray. "She's not for you. You are to marry a real lady and you'd best do it or your mother will make your life miserable."

"There is that," Burkhardt conceded, and Michael couldn't help but smile.

"Is there more?" Kenyon asked with interest.

"Oh, yes, much more." Michael proceeded to tell him

the story of Sir William's formula. He didn't stint on his own culpability; however, he was prudent enough to omit the part when he'd made mind-numbing love to the man's niece in his laboratory. Too much honesty could be a touchy thing.

Angie and Burkhardt listened, and others quickly joined them, all seemingly with a vested interest in Jocelyn's welfare.

"So you *were* burglarizing Mr. Kenyon's house?" Angie clarified with disapproval.

Surprisingly, Kenyon came to his aid. "Sir William's tactics were crude but this isn't the first time this sort of thing has gone on in science, Angie. Especially with something like this where there is the smell of money."

"So what of Sir William's charge that the formula is his?" Michael asked.

"It could be." Kenyon surprised Michael with his answer. He shrugged. "He could have done work that was 'borrowed' by another. However, I did not take the formula and can prove my innocence through my correspondence. I don't know but Randolph Redding could have taken the formula. I'd assumed he'd started with his own experiments. Or Sir William may have had very little to do with the formula's inception and wishes to claim a larger share for himself. This idea of waterproof cloth is not glamorous but has many practical applications. Of course the matter is moot. We can't seem to change the properties of rubber without turning it into a sticky mess." He started to go into a detailed explanation, but his audience groaned with dismay and quickly dispersed to other parts of the room, taking Burkhardt with them.

Alone with Kenyon, Michael leaned back in his chair and admitted, "I'm a fool." His damn single-mindedness had led him to unwise decisions.

Kenyon contradicted him. "You are only a fool if you let Jocelyn go."

Pushing his tankard aside with one finger, Michael said to Kenyon. "You've taken my confession well."

"I like you." He added quietly, "You did me a favor by making my niece see how pompous Burkhardt is."

"Well, now she has shown me my shortcomings," Michael said.

"And they are?" Kenyon asked.

Michael was ruthless. "Pride. Vanity." He thought of the beautiful, mercurial creature Jocelyn had been in his arms last night. "And that Trust is to be valued."

"You can trust Jocelyn," Kenyon said.

"Aye . . . but she no longer trusts me. Burkhardt and I have both hurt her."

"Because you've disappointed her," Kenyon answered. "Who among us has not done that at one time or another? The child disappoints the parent. Parents are not all they should be. Lovers are never perfect." He rapped the table with his knuckles. "What is important is your willingness to make amends. You must win her back."

"I begged—"

"Not beg, man. I said *win*. Do you love her?"

"Yes," Michael replied without hesitation.

"Then show her the very best of yourself. You are a good man. I would choose you for my niece. But winning the battle, storming her senses, and bringing her into your arms—that is up to you."

"You are so certain I could succeed?" Michael asked.

A twinkle appeared in the scientist's eye. "I haven't spent a lifetime studying chemistry without learning how to recognize combustible reactions, and you and Jocelyn are very well-suited. However, the question I have is, do you want to win her? Or are you sitting here feeling guilty over having been caught in your deceits?"

Michael sat back, struck by the shrewd assessment.

"I mean no offense, Colonel," Kenyon added.

"None taken," Michael answered. He sat up. "You are right. I wanted Ivy out of pride. Other men envied such a beauty and I treated her with the arrogance of showing off a prized possession. I can honestly say, I feel no connection to her."

"And Jocelyn? Do you desire her?"

"God, yes. However, my feelings for her run deeper and I am as astounded as anyone. I've known her days, mere hours, and yet I feel I've known her forever. The sight of her curls makes me smile. And when she has an idea, her nose wrinkles . . . and I could listen to the sound of her laughter forever. From the moment I met her, I could think of no one but her. However, she has seen me for the fool I am."

"All women see us for the fools we are. God is merciful though, and also gives them the capacity to forgive us." Kenyon clapped Michael on the back. "Have heart, Colonel. You can win her back."

"How?"

Her uncle smiled. "By being yourself."

Chapter Eighteen

ᘓᘔ

Lord Vaughn's Ball

Jocelyn dried her eyes and forced herself to go on with her daily chores. Uncle Geoff had gone out, which was unusual. It was entirely possible he'd been successful the night before and discovered the elusive result he'd been seeking.

He returned home in the late afternoon looking pleased with himself and smelling of ale.

Because of her lack of sleep the night before, Jocelyn went to bed early and slept hard. She sensed she was in mourning for what could have been. Her feelings for Michael had run deep, deeper than they had for Thomas. She felt as if a part of herself was missing and was powerless to imagine how to make herself whole.

The next morning, Mrs. Jeter personally delivered the dress Michael had purchased. Jocelyn graciously complimented the needlework but later told her uncle she could not wear it.

"I bought this dress for your enjoyment," Uncle Geoff said.

Jocelyn took his hand. "You didn't buy this dress at all. I overheard everything you and Michael said. It is best I wear my yellow muslin."

Still, for all her fine words, Jocelyn couldn't help but open the box and take a peek at the dress Michael had chosen for her. She caught her breath. The overdress of rose tissue was gorgeous. She would have felt very special wearing such a dress.

Jocelyn put the lid on the box, not even bothering to hang the dress up.

Late that afternoon, she began preparing herself, putting on her yellow muslin and styling her hair high on her head. Instead of letting her curls flow freely down to her shoulders, she tied them up with a piece of emerald ribbon so she appeared more mature. At four and twenty, the time had come for her to set aside girlish styles.

Uncle Geoff looked stately in black evening dress. Yes, the style of his coat was perhaps a decade or two old but he still looked remarkable and he acted as if he were anticipating the evening. "Ready?" he asked.

She nodded. "You look very handsome."

He considered her for a moment, then said evenly, "So do you."

She did not comment.

Lord Vaughn's house was filled with light. Candles burned everywhere. Lanterns had been strung in the garden and already half the parish strolled the grounds while listening to the musicians playing for their enjoyment.

The ball was to be held in the house's great hall.

A receiving line greeted Jocelyn and her uncle at the front door. A butler grandly announced their names. He carried a staff embellished with brightly colored ribbons and pounded the floor with it to gain the crowd's attention and add decorum to the proceedings. Announced, Jocelyn and her uncle moved forward to meet Lord and Lady Vaughn. Next to Lady Vaughn stood her daughter, Elfreda. For a second, her gaze met Jocelyn's and in her eyes, Jocelyn saw such unhappiness her heart went out to the woman who had been her rival.

Thomas didn't meet her gaze. He bowed over her hand and acted as if they were strangers. His mother had no such reluctance.

"Why, Miss Kenyon, what a pleasure to see you this evening. I'd heard you had an escort? I suppose he decided not to come?"

Thomas shifted, his embarrassment at his mother's baiting obvious. Jocelyn answered in a steady voice, "He could not be with us tonight."

Elfreda seemed to grow more unhappy and Jocelyn felt guilty.

Uncle Geoff hurried her away. "It's not your fault," he said, accurately divining her thoughts.

"Oh, Uncle, you don't know. I set out to make her miserable and now I am sorry. My behavior was reprehensible. I thought only of myself."

"You were hurting, Josie." He clasped her hand in his. "I should have provided more guidance. I was so involved in my experiments, I didn't know how lost you'd felt until it was too late. However, I am glad you aren't marrying him. He still has a long way to go until he is a man. Witness the stiff way he is toward Lady Elfreda."

Uncle Geoff was right. Thomas seemed to avoid looking at her. "It is unfortunate you and young Sanson could not have met at a different time."

"You know his real name?" Michael must have talked to her uncle.

Uncle Geoff nodded. "Yes, we spoke, and I want you to remember that just as you are sorry for your self-seeking actions, he has regrets, too."

A hurtful lump formed in her throat. "I sent him away."

"I know."

She searched his face. "Was I wrong?"

Uncle Geoff gave her hand a squeeze. "Only you can decide that, my dear. Ah, there is Mr. and Mrs. Lettman."

"I don't want to leave you," Jocelyn said. "You came to help and, if you wish, I'll be happy to stay."

"Nonsense, go and enjoy the party. This is a time to celebrate. I'm going to go find the punch bowl."

Jocelyn walked off but she definitely felt out of place. Speculative glances were often thrown her way and she overheard Mrs. Jeter sigh with disappointment when she noticed the yellow muslin. She knew on the morrow the gossips would be wondering if the new dress had been a fact or a fiction.

Lucy gave her a welcoming hug but she and Kent were busy talking to other married couples about topics they had in common.

Catching a glimpse of another friend, Jocelyn started in her direction—but she saw Ivy and stopped.

Lady Elfreda's beautiful cousin took no notice of her.

She was busy entertaining half a dozen young men, all begging for dances. Obviously Ivy wasn't going to pine for Michael.

Jocelyn turned and saw her uncle deep in conversation with Sir William. What had once seemed a problem to that gentleman was obviously not one any longer.

And Jocelyn realized she was standing alone. Everyone had someone . . . save her.

Like a martyr resigned to her fate, she found a place for herself amongst the matrons, sitting with the likes of the chatty Mrs. Mayes and the Clark sisters.

The dancing began. Although Jocelyn had always liked to dance, she was not in the mood to even tap her toe. She was officially "on the shelf." A spinster. From now on her role would be circumspect, a pillar of volunteer work, and social overseer of such events as this ball without taking part.

The prospect was depressing.

Thomas led Lady Elfreda out onto the floor for the first dance. Soon everyone was up and moving save for the matrons and Jocelyn. The older women attempted to include her in the conversation; however, other than gardening, Jocelyn had nothing to add to the conversation. She'd never had labor pains, nursed a sick child, or worried over a husband's gout. Being a spinster was a bit like being in a no-man's-land. Perhaps she would have to move in with the Clark sisters to learn how to do it right.

If only she could learn to live with this terrible emptiness inside. This loneliness was different than when Thomas had jilted her. This time she knew she'd lost something very precious and would not ever get it back.

There was a lull in the music as one dance ended and couples moved to take positions for the next lively reel. Jocelyn had always loved a reel.

Lord Vaughn's butler pounded his staff against the wood floor for attention to announce a late guest. "Colonel Michael Sanson," he said, his sonorous voice resounding in the sudden quiet.

Jocelyn started at the name. Slowly she turned just as Michael appeared in the doorway—but not the Michael she'd known.

No, this gentleman wore full military uniform. The tailored cut and gold braid made him seem taller and more broad-shouldered than she could remember. He was undeniably handsome with his silver eyes and dark hair.

A murmur spread through the room. Many recognized him as the tea merchant. Others had already learned he had another identity.

The gossipy Mrs. Mayes touched Jocelyn's arm. "Can you believe? Lady Vaughn's cousin just informed me that he is the son of an earl. He must be very busy being a soldier and peddling tea." She dropped her voice to confide, "He never came to my house as I requested."

An earl's son. Well, of course. Michael had never been what he seemed, Jocelyn thought cynically. She crossed her arms, struggling with an almost overwhelming urge to cry. She knew he'd come for Ivy. She'd done all but hand him to the other woman and suddenly, she didn't think she could stand to see them together.

She rose, wanting to escape, and discovered there was nowhere to go without making a scene. Michael spotted her. Like two focused beams of light, their gazes met and she could not look away.

He began walking toward her with purpose.

Jocelyn could have sworn her heart had stopped beating. She waited, hoping against hope, her feet rooted to the floor.

Michael waded in amongst the matrons. He stopped a mere foot from Jocelyn and held out his hand. "Miss Kenyon, would you do me the honor of this dance?"

Chapter Nineteen

❧

Love's True Light

For a moment, Jocelyn stared at his offered hand, conscious that everyone in the room watched them. Part of her feared Michael and his words were phantoms of her overactive imagination.

Then, tentatively, she placed her hand in his.

Strong fingers clasped hers and she almost cried out in thankfulness.

He raised her hand to his lips—and she knew he was real; this moment was real.

Around her, the matrons watched with wide eyes—Mrs. Burkhardt one of their number.

"Forgive me," he whispered.

"I'm the one who should be begging forgiveness," she answered. "We both made some foolish mistakes—"

"That could have cost us dearly," he finished. "Jocelyn, I must know, will you do me the honor of being my wife? I promise I'll never be anything other than I am . . . forever."

He asked her to marry him—right there in the middle of the matrons. Jocelyn glanced around. Uncle Geoff was smiling while Lucy and Kent grinned broadly. The Clark sisters' eyes were as round as an owl's as if they could scarce believe their ears, and Mrs. Banks clasped her hands in anticipation. "Do say yes," she encouraged Jocelyn. "This is the most romantic thing to ever happen in Wye."

Her announcement brought joy to her heart. She looked to Michael. "Yes, I will marry you," she said softly. "And I shall promise you that I will never, ever scheme again."

"Especially to make someone jealous," he cautioned with good humor, then added soberly, "I'll be a good husband to you, Jocelyn."

"And I will be the best of wives."

The Clark sisters appeared to swoon. Mrs. Banks sighed her satisfaction.

Michael led her out on the dance floor and they took their places next to Lucy and Kent, who gave them hugs and handshakes. Jocelyn caught Michael nodding to someone who stood behind her. She turned and saw her uncle. A silent communication passed between the two men, an understanding of sorts.

"He knew you were coming, didn't he?" she asked.

Taking her hand for the set, Michael said, "He made me hope that you would not turn me away a second time."

"I'm glad," she answered and then the music started and they celebrated their happiness with dancing.

However, later, when they'd had enough well-wishes and needed a moment alone, Michael took her hand and led her outside to the stone terrace running along the back of the house. There, they found a quiet alcove away from prying eyes and the light of the paper lanterns hanging from the trees.

He took her in his arms. "I need to hear you say it," he said.

She didn't need to ask him what he meant; she knew. Reaching up to cup his face in her hands, she said, "I love you, Michael Sanson."

"And I love you, Jocelyn Kenyon, and will forevermore."

After a promise like his, she had no choice but to kiss—and do it more than once!

Watching them from the shadows of a large oak tree, Thomas almost couldn't bear to see Jocelyn so happy. In fact, he'd had to leave the ballroom because there was no one who could have looked at her and not known she was in love.

Actually, Thomas had nothing against Donaldson or Sanson or whatever his name was—not after drinking in the Rooster's Den with him. Still, it didn't make losing Jocelyn any more palatable.

He turned his back on the lovers, and leaned against the oak's mighty trunk, his mind a maze of doubts and regrets.

He was so involved in his misery, he didn't see Elfreda's approach until her quiet voice said, "You left the party."

With her hands clasped in front of her, she stood in the moonlight, a few steps away from the dark shadows of the tree. Her expression was unreadable in the silvery moonlight, and yet there was no mistaking the sadness about her.

"I needed a moment of air," he said, lifting his gaze upward to the moon peeking at him through the tree branches.

She was silent for a moment, seemingly accepting his excuse. He expected her to go inside.

Instead, she said, "Thomas, I do not believe we should marry."

"What?" he demanded ungracefully, swinging his gaze back to her.

"You heard what I said," she told him in a firm voice that didn't sound anything like his Elfreda. "I have been thinking and I don't believe you and I will suit."

"Why not?" he demanded, walking toward her.

"Because you are in love with someone else." Her words pierced his conscience.

He stopped, guilty as charged.

"I knew you and Jocelyn had a prior agreement, but I wanted you," Elfreda continued quietly. "From the first moment I saw you walk into church last autumn, I fell in love with you. I know you've never truly returned my affections. You were more attracted to my father's money and the prestige of the marriage. I told myself I could love you enough for both of us and that perhaps someday you would grow to love me." Her eyes were shiny with unshed tears, but she did not give in to them. "But I've discovered something, Thomas. I can't live with this emptiness inside. I can't keep hoping for something that will never happen."

Her words tore at his soul.

For the first time, he truly saw Elfreda as a person and not a trophy to be won. And he came face to face with his own arrogance.

"Good night, Thomas," she said and turned to go inside. "You needn't worry. I will tell Mother and Father that I was the one to cry off. I think they will understand."

Suddenly, he realized he could not let her go, and not just because of scandal or gossip.

No, he couldn't let her go because he fell in love. It happened suddenly and without expectation.

Here, he realized, was someone who didn't see him as a dupe of an overbearing mother. Elfreda had made him feel important and in return, he'd taken her gentle feelings for granted and spent his time longing for what he couldn't have.

Jocelyn had never loved him, not as Elfreda did. He and Joss had *thought* they were in love, but time and time again she'd put off his marriage proposals. First, they had been too young. Then, her uncle had gotten ill. Finally, she'd wanted to wait a year—and he'd been happy to do so.

But Elfreda had always been there for him—and now he was in danger of losing her.

How could he have been so bloody blind?

He caught Elfreda before she started up the steps. Hooking his hand around her arm, he turned her to him. "No, I'm the one who is wrong," he said firmly, and without waiting for permission, he kissed her fully on the lips.

This was no gentlemanly kiss or chaste peck. He kissed her with the recognition of a man who has found his mate. Their kiss blossomed. Hunger, need, desire—all could be tasted, and he knew she hadn't given up on him. Not yet.

He hugged her close, feeling the rapid beat of her heart. It matched the rhythm of his own and this woman in his arms took on an importance greater than gold.

"Elfreda, I have been such a fool."

"No," she protested in a little voice overcome by emotion—and he realized she was crying. "I mean, I know you would prefer someone as bright as Jocelyn or perhaps more ambitious than I will ever be. Thomas, I can't be more than I am. All I ever wanted was to take care of you. Will that be enough?"

"It will," he vowed, "if you are willing to put up with me." He shook his head. "All I seem to do is hurt those who care for me."

"You are a bit spoiled," she ventured in her soft, gentle voice.

"Spoiled?" No one had ever said it to his face before. For a second, he was startled, and then he began to laugh. "Help me be a better person," he said. "Help me to learn to think of others, especially yourself."

Her response was a sigh of contentment, the sound so sweet, Thomas *had* to kiss her again.

Chapter Twenty

All's Well

That night, when the clock struck twelve, two betrothals were announced.

And the following Sunday, two banns were posted.

The young couples drew a line, however, at a double wedding ceremony.

Jocelyn and her uncle traveled to Sussex to meet Michael's large and gregarious family. They welcomed her with open arms. Jocelyn found herself surrounded by something she'd always wanted—brothers and sisters.

She and Michael were married in the family chapel on his father's estate. She wore the white muslin dress with the rose oversheath and red flowers in her hair. Everyone swore she was the loveliest of brides.

Michael resigned his commission. Tired of war, he and Jocelyn purchased a prosperous farm along the banks of the river Avon and not far from Wye. And there they gave birth to and raised three healthy, beautiful children.

Thomas and Elfreda were wed by Vicar Banks and proved to be the happiest of couples . . . even if some whispered she catered to him a bit too much. But then, what had anyone expected? His mother had been the first to spoil him.

Ivy did marry a viscount. Within a year, she'd given him an heir and rumor had it the two never spoke again although they remained married for twenty-two years. Ivy lived her life with her flirts and her husband took his pleasure where he may.

Unfortunately, neither Uncle Geoffrey's or Sir William's venture into waterproof material fared well. Redding denied ever seeing Sir William's formula. After several complaints to the Royal Society, who largely ignored him, Sir William gave up.

Meanwhile, Uncle Geoff's idea of melting the rubber proved to be of no use at all when two years later, a Scot chemist by the name of Macintosh ascertained coal-tar naphtha was an effective solvent for dispersing and adhering rubber onto material. The Scot patented his discoveries in 1823 and started the manufacture of raincoats that bore his name.

The setback did not mean Uncle Geoff stopped tinkering. No, not at all. He returned to his love of gunpowder, invented a new trigger for the pistol and lived out his days content with the faithful adoration of Michael and Jocelyn's children . . . who grew very good at putting out Uncle Geoff's occasional fires.

Hunting Season

Liz Carlyle

To three wonderful authors,
Jo Goodman,
Sabrina Jeffries,
and
Nicole Jordan.

They are the embodiment of
kindness, patience, and generosity.

Chapter One

Beware the fury of a patient man.
—Dryden

*H*e was a young man with old eyes. Eyes which had seen trouble aplenty, and were looking for more, unless the innkeeper missed his guess. The gentleman had blown into the Hart and Hare with a raging thunderstorm at his heels, his coattails flying out behind him, the distant horizon boiling with black clouds as if he'd fled the very gates of hell. His mount had done nothing to soften the image. Big and black, with wicked white eyes, the beast had reared and wheeled about the yard, kicking up dust and gravel with every lightning bolt, until at last the man had soothed him, and passed the reins to a stable boy.

Now, long hours later, the wind was picking up, lashing rain across the door and sending the inn's wooden placard swinging back and forth on rusty iron rings, the rhythmic screech of metal almost painful to the ear. Somewhere in the distance, a shutter began to thump. Another gust sent a sheet of rain spattering across the front windows and forced a damp breeze down the chimney. The sooty back draft roiled into the taproom, but the sullen gentleman sprawled by the hearth scarcely heeded it.

The innkeeper paused in his work, a careful polishing of a pewter pitcher. "A bloody wicked storm," he mused, peering judiciously into the bottom. "Bad for the harvest, eh?"

But the gentleman did not seem predisposed to chat. Indeed, he scarcely lifted his eyes from his task, which appeared to be some strange, solitary card game.

Curious, the innkeeper leaned across the counter, careful of his left wrist, which was splinted and wrapped. The man by the hearth deftly reshuffled, then snapped his cards out across the scarred wooden table, dealing to his imaginary opponents with an expert's hand. *Vingt-et-un*, was it? Over and over the man repeated the process, his movements methodical, his concentration absolute.

With an indolent grace which only the truly dissolute seem to possess, the man occupied the entire length of the settle, one shoulder wedged against the side, a booted leg propped casually up. His eyes, when they were not focused intently upon his table, were cold and narrow. His jaw was hard, shadowed with beard. His long, quick fingers flicked and fanned the pack of cards as adroitly as another man might draw a knife, handling them much like a weapon.

His type was not unknown to the innkeeper. Rowdy crowds of young bucks often cavorted through the village this time of year, migrating into the country for the hunting season, and stirring up all manner of trouble as they came. But this one looked different. More dangerous. More intent. And he was definitely not cavorting. Yes, a young man with old eyes. And he had come alone, arriving at the Hart and Hare to tersely bespeak a bath and a suite of rooms—the very last of their rooms—and had otherwise conversed with no one.

Within the hour, however, he'd stepped back down to demand supper and a bottle of brandy. And there he'd sat, from that hour to this, drinking and shuffling. Dealing and drinking. And occasionally lighting one of his malodorous brown cheroots. Now, with the evening coming nigh on eleven, and the other guests long since abed, the fellow showed signs of neither fatigue nor drunkenness. In fact, he showed no emotion whatsoever. It was just a little chilling.

Gently, the innkeeper cleared his throat. His broken wrist ached like the devil, and he wanted his bed. In response, the gentleman lifted his gaze from his task and shot the innkeeper an insolent, faintly inquisitive look. But at that very moment, the door burst open to admit a whirlwind of rain, lamplight, and green wool worsted. Both men turned their eyes at once toward the door.

"Good heavens!" said a soft, cultivated voice. "Will this infernal rain never cease?"

She was beautiful. Lifting his eyes from his cards, Grayston noticed that much at once. Despite her sodden bonnet, and the damp cloak which hung heavily from her shoulders, any man with two eyes could see that she was an incomparable. Wet tendrils of golden hair clung to her neck, and her stunning blue eyes suffered little from her obvious fatigue.

"Dear me!" she said, giving her umbrella a little shake.

"I'm dripping on your floor." Carefully, she set the umbrella to one side of the door.

Grayston watched as the innkeeper circled swiftly from behind the bar to take her carriage lantern. "Do have off that wet cloak, ma'am," he soothed, urging her toward a table as far distant from Grayston as was possible. "Isn't the weather frightful? I'm sorry to say the kitchen staff is long gone, but I could fix you a nice cup of tea and some toast."

As he set her lamp down on the table, she lifted her bonnet to reveal a coiled rope of golden hair. "Just a couple of rooms, if you please," she said, in a voice which was soft and throaty. "My servants are . . ."

But her words fell away, for she had seen, as had Grayston, that the innkeeper was shaking his head. "I'm dreadfully sorry, ma'am. We've just the five bedchambers above, and all of them bespoken."

"Oh!" she said softly, dropping her gaze to the rough planked floor. "Oh, dear. The price one pays for taking a wrong turn! The village has another inn, perhaps?"

Again, the innkeeper shook his head. "Nary a thing between here and Brockhampton, ma'am."

She lifted her chin, her visage wan in the lamplight, which shone up from the table. The unusual angle of the light, the shifting and flickering of the flame, cast exotic shadows over the delicate bones of her face. A face which reflected her growing alarm. "B-but my daughter," she began unsteadily. "I left her asleep in the carriage."

Clearly, the innkeeper shared her distress. "In what carriage, ma'am?"

"The one which we seem to have mired up beyond

the village." The lady bit her lip uncertainly. "My coachman and footman are working to free it, but it's so late. We . . . we got lost."

"Oh," said the innkeeper again. "Oh, dear."

Slowly, Grayston unfurled himself from the settle and moved from the shadows. "You may have my suite of rooms, ma'am, if it pleases you. I have a good-size bedchamber, and a smaller one adjoining. I'll gather my things straightaway."

Fleetingly, the innkeeper looked relieved. "But sir, where will you sleep?"

Grayston arched one brow and flung down his pack of cards. "Oh, I've never had much trouble finding a bed to sleep in," he murmured dryly. "Perhaps you'll be so good as to accommodate the lady's servants in your stables?"

"Yes, yes, to be sure." Suddenly, the innkeeper's face brightened. "And I've an assembly room above, with a fire already laid in the hearth. If I gave you a few blankets—?"

"It will do," he answered curtly.

The lady looked truly alarmed now. "Really, sir, I cannot put you out," she said, stiffening slightly. "It would be unconscionable."

For a long moment, Grayston studied her. Clearly, the lady had no wish to be beholden to him. No doubt he looked far too much the jaded rakehell for her taste. But beholden she would have to be, for he could plainly see there was nothing else for it. "I insist," he said quietly. "Pray think of your child, ma'am. Where is she to sleep?"

The golden-haired lady sagged with fatigue at that, and then she nodded, pressing her fingertips into her left temple as if her head ached. At once, Grayston flipped up his coat collar and went to the peg by the door for his greatcoat. "Which way is your carriage, ma'am?" he demanded.

She lifted her brows in surprise. "East," she responded, watching as he unfurled the coat over his shoulders. "Just a quarter-mile east on the Cheltenham Road."

Grayston lifted his hat and slapped it on. "Then I shall beg the loan of your lantern to fetch the child," he said, crossing toward the table to take it. "Your servants may follow once your carriage is free."

But to his shock, when he touched the lantern's handle, her hand came out to stay his. "I'm sure you mean to be kind," she said firmly, her fingers cold through her kidskin glove. "But I shall return, with the innkeeper's help. One can scarcely expect a child to go away with a man she does not know."

Grayston studied her face for a moment. Was that true? He did not know. He knew nothing whatsoever of children. He had no notion what they thought about, what they were afraid of. Strange men? Dark, forbidding things? Some would say he was all of those. And the lady did not want him anyway. He should return to his fire and his brandy.

But he wouldn't. This was a matter of honor, and he still possessed at least a shred. Moreover, Grayston was well accustomed to going where he was not wanted. Was that not the very thing which had brought him to this godforsaken place in such miserable weather? Good Lord, who could possibly wish to live in Gloucestershire—or anywhere else in England, come to that? Grayston longed for the sunshine of Italy, the warmth of

Paris. Not this bloody incessant rain. Gotherington Abbey could not possibly be worth owning. But own it he did. At least for as long as it suited him to do so.

Ah, well. That was tomorrow's trouble. Tonight's was already before him. He looked again at the pretty blonde, a mere slip of a woman really, and decided he did not want her, either. But for the nonce, duty called. "We've neither of us much choice, ma'am," he finally answered. The innkeeper has a broken wrist, and you cannot carry an umbrella, a lamp, and a child. Now you may return to your carriage with me, or you may stay here by the fire, as you please."

A quarter-hour later, Elise, Lady Middleton, found herself trudging back uphill toward the tiny inn whose name she'd been unable to see through the downpour. Indeed, she scarcely knew where in England she was. They had crossed the River Windrush in the late afternoon, so they were probably well into Gloucestershire—probably within ten miles of Gotherington Abbey, drat it all. At least the coach had sustained no real damage. Another half-hour would see her servants warming themselves by the fire, and Henriette tucked safely into bed. Someone else's bed, Elise remembered with a stab of guilt.

The tall man in front of her had set a steady pace both to and from her mired coach. Now, his impressive shoulders were bowed about Henriette, as if he hoped the wall of his chest might protect the child from the driving rain. He'd spoken no more than a dozen words since setting out at her side, and Elise could sense his frustration. She hastened her steps in an attempt to keep up, trying very hard to shelter them both beneath her broad, black umbrella.

The dampness squished between her toes now, and her hems were drenched in muddy water. He was soaked through, as well. Really, what had she been thinking to permit a perfect stranger to come out in such weather? At least Henriette had not fully awakened when the gentleman had reached into the carriage to scoop her into his arms. And he had been surprisingly gentle. When Elise had lifted the lantern to better light the interior, she had been touched to see him brush away a lock of Henriette's hair with his long, ungloved hand. It had seemed an odd, uncharacteristic gesture. But really, what did she know of him?

Nothing. He was a total stranger, and seemed perfectly content to remain so. He'd not even bothered to introduce himself. But he was most certainly a gentleman, that much was plain from the expensive cut of his clothes and the arrogant set of his jaw. And so he had bestirred himself from the warmth of the hearth to do what any gentleman would do under such circumstances. But he did not like it. No, he did not.

It was a pity she'd set off from London alone. Why on earth had she not waited for her maid? But Elise had promised her sister-in-law Ophelia that she would arrive at the abbey before the other houseguests. Still, she'd never dreamed that they might take such a wrong turn. And it was all her fault. At that last, fateful signpost, her new coachman had peered down at her, his kindly face fraught with doubt. But foolishly, Elise had persisted. Had she not visited Ophelia and Maynard on countless occasions?

But never traveling directly from London, she belatedly realized. And never without Sir Henry to give the directions. It would have been wiser to have told the coachman to take the route he'd thought best. Now, between her foolishness and the infernal mud, they'd lost at least four hours. And because of that, she was about to put this man—this very dangerous-looking man—out of his bed.

They were walking now on the verge, which seemed marginally more solid than the road. Swathed in a blanket of cloying damp, the tiny village ahead was as still as death. But the man's stride ate up the ground, his heavy boots sure and swift. They approached the narrow stone bridge which arched into the village proper, and this time, it seemed as if the water beneath rushed and tumbled even more treacherously than before. Fleetingly, Elise reached out for Henriette. At once, she felt the man's gaze burn into her, his eyes narrow and suspicious in the dark. She shot a swift glance back up at him and forced herself onward. The water was safe, she reminded herself. Harmless.

But what of her escort? Really, she was not at all sure it had been wise to accept his offer. Had it not been for Henriette, she certainly would not have done so. At least Henriette was perfectly at ease. She had curled herself against her benefactor's chest and was breathing deeply.

When they arrived at the inn, Elise snapped shut her umbrella and grasped the door handle, but halfway open, it slipped from her wet glove. Swiftly, the man thrust out an impossibly long leg and kicked it wide, shouldering his way through. The taproom was empty now, the fire banked for the night, and without any word to Elise, he strode past the hearth and up the narrow stairway to their left.

Still carrying her carriage lantern aloft, Elise followed him to the first-floor landing, where he turned right and strode to the end of the corridor. Tossing a glance over his shoulder, he spoke his first words since taking up Henriette. "The key is in my right coat pocket, ma'am, if you'd oblige," he murmured.

Above the door, a wall sconce burned, its flame dancing in the updraft. Nervously, Elise stepped closer. It seemed a rather intimate thing to do, to put one's hand into the pocket of a man one did not know. A man who, as she could now plainly see, was startlingly handsome. *Rakishly* handsome. But she did it, brushing back his greatcoat and fumbling about inside, enveloped by his masculine scent and warmth until she found it. With unsteady hands, she twisted back the lock, and stepped into a small parlor which smelled faintly of smoke and damp.

The inn was ancient, and the man quite tall, and so he was obliged to duck low beneath the lintel to enter the little parlor. Someone—the innkeeper, no doubt— had already cleared the man's things from the parlor. Crooking one eyebrow, the man tilted his head toward one of two closed doors, and with his boots heavy on the floor behind her, Elise hastened forward to open it. This door connected the parlor to a tiny antechamber, barely big enough for its furnishings. She stepped back, waiting by the threshold as the man settled gracefully on the edge of the little truckle bed, and lowered Henriette onto the mattress.

She could not quite see over his shoulder, but oddly, it seemed as if he lingered just a moment longer than was necessary. And again, the hand came out, his long, elegant fingers brushing the hair back from her face, then drawing the cloak more snugly about her. "Sleep the sleep of the innocent, *ma petite*," he murmured as she put down the lamp. Then he stood and turned to face her, his countenance just a little less wintry than it had been before.

Elise started to thank him, but he cut her off, stepping back into the parlor and pulling shut the door. "How old is she?" For the first time, his voice held a hint of emotion.

The man had drawn off his obviously expensive but hopelessly sodden hat, and now clutched it loosely by the brim. Though his voice had warmed, his demeanor had not. Why would he care about Henriette's age? "Nine," she finally answered. "She just turned nine."

Fleetingly, his face gentled, the softness almost touching his eyes as they swept down Elise's length. They were pale gray, she noticed; a silvery, mesmerizing color. "You are but a child yourself," he said very quietly. "She cannot possibly be yours."

Beyond the black, narrow window, Elise could still hear rain gurgling down the drainpipes, a hollow, lonely sound. She lifted her chin and stared back at him. "Henriette is mine in every way that matters," she responded a little coolly. "She is my stepdaughter. We are quite devoted to one another."

The man seemed to take no offense at her tone. "Well, she is deeply asleep," he said, as if it were not obvious. "I cannot think it worth waking her simply to put on her nightdress."

"No." Nervously, Elise stepped toward the open door,

half hoping that he would leave, but oddly, half hoping he would linger.

The man made no move to go. Instead, he stared at her with his pale gray eyes, as if reconsidering some discarded notion. She had the oddest sensation of swimming in deep, cold water; of having had the breath jolted from her chest.

"Come here," he gruffly commanded.

Strangely, she went. He lifted away her damp cloak and bonnet and hung them on a hook near the hearth, which crackled with a low fire. "Sit down." He spoke with authority, in a voice as mesmerizing as his eyes.

Again, Elise found herself obeying, settling into one of the rickety wooden chairs which flanked the fireside. The fire was blessedly warm. He shrugged out of his own coat, then sat down opposite her. He looked a little peculiar, for the chair had not been made for a man of his stature. His booted legs stretched almost to the hearthstone, and the wood creaked beneath his weight as he pulled the chair nearer. With a dispassionate touch, he took her hands into his lap and tugged off her sodden gloves.

At once, the silvery gaze flicked back up, and the man frowned as if she were a wayward child. "Good God, you really are half frozen," he said, roughly chafing her hands between his own. "Why did you not halt when the storm began?"

"My family," Elise managed to murmur as her wedding ring winked in the firelight. "They—they are expecting me."

"Really?" He arched one eyebrow. "And why were you so frightened on the bridge?"

"Frightened?" she echoed. "Why, I—I wasn't."

Indeed, her instant of panic was almost forgotten. Instead, her mind was slowly turning blank at the fusion of warm sensations, and a feeling of languor was spreading through her belly. The glow of the small fire, the heat of his body, the friction of his skin over hers; all of it was soothing. Seductively soothing. Really, she should not be here. Or rather, *he* should not be here. But the room was his, was it not?

Perplexed by the situation, Elise dropped her gaze to his hands. What lovely hands they were. Thin and elegant, with very long, very supple fingers, they were exquisite, yet unmistakably masculine. And warm, too. She had not realized how chilled she'd become. Blood was rushing into her extremities now, weighing them down with a pleasant lethargy. It had been a long time, Elise realized, since anyone had touched her in a way which was meant to give such unselfish pleasure. In response, she let her eyes drop shut. Oh, yes. This was most assuredly pleasure. His touch felt almost magical. Comforting. And yet, there was an unmistakable element of sensuality in it. She forced her eyes open, forced herself to look at him.

The man had been watching her.

Elise felt her face grow warm. His gaze swept fully over her, and at last, some sort of emotion began to kindle in his glittering gray eyes. "What a queer sort of madness," he murmured. "We are total strangers. We've just met, quite by chance, on a rain-swept night. I don't even know your name—no, don't tell me!—and so this moment seems oddly ethereal."

"Ethereal?" asked Elise lightly, struggling for a return to

normalcy. "What a charming and sentimental notion. I would not have guessed you the type."

A strange half-smile played at his lips. "Charming and sentimental?" he echoed. "Ah, yes. That would be me."

There was, she imagined, a hint of self-deprecation in his voice. Perhaps it was that which tempted her to reach out and touch his coat sleeve. "You are kind, too," she murmured, cutting her eyes away. "I cannot think how I will ever thank you. My goodness, you have given up your rooms to us."

To her shock, he slipped one of his long, elegant fingers beneath her chin, gently tilting her face back toward the firelight. "You could kiss me," he said simply.

At once, Elise jerked away. Still, his invitation had not alarmed her nearly as much as it should have. "I'm afraid you have misinterpreted my gratitude," she managed.

But the man had risen to his feet, and was drawing her from her chair. Drawing her inexorably into the circle of his warmth. And she was not fighting it. "It is a cold, miserable night, my dear," he said very softly. "We shall likely never see one another again. Do you not owe me some small gesture of thanks?"

"But I did thank—"

He caught her wrist in one hand, and jerked her gently against him. "Then do it again."

At the first touch, his mouth was hot and intoxicating. Oh, Elise had been kissed before. Often, and with great affection, by her husband. And twice, with what she'd imagined was real passion, by Denys Roth, her latest suitor. But no one had ever kissed her like this. The man possessed her instantly, molding his lips over hers, spreading his long-fingered hands across her back, and drawing the very breath from her lungs. His mouth moved warmly over hers, his lips pliant, his breath sweet with brandy. And in the narrow little parlor, everything turned topsy-turvy.

Elise tried to make a sound of protest, but it never escaped her throat. Her knees went weak, but her palms went sliding up his back. She meant to pull away, but the scent of tobacco smoke and warm male drew her closer and closer still. Lord, he kissed with a mouth of molten sin, thrusting aside her every good intention as he thrust his tongue into her mouth. And Elise could not pretend for one instant that she was an unwilling participant.

Wildly, the room spun about them. Pure pleasure pooled in her belly and swam in her head. She moaned when his fingers slid deep into her hair, stilling her to his touch, drawing back her head until her neck arched. And when his mouth left hers and slid down the flesh of her throat, almost to her breast, she exhaled on a sigh.

Suddenly, he reached back with one long leg and gently pushed shut the door with his boot heel. Mild alarm shot through her. But oddly, she did not feel unsafe. No, that was half the problem. And the other half was his touch—those long, strong fingers were cupped about her right breast now, weighing it in his warm palm and melting her brain to mush.

He felt it, too. "Lord, you've a blazing fire underneath that ice," he murmured against her skin. "Come, ice princess, keep me warm."

She knew at once what he was suggesting. Heart pounding, Elise jerked her head away. "No," she choked, her fingers clawing at his where they lay upon her breast. "Don't! I c-can't!"

In a flash, his hand turned, seizing hers and dragging it insistently to his mouth. Then, as his gaze held Elise's, he captured her ring finger and drew it deep into the warmth of his mouth, sucking it until the pulsing rhythm sent a ribbon of heat spiraling into her loins.

Elise was unable to tear her eyes from his. "My God—" she gulped. "Wh-What are you doing?"

"*Ummm* . . . leading you into temptation?" he murmured. He let the finger slide from his mouth, then turned her hand to press his lips to the tender skin of her palm. "Just let me take you into that bedchamber, my lovely. I'll lock the door behind us, and your husband need never know." And before she could jerk back in outrage, he flicked his tongue against her palm, and deftly dropped her wedding ring into it, the gold still hot from his mouth.

Elise gasped at his wicked grin. "M-My husband is dead," she choked in a hollow voice. "Else we—I—could never so much as kiss you!"

"Indeed?" With a rueful smile, he let her hand slide from his grasp. "In my experience, few women are hindered by such scruples."

"Then you've had too much experience, sir," she snapped, shoving her wedding ring awkwardly onto her finger. He was so brash, so utterly confident. And wickedly tempting. It was shameful. She went at once to the door, and somehow found the presence of mind to jerk it open.

With one slashing black eyebrow elegantly lifted, the man studied her for a moment. And then his too-handsome face fell with disappointment. "Ah, well," he murmured. "If you mean to throw me out, show at least a shred of mercy and give back my coat and hat."

Her hands shaking, Elise turned at once to seize them. She passed them to him, brushing her fingers against his, then jerking instinctively back. "Ah," he said a little sadly. "You are truly resolved then?"

To her shock and shame, Elise found herself hesitating. She had been courted by a dozen men this season, and none of them had tempted her to so much as smile. But this man, with his silver eyes and sinful mouth, actually made her insides melt.

It was the anonymity of the thing, she swiftly decided. She was alone and lonely, stuck in an ordinary inn in some obscure village with a handsome rake whose name she did not know, and who she would never see again. A man who was obviously schooled in the art of pleasure. And sweet heaven, she was so miserably cold, both inside and out. To feel such a man against her body, to feel his hard weight force her down into the depths of a soft bed and . . . Well, what *would* that be like with him?

He sensed her hesitation. "I've not once left a lady disappointed," he said, as if she were actually considering his offer.

Was she? No. Good heavens, no! But Elise still stood there trembling, apparently struck both dumb and witless. Slowly, his fingers slid past her chin and along the turn of her jaw, lightly cupping her face. "Faith, how a moment's hesitation gives me hope," he murmured, his heavy, somnolent eyelids almost dropping shut again.

Elise jerked back as if his hand had just burst into

flames. Heaven help her, if he got one inch of her skin back inside his mouth, she'd never find the will to ask him to stop. His eyes flared open, the strange, seductive moment gone.

Elise retreated another step. "How perfectly ridiculous this is!" she said. "I don't even know your name." As if that made any difference!

The man gave a sweeping bow. "Easily rectified," he answered, one hand still holding his wet garments, the other tucked elegantly behind his back. "Christian Villiers, the Marquis of Grayston, at your service."

"Oh, my God!" gasped Elise. She slammed the door in his face.

Chapter Two

❦

No more tears now; I will think upon revenge.
—Mary, Queen of Scots

"Bloody hell!" muttered Lord Grayston, dragging a hand through his hair as he stared down at the wrought-iron latch. Had his nasty reputation preceded him even into the wilds of Gloucestershire? Or was he simply losing his touch? At that thought, he spit out a few more curses. But the door could not be intimidated into reopening.

With one final oath, the marquis shrugged, hurled his wet coat over one shoulder, and stomped off down the corridor in search of the servants' quarters. His loins ached with thwarted lust. Blast it, the pretty widow had been a veritable pigeon eating from his hand. She'd even put her hands up his back and her tongue in his mouth! It was unthinkable he'd been refused.

But refuse him she certainly had. Well, bedamned to her. She was too golden and delicate for his sort of sport anyway. In the gloom, Grayston finally found the attic stairs. He'd not forgotten the black-eyed buxom tavern maid who'd as good as crooked her finger at him after dinner. At the time, he'd been unable to bestir much interest. Now he was randy as hell, and short a warm bed. The tavern wench would serve well enough for both predicaments.

Ah, but it would not be quite the same as bedding the ice princess, would it? Grayston admitted it as the narrow, twisting steps squeaked beneath his boots. A frisson of desire ran through him at the memory of her surprisingly full breast in his hand, its nipple peaking urgently against his thumb. Her kisses, too, had been urgent. His reputation aside, given time, he was almost sure he could have bedded her. Unfortunately, time was a luxury Grayston did not possess. He had but one day in which to finish his surreptitious tour of Gothering-ton's tenancies. One day in which to decide if he'd any wish to keep his ill-gotten gains, or whether he should simply toss the place back as one might a too-small fish. So far, he was inclined to toss, unless the Onslows failed to be properly humble and hospitable.

The card game had been too easy by half. Initially, he'd meant to teach that fool Maynard Onslow to keep to a game he could handle, like ha'penny loo with his great-grandmother. A man who could not remember that there were but four aces in a pack of cards had no business in a pernicious hell like Sadridge's. And no business laying everything he had—including his wife's ancestral home—on the table, especially when she'd just invited a dozen guests to a house party. For that folly, Grayston had meant to be merciless.

But then he'd heard about the children. His steps slowed as he again considered it. Onslow had twin daughters. Dowerless little country innocents, much like Lenora, no doubt. But his sister had been far from dowerless, and that had been her undoing. Leaving the Onslow children homeless would be nothing compared to what his sister had suffered. And Major Maynard Onslow was going to be the means of his revenge. Lost in thought, Grayston paused on the narrow attic stairs.

Yes, blast it, it was the children. That was what his conscience kept nagging about. Oh, he'd done some cruel things in his life, but he was not sure he could leave two little girls without a roof over their heads. Since learning of his sister's death, Grayston had oddly found himself reassessing his old instincts. Every debt he called due, every hand he forced down, and every swaggering young buck he pressed until the swagger was gone and the fellow's bowels began to nervously rumble—oh, yes!—Grayston had begun to second-guess it all. A damned inconvenience, a burgeoning set of principles, when it was so much easier to run roughshod over fools like Onslow.

But he could not get Lenora out of his mind. What a sweet, sweet child she'd been. He'd been stunned nearly speechless tonight when he'd reached into the carriage to pick up the little girl—*Henriette*, the woman had called her. With her coltish legs and heavy black hair, she had looked so startlingly like Lenora. Or Lenora as she'd been a dozen years ago. Which had been just about the last time he'd laid eyes on her. But that was not his fault, was it? No, it was his father's, and Grayston hoped the old man's spite was keeping the devil warm in hell.

Good Lord, he was becoming maudlin again. He must get moving, focus on his plan, plot the course of his revenge. With righteous fury coursing anew through his blood, Grayston laid his hand on the attic doorknob. Tomorrow would bring another long morning. And then on to Gotherington Abbey, where another reputed beauty awaited him. Though frankly, Grayston held little hope that she would be as lovely as the one who'd just slammed his bedchamber door in his face. He just prayed to God that she had breasts half as fine. But then, God had never been particularly good about listening to Grayston's prayers.

At Gotherington Abbey, the following day dawned golden with promise, as mornings which follow a thundershower are wont to do. Ophelia Onslow stood at one of the deep Venetian windows which lined her red and gold salon, absently watching this miracle of nature unfold, and feeling in perfect charity with the world. All was in readiness for this, her social triumph of the year, her first autumn house party at her much admired ancestral home.

For a time, it had felt as if Grandmama Hilliard might never pass on to her great reward and leave Ophelia to savor hers in peace. Of course, she'd long known that she would eventually have Gotherington, and she'd paid well for it, too. For twenty years, she had catered to the irascible old woman's every whim, as her mother before her had done. But while Grandmama had lived—and ninety-three long years it had been—lavish entertainment had been out of the question. Grandmama had been neither the gregarious nor generous sort.

But the death of her grandson Sir Henry nearly two years past had finally sucked the wind from her sails, and permitted the family to enjoy the convenience of putting on their black but once. Henry's entailed property, a drafty old pile in the north, had passed to a distant relation, and good riddance. His remaining properties and fortune had gone to Elise, his widow, and Henriette, his only child. But Gotherington! Ah, yes, Grandmama had kept her word, and at last the plum had fallen into Olivia's outstretched hand. And now she meant to enjoy it, no matter the cost.

So as she stood awaiting the arrival of her brother's widow, Ophelia watched the sun rise high over her kingdom while she studied the abbey grounds with a narrow, persnickety eye. The canal which encircled the Dutch garden had been seined of leaves, the topiary sculptures had been pruned and plumped, and the outside of the vast octagon maze had been shaped and sheared within an inch of its arborescent life. In the larder lay a small fortune in fine foodstuffs, and in the cellar sat a sultan's ransom in wine. Ophelia bit her lip at that. A pity they had not thought to kidnap a sultan with which to pay for it.

Oh, well! Ophelia was never one to let penury spoil her plans. Maynard would think of something before the duns floated in. He always did. Suddenly, from the adjacent breakfast parlor, a small commotion erupted. Ophelia lifted up her skirts and sailed through the connecting doors, her shrewd gaze falling at once upon her sweet, golden-haired darlings, and upon their father, oblivious behind his newspaper.

"Spiteful cat!" wailed the first darling, reaching across the table to yank a yellow ribbon from her sister's hair. "That's mine! Mine, do you hear!"

"Is not! Is not!" shouted the second, pressing both hands against her scalp to defend her prize.

Belinda's eyes sparkled maliciously. "I bought it not a fortnight past in Bond Street, you shrew!"

Lucinda sneered across the table. "Not this one, you jealous little witch!"

Ophelia darted toward the table with unseemly haste. "Belinda! Lucinda! Stop this at once!"

"But it's mine!" burst the twins in unison. Still, each settled back into her chair, poking out an identical set of pouty pink lips.

Ophelia collapsed into her chair and pressed her fingertips to her chest. "Oh, vipers in my bosom!" she moaned dramatically. "How am I to find husbands for either of you?"

From behind his paper, Major Onslow harrumphed. "Can't think who'd be fool enough to have 'em."

Ophelia's chin snapped up. *"Maynard!"*

Major Onslow simply rattled his paper and kept reading.

"You!" challenged his wife, looking daggers at the back of his newspaper. "You'd best pay a little attention to their comportment! In two days' time their godfather will be here. Amherst is your oldest friend, and his wife is well connected."

Belinda made a most unladylike sound. "Oh, he isn't even a half-pay officer now!" she muttered, throwing herself against the back of her chair. "Just a pokey old vicar."

"Foolish child," snapped Ophelia. "He'll be a bishop before all is said and done, mark me."

"A bishop!" snorted Lucinda, crossing her arms over

her chest. "Who gives a snap for that? It was exciting when he was a Royal Dragoon with Papa."

"Ooh, in those snug regimentals!" Belinda leaned companionably toward her sister. "Do you not think, Lucy, that blond men look splendid in red? I'm sure he wears only black and is very dull now. Really, I wish he wouldn't come at all!"

Their father peered from behind the paper. "Then I shall write straightaway and tell him so, girls," he murmured, feigning solicitude. "And I shall tell him to keep his dull stepsons at home, too. Between them, they cannot have but a half-dozen titles and fifty thousand pounds a year. Not worth our notice, to be sure."

Two mops of yellow ringlets jerked up at once. "Papa!" they gasped in unison.

Major Onslow returned to his paper. "Oh, Papa indeed!" he said sarcastically. "Hold out for dukes, the both of you. Don't let your lack of a dowry stand in the way."

"Maynard!" Sensing that her husband's feelings were wounded, Ophelia leaned across the table to pat his hand. "Of course we wish to see dear Mr. Amherst and Lady Kildermore! And her handsome boys, too!"

"Boys!" harrumphed the major. "Why, the Marquis of Mercer is near twenty, and Lord Robert not much younger."

"Oh, Maynard, my love, your cup is quite empty! Do let me fill it." Ophelia flashed her husband an ample expanse of cleavage as she stretched toward the teapot. "Now, tell us all about their daughters. Are they darlings?"

"No idea," muttered the major, peeking from behind

the paper to eye his wife's bosom. "Gaggle of chits with names devilish alike. Marianna, Pollyanna, Arabella. Can't keep up."

"*Pollyanna—?*" Ophelia drew her brows into a frown. "Maynard, I don't think so. And aren't there four?"

His answer was forestalled by a noise deep inside the salon. The butler had thrown open the door. With a shriek of delight, Henriette burst in, rushing along the red and gold carpet in a beeline for the breakfast parlor. She launched herself at the major, who promptly hurled his newspaper aside.

"Uncle May! Uncle May!" she cried as he hoisted her onto his lap. "Mama and I have had the awfulest journey ever! We stayed at a smelly inn. Oh, Aunt Ophelia, is it true? Are there to be other girls here? Do you know their names? Is Ariane to come? Can Bee and Lucy stay in the schoolroom with us?"

To their credit, Belinda and Lucinda had risen at once, one to hug Henriette, and the other to greet Elise, who was drawing off her gloves and smiling brightly as she came into the room. A flurry of activity ensued, with cheeks kissed, chairs pulled out, and tea poured all around. But Henriette was still chattering at her uncle. "And then Mama said I mustn't bring my toy soldiers, for the other girls mightn't like them. What do you think? Would they? I've a whole regiment of dragoons now. I daresay our coachman would go back and fetch 'em for me."

Major Onslow tweaked her nose. "Save the soldiers for me, my sweet," he encouraged. "We'd best stick with Roll the Hoop this visit. The Amherst girls are doubtless quite tame, and Lady Ariane is too old for toy soldiers."

Ophelia leaned solicitously toward her widowed sister-in-law. "My dear Elise, how was your journey? Will you take a bite of breakfast?"

"No, thank you, just tea," said Elise a little breathlessly. "And the journey really was dreadful. I managed to get us lost, else we'd have arrived last night." She turned her gaze on the major and smiled. "Maynard, you are well? Oh, how glad I am to see all of you. Belinda, Henriette tells me you've a new pianoforte in the music room. May I prevail upon the two of you to show her?"

"It is a Graf, all the way from Vienna," answered Belinda, drawing herself up proudly. "With six and a half octaves. Mama says with my promise, I need the very best."

Elise's brows flew up as she turned to her sister-in-law. "A *Conrad* Graf?" she said in an undertone. "Good heavens, Ophelia!"

Ophelia's full bottom lip came out. "Oh, pray don't scold me again, Elise! You shall give me the megrims. Besides, it was not so dreadfully expensive, and young ladies must have a few fine things."

The young ladies in question hastily departed, and just as swiftly, Ophelia changed the subject. "Elise," she began. "We were just speaking of who is expected. Most guests will arrive the day after tomorrow, but I took the liberty of asking that Mr. Roth come early."

Elise's cheeks turned faintly pink. "Ophelia! Really! I think you are altogether too sure of yourself."

At the head of the table, Major Onslow snorted. "Sure of that popinjay Roth, belike."

Ophelia ignored her husband. "And of course, Mr. Amherst and his family will be here," she preened. "And the *coup* of the season—Lord and Lady Treyhern have agreed to come for at least a few days! With Lady Ariane and little Gervais!"

"They are lovely people," agreed Elise as she sipped delicately at her tea. "We have some vague connection there, do we not? I confess, I've never understood it."

"It is through Uncle Henry, for whom your husband was named. He was Lady Treyhern's stepfather." Fleetingly, Ophelia's brows snapped together. "Of course, her mother was not quite *bon ton*—but that is neither here nor there, for Lady Treyhern has since married well."

"Ah, yes," Elise dryly responded. "Much can be forgiven after a good marriage, can it not? Who else is to come?"

Ophelia was oblivious to the mild rebuke. "Oh, no one quite as exalted as Mr. Amherst or Lord Treyhern," she admitted, and then she mentioned a few more names, most of whom Elise vaguely knew.

When she finished, Major Onslow rattled his newspaper again, then cleared his throat almost nervously. "Hang me if I didn't forget to tell you, Ophelia!" he remarked. "I did invite another fellow. Invited Grayston."

With a faint gasp, Elise sat her cup down, splashing coffee across the ivory linen tablecloth.

Beside her, her sister-in-law went completely rigid. "I do beg your pardon, Maynard!" said Ophelia quite distinctly. "You did not say . . . oh, pray tell me I did not hear—"

"*Grayston*," interjected the major, more firmly. "You're wanting another chap to even our numbers. Invited Grayston. Expect everyone to be civil, Ophelia. Fellow's a marquis, for God's sake. Old money, and plenty of it. Outranks us all."

Ophelia half rose from her chair, her legs unsteady. "B-But why? My God, Maynard! The man is hardly received."

"Not true, Ophelia," countered her husband defensively. "Grayston has been invited to some of the best houses in town since returning from France."

"Blackmailed his way in, more like!" snapped Ophelia, flinging herself back down again and pressing her fingertips to her temple. "Is that not his method? Besides, I cannot think why *we* must have him, Maynard! Gotherington Abbey is one of England's finest homes! The pride of my Hilliard ancestors!"

Elise thought the major had lost a bit of his color. "Knew his father," Major Onslow explained, folding his paper clumsily. "Belonged to White's, as does his son now."

"Does he indeed?" challenged Ophelia. "I heard Lord Bothwill was coerced into supporting the blackguard's membership. Besides, a country house party will be quite dull entertainment for one of his ilk."

"It is a shooting party," growled Major Onslow irascibly. "Grayston likes to shoot."

"Yes, but at people!" wailed his wife. "It's not at all the same thing as shooting pheasant or partridge! And this is a family gathering to celebrate the twins' seventeenth birthday! I cannot think it seemly to expose them to such a man."

"Isn't Denys Roth to be here, Ophelia?" challenged her husband. "Are you fool enough to think him an innocent?"

Ophelia blushed very prettily. "Perhaps he has sowed a few wild oats, Maynard. What man has not? But Roth has fallen in love with Elise. If they've not set the date by Martinmas, it won't be my fault."

Major Onslow jerked to his feet, eyeing Ophelia over the tall, silver epergne which sat in the center of the table. "You always wanted to be the talk of the town, m'dear," he warned. "And with Grayston coming, you shall."

"Not that sort of talk!"

But the major looked grim. "I've an appointment with my steward at half-past." He yanked a gold pocket watch from his waistcoat. "The marquis is to arrive tomorrow, and I expect—no, I *demand*—that he be treated warmly by everyone. If not, there'll be hell to pay. Do I make myself plain?"

Ophelia sniffed miserably. "Oh, we are ruined!"

Major Onslow rolled his eyes, then turned to Elise with a bow. "My dear, I beg your pardon for shouting. Glad you're here. I know I may count on you to make everyone feel at ease."

"Yes, of course, Maynard," Elise managed to answer. But her stomach was already twisted into a sick knot.

His smile tight, Major Onslow turned and strolled toward the door, but Ophelia sprang to her feet at once. "I cannot like the smell of this, Maynard! Never think that we are finished with this discussion!"

"No, no, I don't, my dear!" The major slumped a little as he passed over the threshold. "Not in my wildest dreams!"

Chapter Three

❦

Love and scandal are the best sweeteners of tea.
—H. Fielding

The following afternoon, Elise found herself alone in the small family parlor in the oldest wing of the abbey. Though a bit shabby, the room was warm and comfortable, and the light perfect for sewing. Maynard and Ophelia had been called to the bedside of an injured tenant, leaving Elise to enjoy a few blessed hours of solitude. And she very much feared she needed them.

With a sigh, she let her hands fall into her lap, crushing the embroidery which she'd so industriously been stitching. She'd long ago learned that needlework was the perfect outlet for disordered nerves, and since Maynard's announcement at breakfast yesterday, Elise had felt as if she could have completed a set of sofa cushions. Blindly, she stared across the room, seeing not the tall cherry-wood armoire in the corner, but something almost as dark and implacable. *Christian Villiers.* The Marquis of Grayston. As if the vision had been burnt into her mind, Elise could still see his mocking eyes, his odd half-smile. His elegant bow, which held not one whit of humility or deference. She could remember some other things, too. . . .

No, she *couldn't*.

Elise took up her needlework again, and began to stab at it viciously. She really could not fathom how Maynard had come to be friends with such a person. Elise's brother-in-law was a bluff, hearty military man, highly decorated and deeply respected. Oh, perhaps he occasionally drank a bit too much or played just a little too deep. What gentleman did not, from time to time? Well, her husband Henry had not. Still, Maynard did not keep bad company.

As to Lord Grayston, she'd recognized his name the moment he'd spoken it. In town it was said that he was the worst sort of blackguard; a libertine who had spent most of his life flitting about the Continent, living by his charm, his wit, and his gaming skills, all of which were reputedly impressive. He'd fled England in disgrace as a very young man after being caught in bed with the Belgian ambassador's wife *and* her lady's maid. Rumor had it that he had ruined more European noblemen than Wellington, and hadn't needed an army to do it. It was said that in Naples, he kept *five* mistresses, sometimes openly sharing them. That he had been seen sipping champagne from the late queen's slipper whilst they lay sotted in the sand at Saint-Tropez. That he had won a harem of virgins from the Sultan of Malkara, and sold them off to buy a French brothel.

Surely it couldn't all be true? Even Elise, in her inexperience, doubted it. He had returned to England just this spring following the death of his sister and his father. But instead of observing a full mourning, he'd passed but a fortnight at his seat in Northamptonshire, then scandalized London by turning up for the Season. Still, Elise had never met him. Not until last night.

Well, soon he would be arriving at Gotherington. Somehow, she must find a way to be civil. And to be honest, what did she really know of Lord Grayston? He had looked rakish, yes, but not hopelessly hell-bound. He had slogged half a mile through the mud to help her. He had willingly given up his bedchamber. It was only at the end that he had . . . that he had made her feel uncomfortable. Out of her depth. *Naïve.*

Elise sighed deeply. Despite her twenty-five years, she was still little more than a governess who'd had the good fortune to marry her wealthy employer. And too often, it showed. She had just spent her first Season in London, where she'd learned a great deal. From Ophelia's friends, she had discovered that widows, and sometimes even married ladies, were permitted discreet dalliances. And that some gentlemen were very much sought after for their talents in that regard.

Was Lord Grayston such a gentleman? Elise very much suspected that he was. He had a dangerous sort of magnetism in his eyes. And there had been an awful lot of tittering and fanning amongst the ladies every time his name was mentioned.

And then there was that wicked thing he'd done with her finger. . . . Distracted, Elise caught a knot wrong. Good Lord, she thought, biting through the thread and stabbing the frazzled end back through the needle. Why hadn't she discouraged Ophelia from all this nonsense? This party had been designed, she feared, in the hope that she and Denys Roth would announce their betrothal. But Elise was not at all sure she could fall in love with him, no matter how much time they spent together, nor how ardently he kept asking for her hand. He was charming and handsome, yes. But try as she might, Elise did not feel that shivery, quivery feeling one was supposed to feel when one fell in love. Oh, she had cared deeply for Henry. She did not for one moment regret having married him. But she had not been in love with him, nor he with her. They had done it, both of them, for Henriette.

And so this house party—Ophelia's scheme—would be all for naught. And now there was Grayston to put up with! Worse still, Elise had a deep suspicion that Maynard could ill afford the affair, which was supposed to last much of the hunting season. The other guests, better than a dozen adults and children, would arrive in two days' time. And during the second week, there was to be a Hunt Ball, with over a hundred neighbors invited! It had gotten wholly out of hand, as did most of Ophelia's endeavors. Elise wished there were some gracious way of offering financial help.

At least the twins would be well dowered now. That was going to be a bit of a trick, convincing Maynard that Ophelia's dead brother had provided for Belinda and Lucinda. He had not, of course, for Sir Henry had secretly thought his nieces vain and silly. He'd held a similar view of his sister, but Ophelia did mean well. Moreover, Elise was sure Bee and Lucy would settle down once married—especially if they could afford to marry someone who made them feel shivery inside.

With grave disapproval, Henry's solicitor in Sussex had drawn up the documents so that Elise could bring them with her to Gotherington. Elise had taken the money from the generous widow's portion which Henry had left her. And on the twins' birthday, Elise was going to do something she had never done in the whole of her life. She was going to tell a lie. She was going to say her husband had set aside the money as a gift for the girls' come-out. And she would make Maynard believe it. Ophelia, unfortunately, would believe anything.

The sound of jingling harnesses startled her from her reverie, causing Elise to stab herself in the thumb. With a muttered oath, she flung down her stitchery and rushed to the window. Her heart in her throat, she watched the shiny black traveling coach turn into the upper carriageway, preceded by a tall, broad-shouldered man on a snorting black beast. The animal was tossing his head wickedly and dancing about the gatepost in marked dislike.

Elise felt her stomach flip-flop. Denys was a handsome man, but not an especially tall one. And Elise was willing to bet he'd never ridden a horse like that in his life. Dear Lord. That could only mean one thing. But at least she was alone. Elise went at once to the bell and jerked it firmly.

"There is a guest arriving below, Pratt," she said when the butler entered. "In my brother-in-law's absence, I shall receive him here."

"Very good, ma'am. Shall I have his drapes drawn and his water sent up?"

"Yes." Elise managed a tight smile. "The name is Grayston. *Lord* Grayston."

She returned to the window, watching as the footmen swarmed about his lordship's carriage, unstrapping a huge traveling trunk and an exquisite, brassbound dressing case. A gun case, a small rosewood chest, several hatboxes and two glossy leather valises followed, their unloading directed by a stately, silverhaired man whom Elise took to be Grayston's valet. How odd. At the inn, she'd had the clear impression that Grayston was traveling alone.

His valet must have been quite skilled, for the marquis looked little like the brooding ne'er-do-well he'd seemed two nights ago. Today, he oozed Continental sophistication. Gone was his sodden, misshapen hat; in its place was a stiff, tall-crowned top hat with a shallow, curved brim. His coat was not the common cutaway usually seen in the country, but a sweeping, elegant frock coat of deep charcoal, with very wide, very chic lapels. His double-breasted waistcoat and snug, strapped trousers were a matching shade of gray. A simply tied cravat was bound high about his throat, his linen sported not an inch of lace, and in his gloved hand, he carried a gold-knobbed stick of polished ebony.

Formal. Forbidding. Urbane. The merest glance at the man left Elise feeling tongue-tied and out of place. But Pratt was going down the steps into the bright sunshine to greet him, and bowing more subserviently than Elise had ever seen. Then together, they turned, and the marquis came swiftly up the sweeping turn of the steps, disappearing from view as he entered the house.

Running her damp palms down her skirts, Elise turned to face the inevitable. Within moments, she could hear them coming up the winding staircase.

Down the long, heavily carpeted corridor. Her heart pounded in her ears. Pratt's voice echoed as he paused by the door. "A nasty compound fracture, my lord," the butler was saying. "Major and Mrs. Onslow went at once to his bedside. But Mrs. Onslow's sister-in-law will make you comfortable."

And then the door to the parlor was swinging open. As if her feet were frozen to the floor, Elise could only stare. "His lordship, the Marquis of Grayston," intoned Pratt very solemnly.

But if Elise's feet were frozen, his lordship appeared to have suddenly altered into a solid block of ice. He jerked to a halt just inside the parlor, barely leaving Pratt room to pull shut the door as he departed. The marquis did not look the sort of man who was easily taken aback by anything, and yet he was. Oh, he most definitely was.

His astonishment gave her courage. Swiftly, she closed the distance between them and swept into her deepest curtsey. "Welcome to Gotherington Abbey, my lord." The words came out deeper and throatier than she had intended. "I am Elise, Lady Mid—"

Almost rudely, Grayston cut her off. "Good God!" he choked. "You are . . . *you* are Lady Middleton?"

At first, his use of her full title did not strike her as odd. Elise rose and, remembering her promise to Maynard, placed her hand on his arm and led him deeper into the room. "I'm Mrs. Onslow's sister, by marriage."

"Yes, yes, I did know that much." His expression shifted to one of impatience.

Elise laid her embroidery on the tea table and settled back into her chair, motioning him to sit opposite. "I am often at Gotherington," she said stiffly. "I was on my way here, you see, when we . . . when our paths crossed."

He recovered his composure quickly, Elise would grant him that. All semblance of surprise had vanished, and in its place was the usual cool expression on his long, thin-lipped face and in his calm, ice-gray eyes. Grayston folded his lean form gracefully into the chair, then let his gaze drift indolently over her. "I was disappointed to find you gone when I awoke." His voice was soft but his eyes were not. "And since you'd never signed the register, the innkeeper could not be bribed to help me."

Elise was taken aback. "Why, I can scarce imagine you thought ever to·see me again."

Some strange, nameless emotion flitted across his face. "But what if I'd wished to, my lady?" he answered suggestively as he fiddled with his watch fob. "You are very lovely—especially when . . . a little wet."

Elise felt her heart leap into her throat. "Really, Lord Grayston, it is hardly appropriate to . . . to—"

"To flirt with you?" he supplied thoughtfully, his silvery gaze capturing hers, then trailing quite boldly downward. "But it heightens your color so charmingly. Indeed, ma'am, you look quite warm and pink . . . all over. It is a lovely sight."

"You may save your breath, sir."

Grayston smiled his lazy half-smile. His teeth were very large and very white. "I collect you are still angry over my invitation?"

She was, rather. But Elise was not perfectly sure how to answer him. Worse, she had the deeply disturbing feeling that his words were laced with nuances she did not understand. She wished she did not owe it to Maynard to be civil. "I was not angry, my lord," she finally answered. "Just taken aback. As you've discovered, I am encumbered by what some might consider dreadfully old-fashioned morals."

"Ah!" he said softly. "So you are not *that kind* of woman? You regret having kissed me with such passion?"

She felt heat flood her cheeks. "I'm glad you understand."

But to her undying frustration, Lord Grayston threw back his head and laughed. "My dear Lady Middleton!" His eyes glittered wolfishly. "We are all of us just a shade immoral when it suits us to be so. And all I regret is that you did not think having me in your bed would be worth singeing your soul on a little brimstone."

"Really, Lord Grayston!"

But he just laughed again. "Oh, do not scold, ma'am. I felt the stab of your old-fashioned morals most keenly. I persuaded one of the serving maids to share her attic bed with me, only to find I wasn't quite capable of expressing my gratitude, if you take my meaning. She was not amused, and my masculinity has not yet recovered."

Elise went rigid in her chair. "How sorry I am to have disappointed you both."

"Ah, disappointment!" Grayston leaned forward in his chair, and seized her hand as if he meant to lift it to his lips. "But satisfy my curiosity, Lady Middleton, if you'll satisfy nothing else," he whispered, staring at her across her knuckles. "Did I not tempt you, even just a little bit?"

Those eyes. Good God, those sinful, silvery eyes! Were *they* the reason she wasn't slapping him across the face?

"You did not tempt me," she lied, jerking her hand from his long, warm fingers.

Elise could not hold his gaze. Good Lord, he really was quite wicked. She'd never met such a man in her life, or if she had, he'd been civilized enough to hide his true nature. But Grayston wore his sensuality as openly as other men wore clothing. Desperate for some distance, she sprang to her feet and paced back to the window. "Lord Grayston," she said, her back to him. "I cannot think a civilized man would keep revisiting this topic."

To her shock, she heard him leave his chair. But of course he would rise. He was a gentleman—in that way, at least. "My dear, have you not heard the gossip? I am hopelessly uncivilized." His voice was teasing as he approached her. "Come, may I not even kiss your hand? My masculine pride is mortally wounded now. Does that please you?"

"I would not willingly wound anyone, sir," she said, staring blindly down at the carriageway. "I simply don't wish to flirt with you. Maynard—Major Onslow— wishes you warmly welcomed to Gotherington. You are his friend, his guest. Let us leave it at that."

She could sense that Lord Grayston stood behind her now. It was as if she could feel the heat radiate from his body, warming her back. "But what of you, Lady Middleton?" His soft words stirred the hair at her nape. "Do you not wish to warmly welcome me?"

Elise ignored his suggestive tone. Instead, she lifted her eyes from the green expanse of lawn, but as she did so, she caught his reflection in the window, looming impossibly large behind her. Her head did not reach his shoulder. Her breath was hard to catch. "I am pleased to abide by my brother-in-law's wishes, my lord," she managed. "As long as you are courteous."

He held her gaze in the glass, a bitter smile twisting his mouth. "An obedient woman," he softly remarked. "I like that."

She whirled about at that, then wished she had not. He stood very close. Too close. But Elise sensed that she must not let him intimidate her with his physical presence. "I'm trying to be civil, Lord Grayston," she retorted. "But don't dare push your luck. You'll find I'm not subservient."

His smile relaxed ever so slightly, and he lifted his hand as if to dust some imaginary bit of lint from his coat sleeve. But Elise mistook the motion, and jerked away.

His silvery eyes flicked up, capturing her gaze. "Do I make you nervous, Lady Middleton?" Grayston asked, the odd, emotionless smile tugging sideways again. "My nasty reputation has preceded me, perhaps? But rest assured that I have not accepted Major Onslow's hospitality simply to strip young men of their fortunes, or to ravish lovely young women. Well, not unless . . ."

Not unless they wish to be. The unspoken words fairly sizzled and snapped between them. Elise itched to box his ears.

Grayston had the good grace to look away. "You spoke of civility, ma'am," he said blandly, as if a jolt of electricity had not just passed between them. "I confess, I am parched. Might you find it in your heart to ring for tea?"

"Tea?" she said archly.

Grayston whirled back around, both his slashing

black brows going up. "I believe the butler said you'd make me comfortable," he murmured. "Be glad, my lady, that at present, it is only tea which my comfort requires."

Elise went at once to the bellpull, and yanked it far harder than was necessary. "You quite waste your time with me, Grayston." Her gaze held his firmly. "We have nothing whatsoever in common. You would find me very dull company."

"Oh, but I don't." His voice was surprisingly soft. "That's the bloody problem, isn't it?"

From his position by the window, Grayston watched his hostess. Unless he misjudged, which it was his business never to do, Lady Middleton burned to wrap that bellpull firmly around his neck, or perhaps somewhere even more painful. Good God, she was china-doll pretty, with eyes as blue as a Tuscan sky, and a mass of soft gold curls which fought their conventional constraints by occasionally tumbling out of place.

Inwardly, Grayston laughed. He rather suspected that Lady Middleton's morals were a bit like her hair. After all, he had put his hands all over her body, and felt the unmistakable heat within. Yes, she kissed like an innocent, but she only wanted a little educating. And Grayston found himself just a little too eager to enlighten her. He watched her walk back to her chair, her slight body trembling with restrained emotion. Beneath the dark blue skirts of her gown, her round hips swayed, stirring something deep and hot inside him.

Lord, he'd best have a care with this little pigeon. He could not misplay one hand, lest his game be lost. Oh, he might leave this house in a week or two, having freely given it back to that idiot Onslow. And it was remotely possible he might leave without having bedded the lovely Lady Middleton as he'd planned. But he would not leave here without having put a bullet through Denys Roth's black heart. And everyone knew the quickest way to a man's heart was . . . well, through his heart.

Still, it was going to prove more difficult than he first imagined to openly seduce Roth's intended bride, then simply walk away. She really was quite . . . *charming.* How strange. That had never been one of his requirements in a bedmate. Voluptuousness. Audacity. Skill. Oh, yes, those things. But he was not accustomed to this, the perverse pursuit of a woman who clearly did not know the rules of the game. He would have to be very, very careful. But then, all appearances to the contrary, Grayston was a very careful man.

They were seated again, she on the little brocade settee, he opposite the tea table in a leather armchair. With quiet dignity, she attempted to make idle conversation until the tea was brought and the servants withdrawn again. She leaned forward to pour, and Grayston found himself suddenly captivated by the swell of her breasts as they shifted. Her brilliant blue eyes flicked up at him. "Sugar, my lord?"

He swallowed and focused his gaze on her face. "I beg your pardon?"

Lady Middleton made a small sound of exasperation. "Do you take sugar? Or milk?"

"Neither, thank you." He reached across the table to take the cup from her outstretched hand, admiring the fine bones of her wrist. Dimly, he heard the rattle of carriage wheels on the gravel below, but she did not seem to notice.

"You had a pleasant journey from London yesterday?" she asked stiffly, passing him a plate of tiny cucumber sandwiches.

He took one, though he had no appetite. "The day before," he answered hesitantly. "I'd not spent much time in Gloucestershire, and wished to see the countryside."

He hoped she did not raise the question of why he'd been sleeping in squalid inns rather than staying at Gotherington. She was looking at him, her full lips parted as if she might ask, but Grayston was saved when the doors burst open, and the little girl darted into the room.

"Mama, come listen! I just played my new Mozart piece the whole way through without one mistake!" The child almost hurled herself at Lady Middleton, but at the last moment, she noticed Grayston and jerked to a halt. "Oh!" she said, bobbing an uneasy curtsey.

Elise watched Grayston rise from his chair just as Gotherington's governess entered. "Your pardon, my lady," she said, placing a hand on Henriette's shoulder as if to draw her away. "We did not know you had a guest."

But Grayston interceded. "What, is this my Sleeping Beauty, Lady Middleton?" He bent down to Henriette, and lifted her hand to his lips in a theatrical gesture. "She is even more lovely when awake."

Henriette giggled, her uncertain gaze going at once to her mother.

Lady Middleton was blushing. "My daughter, Henriette, my lord," she said. "Henriette, this is Lord Grayston.

He carried you from the carriage to your bed last night. Do you remember?"

Shyly, the child shook her head.

Grayston let her hand drop. "And so you have mastered Mozart, Miss Middleton?" he asked, gazing at Henriette quite seriously. "I confess, I was all of eleven before I played with any confidence."

Henriette's dark eyes grew round. "Do you play the pianoforte, sir?" she asked eagerly. "Uncle May has a new one in the music room. A Graf all the way from Vienna. I could show you, if you wish?"

Elise put down her cup with an awkward clatter. "Lord Grayston has come to hunt, my love," she said softly. "He shan't have time to—"

"Oh, but I'm sure I shall," the marquis smoothly interjected. "After all, one cannot hunt all day. I shall place myself into your capable hands, Miss Middleton. And if I am very good, perhaps you'll play a duet with me? Do you have a favorite?"

The child smiled and shook her head.

"Then I shall search through Gotherington's sheet music until I find something," he promised.

Inwardly, Elise sighed. Henriette's rapt gaze was now transfixed upon Grayston's face; a face which seemed suddenly less harsh, far more animated. His voice, too, seemed gentler. But how fanciful she was. The arrogant devil probably had tricks calculated to charm females from nine to ninety.

"Back to the schoolroom, my dear," said Elise as the governess took Henriette's hand. "I shall see you at three for our botany walk."

The door clicked softly shut. "So lovely in their innocence, are they not?" murmured the marquis, staring at it almost sadly.

"Children should be innocent," Elise answered a little waspishly.

"Indeed." His gaze snapped to hers, and suddenly, it was if a door had closed on his emotions as well. Gone was the almost avuncular warmth, and in its place, the look of jaded boredom had returned. "But when the epithet is applied to men or women," he continued, "it is but a civil term for weakness, is it not?"

Elise felt her eyes widen in shock. "Sir, I find that insulting."

His mouth curved into a bitter smile. "I am sure Mary Wollstonecraft meant you no personal ill when she wrote it," he murmured.

"I b-beg your pardon?"

"Peruse the second chapter of *A Vindication of the Rights of Women,* Lady Middleton." His voice was low and languorous. "I daresay you'll find it there."

"You have read that sort of thing?"

"I have read a great deal of every *sort* of thing," he retorted. But suddenly, his expression shifted yet again. "Ah, but I tease you cruelly. Your daughter is lovely. That is all I meant to say."

His ever-changing personality set Elise on edge. She wished he would remain either the arrogant rake or the cold aristocrat. Either of those she could deal with. "I'm doubly proud of Henriette," she responded awkwardly. "I was her governess, you see, before Sir Henry and I wed."

"Ah!" said Grayston, as if the mysteries of the universe had just been unveiled. "I had a governess myself once.

Had she been half as lovely as you, no doubt my lessons would have held more interest."

"Lord Grayston, please!"

Grayston sat down his teacup and leaned halfway across the too-narrow tea table. "Oh, I should love to please you, Elise," he said softly. "I may call you Elise, may I not?"

"Certainly not!" She drew back as far as possible. "I am Elise only to those with whom I'm close."

"But we have been very close, Elise," he said, his face breaking into a sudden, and very real, grin. "Indeed, my dear, we have shared the sort of intimacies which I hope you don't casually bestow on men whose names you don't know. I am Christian, by the way."

"I recall it!" she snapped. "May I gather, sir, that you mean to keep tormenting me?"

"*Flirting*, Elise." He relaxed lazily into his chair and let his silvery eyes drift over her. "One calls it flirting. *Tormenting* is something quite different. Would you like to be tormented? I would most cheerfully oblige."

Elise jerked to her feet. "I've never thought to say such a thing, sir, but I'm sorely tempted to slap your face!"

The grin deepened. "Might a good spanking do as well?" he asked, unfolding his height languidly from his chair. "No doubt my first governess shorted me a few, thus the scoundrel you see before you. Perhaps you could redeem me, Elise? I have no mistress, and you would do admirably."

She drew herself up to her full height and pinned him with her best glare. "I do not know, my lord, what sort of witless females you are accustomed to tricking with that tripe of yours, but I shan't fall for it. I don't *flirt*.

I won't be your *mistress*. And I don't believe in fairy tales, leprechauns, or fortune-tellers, either. You are arrogant and asinine and you—you—why, you are an arrant rake! And I'm certainly not fool enough to think arrant rakes can be redeemed."

Grayston grew very still, the glitter slowly leaving his gaze. And then, ever so gently, he dropped his napkin down upon the tea table. "My dear Lady Middleton! You are about to run out of insults which begin with A," he said. "I shall relieve you of your burden before you proceed apace to the B's. I am suddenly quite certain which of those you'd hurl first." And to her shock, he spun on one heel and headed for the door.

Suddenly panicked, Elise recalled Maynard's edict at breakfast. Was this man really her brother-in-law's *friend?* Could she be naïvely overreacting to his flirtation? Somehow, she jerked into motion and followed his long, powerful strides toward the door.

She caught him by the shoulder as he crossed the threshold, and felt a coiled strength ripple through his arm. "I am sorry, my lord," she said. "I did not mean to insult you."

His eyes were gray as a stormy sea. "Oh, Lady Middleton, I think you did."

Elise pursed her lips for a moment. "Perhaps," she admitted, and felt him relax ever so slightly. "But while we are both Maynard's guests, can we not agree to be civil and keep our distance?"

"Be predictably English, do you mean?"

"I—good God! I'm so confused I don't know what I mean." Elise let her shoulders fall. "But you did not finish your tea."

As it shafted through the window, the pale autumn light touched his face, softening his expression. "Do you wish me to finish?"

Elise cut her eyes away, then back again. "I would not wish Maynard to return and realize I had argued with you."

As Grayston let his hand fall from the door, something in his quicksilver gaze made her breath catch. "Ah, Elise, have we just had our first lovers' quarrel?" His voice sounded genuinely tender. "Perhaps I can manage another of those little sandwiches, then, if it will please you. I shall endeavor to mind my manners."

Elise tried to ignore the strange sensation in the pit of her stomach. What a conceited devil he was! She opened her mouth to tell him so, but suddenly, the sound of heavy footfalls could be heard around the corner. The butler came into view, and behind him, to her great relief, was Denys Roth.

Elise stepped forward. "Mr. Roth!"

Swiftly, the man closed the distance between them. "Elise, my dear," he murmured, catching and lifting her hands in his. "How lovely you look!"

"We did not expect you so soon," she said breathlessly. "Oh! Forgive me. Do you know Lord Grayston? My lord, Mr. Denys Roth, a friend of Ophelia's."

Roth shot her a chagrined look. "And of yours, my dear, I hope?" And then he turned his gaze on Grayston, and his expression seemed to falter. "Grayston, did you say?"

Elise watched, mystified, as the marquis' spine went rigid. "I believe I've not the pleasure, Mr. Roth." His eyes were quick and glittering, like some taut, untamed creature watching his prey. "I'm newly returned from many years on the Continent."

Roth smiled tightly. "I am pleased to meet you, my lord."

Uneasily, Elise motioned them toward the tea table. Denys settled into the chair Grayston had just vacated. To her shock, Grayston passed by the matching chair and settled down beside her on the narrow settee. She cut a sideways glance at him, but the marquis merely smiled and . . . what? *Winked?* Good God!

"Elise, my dear," he said leaning companionably toward her as if they were old friends—or something worse. "Why don't you serve Roth one of those delicious cucumber sandwiches?"

She cut another look at him. "Y-Yes, of course."

"Have I interrupted something?" asked Roth.

"No," answered Elise, too sharply.

"We were just enjoying a quiet little tea for two, Mr. Roth." Grayston smiled faintly at the newcomer. "But I've quite had my fill. You won't mind taking another man's leftovers?"

The skin drew tight about Roth's mouth. "I had a late luncheon in Cheltenham," he murmured, his eyes darting back and forth between them uneasily. "You've known Major Onslow long, Grayston?"

"He was at Cambridge with my father." Grayston reclined lazily against the settee and stretched his arm along its back, almost around Elise's shoulders. "You knew him, did you not? My father?"

Roth shifted awkwardly in his chair. "Indeed, yes. A fine man. In fact, he had me up to Northamptonshire last year. A lovely home, Hollywell Castle."

"Ah, yes." Grayston sounded as if he were reminiscing. "That was my sister's doing, you know. She was quite devoted to hearth and home. Did you meet her, by any chance?"

Fleetingly, Roth hesitated. "Lady Lenora, you mean?" he answered. "Indeed, I recall her very well. She made her come-out in Town last Season."

"Did she?" asked Grayston absently. "As I said, I've been away."

Roth relaxed slightly. "I was dreadfully sorry to hear of her . . . her—"

"Her *accident,*" supplied Grayston firmly. "She fell and broke her neck."

Elise gasped. She lifted her hand in an uncertain, fluttering motion, then put it down again.

Swiftly, Grayston covered it with his own, and gave it a little squeeze where it lay upon the settee. "She did not suffer," he murmured, turning slightly to face her. "It was very sudden."

Elise was not sure whom he wished to convince. "My lord, I am so sorry."

"A dreadful accident," he reemphasized, returning his gaze to Roth. "And now, what little light my life held has been snuffed out. One finds one's self quite desperate to exact some sort of revenge for such a cruelty. But alas, one can hardly punish fate, can one?" His voice was devoid of emotion.

Elise looked up to see that much of the color had drained from Denys's face. He was distressed, perhaps, that the marquis had grasped her hand? But Grayston's touch had brought her a moment's comfort. And oddly, Elise began to resent Denys's intrusion into her argument with Grayston. It made no sense, but there it was.

At last, he relinquished her hand, and to occupy herself, Elise poured tea all around while the gentlemen began to converse more casually. But there seemed nothing more of interest to discuss. Lord Grayston's silvery eyes had become as opaque as a lake at sunset, and it felt as if the tragedy of Lady Lenora's death lay over the room like a shroud.

But Denys seemed not to notice. Instead, he settled back into his chair as if he were rooted to it, and took up the safe, dull subject of his newest fowling gun.

Chapter Four

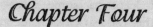

Nothing is sacred to a gamester.
—Saurin

It was some two hours after dinner had ended that evening when Grayston was ushered into Major Onslow's study for a private *tête-à-tête*. The summons from his host had not come unexpectedly. Indeed, Grayston would have been disappointed in his ability to predict human nature had he not been beckoned.

He'd shown his opening hand to Roth during tea, but he'd set about playing a serious game just prior to dinner. The household had met to take a glass of sherry in the gaudy red and gold salon, a room so appallingly vulgar that Grayston made a mental note to rip it apart from rug to rafters should he decide to keep Gotherington. Over drinks, Grayston had been at his most charming, fawning over Mrs. Onslow's hand until the lady succumbed to blushing twitters, and managing not to grit his teeth at the sight of her impertinent daughters.

And there was another mystery! How on earth had he come to think them a pair of mop-haired toddlers? Evidently someone had uttered the phrase *twins*, and

Grayston had leapt to some sweet, sentimental assumption. The Misses Onslow definitely weren't mop-haired toddlers. They were buxom, blue-eyed, and blatantly coquettish. Still, Grayston had done the pretty to each in turn. In fact, he'd been the perfect gentleman. And then, when the bell had sounded for seating, he had quite cleverly—and most improperly—managed to take Lady Middleton in to dinner. The Onslows had been aghast. Roth had quite literally choked on his wine. And the blue-eyed coquettes had very nearly burst into giggles.

Throughout dinner, he had monopolized Elise's attention until she was blushing three shades of pink. He'd sat too close, stared too often, and even offered her a sip from his wineglass when the footman had been slow to pour. And then, he'd looked down her bodice and offered to help her cut her venison. Roth, who had started to simmer over the curried lobster, had rolled to a near boil by the time the apricot blancmange was brought round.

After dinner, remaining for port had been a testament to Grayston's patience as a gamester. It was a perverse sort of pleasure, this slow, deliberate torment of Denys Roth. He wondered how long it would take before Roth called him out. A while yet, Grayston predicted. Like the craven bastard he was, Roth would try counteroffensives first. And so, when the house had retired to bed after coffee, Grayston had strolled through the wide Venetian windows of the salon to have a smoke on the veranda while he awaited Onslow's summons.

It came, and Grayston was shown into the long, galleried library and escorted through a side door which connected the room to Major Onslow's study. Grayston sat down in a chair which was still warm. Inwardly, he smiled. He sincerely hoped the door had hit Roth in the arse on his way out.

The old ormolu clock in the family parlor was striking half-past eleven when Elise pushed open the door and felt her way into the gloom. Fleetingly, she hesitated. Then, remembering her promise to Denys, she groped about until her fingers found the branch of candles which always sat atop the mantel. By the glow of the smoldering fire, she knelt and lit one, and soon the room was bathed in a flickering yellow light.

The air had grown chilly; the draperies had long since been drawn for the night. Restless and moody, Elise slid her hands up her arms and sank down into the bay of one of the low, Gothic windows which were so prevalent in the original part of the abbey. Allowing her skirts to pool carelessly onto the floor, she leaned forward to draw open the draperies with one finger. Beyond was a cloudless night, the sky vibrant with stars. Cold air shimmered off the glass, bathing her face. Elise drew it deep into her lungs, then exhaled sharply with some vague hope of clearing her mind.

Oh, she was so miserably confused! This visit to Gloucestershire was not turning out as she had hoped. Dinner had been nerve-wracking. Seated next to Lord Grayston, her ears attuned to his deep, rumbling voice, and her skin shivering with life at his merest brush, she had felt . . . oh! She dared not put a name to the emotions Lord Grayston engendered.

And after dinner, when Denys had approached her in the drawing room, that had been worse. "Really, my dear, what can your brother-in-law have been thinking?" he'd said bitterly. He had pulled her aside on some pretext and placed his lips close to her ear, but always, his eyes followed Grayston. "That scoundrel is not fit for decent company, and his conduct tonight proves it. I shall speak to Maynard at once. He ought to be sent packing."

They had spent an hour over coffee before Ophelia declared it time to retire. Then Denys had left for Maynard's study after extracting Elise's promise to meet him afterward in the parlor. But Elise found it vaguely dissatisfying that Denys meant to approach Maynard when the problem was Lord Grayston. It seemed somehow . . . well, *cowardly*. But really, what had she expected? Had she wished him to jerk from his chair in the midst of the soup course and fling a glove into Grayston's face? Lud, that would have provoked a scandal! She might very well marry Denys. She should be happy he was both prudent and sensible.

So why was she not happy? In the soft glow of moonlight, she watched as a huge bird sailed from one of the oaks which lined the carriageway and swooped over the tall grass beyond. A barn owl, no doubt. Elise could well imagine the panic of those lesser creatures who now scurried through the weeds in search of some hiding place. She had felt much the same when she'd realized Lord Grayston had no intention of going up to bed. Instead, he'd strolled out onto the veranda to smoke. It was as if the man were a threat to her sanity so long as he wandered unchecked through the house—and through her mind.

Oh, she wished she could go upstairs to her bed-chamber! She wished she had not promised Denys she would wait. But at that very moment, Denys thrust open the door and stomped into the room. "Good God!" he exclaimed, setting one fist on his hip. "I think Maynard has gone quite mad!"

Elise stood. "What is it, Denys?"

"Why, the man seems to be both blind and stupid!" And then, as if it were an afterthought, Denys closed the distance between them, and lifted both her hands to his lips. "Oh, my dear, I have looked so forward to these weeks with you. I have told you, Elise, how I feel. Now I beg you to make me the happiest man on earth, and allow me to announce our betrothal."

Elise was taken aback. "Denys, I thought—"

"Yes, yes!" Denys cut her off impatiently. "But it is best we make plain our intentions, Elise. I wish you to have the protection of my name. Surely you cannot welcome that disreputable rogue's flirtations?"

Elise widened her eyes. "No, I do not!"

Then, as quickly as it had come, the impatience melted away. Perhaps she'd even imagined it. "No, my love, of course you do not. You are too honorable and virtuous for his sort. I am worrying myself for nothing." And then, Denys smiled, drew her near, and bent to kiss her.

Their lips met chastely. And suddenly, it felt to Elise as if the room, which had once been merely chilly, had grown as cold as the grave.

With a cool nod, Major Onslow crossed to the satin-wood sideboard and offered the Marquis of Grayston a snifter of cognac. Then after pouring a second for himself, he sat down behind his desk. A gruff, plain-spoken man, Onslow's displeasure was writ plain upon his face, and he went up a tiny notch in the marquis' estimation when he did not trouble himself to soften his words. "Listen here, Grayston," he challenged. "I'm given to understand that you've been riding about Gotherington asking questions of my tenants."

"Have I?" Grayston lifted one brow. "How very awkward. I thought they were *my* tenants."

Onslow's face lost a little of its ruddiness. "We had a gentleman's agreement, sir, that I might have the use of my home until after the hunting season."

"Ah, that!" mused the marquis, cradling the brandy low against his thigh. "And you wish to extend the scope of my charity, is that it?"

The major bristled visibly. "I have no wish for your goddamned charity, Grayston," he boomed. "What I want is the opportunity to win back what I have lost. An opportunity you have thus far refused me."

"A skilled gamester quits the table when he has won what he seeks," murmured Grayston. "There is no gentlemanly requirement to continue playing when one is done. And I am done with you, Onslow. Perhaps you'll get this house back. Or perhaps not. But I will not sit down with you again, sir. Indeed, you would be a fool to even attempt it. Think of your duty to your family."

But Onslow did not back down. "I do not need a lesson in family duty from you, of all people, sir!" he snapped. "Where the devil were you for the last ten years? Or when your sister mysteriously died? Or when your father fell ill, come to that? Do not lecture me about duty, you young pup, when you've not even troubled yourself to put on mourning."

Faintly, Grayston smiled. "You may say what you wish, Major Onslow, of my father or me," he said very quietly. "But if the breath of scandal so much as taints my sister's memory, you'll lose a vast deal more than your home. And that, sir, is a promise."

Onslow lost the rest of his color. "Damm it, I meant no ill toward your sister's good name," he sputtered, his hand shaking as he pushed away his glass. "A prettier, sweeter-natured girl I never met. A pity mine couldn't take lessons from her, truth be told. But there's no denying the mystery about her, Grayston, and others *do* talk."

"There is no mystery."

"Well, to stay buried in the country like that until she was—what? Twenty-something?" he pressed. "And to turn up for half the Season, take London by storm, then vanish as quickly as she'd come, only to die within the year? It's just queer, that's all."

"I believe it is common knowledge that my father did not wish to be troubled by either his wife or her children, Major Onslow," Grayston stiffly responded. "Indeed, it was his wish that Lenora remain sequestered in the country until such time as he had run out of excuses for not taking her to Town."

Onslow simply raised his bushy brows and opened his hands expansively. Setting down his half-empty glass, Grayston rose. "I think that's enough family gossip," he said smoothly. "If you'll excuse me, I'm for bed."

"I—well, I . . ."

Grayston smiled as if there had been no disagreement at all. "By the way, that is an exceptional painting above your chimney-piece. Holbein the Younger, is it not?"

Onslow seemed mystified by this turn in the conversation. "Er—some German fellow, I reckon. So bloody old now you can scarce make it out."

"It's a dark work, yes, but his use of symbolism was extraordinary, don't you think?" asked Grayston, clasping his hands behind his back as he studied it. "I should find that particular piece a true joy to own."

Onslow stiffened noticeably. "Let us get one thing straight, Grayston, before you start counting your goddamned chickens," he said gruffly. "You may have some claim to this house and its contents, but there is one thing which is off-limits to you, and that is my sister-in-law. I feel for Elise much as you felt for your late sister. Try to understand that."

"Again, Onslow, your point escapes me."

"You are a guest in this house. I expect you to act like a gentleman."

Grayston felt his blood grow cold. "I do hate to be tedious, Major Onslow, but you are the guest. And while I'm guilty of many sins, ill-breeding is not amongst them."

Major Onslow looked slightly apoplectic. "Nonetheless, sir, you will leave Lady Middleton alone."

"Will I?" asked Grayston pointedly. "I am not at all sure. She is a very lovely widow."

"She is intended for Mr. Roth." His voice was flat and cold.

"Has Lady Middleton accepted his suit?" Grayston demanded, caring more about the answer than he wished to admit.

Onslow drew himself up stiffly. "It is expected that before the month is out, their announcement will be made," he said. "In the meantime, I am responsible for her."

Grayston suppressed a flash of rage. The man spoke as if the marriage were a certainty. "Don't be a fool, Onslow," he snapped. "*Responsible* is hardly a term applicable to you. If it were, I would not now own the very roof beneath which your family sleeps."

Onslow shoved himself violently away from his desk. "You really are the bastard people call you, aren't you, Grayston?"

"I have often wished, sir, that I had been." And with that, Lord Grayston bowed and left the room.

Chapter Five

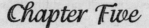

A little disdain is not amiss; a little scorn is alluring.
—Congreve

*G*rayston arose the next morning in a very foul humor, and immediately managed to tie his cravat so tightly he had to ring Stallings to unstrangle him. And the day was not looking up. Over dinner the previous evening, he had learned who else was expected to round out the house party. A pack of dull Scots and a bloody parson were to make up the largest entourage, followed by a reclusive earl who had married Ophelia's cousin or some damned thing. They apparently lived but a dozen miles away, and thus would benumb the conversation with local gossip and rural chitchat. After that, the guest list went downhill.

The horde was expected to descend around mid-morning, and Grayston was determined to plot an escape. After breakfast, he wandered into the old abbey and found Elise sewing in the family parlor. Henriette sat at a Pembroke table executing a charcoal sketch. They looked up in mild surprise when he entered. Perhaps guests were expected to keep to the newer, more formal rooms? But Grayston was undeterred. "May I join you?"

"Anyone may do so," Elise murmured, shrewdly laying aside her stitchery such that it blocked the other half of the tiny settee. "I trust you slept well, my lord?"

He had not, but Grayston lied with alacrity. He sat down opposite her, and they chatted idly for a time. Today Elise wore a silk gown of deep rose. It was the same color as her cheeks when she blushed, he thought, a lovely, innocent shade. He'd set her to blushing more than once during dinner last night, and it was clear she'd neither forgotten nor forgiven him.

He leaned forward to study her embroidery frame where it lay upon the settee. "A fine piece, ma'am," he said. "You've a clever hand."

"Thank you."

"I find delicate work with the hands most soothing," he murmured, stroking his fingers almost lovingly over the silk threads.

"Oh," she said vaguely, too innocent to catch the double entendre. "Is that why you play the pianoforte?"

Grayston lifted one brow and studied her for a moment. "In my line of work, ma'am, a man must keep his fingers supple and deft." She looked at him in some surprise, and so he continued. "I am a professional gamester, Lady Middleton. A wicked *fileur de cartes*. But then, you knew that, did you not?"

Elise looked at him unblinkingly. "But you are now the Marquis of Grayston," she said simply. "Surely you no longer need—"

Softly, Grayston laughed. "Need has little to do with it," he answered. "A man's character never alters, ma'am.

Women would do well to remember that about the men in their lives."

But Elise would not be led. Instead, she narrowed her eyes and forced the conversation toward something more mundane. Soon Henriette brought her sketch to be admired, and with a shy smile, reminded Grayston of his promise to see the pianoforte.

"I have not forgotten," he assured her. "Indeed, I have been pilfering the sheet music in your uncle's library. I found two pieces which I thought we might try together this afternoon. My lady, will you join us?"

"I have plans," said Elise, seizing up her embroidery and beginning to stab at it once again.

"Ah." Grayston watched her nimble fingers work. The piece really was quite lovely. "Then would you consent to spend the morning with me? I should very much like a tour of Gotherington's grounds."

"I'm sorry, but I mean to take a walk with my daughter, my lord. Until Lady Ariane Rutledge and the Amherst girls arrive, Henriette has no one to play with."

"Excellent!" returned Grayston smoothly. "Then I shall have two ladies, one for each arm."

He really had left her no choice. Within the hour they were walking arm in arm along the path which wound from the rear entrance through the topiary garden. Elise was awkwardly transparent in her efforts to hasten him along, while Grayston was equally determined to stop and admire every sculpture. He considered with great satisfaction the picture of domestic bliss which would greet Denys Roth should he happen to glance out his bedchamber window.

It was an easy enough matter to engage Henriette's

complicity. At her instigation, they would pause alongside each carefully pruned shrub and take turns making up fairy tales to suit its shape. Thus, the prancing boxwood unicorn became a princess forever frozen by the spell of a jealous witch, while the gaggle of green geese around the fountain became an army of elves called to her rescue. Henriette was a lively, fanciful child, and their game made for slow progress. Christian held Elise's arm firmly against his side throughout it.

After half an hour of their relentless good cheer, Elise began to wear down, the chilly edge receding from her voice. And soon, despite his delaying tactics, they ran out of topiary and crossed into the walled flower garden. There the three of them strolled slowly along the brick paths, looking, he supposed, very much like a happy family.

But how would he know? Christian could not once remember strolling through the gardens at Hollywell with anyone other than Lenora toddling on his heels. They had scarcely even known their parents. His father had always lived in London, returning reluctantly to Northamptonshire only for a few weeks at Christmas. His mother had lived far away in Bath, where his father had sent her when Christian was four, with instructions to never again darken their door. And she had not done so. Not until she was six months' gone with a second child, leaving Christian's father with an unpleasant choice. He could leave his wife to give birth alone in Bath, thereby making it plain to the world that he had been cuckolded for the hundredth time. Or he could hide her away in the country in an attempt to mitigate the embarrassment.

For Lady Grayston, the embarrassment had lasted but nine months. She died in childbed, leaving behind a squalling, black-haired infant of uncertain parentage. Christian watched Henriette Middleton dance down the path before him, her raven braids swaying as she went, and remembered his sister with an abiding sweetness. The circumstances of her birth had marked a drastic change in his life. He had not missed his mother, for she'd never been overfond of children, and even before her banishment, had lived most of the year in London. No, the change had been Lady Lenora Villiers.

Despite the difference in their ages, there had existed between them an instant bond, not unlike that of two souls cast adrift in a lonely sea. No longer was he left alone in a three-acre mausoleum with only a tutor and a housekeeper for companionship. Fool that he was, he had believed his childhood suddenly idyllic. He had believed his life perfect. For a few years, it had been. And then the façade crumbled.

On his twelfth birthday, his father had announced that it was time to make a man of his son. And Christian *was* his son. None but a Villiers, it was often said, could beget a child with eyes which were at once so cold and so silvery. But the rest of him was his mother's. He had her dark coloring, her voluptuous mouth, and—as his father was ever fond of reminding him—her reckless appetites. To ensure that such tendencies were beaten out of him, Christian had been sent not to Eton or Harrow, but to Rugby School, whose motto was "By prayer and by work."

It was an accurate assessment of the curriculum. Christian had never prayed so much nor worked so hard in all his life. For a couple of years, anyway. Then, after having been repeatedly told by his father that he was irredeemably wicked, Christian had decided that no prophecy should go unfulfilled. At fourteen, he ran away from Rugby. At sixteen, he ran off to join the Royal Navy. At seventeen, he ran away to the Strand and fell in with a gang of blacklegs who'd taught him the first of many hard lessons in cardsharping. And at eighteen, he ran away with the Belgian ambassador's mistress. It never occurred to him that while he was running and running and running, his young sister was left to the mercies of their overbearing father.

Finally, when he was twenty, Christian ran into a very beautiful—and very married—countess. After being caught in a moment of bliss between the lady's thighs, Christian almost killed her husband in a duel, and was obliged to flee to France. The old marquis declared it the last straw. Christian had been whoring and drinking and gambling his reputation to ruin, and so his father banished him from England. As long as Christian would stay on the Continent, his father promised he would continue to give Lenora the protection of his name and provide her with an enormous dowry. If not, he'd wash his hands of his dead wife's bastard, and Christian could deal with Lenora's future as best he could.

By then, the truth of Christian's exploits had been magnified times ten in the telling, until his reputation was even worse than he deserved. But Christian still knew he had rendered himself unfit to raise a child. And so he left his little sister behind for good. At the time, it had seemed his only choice. Damm it, it *had* been his only choice.

He was jerked back into the present when Henriette

shrieked with delight, splintering his maudlin mood. Christian looked up to see that she had espied a pair of young rabbits sunning themselves beyond a row of rose bushes, and had darted around the distant wall in hopeless pursuit. "Henriette!" cried Elise after her. "Stay away from the canal!"

But the child did not seem to hear. Christian watched her go, amazed to find himself genuinely smiling. "She is headed the other way," he soothed. "She will be safe."

Elise caught his tender tone. "Have you some fondness for children, my lord?"

Christian crooked his head to look down at her. "I hardly know," he lightly confessed. "I've rarely been around them. Still, it is a pleasure to watch Henriette."

"Is it?" Elise sounded skeptical.

Christian shrugged. "She has such a natural exuberance beneath her shyness," he explained, feeling suddenly ill at ease. "I knew someone once who was very like that as a child."

Elise seemed taken aback. "Really? Who?"

He hesitated for a long moment. "My sister," he said softly. "She is—*was*—six years my junior."

"Oh, yes," she said softly. "How odd that I did not realize Lady Lenora Villiers was your sister." Distance had crept back into her tone, as if she, too, found their conversation awkward. "But then, I hardly know you, do I?"

"Don't quarrel with me just now, Elise," he said very quietly.

"Forgive me," she said stiffly. "I did not realize I was quarreling."

"Forgiven."

For a time, they simply strolled along the path which

Henriette had taken, the hems of Elise's dress sweeping over the leaves which had started to fall. "I only saw her once, you know," Elise mused, pushing a branch of forsythia from her face. "At Lady Morton's ball last Season. She was so very lovely."

"Lenora—?" he murmured, as if returning again to the present. "Yes, Lenora was lovely inside and out."

They were still strolling along the main path. Elise looked up at him strangely. "How long has it been since you lost her?" she finally asked. "And your father passed away shortly thereafter, did he not?"

He thought of Henriette dashing after the rabbits in her yellow muslin pinafore, the sun glinting off her hair, the very picture of well-bred innocence. Such were his last memories of his sister. *How long since he'd lost her?* Ten long years, really. Ten years since he'd betrayed her by capitulating to his father's demands, leaving Lenora alone to bear the brunt of his hatred. But how long since she was murdered? Tricked, debased, and abandoned by the man she'd loved? Ah, that betrayal was more recent.

"Last August," he answered, turning to fully face her, preparing to tell Elise the same awful lie he'd been telling for months now, ever since Lenora's last letter had finally caught up with him in Venice. "She died last August in a fall from a parapet at Hollywell Castle. A portion of the wall gave way. It was a dreadful accident. And yes, my father followed not long after."

Elise's expression softened. "How horrible for you," she said quietly. "But you must not blame yourself, my lord."

He looked at her sharply. "Why do you think I blame myself?"

Elise shrugged. "I do not know why," she answered. "But I can hear the pain and doubt in your voice. And yet, there was nothing you could have done."

Christian jerked his eyes from hers and stared straight down the path before them. "You do not know that," he said swiftly. "I should have been with her. Perhaps . . . perhaps things would have been different."

Her gaze flicked up at him. "Your pain is deep, my lord," she murmured. "But you must cut out the bitterness, and cleave only to the pleasant memories of your sister. I am glad that you had her for a time, and that you loved her."

He realized at once that it had been a mistake to speak his thoughts of Lenora aloud. He had no wish to share any part of his sister—or his sin—with anyone. They were crossing from one walled garden into another. Suddenly, Christian halted and swung around to face her, almost trapping her with his body. "I do not wish to speak of my sister, Elise. I should much prefer talk about us."

Her blue eyes shifted nervously. "There is no *us* to talk about, my lord. Please do not start this again. I have not yet lectured you for your behavior last night at dinner, and I mean to do so."

He lifted one slashing black brow. "You did not enjoy it?"

Elise felt heat flush up her neck. "You know I did not!"

He gave a dry, doubtful smile. "You are not flattered by the fact that a man finds you infinitely more desirable than his dinner? Almost more desirable than the air he breathes? I want you as my mistress, Elise. Have I not made that plain?"

"The only thing you've made plain is that you have lost your hearing at an abysmally young age." Elise tried to keep her expression stern. "I said no. And I meant it."

Quietly, he laughed. And then, after cutting a swift glance to be sure Henriette had not returned, he gripped Elise lightly by the shoulders. "Elise, my dear," he said. "You have been a widow for—what? Two years? Did you take no pleasure from the physical aspects of marriage? Do you not miss having a man to warm your bed?"

Her eyes blazed with anger. "My bed is none of your business, my lord," she hissed. "And I am not interested in your quick, cheap pleasures."

Christian pursed his lips for a moment. "Do you think that sexual pleasure between a man and a woman is cheap, Elise?" he murmured. "I could show you that, properly done, it is the ultimate luxury. And it certainly is not quick. Let me come to you tonight and show you just how rewarding an *affaire d'amour* can be."

Elise felt herself unaccountably trembling inside. "A love affair!" Her hands came up to push defensively against his chest. "Don't pretty up your offer with French, my lord. There is no love between us. That is what *cheap* means."

She watched as faint humor flicked across Grayston's face. "But I love the look on your face when you are ringing a peal over my head, Elise," he laughed. "Doesn't that count?"

Elise lost what was left of her temper. "Oh, devil take you, Grayston!" she snapped. "You are maddening."

But the devil did not seem to want him either, for Grayston did not vanish. Instead, his smile merely deepened. "You are not by chance holding out for marriage, are you, Elise?" He chuckled when she gasped in horror. "You could almost tempt me, my love," he continued. "But what if I am all brag and no brawn? Many men are, you know. It is best to put a horse through his paces before you bid."

"I will not be bidding, my lord. Indeed, we know nothing of one another."

"That excuse has become shopworn, my dear." He dipped his head as if he might kiss her right in the middle of the rose garden. To her shock, she did not jerk away as any sensible woman ought to have done. But at the last possible instant, he drew back, a mischievous grin spreading across his face. "Do I not know everything about you that a man needs to know?" he asked in that wicked whisper of his. "I know that your nipple hardens sweetly to my touch, that your mouth tastes of cinnamon, and that the sway of your hips can hold me in thrall. And I know you make the most exquisite sounds of pleasure in your throat when my tongue teases yours."

"Why—*good Lord!* I do not make noises of any sort!" Elise took a step back, her heel sliding awkwardly off the brick path. Oh, how she wished Henriette would return!

The marquis caught her firmly beneath the elbow, and drew her back to him. "I lied, Elise, when I said that I slept well last night. I did not. Shall I tell you what I dreamed of? You were so very, very good, my dear. It was sheer torment. I awoke shaking with fever, and aching with disappointment."

"I fear your torment is destined to continue," she snapped. "In this world, certainly, and right into the next, I don't doubt."

"You shrew!" he chuckled. "For my part, I don't think it will last much longer. I think bliss is just around the corner."

"You are an ass, my lord. And an arrogant one, at that."

His silvery eyes glittered with something, but it was not humor. "Back to those insults again, are we?"

"Yes," she hissed. "And I shan't apologize again. Not when you keep teasing me."

"You do not want me to tease you?" he responded, his voice laced with a challenge. "You do not wish me to continue inviting you to my bed? Then keep your lips perfectly still, Elise, while I kiss you very thoroughly. Don't move, and don't let me coax out any of those sweet little noises. If you can, then I swear I will never again lay a hand on you."

Her eyes widened, the color deepening across her face. Christian waited for a heartbeat, waited for her to step back, or lower her gaze. But instead, the lady set her palms more firmly against his shoulders and gave him a scolding look. *A governess look.* She did not wish him to kiss her, but he was not at all sure she would try to stop him.

But then again, he might be wrong. Perhaps she would strike him a cracking good blow across the face. Suddenly, he did not care. Instead, Christian had the sensation of standing on unsteady ground, as if he had ventured into quicksand from which there was no turning back, and was finding it oddly exhilarating to be dragged under. He had forgotten where he was. He had even forgotten about Roth. He dipped his head again. "Now hold very still, my love," he whispered near her mouth. "You must try to prove your point."

"You are insane," she hissed. "I shall scream."

"No, you won't," he whispered, his lips brushing lightly over hers.

I will! she thought. *I swear to God I will!*

But when his lips touched hers, so sweet and lightly teasing, Elise sucked in her breath. With it came the dizzying scent of him, his musky warmth, his freshly starched linen, and the hint of sweet tobacco, all of it so achingly familiar. And as if drawn by powerful magnets, Elise turned her face into his and kissed him back. The resolve seemed to drain from her every muscle, only to be replaced by something which spiraled sweetly into her belly.

Ah, God! She had known it! Known that she would weaken, and then capitulate. And yet, it was another of those otherworldly moments, as though her impulses and her mind were controlled by someone else. She leaned into his heat, felt the soft wool of his lapels firmly against her breasts, and opened her mouth beneath his. And then he did it again; melted her world with his lazy, stroking tongue and his warm, knowing touch.

The marquis soothed her gently, sliding inside her mouth and back out again, raking her skin with the faint stubble of his beard, and drawing her fully against him. Into him, it seemed. And Elise felt herself rise up onto her toes, intuitively searching, instinctively aching. Gently, he set her back against the stone gatepost, wrapped a powerful arm about her waist, and plumbed her mouth again. Elise let her hands drift from his chest down and around to the small of his back, remembering the hardness of his muscles there.

At her touch, Grayston groaned faintly, deepened the kiss, and slid one hand under her behind, the silk of her gown softly rustling as he circled and caressed her through the fabric. On another moan, he lifted her against him, easing her up the warm, hardening length of his erection. Elise fought down an almost unbridled emotion—not panic, but something worse. Something *wonderful.* She fought the urge to curl one leg about his waist; battled the wanton wish to press herself higher, harder, against him. It felt delicious and wrong and wicked and perfect all at once. Suddenly, she cared not one whit that he was a rake and a rogue, as long as he would soothe her aching torment.

And then she remembered Henriette! At once, Elise stiffened and tore her mouth from his. She might hear the child's footsteps running back down the path at any time. The walls and bushes might not be enough to hide them.

Slowly, with obvious reluctance, the viscount lowered her back down the hard swell of his trousers. Then came the moment she had instinctively dreaded. The moment when he would look into her eyes and laugh. But he did not laugh.

Soon, she wished he had. Elise had expected him to mock her, had expected at the very least that his face would be alight with unholy amusement. Instead, Grayston looked down at her, his expression tender, and a little mystified. And there was a sense of grief and loss there, too. Then very gently, as if she were a way-ward child, he set her away from him, and looked down to neaten the fabric of her bodice.

It was a long moment before he lifted his eyes to hers again. When he did, the tender expression—if it had existed at all—was gone.

"Ah, my dear Lady Middleton," he whispered, his sil-very gaze catching hers once more. "It seems hunting season is destined to continue."

Chapter Six

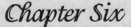

I have no relish for the country; it is a kind of healthy grave.
—Smollett

Much later that same evening, Lord Robert Rowland found himself attempting to alleviate the boredom of Gotherington's drawing room by lifting his wineglass to the candlelight and peering discreetly through his sherry. To those who did not know the young man, such a gesture made him appear almost introspective, as if he were contemplating the fine quality of the vintage, when in truth, all he was contemplating was the quality of the Misses Onslows' bosoms. Those were very fine indeed, he noted, when Belinda leaned over the harpsichord to turn her sister's music.

The room in which Lord Robert languished was stuffed cheek-by-jowl with the Onslows' newly arrived guests, most of whom lingered about a pair of whist tables which had been set up after dinner. Lord Robert gazed past them most carefully. It would not do, his elder brother had warned during their tedious journey from Cambridgeshire, to be caught paying overmuch attention to the oh-so-eligible Misses Onslow.

"Well, Stu, at least they have their mama's luscious bosoms," he said, stretching back into his chair on a huge yawn. "Perhaps these two weeks in the back of beyond won't be such a great snore after all?"

From his adjacent chair, his elder brother, Stuart, Lord Mercer, shot him a speaking glance. "They are young ladies, Rob," he grumbled. "Not Green Room talent to be ogled at your convenience."

Lord Robert laughed. "Oh, don't be such a stick, Stu," he sagely advised. "Lucy's been batting those big blues at us since we arrived. I daresay a fellow could coax her into a dark corner without too much trouble."

"Thank you, but I've no wish for a leg shackle at my age," snapped Lord Mercer. "And that's what we'd likely get. Do you imagine for one instant that Papa wouldn't drag your young arse to the altar for it? They are his goddaughters, never forget."

But as usual, Lord Robert was undeterred. "Then what about a pretty widow or a bored wife?" he asked just as Lucy struck up her next tune. He motioned with his wineglass in the direction of the two whist tables. "Helene Rutledge has very long legs."

"She is also Bentley Rutledge's sister-in-law, you lackwit!" Mercer's voice was thick with disgust. "And Lord Treyhern's wife. Really, Rob, you're such a puppy. If a woman of Lady Treyhern's caliber so much as winked at you, you'd likely just come all over her slippers."

Across the room, Belinda began to sing to Lucy's accompaniment. Lord Robert winced, and turned away. "You are just jealous of my looks, Stu," he drawled. "Fifty guineas says I can bed her within the week."

"Your fifty guineas will get your brains blown out by

that hard-nosed husband of hers," retorted his elder brother. "If Hell-Bent Rutledge doesn't do the job for him. What kind of friend are you?"

At last, Lord Robert fell silent. "You are right, of course," he finally agreed, watching Lord Treyhern sweep up a trick and stack it neatly by his elbow. "It would not be at all the thing to sleep with old Bentley's sister-in-law, would it? But what of Elise Middleton? I hear widows are always eager for bed-sport."

Now it was Lord Mercer's turn to snort with laughter. "Even a fool can see which way the wind blows there."

"Who, Roth?" Lord Robert scowled just as Belinda hit a sour note. "Mama says he's just a fortune-hunter who's been hanging out after Lady Middleton all Season. If she wanted him, she'd have had him ere now."

Lord Mercer hissed between his teeth. "She does not want *him*, you noddy. She wants the Marquis of Grayston."

"She *what*—?"

Lord Mercer jerked his head toward Lady Middleton's card table. "She can scarce take her eyes off the man, Rob. They've been cutting sidelong glances at one another since we arrived."

Lord Robert put down his glass and commenced a careful study of his manicure. "So—?"

"So stay well out of that one, Rob. They say Grayston would as soon put a bit of lead between your eyes as look at you."

Just then, the would-be assassin stepped from the shadows where he'd been standing since declining a seat at the after-dinner card games. With a slow, indolent gait, he wandered across the room toward them, a half-empty brandy glass held low and loose in his fingertips. Both young men twisted uneasily in their chairs when Grayston halted, looming over them like a thin, black shadow. He was tall and very lean, with eyes like well-polished pewter; silvery and emotionless.

"I collect, gentlemen, that your evening lacks excitement," he said very quietly. "Might I be of service?"

"In what way, sir?" asked Mercer politely.

Grayston cast a jaded eye about the room. "Perhaps we should play at something more challenging than whist?"

Lord Robert forced himself to sit up very straight. "What is your game, Grayston? We might be interested."

Swiftly, Mercer's elbow jabbed into his brother's ribs.

"*Vingt-et-un* is the only game I play," murmured Grayston. "Usually," he added, lifting his glass to his lips and staring quite blatantly over the rim at Lady Middleton.

Vingt-et-un! Bloody hell. It was a very dangerous sport, and one which it was said a very clever man could master. Lord Robert Rowland had not mastered it. Truth be told, he'd not mastered much of anything, cards or copulation included, loath though he was to admit it.

Thankfully, his brother saved him from his fate. "Perhaps another time, Grayston," Mercer said, feigning his mother's most world-weary tone. "Our stepfather frowns upon serious gaming when ladies are present. You understand, I hope?"

A strange half-smile crooked Lord Grayston's mouth. "Ah, the Reverend Mr. Amherst as a stepfather," he murmured. "I quite perceive your problem."

"We do not find it a *problem*, sir," said Lord Mercer very softly.

For a long moment, Grayston stared at him. "A poor choice of words on my part," he finally acknowledged with a nod. "And I meant only that we might play for practice, not serious money. But perhaps another time?"

Just then, one of the whist games ended, chairs sliding back amidst a great deal of laughter. The harpsichord, too, halted. Grayston crooked one brow. "Your pardon, gentlemen," he remarked, turning away with some haste. It was quite clear where he was headed.

Lord Robert felt the stab of his brother's elbow yet again. "Observe now, my brother, " hissed Mercer. "And behold a master at work."

The game had not gone well for Elise, who had finished the rubber badly by tossing down a trump, which quite obviously ought to have been played earlier. She was partnered by Mr. Amherst, who merely smiled, slid the trick to Helene, then suggested they pause for refreshments. At Elise's elbow, Denys pushed back his chair and stood. Suddenly, it was as if her breath came more freely; as though she'd been unconsciously ill at ease in his presence. There was an undeniable tension between them now, and she was not quite sure what, if anything, she ought to do about it. She had made Denys no promise, and was feeling less and less inclined to do so.

But even that discomfort had been surpassed by the disquieting sensation of Lord Grayston's cold gray eyes on her face, where they had remained for much of the evening. He was without a doubt the most relentless gentleman she'd ever known. And the most commanding. Since his arrival at Gotherington, she'd been almost intuitively aware of his presence each time she entered a room. His gaze seemed somehow to command hers, willing her to look at him, drawing her eyes down his length. And no matter what he wore, he was always startlingly handsome. The arrogant devil.

Denys had been very much aware of him, too. In fact, if he came within three feet of her, it seemed that Grayston was at once by her side, touching her on the shoulder, or murmuring some compliment into her ear, and making Denys's eyes flash with resentment. Elise felt confused, and wretchedly out of her depth. Suddenly, the hair on her neck prickled, and Elise turned her head just as the marquis slid a strong, warm hand beneath her elbow.

"I find the air has grown overwarm, ma'am," he said in a voice which was clearly meant for her alone. "Might I prevail upon you to take a stroll through the gardens?"

"The gardens?" Elise managed to stand without stumbling.

Across the table, Denys cleared his throat. Grayston seemed oblivious. "I have a particular wish to see the ornamental canal by moonlight," he urged, his breath warm on her ear. "I am told it is very romantic."

Denys coughed sharply. "Lady Middleton is playing at whist, Grayston."

Finally, Grayston lifted his cool gaze. "Is she? I was under the impression the game had ended."

"Just the rubber," snapped Denys. "Lady Middleton will wish to finish the match."

Elise, however, found herself just a little wary of having someone else decide what she wished. Perhaps she did not know her own mind, but that was her problem.

At that moment, Lady Kildermore reentered the drawing room. "The girls are finally asleep!" she announced, her eyes going at once to her husband, Mr. Amherst. "Oh, are you being forsaken, my love? I should be pleased to take Elise's seat, if she would like some air."

Elise stepped away from the table. "Thank you, Jonet," she said, telling herself she could hardly refuse either Grayston or Jonet without being rude.

For much of the evening, the marquis had stood aloof and alone by the fireplace, while Elise remained almost shockingly aware of his presence—which was just what he'd intended, she did not doubt. She did not wish to be aware of such a man. She did not wish to feel the heat of his eyes almost consuming her flesh. Certainly she did not wish to leave the warmth and safety of the drawing room on his arm. Or did she? Good heavens, his strange, twisted logic was taking root in her head!

"I'll just go and fetch my shawl," she heard herself murmur. Good God, she never *murmured*.

"Splendid." Grayston curled his hand more possessively beneath her arm. "I shall see you upstairs."

Elise turned to go, but from across the table, Denys's eyes caught hers. A flash of something unpleasant twisted his features, but before Elise could make it out, he spun about on one heel and crossed to the sideboard. "Will you take sherry with us, Lady Kildermore?" he asked, jerking the stopper from the decanter with an ugly scrape.

Elise was very much aware of Grayston as he followed her up the curving staircase. She was a mindless idiot, no doubt, for provoking Denys Roth over the likes of Lord Grayston. Why could she not behave sensibly? Why could she not keep this man in his place? She should not have angered Denys. Suddenly, it seemed as if her weakness was the marquis' fault, and she wanted to strike out at him for it. "Well," she said over her shoulder. "You have got your way again, it would seem."

They had reached the landing. Abruptly, Grayston seized her by the shoulder, forcing her to turn and face him, his expression and his words suddenly grim. "Do you accompany me against your will, Lady Middleton? If so, feel free to return at once to the drawing room before I do something untoward."

Elise could not hold his gaze. Her words had been unfair. "You've done nothing," she whispered. "Nothing *yet.*"

He slid one finger beneath her chin and forced her face back to his. Tonight, there was a noticeable strain about his eyes. "Perhaps, madam," he said quietly, "you'd best decide which of us you're most afraid of."

Elise felt heat flood her face. "Why, I cannot think what you mean."

"Can you not?" He let his gaze roam slowly over her features, as if he meant to memorize them. "Isn't it just a little unfair to return my kisses with such ardor, and then lay the whole of the blame on me? Be warned, my dear. It is a burden I'll bear but so long."

Elise opened her mouth to argue, but no words came out. And after all, what could she say? "I do not wish for your kisses, my lord," she managed. "If I've misled you, I apologize."

The tight lines about his mouth deepened to a frown. "So why are you here, Elise?"

"To—to walk."

"But an arm's length away, is that it?" He crooked one brow. "No flirting? Touching? Kissing? Are those your terms?"

"Yes." The word was a whisper.

Grayston nodded curtly. "If that is what you think you want, ma'am, then so be it."

Elise shot him another uncertain glance, and hastened in the direction of her bedchamber. She would not permit herself to slow down, did not wish to reconsider the folly of her choice. She told herself that she was leaving with Lord Grayston merely to make a point to Denys. She was her own mistress, and made her own choices. But Elise very much feared that was only a part of the truth. The rest of it she was not at all ready to examine.

It took but a moment to fetch her shawl, and soon they were making their way through the topiary garden. It really was a gorgeous night; the air autumn-crisp beneath a sky which was washed with starlight. A night for romance, she thought impulsively. But what a foolish notion. There was nothing in the least romantic about a handsome rake, unless one was a fool.

The walled gardens of Gotherington were vast, one connecting to another through a series of gates, arches, and arbors. Grayston strolled through them in silence, Elise's fingers resting warmly on his arm. True to his word, Grayston did not allow himself to draw her near. Instead, he struggled to control the frustration he'd been suffering since dinner. A frustration which was not waning.

Having caught on to Grayston's tricks, Mrs. Onslow had seated him between Lady Treyhern, a passionate, dark-haired beauty, and the effervescent Lady Kildermore, who had turned out to be so vastly different from the dour Scot he'd expected, it was laughable. Of course, he had flirted shamelessly with them both. But strangely, it was Elise with whom he wished to converse. Elise with whom he wished to laugh and whisper. And the worst part of it was, with every passing hour, his wish was having less and less to do with that bastard Roth.

Tonight as Roth had hovered about Elise, there had been no mistaking the proprietary look in his eyes, the sense of ownership in his touch. He was sending Grayston a message. Roth was rattled, and that was, of course, deeply gratifying. So why was he here now, strolling through the moonlit gardens with the man's intended wife? Grayston had incited Roth's wrath by taking her, yes. But would not his purpose have been better served by remaining in the drawing room to flaunt his flirtation? Instead, he had slipped away with Elise into the darkness, which was precisely what he'd wanted to do. And therein lay the problem. He was losing sight of his goal.

Even worse, he had agreed to Elise's ridiculous notion of propriety, simply to ensure that she would not scamper back into the relative safety of the drawing room. *An arm's length away.* She did not wish to be touched. Kissed. Flirted with. So this walk did him no good at all. Except that he was enjoying it. He loved the feel of her properly gloved hand on his arm and the scent of her soft, simply dressed hair. He loved the way her dinner dress laid bare her dainty collarbones and the way her shawl was inching down her right shoulder. And he especially loved the way she had gasped when first she'd caught sight of the moonlight reflecting down the length of the canal.

God help him, what he wouldn't give to hear her gasp in just such a way beneath him. Oh, how he would love to strip away that dress, spend his frustrations inside her, and then—and here was the most disconcerting part—spend the rest of the night with her enfolded in his arms. Good God, he wanted to murmur sweet nothings against her temple. And why? *Why?* What on earth had got into him?

But there was one thing about Elise which rattled him. In the quiet of the night, it was easier to admit that he was disconcerted by how easily she saw through him. Her sudden insights always left him vaguely ill at ease. The ability to cloak his thoughts, sometimes even from himself, was a skill he had honed carefully through the years. He did not need Elise Middleton to lift the wool from his eyes. And yet that same emotional acuity drew him. Drew him, and left him feeling strangely raw and vulnerable. He did not want to feel vulnerable. It would be wise to carefully guard his emotions when he was with her. And Elise would be well worth the effort.

The moon was a silver crescent in the sky, its light shimmering off Elise's bare skin. He wanted to draw her close, but he had sworn he would not. Grayston crooked his head to better see her face. "Elise, you had best say something," he warned.

She looked up at him uncertainly. "I beg your pardon?"

"Amuse me, Elise," he advised. "Chatter idly about something, for God's sake. Else I might resort to those very things I've promised not to do."

Even in the cool night air, he could sense her skin growing warm. "What shall I talk about?"

He made an exasperated sound through his teeth. "Tell me about yourself."

She lifted her shoulders in the merest shrug, sending the shawl slithering off the other arm. "Oh, I fear I've lived an unremarkable life."

"Unremarkable—?" Absently, Grayston tucked her shawl back up again. "That has a certain appeal."

Elise lifted her gaze from his fingers to his eyes. "To you—?" she asked on a laugh.

Grayston refused to be baited. "Tell me, Elise, how did you like being married? Was it a love match? Do you yet grieve for your dead husband?"

"So many questions, my lord!" Her voice was soft but chiding. "However, in the interest of amusing you, yes, I liked being married. I liked having someone to care for, and someone who concerned himself with my welfare. And yes, I loved my husband, but it was not a love match. There are many kinds of love, you see."

"Ah, and I would know nothing of such tender emotions?" remarked Grayston mordantly. "I assume your paragon wed you because your sharp little tongue and pale blond beauty stole his breath away, as it has mine?"

She pressed her lips firmly together. "What folderol! Never was a man more full of breath than you."

"Ah, I'm flirting again, am I not?" he murmured. "A nasty habit I shall strive to restrain. Now tell me why two people who were not in love decided to wed?"

For a moment, her eyes sparked, and then Elise relented. "Because we were fond of one another," she said. "And because his lungs were . . . not strong. The doctors could do little. H-He did not wish Henriette to be orphaned."

Grayston lifted one brow and looked down at her as they strolled. "I'm very sorry," he said quietly. "But is Ophelia not his own blood kin?"

Elise hesitated, her blue eyes flicking up at him beneath a fringe of dark lashes. "Henry felt that Ophelia had her plate full."

Grayston laughed softly. "Henry thought his sister a hen-wit, more like," he returned. "But that was nicely done, Elise. You are every inch a lady. Now tell me, where does such a well-bred lady hail from?"

"A village in Sussex, near the South Downs," she answered. "I've lived within twenty miles of it all my life."

They had begun to stroll along the wide graveled path which verged the canal. Carefully, Grayston set her to his left, away from the water's edge. "You have property in Sussex, do you not?" He knew, of course, that her husband must have left her quite well off. A predator like Denys Roth did not fish in shallow water.

"My late husband left me one of his lesser properties, yes," Elise murmured. "It is a small manor, but very lovely. And it has always been Henriette's home."

"Ah! You had said you were her governess. How did that come to pass?"

"Sir Henry was a widower, and when he moved into my father's parish, we were intro—"

"Oh, Lord!" interjected Grayston, halting on the path. "You're going to tell me that your father was the local vicar, aren't you?"

"You needn't make it sound like some sort of cliché, my lord," she murmured.

At once, he drew her back into motion. "But it is a bit, isn't it?" he carefully suggested. "The virtuous vicar's daughter becomes a governess, then earns the undying love and respect of her employer? It happens often enough, does it not?"

"Oh, to be sure." He felt her body go stiff with anger. "Almost as often as spoilt young noblemen seduce other men's wives, then bolt off to the Continent to forever wallow in vice and dissolution. If we're to discuss clichés, my lord, let's not miss any of the more salacious ones."

"Touché, Elise," he murmured. "But my exile was not quite forever, was it? I am here with you, behaving myself with relative grace, whilst the vice and dissolution of Paris wallow on without me. Still, if you mean to wound me, you are making progress."

Elise slowed her pace. "Oh, I am sorry," she said on a sigh. "I didn't exactly mean—"

"Oh, but you did!" He gave a bitter laugh. "Elise, you are the most egregious liar! To yourself, and to me. And what now? Must I deny my wicked reputation? Well, I shan't. I hardly know what is said of me here in England, but I do not doubt for one moment that at least half of it is true. Unlike some men, I will never hide from you my true nature—or my motives."

On his sleeve, her fingers tightened. "What is that supposed to mean?"

Grayston pursed his lips and shook his head. For a heartbeat, he considered. No, his job was not to save Elise from her folly, but rather, to avenge Lenora's. Elise was capable of making her own choices; she was no green girl. Or was she? He did not know, nor did he wish to. In fact, Grayston wished he need know nothing more about her. He wanted only to bed her, and for reasons which went far beyond pleasure. It would be less of a torment to tumble her as publicly as possible, then meet Denys Roth over pistols at dawn to settle the matter.

Oh God, how awful that now sounded! Suddenly—and very desperately—Grayston wished that his hunger for revenge need not consume another human being whilst it was being satisfied. The thought of hurting her was almost unbearable. It was not just her innocence. Not just the fear that she might love Roth, perhaps even deeply grieve for him when he was dead. No, it was worse than that. For if she loved Roth, then it would mean that she would never . . .

But he must not think of that. He must think of Lenora. If guilt and grief and yes—perhaps even a measure of loneliness—began to choke him, then he must throw off that emotional stranglehold by reminding himself of hers. What must it feel like to be seduced, betrayed, and abandoned by someone you loved? To feel his child growing in your womb, and know that you had been forsaken to bear your shame and punishment alone?

Good God! For months now he had seen her in his dreams, as clearly as if he'd stood on the ground beneath, begging her not to do it. Again and again, he watched as her silky black hair tossed lightly in the updraft and her pale linen nightgown billowed in the moonlight. In his mind's eye, his sister stood alone at the top of a cold stone parapet, staring down into fate's abyss. And there was nothing he could do to stop her. Not now. It was too late. He could only avenge her death, but in the process, might he be committing a sin blacker than any of those which already shadowed his soul?

They had reached the end of the path. And perhaps they had reached the end of something else as well. Grayston was not perfectly sure. Gently, he slid his hand over Elise's and lightly patted it where it lay upon his coat sleeve. "We should go in, my dear," he said quietly. "It grows late."

Elise looked up at him in mild surprise, then nodded. Was it his imagination, or did she look disappointed? Despite her protestations, had she secretly wished him to pursue her? Well, he was in no mood to oblige her. No, not tonight. Tomorrow, his cold resolve would no doubt rise anew from tonight's ashes. But at the moment, it had somehow escaped him, leaving him feeling melancholy, and absurdly world-weary.

Elise felt a jumble of emotions as the house came into view. When they reached the short flight of stairs which led up to the veranda, Lord Grayston pulled her gently to a halt. Elise lifted her chin and looked up at him expectantly, her heart beating an odd tattoo. For a moment, their eyes met, and Grayston let his gaze roam over her face in that odd way which made her insides go limp and her stomach flip-flop. Her pulse ratcheted up and her lashes fluttered almost closed.

He is going to kiss me, she thought. *No matter his promise, he is going to kiss me.*

But he did not. Instead, with a faintly mocking smile, he lifted her hand from his arm and let her heart fall back into its proper place. "I'll bid you goodnight here, Elise." His voice rumbled softly in his chest. "I wish to stroll the veranda and smoke."

His meaning was obvious. He wished to be alone. She should not have been surprised; he was a solitary creature. She watched his long, elegant fingers withdraw a burnished cheroot case from his pocket, and felt an odd and acute disappointment that those long fingers weren't sliding into the hair at the nape of her neck, stilling her mouth for his kiss. Worse, she had the strangest notion that he sensed her disappointment, and found it faintly amusing.

Well! She did not really want him to kiss her. She had specifically requested he refrain from doing so, and he had honored that request. She was grateful. She *was*. And so with a few quiet words of goodnight, Elise turned and went lightly up the steps and across the veranda, her arm still warm from his touch. But before she reached the long row of French windows which lined the back of the house, one of the handles rattled, and she looked up to see Denys through the glass.

"Elise, my dear," he murmured, pushing it open. "We were worried."

Elise stepped in, sliding her hands up and down her arms as if she were still cold. Inside, the house felt almost chillier than did the brisk autumn air. "There was no cause for concern, Denys. I merely went for a walk."

Denys looked troubled. "Yes, and with that scoundrel Grayston," he murmured, placing his hands lightly on her shoulders. "Everyone has been concerned, Elise. No one understands why Maynard invited him here."

Elise bit back the retort which sprang to her lips. Perhaps Denys *was* concerned. And Grayston's reputation was by no means pure. "Yet as you see, I am fine." She forced a tight smile. "But I am tired, Denys. I am going to bed. Please make my apologies to the others."

He must have caught the irritation in her voice.

"Come now, Elise," he whispered. "Surely you understand my concern? You are good and virtuous, and nothing Grayston can do will change that. But you are also very innocent, and I want so desperately to protect—"

"Oh, Denys!" she interjected, lifting her hand. "Please! Do not—"

He pressed his finger to her lips, cutting her off. "Elise, love, I know that you are not sure," he gently answered. "But I am patient. In time, my dear, you will be as convinced of the rightness of this match as am I. Now, come, may I kiss you goodnight? Let me show you, Elise, just a hint of what I feel for you."

With another weak smile, Elise allowed Denys to draw her near and press his mouth coolly against hers. Fleetingly, she closed her eyes and tried to feel some enthusiasm. But it was a cold comfort, this kiss she had not wanted, and a dreadfully stark comparison to the kiss she had secretly wished for.

On a sigh, Denys set her away. "There, you see?" he said, his voice low and suggestive.

And Elise saw. Oh, she certainly did. Beyond Denys' s shoulder, in the shadows which edged the veranda, she saw Lord Grayston. He was silently watching them, like some lean, dark creature of the night, his eyes burning through the glass and radiating a white-hot malevolence.

Chapter Seven

They love indeed who quake to say they love.
—Sidney

Over the next few days, the gentlemen began their shooting in earnest, while Ophelia busied the ladies with plans for the Hunt Ball, an event which was to mark the twins' birthday, and their first appearance in society. Elise, who rose far earlier than Ophelia, usually spent the breakfast hours in the family parlor, feeling just a little neglected by Henriette, who was having the time of her life with so many children about. And each morning, something inevitably drew Elise to the window which overlooked the carriageway. There she would stand, still and silent by the cold panes of glass, as the dogs and horses were brought round to the gentlemen who were assembling for the morning's hunt.

And as she stood there, with each passing day, she became more and more confused about her feelings for Lord Grayston. In truth, she could not take her eyes off the man, and it was no longer just his sinfully good looks which drew her gaze. Ophelia, too, noticed her wandering eye, and sharply pointed out what a goose Elise was making of herself.

Perhaps Ophelia was right. Since their moonlit walk, the marquis had continued his flirtation with her, but no longer did he whisper inappropriate things into her ear, nor contrive to sit with her at dinner. No, he treated Elise much as he treated all of the ladies, behaving like an arrant but charming scoundrel.

So, thought Elise, she had gotten her wish in spades. Grayston was no longer trying to seduce her into his bed. Then why was she not happy? Why, on this morning and every other, did she stand at the window watching him as he laughed and joked with the other gentlemen? And why was she glad when, with each passing day, he seemed more and more a welcome part of the group?

Oh, Maynard seemed a little preoccupied, and Denys was coolly civil, but the others were warm, and it seemed that the marquis had kindled something of a real friendship with Mr. Amherst, despite the fact that he flirted outrageously with the gentleman's wife, Lady Kildermore. What a contrast in character they seemed; the understanding vicar and the unrepentant rake. But were they really that different? Certainly there was a strong visual contrast. The vicar's golden good looks and Lord Grayston's dark, satanic beauty could not have been more disparate.

This morning they stood on the graveled carriageway along with Mr. Amherst's grown stepsons. Their four heads were bent together in companionable conversation as a pack of speckled pointers milled and wove between their legs. Grayston—*Christian*—was attired much as he had been on the evening she'd first met him; in dusty brown boots which reached to his knee and a soft-brimmed hat which had seen better days. And in the crook of one arm, he balanced a fowling gun with a grace which seemed second nature.

Beside him, Mr. Amherst made a remark—some witticism about the weather, perhaps—then threw back his head and roared with laughter. In response, the marquis looked up and spun about, almost losing his hat as he pointed to the clouding horizon. His long, canvas coat billowed about his boots, and Elise could not miss his expression of almost childlike exuberance. Yes, he did look younger. Happier, somehow. And oddly, for the first time, Elise found herself wondering at his age. Those wintry, all-seeing eyes seemed ageless, as if they had beheld a lifetime's experience. And yet his body was strong and lithe, his hair as black as well-polished onyx.

Six years, he had said, was the difference between him and his sister. Lady Lenora had stunned society by coming out when she was well past twenty. Elise counted on her fingers and gasped. Why, Grayston was probably not yet thirty! Better than half his life lay before him, and yet a certain despair, a kind of world-weariness, seemed already to hold him in its grasp. He was a rake, yes. And he had done some wicked things, she did not doubt. But it was hard to believe that three decades formed the whole of a man's character, and left him irredeemable. Or was she simply trying to fool herself?

On that thought, Elise caught sight of Lady Kildermore dashing down the steps to kiss her husband good-bye. In her arms she carried an infant, and about her heels a tide of little girls surged like lacy foam. Mr. Amherst bent down and swept up the smallest, a golden-haired toddler of perhaps three years, leaving the other three to dart about petting the dogs and pestering their elder brothers.

Three—? Elise swiftly recounted. One of the girls now stood alongside the Marquis of Grayston, pointing at his gun. In response, Grayston went down on one knee in the gravel, and began to demonstrate the mechanical workings of his weapon. Oh, yes! That was Henriette. Something as hazardous as a loaded weapon was just the sort of thing to incite her curiosity. But Grayston, she was strangely confident, would keep the child safe.

Suddenly, something caught her attention. Elise shifted her gaze to see that Lady Kildermore's sons had hefted their sisters onto their backs, and were riding them piggyback. Together, Lord Mercer and Lord Robert darted around the crowd in some sort of silly game which was apparently intended to drive the dogs wild. In a frenzy of flopping ears and flying feet, the pointers dashed madly about, chasing trailing sashes and barking at dangling petticoats until the entire pack was caught up in a wild, canine tumult. But Henriette, as so often happened, was left out. Then, with a casual motion, Grayston flung his weapon onto the seat of a nearby curricle, and tossed Henriette onto his back like a sack of potatoes.

Even three stories above the fray, Elise could hear her shrieks of joy. Of course, Henriette seized her good fortune with exuberance. Apparently dissatisfied with his speed, she snatched the marquis's hat from his head and began to flail him across the backside with it. The shrieks grew louder, and the dogs more frenzied, until at last Lady Kildermore clapped her hands over her ears and ordered the children back into the house. At once, the gentlemen packed up and set off. Elise watched them go with a strange sort of sadness weighing down her heart.

"Sunday!" muttered Grayston to himself as he stood warming his hands by the fire which roared in the breakfast parlor. Of all the bloody days, this one would have to be the Sabbath. For the fifth night in as many, he had slept fitfully, his mind tormented by indecision. He had come to Gotherington, he kept reminding himself, to wreak havoc on the man who had seduced his sister, not to ruin his sleep over a woman who'd rather not give him the time of day. And certainly not to attend an endless string of tea-parties, the latest of which was holding forth behind his back this very minute.

This one had been brought about, in part, by a sudden and unseasonable cold snap—weather which had not, mind you, dissuaded Ophelia Onslow from marching them all off to the parish church like a line of Prussian infantry. Nowadays, sharing a bottle of well-aged cognac with the Reverend Mr. Amherst was about as close to God as Grayston wished to get. But he'd seen early on there was to be no escaping Mrs. Onslow's sense of Christian duty. And so Grayston had put on his plainest waistcoat and ordered Stallings to tie his cravat in the simplest style imaginable, and had desultorily brought up the rear on the trek to the nearby village.

The hike back had been worse, for on the return trip, he'd been weighed down by a whole chapter of Deuteronomy and a couple of very grim warnings about just who it was that vengeance belonged to. Oh, he'd rather enjoyed that passage about the teeth of beasts and the poison of serpents being set upon one's enemies—that sounded like just the sort of retribution he was after. But he had not liked one whit the suggestion that his hand should be stayed in favor of God's. Now, two hours later, the Onslows and all their guests were milling about the tea table, gratefully clutching their scalding cups between their bloodless hands, whilst he stood by the hearth feeling just a little bit like a chastised child.

In disgust, he turned around to roast his other side and caught sight of Elise, who smiled, lifted her teapot, and tilted her head in obvious invitation. And there, heaven help him, was another problem. Moses and Deuteronomy notwithstanding, Grayston still meant to dispatch Denys Roth from the face of the earth, and the look on the bastard's too-pretty face when he found out would be well worth spending an eternity in hell, which was where Grayston was headed anyway. But he no longer knew precisely how he was going to seek his revenge. He couldn't very well slap a glove in Roth's face and announce his intention of avenging his sister's death. That would be tantamount to proclaiming Lenora's suicide. Two heartbeats later, the assumptions about her character would begin, and on the heels of that would come the rumors of her pregnancy. No, he couldn't do it.

Nor could he use Elise as a means of his revenge. He knew that now; had probably known it from the first. It was one thing to strategize about the means and opportunity of one's retribution, and quite another to hurt someone who was very real and very innocent in the process. It had seemed easy enough when Lady Elise Middleton was no more than a name to him. When he'd not known how soft her hair felt between his fingers, or how furiously she stabbed at her needlework when she was in a temper. When he had not known how faithfully she could love another woman's child.

Oh, yes, Elise had become frighteningly real to him. Indeed, he was almost grateful that his hunger for vengeance had all but consumed him, else he was very much afraid he might have been consumed by an altogether different emotion. He watched as Elise passed by Roth, pausing just long enough to refill his cup. She certainly did not look as though she was in love with the fellow, and that brought Grayston some small comfort. He did not think she would suffer when Roth was gone.

Sometimes when he looked at the gentle lines of her face, as he did now, Grayston found himself wishing he was a different sort of man altogether, or that he could go back and undo this last decade of his life. But there was no changing the truth of what he was. Oh, he had toyed with the notion of flinging himself at her feet and saying something wildly foolish as soon as his work here was done. But what did he think would happen then? Did he imagine for one moment that Elise would not be horror-stricken by the blood on his hands? Did he somehow harbor the insane hope that she would simply give up her home, turn her back on her friends, and drag a nine-year-old child off to a life of exile on the Continent? Oh, that would never happen. And he would never ask it; neither of her, nor of the child.

No, all he could hope for was just the chance to make love to Elise before he bolted for France. He doubted it would happen, but a man could dream. Though honestly, he did not know what it was about her that so captivated him. She was lovely, yes. But he'd known dozens of women who were just as beautiful, not to mention more willing and better skilled. But the attraction was growing undeniable. And it was complicating his life.

Elise picked up a platter of seeded cakes and began dropping them onto the children's plates. When she moved to set it down again, she caught his eye and smiled, then swished her skirts around the tea table and sat down near Henriette and her playmate, Lady Ariane Rutledge. He was tired, so damnably tired, of keeping his distance from her. Now that he had decided what to do—or rather, what he could *not* do—perhaps he could at least enjoy her company. He could even pretend, just for a while, that he was that different man he sometimes wished to be. So this time, Grayston accepted the invitation in her smile and headed across the room for a cup of tea.

And so it was that, quite by accident, he overheard Henriette pleading with her stepmother to allow her to explore Gotherington's maze. And quite by accident that he heard Elise promise that they might do so during their botany walk on Tuesday, when the warm weather was expected to return. But it was no accident at all that, a full quarter-hour before their appointed stroll, the marquis himself was comfortably ensconced inside the summerhouse which sat at the maze's center.

The summerhouse was just an old wooden folly with double doors which could be thrown open on two sides. Though it looked little used now, it had been furnished for summer entertaining, and still contained a well-padded chaise and several chairs. After sweeping away a few cobwebs, Grayston stretched out upon the former, his hands folded behind his head, his freshly polished hessians crossed quite lazily at the ankles. Sheltered thus from the autumn breeze, he had very nearly fallen asleep before he heard their approach.

"Chamomile," he suddenly heard a small voice say through the greenery. "*Chamaemelum nobile*—? And this . . . I think this is *potentilla reptans*, cinquefoil."

"Very good, my dear!" He recognized Elise's encouraging tone, but they were still far away. "And this?"

"Goldenrod." The small voice carried on the breeze. "It is . . . *solidago virgaurea?*"

Elise laughed. "Splendid, Henriette! We'll make a botanist of you yet."

"But Lucy says I must be careful," said the worried little voice as they circled nearer the entrance to the maze. "She says someday I'm to have a come-out, and that I mustn't be a bluestocking if I want a husband and children."

Hidden deep inside the evergreens, Grayston listened to the pregnant pause which ensued. "Of course you'll have a come-out, and someday a family, too," said Elise consolingly. "But you will also be intelligent, Henriette. That way you'll choose wisely."

"Oh," said the child. "Did you choose wisely?"

Again, a long silence. Grayston got up and began to follow their voices along the inner circle of the maze. He would have given last month's card winnings to see Elise's face. *Had* she chosen wisely? How deeply had she come to love her husband? And why the hell did he care? A gentleman, he knew, would not eavesdrop so deliberately. He was very glad he was not a gentleman.

"I did indeed, Henriette," Elise finally said. "Your Papa was the most wonderful man on earth. He was good and honorable. And very kind."

He heard the child kick a stone down the path which circled toward the maze's entrance. "Bee says you're to marry Mr. Roth next." She sounded less than enthusiastic. "Is it true?"

"Oh, Henriette!" Here, Grayston heard the crush of her petticoats as she knelt in the grass. He could all but see Elise holding the child's face in her small, fine-boned fingers. "Perhaps I shan't marry anyone at all. But do you not like Mr. Roth, my dear? Has he been unkind to you?"

Henriette avoided the question rather neatly. "Well, perhaps you might find someone taller and handsomer?" she returned. "Maybe Lord Grayston would marry you? He plays the pianoforte. And I think that if you married him, he might let me shoot his gun."

"Henriette!" Elise jerked to her feet in a rustle of silk. "His lordship is very charming, but he is not the sort of man one marries."

"Why not?" she asked simply. "Lucy says he's a wicked rake, whatever that is. But Ariane's mama just laughed, and told her that leopards can change their spots. I think Lord Grayston looks kind of like a leopard. But a black one. What do you think?"

Finally, Elise laughed. "Oh, never you mind what I think, Henriette! And stop listening to Lucy's tittle-tattle."

Again, a long, companionable silence. Soft footfalls

crunched on gravel as they circled closer, like little rabbits toward a snare. "Oh, Mama!" Henriette suddenly cried. "Here is the entrance! Hurry, hurry! Race you to the summerhouse!"

And then the child was off and running, her light steps pelting along the gravel and into the tunnel of evergreen. "Not so fast!" he heard Elise cry in exasperation. "I don't know the way!"

Lazily, Grayston withdrew a cheroot from his case and strolled back toward the folly at the heart of the maze, now some twenty feet distant. They would be a while, he predicted. It had taken him six wrong turns and ten minutes to wander through the twisting, overgrown verdure. He went up the creaky steps, then reconsidering his cheroot, tucked it away and stretched out across the cushioned chaise so that he might pretend to be asleep. That would at least save Elise a little embarrassment.

He could hear the shrieks of laughter and muttered complaints as the pair meandered down blind passageways and dead ends. Closer. And closer. Henriette was just a bit slower than he expected. Or perhaps he was more impatient than he wished to believe. Still, he'd not lied when he'd called the child bright. There was a look of keen intelligence in her eyes; eyes which were a dusky brown, and far too big for her face.

Over the past week, he had passed several pleasant hours in the music room with Henriette and Lady Ariane, playing the piano and singing silly songs as if he were some cheerful, slightly dotty uncle. He had begun it, or so he'd told himself, in order to win Elise's confidence and to aggravate Denys Roth. But Denys paid the child little mind, and to Grayston's surprise, he had enjoyed the girls' company. There was something refreshing, almost purifying, in the innocence of children. Not that his sins could be so easily wiped away. Still, he always left the music room feeling oddly buoyed by the experience.

When at last they burst into the clearing, Henriette was still giggling. Elise's arm was circled lightly about her waist. "I told you!" cried the child, beaming up at her stepmother. "I told you I could find it!"

"And so you did, my dear." Just then, Elise caught sight of him, snoozing in the shadows of the folly. "Oh!" she exclaimed softly. "We have interrupted your nap, my lord."

Grayston looked about himself in feigned confusion. "What? Oh, yes," he murmured. "It seems I am the Sleeping Beauty today, doesn't it? Perhaps one of you ladies will awaken me with a kiss?"

Henriette laughed and darted up the steps. "But you are awake now!" she said, gurgling with laughter. "You oughtn't have a kiss." Still, she held back her braids with one hand, and bent to press her lips lightly to his forehead.

"Ah, Henriette, you are both wise and generous," declared Grayston, sitting up and rising to his feet. "The young gentlemen will never pull the wool over your eyes."

Elise stood at the foot of the steps. Her lips were pursed, but her eyes were laughing. Grayston stepped lightly down to greet her, and the child followed. "Is this not a fantastical maze, Miss Henriette?" he said, after bidding Elise good afternoon.

"But I came almost straight to the center," bragged the

child, her eyes shining. "Mama was slow, so I had to go back for her."

Grayston stood up and winked at Elise. "Oh, ladies should be very, very slow," he answered. Elise turned faintly pink and opened her mouth to give him one of those veiled set-downs which she seemed to forever have ready, but in that instant, a feminine voice rang out, yoo-hooing through the shrubbery for Henriette.

The child's eyes flew wide. "That's Bee!" she cried. "Mama, Bee is going to the stables! She promised to show me the new colt! May I go? May I?"

Grayston could not believe his good fortune when Elise nodded. "But go straight to the schoolroom after, mind! And within the hour, too, for Lady Ariane and the Amherst girls will want their cakes and chocolate."

Grayston watched the child's yellow muslin skirts as they vanished down the corridor of greenery. Then he turned to face Elise. And suddenly, he could not help himself. Could not wait. He caught Elise by the hand, and turned her back toward him. "Elise." He did not know what else to say. It had been so long. Her hand felt so right in his. Another gentle tug brought her almost against him.

Her eyes flared wide, and she made a sound of protest. But he slid one hand behind her neck and kissed her anyway. The heels of her hands dug into his shoulders, but her mouth softened at once beneath his. She tasted of tea and cinnamon. Sweet. Spicy. He kissed her long and hard, until her cashmere shawl slithered from her shoulders into the grass. And then, on a faint shudder, Christian bent his head to the turn of her neck and let his forehead rest on her shoulder. "I have tried,

Elise," he whispered. "I have tried, and it is no use. I cannot stay away."

They were, quite probably, the truest words he'd ever spoken to her. Words meant neither to flatter nor seduce, but simply to state an awful truth. Her hands slid up his back, skimming lightly over the wool of his coat, and it felt as though she shook her head. "Oh, Christian!" Her whisper was rich with disbelief, and yet, there was surrender in it, too. "Just kiss me again. Please just kiss me."

He did better than that. He swept one arm beneath her knees, and with her skirts spilling over his arm, Christian carried her up the steps of the folly. He sat down on the chaise and settled her across his lap. Elise turned her face into his, and then his mouth touched hers, a sweet, delicate kiss at first, his lips just teasing at the corner of her mouth. Elise's hands went around his neck and she pressed her chest to his. In answer, Christian let his mouth drift lazily over her bottom lip, lightly sucking it between his own. "So good, Elise," he whispered against her mouth. "Such fine, forbidden fruit."

Elise shivered and opened beneath him. As his hand lightly massaged her back, Christian tasted her upper lip, then let his tongue glide into her mouth ever so slightly. With sweet, delicate forays, he tasted and teased, allowing Elise to set the tone. But on his lap, she squirmed impatiently closer. Christian groaned, the pressure of her hips an agonizing temptation.

At once, Elise drew back with a look of faint alarm. Christian flashed her a crooked smile, and returned his mouth to hers in a proper kiss, his mouth covering her lips and his hand covering her breast. Slowly, he stroked the generous swell through the silk of her gown, feeling her nipple harden to his touch.

"Do you want me, Elise?" he murmured, feathering kisses over her collarbone. "Oh, God, please say *yes.*"

"Oh, I shouldn't." Her voice was husky. "If I had any sense at all . . ."

But she did. Christian knew the signs as surely as he knew the taste of her mouth. He plucked lightly at her nipple and she whimpered, arching against his hand. *Too fast*, his mind cried. But he had denied himself for too long. He had to have her. The swell of her hips, the taste of her mouth, the sweet, soft noises in the back of her throat—it was just too much for a man to bear. Already he burned to shove himself inside her; the hunger like nothing he'd ever known. She slid her tongue sinuously around his, then very tentatively into his mouth, and Christian realized he was going to do it. Right here. Right now.

"Elise," he whispered. "Please. Let me."

He did not wait for her answer. Instead, with one arm curled about her waist, he shifted their weight around, lowering her onto the chaise and following her down, easing her against the cushioned back, and returning his hand to tug at the fabric which guarded her breast from his ravenous eyes. But she broke the kiss, jerking her face away. Her eyes were nearly closed, the long, brown lashes fanning over her cheeks. "Don't," she whispered. "Oh, please don't!"

Grayston brushed his lips over her brow. "Ah, Elise, must I stop? I don't wish to, you know."

She laughed, a small, pathetic sound. "But I've never . . . I don't . . . do this."

Not *I won't*. Not *I don't want to*. Relief surged through him. To hide it, Grayston let one fingertip trail gently over her face, stroking the arch of her brow, the turn of her cheek. "You are a passionate woman, Elise," he whispered. "Let it go. Set it free. Please, please, let me teach you."

Above her head, one fist curled against the cushion. She shook her head, her gold tresses scrubbing against the fabric. "Not here," she softly pleaded. "Please, oh, Christian—you stop. I *can't*."

But he could not, and her lithe, young body thrummed with desire. Eager. Passionate. He'd never known the like. Despite her sweet plea, he knew he could have her, here and now, with no force at all. He could tease up her skirts, release himself between her warm thighs, and rut with her like the beast he probably was. And she would enjoy it, too. For about as long as it took for the world to stop splintering about them.

And then she might hate him. Hell, he might hate himself for taking her so carnally. But all Christian might have was the here and now. He looked down to see her wide, blue eyes holding his, confused but not angry. "Let me, Elise," he whispered. "Don't lie to yourself about what you need."

She squeezed her eyes tight. "Oh, God," she whispered.

"Elise," he murmured, sliding his hand up her stocking until his fingers stroked her bare inner thigh. "Just let me have you, love. No one can come upon us. Let me show you how the breeze will feel on your bare flesh. Let me show you what a sensual creature you are."

Without opening her eyes, she sighed and opened her legs to him. Grayston slid his hand higher, dragging up her skirts until he found the opening in her drawers. He cupped her mound, savoring the heat, and then eased one finger into her welcoming wetness. Elise arched, and made a small, sweet sound in the back of her throat, and then something inside her seemed to awaken, rip free, and come to him on a shudder.

Christian felt it, thrilled to it. "Aaah," she moaned, unabashedly urging herself against him. Kissing her more deeply, he cupped her face with one hand, and with the other, he stroked slowly into the folds of her flesh. She was hot and shivering, already easing slowly toward the edge. It was a good thing, Christian grimly decided. After watching this, he might not last long enough to thrust himself inside her.

Beneath him, she moaned and arched again, drawing the fabric of her gown low across her breasts. She was the very picture of feminine decadence, with her skirts hiked up and her knees spread. Elise had one arm behind her head now, her face turned away, her mouth slightly open. Christian's cock throbbed insistently as he eased a second finger inside her, stroking her inner wall as his thumb found the delicate treasure buried in her wetness.

Elise sucked in a gasp through her teeth, and pressed herself against him. Gently, Christian leaned forward to plumb the recesses of her mouth with his tongue. For long, sweet moments, he touched her, using the same slow, stroking rhythm with his tongue and his fingers, until she was writhing beneath him. He felt her need, sensed her urgency.

But suddenly, Elise jerked her mouth away. "Oh, God, what—" she panted. *"What* are you doing to me?"

Christian did not slow the motions of his thumb. "I am going to watch you orgasm, my love," he whispered. "Just let it happen, Elise. Just let it happen. Then let me put myself inside you and make it happen all over again."

"I—I can't," she panted, her eyes still closed. "I *can't!"*

"Shh, love," he whispered. "You *can.* Just let me touch you." He delved inside to taste her mouth again, this time more demanding, more insistent. And suddenly, Elise exploded, her entire body shuddering and trembling on the chaise. Her eyes flew open and her head strained backward. Her breath came in sharp little gasps as she rode down on his hand, whimpering his name.

For a long moment afterward, Christian just held her, drawing in her essence. Innocence and lust. A cloud of lavender water. Her sun-warmed hair. All of it blended together in a heady fusion which played havoc with his judgment. And then he could wait no longer. He shifted his weight again until he was on his knees between her legs. With rough, impatient motions, he tore at the buttons of his trousers, and shoved down the linen of his drawers until his cock sprang free, throbbing hot and hard to the touch.

Elise watched, her eyes wide on his erection as Christian eased one hand along his length, then back again. It felt as if his very breath seized at the thought of what he was about to do. *Had* to do. Unable to wait, unable to choke out any words, he set one hand on her mound and spread her flesh wide to take him, shoving her legs apart with his knee as he bent nearer.

But her wary eyes were fixed on his erection, the long white column of her throat working a little desperately. "Oh, Christian . . . !" she choked. "That s-seems . . . the wrong size—" Almost frantically, she turned her head away again, and tried to scramble up.

Christian knew he was generously made, but hers was hardly the expression of gratitude he'd come to expect. Instead, Elise looked terrified. Good God, he was forgetting her inexperience! He was accustomed to bedding ravenous, well-tutored women. Suddenly, his newfound scruples were wrestling with his raging desire. But Elise's expression of doubt did not lessen. Good Lord, he could not do it. Not with her eyes so wide and her expression so skittish. No, not even if his body imploded from unslaked lust.

He looked at her again, and suddenly, Christian felt just a little ashamed. In response, he eased one hand beneath her elbow and felt a bitter smile curve his lips. "I am a cad, Elise," he quietly admitted. "I am pushing you to do something you are not ready for."

At last, she lifted her gaze from his cock. "I am n-not a virgin." She was so obviously trying to sound brave. "And I do want you."

Grayston bent forward and kissed her lightly on the lips. Oh, this would not do. Despite the awful, heavy ache in his loins, it simply would not do. He might be a libertine. A jaded and dissolute scoundrel who'd had more women than he could count. But Elise was not ready for . . . for *him*. Her dead husband had probably visited her bed once a fortnight, snuffing the candles as he went. And this place—! With reality dawning, Christian looked about him. They were in the middle of the outdoors, sprawled on a chaise in broad daylight with her skirts rucked up and his trousers half down. That was not right, either. He had never meant things to go this far. Good God, he was not even prepared! If he took her here, he might inadvertently leave her with child. And by the time she knew, he'd be an ocean away, unable to return.

Stoically, Christian drew down her skirts and restored his clothing to order, biting his lip so hard he tasted blood. And when he was done, he lifted one of her legs over his lap, wrapped his arms tightly about her, then gently settled his head against her breast. She was full of questions, he knew. But he was not sure he had answers. And so for a long, quiet moment, they simply stayed as they were, breathing in the same rhythm, their bodies warming one another, as the shadows of the summerhouse angled across the maze and the sun began to soften into a puddle of pink and gold along the westerly sky.

"Ah, Elise," he finally whispered into her hair. "You are not quite ready for a man like me, are you? But please do not tell me it is Roth. Please tell me you will never give yourself to that fortune hunter."

Her fingers, which a moment earlier had been trailing through his hair, froze. "A f-fortune hunter?"

Grayston bit back his frustration, only to find it tinged with fear. "You cannot care for him, can you, Elise? Please promise me you don't."

Her tone was cooling. "What are you talking about—?"

Grayston tried to keep his fingers from digging into her back as his mind began to race. Good God, he had best be careful. He had to think this through. Not just his words, but his actions. In his arrogance, the possibility of losing a duel with Roth had never occurred to him. Now a specter more frightening than death loomed. If he lost, who would protect Elise from Roth?

"No matter what happens, Elise," he rasped, "for God's sake don't marry that man."

She pushed Christian away and looked squarely into his eyes. The desire and confusion which had clouded her eyes was melting. "Should I be touched by your concern, Christian?" she asked a little too lightly. "Can it be *you* are coming up to scratch?"

Coming up to scratch? What the devil? And then he remembered Henriette's words, and felt a blinding moment of panic. He must have jerked backward. "I—I beg your pardon?"

Elise's gaze did not falter. "You mean to offer for me, do you not?" she teased, but her tone was a little bitter. "Of course, I realize we've known one another a scant ten days. But since you presume to make love to me in public, and tell me how to live my life, then might I not gather you mean to make some sort of commitment to me?"

The panic slowly subsided. Good God, she was jesting. She was merely angry, not serious. Besides, he needn't have worried. He was not *the sort of man one married.* But still, he'd best make plain his position before the woman started wishing for something she definitely did not want. "Elise, you wouldn't be fool enough to have me," he murmured, lightly cupping her cheek. "I'm the sort of rogue a woman takes a night's pleasure from, not the sort she leans on for a lifetime. Besides, I shall soon return to France. And this time, I won't be coming back."

The evening breeze was picking up, lightly whipping a tendril of golden hair about her throat. "I see," she said quietly. "So if I wanted you to warm my bed—just for tonight—you'd gladly oblige?"

A vision of Elise spread across a tangle of bedcovers danced through his mind. "Oh, not just gladly, Elise, but *gratefully*," he answered, and he meant it. Lightly, he brushed his lips over her cheek. "You are a little frightened, Elise, I know. But if ever a woman's body cried out for pleasure, it is yours. You should make use of me, my dear. Take me—but only to your bed, not to the altar."

Elise looked at him uncertainly, and he dropped his voice an octave. "Shall I come to you tonight after dinner?" he murmured. "I swear I will be discreet."

For a long, uncertain moment, she held his gaze. "Oh, God, I don't know—!" she finally answered, cutting her eyes away. Her hands toyed almost nervously with the buttons of his waistcoat. Setting his hands wide on either side of her face, Christian leaned forward to kiss her just soundly enough to persuade her. But their lips never touched. Suddenly, a heart-stopping scream tore through the air.

"Oh, my God!" Elise jerked upright, almost bumping their heads. *"Belinda*—! Christian, that's Belinda!" But Christian had already torn himself away, and was running out of the summerhouse.

"Henriette!" came the scream again. Belinda's voice was desperate now. "Oh, my God! Help! Help—!"

Chapter Eight

❧❧

A man that studieth revenge keeps his own wounds green.
—Bacon

Christian had no memory of bounding down the steps of the folly; no clue as to how he found his way through the maze. It seemed to take hours; it must have been mere seconds. The voice kept shrieking, rising to a hysterical pitch now. Christian did not stop to see if Elise was behind him. He bolted from the maze and turned the corner, running down the path toward the Dutch Garden. Toward the ornamental canal which encircled it.

Water came into view around the next corner, sheened with gold in the fading light. Belinda squatted awkwardly in a flat-bottomed rowboat. One hand was pressed to her mouth, the other was holding an oar, poking at something floating in the water. Something—*someone*—wearing pale yellow muslin.

"Her head!" wailed Belinda. "She struck her head!"

Christian did not pause to think. He had no need to. Instead, he hit the canal at a run. But the water was not deep; he struck bottom almost instantly, surfacing only yards from Henriette. By now she was flailing wildly. Her head went under, her arms wheeling in the water. "Oh! Oh!" sobbed Belinda, kneeling in the boat now, her knuckles white against the wood.

But Christian had his arms around the child. In one swift jerk, he forced her head to the surface. She came up wild and sputtering, water weeds clinging to her hair. Christian fought for purchase on the slimy bottom, Henriette gagging as he dragged her backward. His boots were like lead weights in the water. He reached the stone wall of the canal, slapping his free hand up on the ledge to anchor them. And then Elise was there, screaming and clawing at the child, her face a mask of terror.

"Henriette! Oh, my God! Oh, my God!" Her hands shook as she forcibly dragged the child, sodden skirts and all, onto the graveled path. Her face was bloodless; her entire body trembled.

Christian planted both palms on the ledge, and somehow hefted himself out. He went at once to the child, squatting down beside Elise, trying to restrain her. She was hysterical with fear, clutching and clawing like a madwoman at the child. Christian seized her hands, forcing them into her lap. "Get back, Elise, you are making things worse," he demanded.

"My baby, my baby!" Elise was crying now, tears pouring down her face as she reached again for Henriette, trying with all her might to drag the child onto her lap. "Oh, give her to me! Oh, God, *give her to me!*"

Christian pushed her away. "Calm down, Elise!" he roared. "Don't drag her upright! She must retch up this water."

Still shaking uncontrollably, Elise fell back onto her heels, her eyes wild, her fingers digging into the gravel as if it might anchor her. Tenderly, Christian turned the child on her side and began to pound between her shoulder blades. Suddenly, a spasm wracked her slender body, and Henriette began retching up green water. Three times. Four. And then she fell back, her eyes fluttering.

Belinda had somehow gotten the rowboat to the canal's edge and scrambled up. She fell onto the path beside Christian. "Oh, Aunt Elise!" sobbed the girl. "Oh, I'm so sorry! Sh-she stood up. I turned my head, and—and she just lost her balance! She hit her head on the boat."

Christian shut out the racket. Murmuring quietly to Henriette, he pushed the hair from her eyes and surveyed the damage. Beside him, Elise was stifling her sobs and clutching her hands in her lap as she watched him. "It is not bad, Elise," he said confidently. "Miss Onslow, go send someone for a doctor at once. She has a mild concussion, I'll wager."

Her face pale, Belinda hastened away. Elise was leaning over the child now, obviously struggling to sound calm as she slicked the hair back from Henriette's forehead. "Poor baby, my poor baby," she murmured.

"Oooh, my head," whispered Henriette faintly. "Mama, I . . . I hit my head."

"Yes, we know you did, sweetie," clucked Christian, stroking Elise's back with one arm. "I am going to pick you up now, Henriette, and your mama and I will take you into the house." A little awkwardly, he scooped up the child and stood, water streaming off his coat.

Elise was still at his side, her eyes fixed on Henriette. "Thank you," she whispered. "Oh, Christian, thank you."

"She is fine, my dear," he said with a sidelong glance. "The water was hardly deep enough to drown in. Had she not hit her head, she could have walked out on tiptoes."

"But a concussion!" whispered Elise in a horrified voice.

"Yes, she likely has one," said Christian gently, striding through the topiary garden. "She'll want watching through the night, and perhaps need a plaster. But by morning, she'll be on the romp again."

Elise jerked to a halt and burst again into tears. "Oh, God, it is all my fault," she wailed. "I did not tell her to keep away from the water. I *always* tell her that. I tell her to *be careful*. But this time, I forgot. I forgot—and now look what has happened!"

Christian turned to face her, Henriette still limp in his arms as she drowsed against his shoulder. Elise was still far more distraught than the situation warranted. Moreover, she was not the histrionic type. "Elise," he said gently, resuming his stride and forcing her to follow. "Can you swim?"

Wildly, she shook her head. "N-No." It was a horrified whisper as she rushed to keep up with him.

"Can Henriette swim?"

Just a shake of the head this time.

"Then you must learn," he said very calmly. "*Both* of you. I shall teach you. It is a dangerous thing to be unable to swim, Elise."

"No!" Eyes wild, Elise shook her head again. "No! Don't ask it of me. We *cannot*."

Christian shot her a steady look. "Can and will," he said firmly.

Elise was white-faced now. "My m-mother," she blurted. "Sh-she drowned. When I was six, she f-fell from our boat. Papa jumped in, but he c-could not save her. Oh, Christian, I am afraid. Sometimes I think . . . yes, I think water is the only thing I truly fear."

Grayston could well believe that. Certainly she was not afraid of him, and God knew she should have been. They were going up the steps now. Lady Ariane Rutledge was standing on the veranda, the wind whipping through her hair. "My papa is coming," cried the girl, her face pale. "Major Onslow has gone for a doctor. Will Henrie be all right?"

Just then, Lord Treyhern burst through the windows of the salon. "Good God, man," he said, striding across the veranda in an instant. "You are soaked, Grayston. Here, give the child to me. Ariane, fetch a footman. He is to build up the fire and take hot water to his lordship's room at once."

With a determined nod, the girl darted away. Together, the rest of them hastened through the salon and down the corridor, Elise leaning on Christian's arm now. When they reached the top of the curving staircase, he paused. "I am ruining Onslow's carpet, Elise," he said softly. "Go. Go with Treyhern. I'll join you shortly."

With obvious reluctance, Elise tore herself away and started down the corridor after the earl, who was striding in the direction of the schoolroom wing. But at the last possible moment, she turned back, her face a mask of gratitude. "Christian, wait!" she cried, wringing her hands as she stared at him. "You are right. About th-the swimming. If you will teach us, we . . . we will try." And then she turned around and ran to catch up with Lord Treyhern.

For a long moment, he stood stock-still in the middle of the corridor. Suddenly, his heart felt heavier than his sopping boots. He watched Elise's small, neat figure hasten around the corner and vanish.

If you will teach us, we will try.

Her brave acquiescence cut him to the quick. Good God—he had said that *he* would teach them to swim? Yes, and he had said it sternly and instinctively. He had said it from the heart. But he wasn't going to be around long enough to teach anyone anything, was he? Not unless one counted the hard lesson he would shortly be teaching Denys Roth. And suddenly, it was as if that aching sense of despair were dragging him under again, as immobilizing and as hopeless as it had been after reading Lenora's last letter.

Christian found himself seized by the urge to flee, to run away, as if the pain were something he might out-distance. But it was not. He had long ago learned that pain could traverse oceans, could sneak insidiously into the darkest and most distant corner of any hell or whorehouse—could always manage to find him. Still, he turned away and strode toward his bedchamber, almost at a run, half-afraid he might meet someone, afraid that his grief was so plainly written on his face, the whole world might see it. His breath rapid and shallow, Christian reached his door and threw it open.

The room was the same, everything just as he had left it. So why did it seem as if his world had been suddenly turned upside down? Why did he feel as if some sort of chance for salvation had just slipped from his grasp? He had selfishly abandoned his sister, and for that, he had to atone. Was he not on the path to expiation? Or was he about to do something unutterably destructive? If Denys were dead, where would Lenora be?

Still dead.

That was the answer. Or a part of it. Grayston shut the door and let his weight fall back against it, as if he feared the whole truth might burst through and overcome him. He had no notion how long he stood there, trying to force his brain to make sense of his muddled and miserable life. Trying to decide what next to do. He knew only that when a sharp knock rang out, he leapt away from the threshold, only to realize he'd been standing in a puddle of water.

Blindly, he stared down, trying to remember where it had come from. The knock sounded again. "My lord—?" called a footman. "You requested hot water?"

Henriette, as it turned out, suffered little from her accident. In fact, she suffered scarcely at all until she had fully recovered from it. And then the bad news had thundered down, so stern it might have been carved in stone. Henriette knew the rules; she was never to go near water, no matter the circumstance. And she knew the punishment for deliberate disobedience.

It was a lowering thing indeed for one of her mature years, she complained to Christian over their piano duet on Thursday afternoon. For one full week she was to be put to bed at half past seven—right along with *"the babies,"* Gervais Rutledge and the littlest Amherst girls—

none of whom was above age four! And the worst of it was, this was the night of the Hunt Ball! In honor of the grand event, Ariane, who was all of eleven, along with Arabella and Davinia Amherst, were to be permitted to stay up an extra hour so that they might peek down from the long gallery as the guests arrived in the great hall.

Before the wheedling was over and done, those big brown eyes—the ones which Christian had already noted were far too large for her face—had seemed as if they might swallow him whole. And so he gave the child a tight smile, and like some foolhardy knight with a dull lance, left the ballroom in search of Henriette's dragon.

It was, Christian supposed, as good an excuse as any to seek out Elise. For two whole days, he had subtly avoided being alone with her, simply because he was not yet certain what he ought to say. He had no notion where he ought to go from this point. And had he even reached a point? He no more knew the answer to that one than he knew what ought to be done with Denys Roth. Perhaps he should just tell Elise the truth, or a part of it, then take his quarrel with Roth elsewhere. Handle it in some other way. But where? How? And there was something else which had to be done before Christian could even begin to wonder about his future. For if Elise discovered the truth about what he'd done to Maynard Onslow, there would be no questions worth answering, and no future save the bleak one he'd come to expect.

With each passing day, the major had lost a little more of his vivacity. And with each passing day, the guilt of what Christian had done in that London hell had weighed heavier and heavier on his mind. Oh, perhaps he'd done nothing strictly unethical. He never did. But he had very skillfully and very easily enticed an amateur gamester into playing too deep and drinking too much. Despite his military skill, Onslow was too naïve and trusting for his own good. Yes, it had been a simple matter to persuade the fellow that he was playing a game of chance, when the truth was, he'd had no chance at all. Christian had acted almost unconscionably. And a conscience, he was belatedly discovering, was an onerous, yet delicate thing.

Chapter Nine

ℰℐ

The ruling passion conquers reason still.
—Pope

The house was already filled with the sweet vibrato of violins as Gotherington's doors were flung open for the Hunt Ball. Despite the fact that Elise had attended countless such evenings, she could not suppress a little thrill of anticipation as she hastened toward the entrance of the red and gold salon to better survey the crowd. This salon, along with many of the other ground-floor staterooms, had been flung open, one onto another, by a series of connecting doors, so that the crowd might surge back and forth. A dozen couples now twirled beneath the brightly lit chandeliers of the ballroom, while as many more lingered about the feast which had been laid out in the drawing room. For those too old to dance, the breakfast room had been filled with card tables, and for those young enough to flirt, the lights along the veranda had been lit.

Slowly, she looked over one shoulder to see that Maynard and Ophelia were greeting the last of the guests. In the long gallery above, she could see the four little figures in white nightclothes which peeped down from the balustrade. Elise shook her head in bemusement and returned her attention to the crowd. How on earth had she been persuaded to let Henriette postpone her punishment? Christian Villiers seemed to possess quite a talent for persuading her to do things which she knew were rash and imprudent.

But Elise's weaknesses aside, at least the Hunt Ball was an unarguable success. The neighboring gentry had poured from their manors and villages to gossip, to dance, and to drink to the health of the young Onslow sisters. The last of them—an elderly squire whom she vaguely knew—passed from the hall into the salon, greeting Elise warmly as he crossed the threshold. Ophelia came in on his heels, her chest puffed out like an overdressed pouter pigeon. "Quite the crush, is it not?" she murmured, sweeping her hand in an expansive gesture. "You see! Did I not tell Maynard we mustn't spare any expense?"

Just then, the Reverend Amherst approached. "The twins look lovely tonight, Mrs. Onslow," he said with a bow. "I believe you may consider them properly launched."

Beaming, Ophelia drew breath to answer, but at that very moment, her butler gave a mildly panicked wave from one of the buffet tables. Murmuring vague apologies, she hastened off, abandoning Elise to Mr. Amherst. As had been the case all evening, Bee and Lucy were dancing. Amherst was watching them, too. Impulsively, she leaned a little nearer. "You are the girls' godfather, are you not?"

"Yes, and honored by it," he answered cheerfully. "But

I am very glad I do not have the job of firing them off. I collect my old friend Maynard has his hands full." His smile was brilliant against his sun-bronzed skin, and a shock of heavy gold hair had fallen forward to make him look more than a little rakish. In fact, he looked nothing at all like a staid country vicar.

The music had ended, and the dancers were flooding from the ballroom in search of punch and champagne. Elise moved a little away from the tables which flanked the door and smiled back at Mr. Amherst. "I wonder, sir, might I have your help with a nefarious plan?" She spoke in a nervous rush. "You see, I wish to dower Belinda and Lucinda. My solicitor has set aside half of everything I have in the funds. It is all arranged."

Amherst looked both surprised and puzzled. "How exceedingly generous," he murmured as a boisterous group pushed past them in search of the punch bowl. "But how may I be of service in this—er, nefariousness?"

Elise smiled weakly. "Such a thing might be hard on Maynard's pride, Mr. Amherst, and so I mean to tell him this was my husband's dying wish." At his look of bemusement, she lifted a staying hand. "No, no, I do not wish *you* to lie."

Mr. Amherst crooked one eyebrow. "No?"

Someone brushed past Elise, jostling her elbow. "Not exactly," she answered, edging closer. "Sir, may I speak frankly?"

"I am a vicar, Lady Middleton." His sparkling gold eyes teased her. "Between you, me, and the good Lord, you may confess your sins if you so choose."

"My fib does not quite sink to the level of sin, I hope," she answered, dropping her voice. "But I realize, as you do, that the girls are a little—oh, capricious? Still, they have their mother's beauty and their father's kind heart. Can you convince Maynard to accept this dowry? Sir Henry provided for me far in excess of my needs, and I wish the girls to be happy. And as foolish as it may sound to you, Mr. Amherst, I wish them to marry for love."

The teasing light left his eyes at once and he smiled softly. "Oh, that is wise, Lady Middleton, not foolish," he said gently. "Depend upon me to take care of old Maynard."

Just then, the violins struck up again, and someone brushed Elise's elbow. She turned to see Denys standing at her side, holding a glass of champagne. "Amherst," he interrupted, greeting the vicar with a tight nod. "My dear, may I have the pleasure? We've not had a chance to chat all evening."

The orchestra was playing a waltz. Elise shook her head. "Thank you," she murmured, oddly annoyed. "I am in the middle of something with Mr. Amherst."

Denys nodded again, even more stiffly, if such a thing were possible. He was quite clearly angry. And then as abruptly as he had come, he left. Good Lord, could she do nothing right as far as Denys was concerned? Though she now realized she could never love him, she had no wish to make an enemy of the man. Elise shook her head and returned her gaze to Mr. Amherst, only to catch sight of Lord Grayston striding across the dance floor toward them.

"Ho, Amherst!" announced the marquis brightly. "You're on the verge of calamity, sir. Your wife says you were to dance this one with her, and she doesn't look like the sort of woman a fellow ought to antagonize."

Amherst lifted both brows at that, and promptly put down his glass. "No, by Jove, she isn't!" he murmured, swiftly bowing to Elise. "Lady Middleton, your pardon. Even a man of God must first see to his own preservation."

Elise stared after him as Amherst melted into the crowd. "Ah, alone at last," whispered a pair of warm lips very near her ear. "Can I persuade you to waltz with me?"

The strangest sense of relief flooded through Elise. Christian had not sought her out all evening. In fact, he'd kept his distance since Henriette's accident, approaching her only in company—until this morning, when he'd come to plead the child's parole. Then, although his touch had been tender and his words persuasive, his eyes had held a look of quiet sadness.

Now, as if impatient, he moved nearer and set his warm, heavy hand at the small of her back. It was a possessive and inappropriate gesture. Elise tried to shoot him a daunting look, but her traitorous mouth twitched with amusement. He glanced down at her, his silvery eyes flashing. "Do you dance, my lady, or no?" he demanded.

"And be reduced to blushes in front of an audience?" she whispered over her shoulder. "No, I fancy not."

The lips returned to her ear, his warm breath stirring the hair about her temple. "Then do you fancy a walk in the dark with me?"

Elise pressed her lips tightly together and shook her head. "Go *away*," she hissed.

She felt his arm snake about her waist. "Come with me," he growled. "Or I shall make a scene."

And he might, she realized. Oh, he would never truly humiliate her; she knew him well enough now to realize that. But Christian would somehow manage to set her face to blushing, and with no hesitation at all. And in truth, she wanted a few moments alone with him. She felt rather light-hearted as she gave a quick glance about the room to make certain no one was looking. Impatient, Grayston seized her by the hand, almost dragging her through the salon and into the dimly lit corridor. They had swept past a half-dozen doors before she managed to shake off his hand.

"This is not the garden!"

Christian slowed to a halt. "I said nothing about the garden," he murmured, lifting one demonic black brow. "I said *dark.* The library is dark—and very, very empty."

Before Elise could protest, he pushed open the heavy oak door, snapping shut the lock as soon as they plunged into the gloom. She had not a moment to draw breath before he pulled her backward against him, urging her shoulder blades against the powerful width of his chest. His arm tightened around her waist as he bent his head to set his lips against her neck. Crooking her head, she felt him nip at her skin, and she gave a little gasp of surprise.

Christian took her mouth with his, surging inside on a kiss that fired her blood and made her knees go weak. His every touch was hot and demanding, and against her better judgment, Elise fell fully back into his arms, reveling in the feel of his hands as they flowed over the front of her body. She let her head fall back against the strength of his shoulder as his hand stroked her cheek, her hair, and then slipped to the curve of her throat.

With one arm banded about her waist, Christian dragged her hips back against the hardening ridge of his arousal while his other hand slid down her belly and lower still, imprisoning her in sweet sensation. His hand eased between her thighs, crumpling the fabric as he caressed her, his breath hot and fast against her temple now.

Elise knew she should argue, but she could no longer remember why she had once resisted his touch. And so she simply surrendered to it, allowing that slow, familiar ache to pool in her belly and weigh down her good intentions. His hand moved back to her breast, his broad-tipped fingers skimming beneath the neckline of her gown to pinch and tease at her nipple. Dimly, Elise knew she should be frightened, but she was not. He turned her about and dragged her hard against his chest. "Elise," he whispered.

His mouth took hers with a new urgency, moving almost desperately as he explored her with deep, hungry strokes. Christian urged her deeper into the shadows until Elise felt as if she were drowning in his touch. It felt as if the darkness swirled about them, absorbed them, and drew them inescapably into its depths. She was lost, swimming in sensation. And as he plunged into her mouth again, she let her hands slide beneath his coat and up the rock-solid muscles of his back as his heat and scent surrounded her. Warm male musk mingled with the smell of starch and cologne, making her wish she could strip away his every stitch and feast her eyes on his beauty.

But he is just a beautiful rake, she tried to remind herself. *And he wants only one thing.*

But the knowledge no longer dissuaded her. Elise wanted that one thing, too. What did that make her? She wasn't sure she cared. She ached for his weight to settle over her, to press her down into the depths of sensation until he eased the torment his touch engendered.

Christian's nostrils were flared wide now, and his warm, heavy hands were on her breasts, molding and caressing them through the fabric of her gown as he urged her backward. Suddenly, she felt something hard strike the backs of her thighs. Her eyes flew open. *A table—?* She'd backed into one of the reading tables. And the room was not quite pitch black, after all. Along the row of windows, a lamp burned, its wick cut back to near nothing. But it was enough to see the ferocity which burned in Christian's eyes.

"Elise," he whispered, his voice almost grim. "God. Elise."

His teeth raked down her throat, and Elise felt him push her back onto the table. Felt his arm come out and sweep a stack of magazines onto the carpet as he crawled over her. Dragging her farther up the table, Christian set his powerful arms on either side of her head, and took her mouth again, thrusting into the recesses of her mouth, almost into her throat. It was good to feel his mouth possess her, to yield to his unrelenting pressure and draw his tongue deep into her mouth. In the dim light, she listened as her own breath sped up. Listened to her heart pound against his. Felt his hand cup her breast and rub her nipple until it hardened and made her arch, aching for more.

It was so easy to let him seize control, to shut away all thought of discovery, and simply lie beneath him, savoring the raw, sweet pleasure of his touch. Unable to hold back, she strained instinctively upward, urging her body against his as a physical need built inside her, drawing her to him as if only Christian could assuage it. As if of its own volition, her hand went to his trousers, molding the hard ridge of his erection with her palm and fingers. She was oddly emboldened by the darkness. "Christian, now please . . ." she heard herself whisper.

"Elise," he choked, his tongue sliding down her neck, down her chest, delving hotly into the cleft between her breasts. "God almighty, Elise."

She lay halfway up the length of the table now, the baize surface rough and cool beneath her back. She felt his hand go skimming up her stocking, felt her leg bared to the thigh and higher still. Christian fumbled with the slit of her drawers and tore it open. She gasped when his fingers stroked her flesh, gliding between the folds already swollen and moist to his touch.

"Elise," he muttered again. "So sweet."

Elise closed her eyes and fought for sanity. Alarm bells should be ringing in her head. The word *no* should spring unhesitatingly to her lips. But Elise seemed unable to form intent. Could think of nothing but having him inside her, easing her torment. Again, as if she'd willed it, her hips lifted, inviting him to claim her. Christian's hands worked frantically at the close of his trousers. His lips were pressed tight, his breath dragging in and out through his nose as he released himself. She could see the swollen head of his shaft rise up. In the dimness, it was not so intimidating.

Oh, she should *not*. What sort of fool did this? But the chance to love swiftly and mindlessly was too tempting to resist; the risk of being caught was like a wicked aphrodisiac. On a soft cry, she reached out and seized him, slicking her hand down his length, awed by the power she felt stir inside the warm, bulging veins and satiny flesh.

On her next stroke, Christian's head went back, and Elise sensed his spine draw taut as a bowstring, felt his whole body shudder with restraint. "Christian, please," she whimpered, lifting her hips, aching for the weight and power of him. "Now. *Please.*"

He hardly needed to be told twice. On her second *please,* he shoved her legs wide with his knee, and without a word of warning, thrust himself home—deeply home—on a desperate grunt. Swift. Furious. Elise jerked at the sudden invasion. The heavy, searing heat filled her, stretched her beyond belief. But Christian clasped her hips, stilling her to take his powerful thrusts. "Oh, Elise. So—sorry. Can't—oh, God. Can't wait."

The rhythm was driving, pounding, and dragging her with it. It should have hurt. It should have seemed cheap and crude to ruck up her skirts and let herself be mounted on top of a table. But it was neither. Instead, the relentless pounding became a pleasure. She wrapped both legs around his waist and clutched at him. Christian's soft sounds mingled with hers as his fierce rhythm caught her up in its cadence. Pleasure and pain simmered and swirled, then leapt to full flame.

Elise fought him, and fought to pull against him, hungering for something she barely understood. Yearning to drown in that sweet, pulsing sensation which he'd shown her once before. Willingly, she arched her hips and let him drive deep. And when his long, warm fingers drew down the ruching of her ball gown, and the heat of his mouth found the hard peak of her breast, biting and suckling like some wild animal, Elise thought she would die. An invisible spiral of lust writhed inside her, twisting from her breast to her belly and into her womb. Uncontrollably, her back bowed and her climax seized her, fast and hard, jerking at her insides with a searing pleasure.

Holding her gaze with a wild, shocked expression, Christian arched his spine and withdrew almost fully, then sank himself deep on one last stroke. His head went back until the tendons of his neck strained, and then he exploded, washing her with the warmth of his seed as he jerked and shuddered. "Oh, Elise, Elise." He whispered her name with every spasm.

It seemed a very long time before he finally fell against her, his breath heaving in and out of his chest as though driven by bellows. Christian dropped his forehead to hers, and she felt his perspiration cool against her skin. "God almighty, woman," he groaned. "Loving you will surely be the death of me."

But Elise could not find her voice to ask him what he meant. It had all been too raw, too visceral. *Too magnificent.* Her heart still pounded in her chest. But one thing was now crystal clear. However exaggerated his other habits might be, the wicked marquis had fairly earned his reputation as a lover. Elise no longer cared if Christian made her act more like a whore than a lady, and if she were dancing down the road to ruin, at least she liked the tune.

But Christian, it seemed, was suffering a pang of conscience. He lifted his weight onto his hands and sat back, allowing his trousers and drawers to slide halfway down a pair of thickly-muscled thighs. His eyes drifted about the room, as if he were not perfectly sure where they were. "God, Elise." It was a horrified whisper. "I cannot believe I did this. To you. *Here.*"

Elise held out her hands, and he grasped her fingers in his. "I cannot claim to have voiced any complaint," she murmured. At that, Christian closed his eyes and shook his head, a soft laugh escaping his mouth.

And then, they heard it.

The muted squeal of a door hinge. Then a muffled, bubbly giggle.

"*Christ Jesus—!*" Christian was off her in a flash, shoving in shirttails and yanking down skirts as if the house were suddenly afire.

"*Shh—!*" Elise sat up, jerking her bodice up as she tilted her head toward the left wall. "Through the door," she softly mouthed. "It's *Lucy!* In Maynard's study!"

Christian hitched up his trousers, casting an assessing eye over Elise as he buttoned them. Another light, feminine laugh could be heard through the heavy wood panel. "Come on, Elise," he whispered, extending his hand to her. "Out! Now!"

But Elise shook her head and clambered off the table. "Christian, I know that giggle. Someone is up to no good."

"Yes," he murmured dryly. "And we know just how easily that can happen, do we not?"

Elise blushed. "Well, at least I am no innocent virgin," she answered. "And if we don't sort this out, someone else might."

For a long moment, he hesitated, and then with a

shrug, Christian crossed to the window and took up the lamp. With Elise dogging his footsteps, they tiptoed through the shadows toward the door. Christian laid his hand on the brass doorknob just as something thumped hard against the adjacent wall.

"Oh, Lord!" groaned Elise.

With a soft oath, Christian jerked open the door and entered, Elise hard on his heels. But at once, he stopped short and spun about, his elbow almost clipping Elise's temple as he slapped a hand over his eyes. "Good God!" he exclaimed. "Miss Onslow!"

On an angry gasp, Elise pushed past Christian just as Lord Robert Rowland shoved Lucy off his lap. But Elise could not miss Lucy's wet, just-kissed mouth, nor the ample display of feminine flesh which Lord Robert had apparently been admiring. "Lucinda Onslow, you minx!" declared Elise.

Lucy burst at once into tears. "Aunt Elise!"

As Lucy struggled awkwardly to hitch up her gaping dress, Lord Robert jerked to his feet. He was shifting anxiously back and forth, as if unsure whether he'd be better served by soothing Lucy or placating her aunt. But the young man hesitated a moment too long, giving Elise the opportunity to turn on him. "What are you two thinking?" she demanded of him. "I daresay your mother will have you whipped within an inch of your life! I ought to do it myself! *That* is an innocent, untouched girl!" Her voice was steadily rising as she stabbed one finger at her cringing niece.

Christian caught Elise firmly by the shoulder and shoved his weight between them. "Shush, my dear," he demanded, drawing her gently against his side. "Should anyone overhear you, we'll have a worse scandal than this on our hands."

Elise's hand clamped over her mouth as her eyes flew open wide. Lucy drew one last pitiful snivel, and Christian raked his gaze down Lord Robert. "Boy, how old are you?" he gritted out.

"Eighteen, s-sir," he stammered. "Almost."

Christian eyed him in cold disapprobation. "Then there's little question what must happen next, is there?"

Lucy gave another withering sob and pressed one fist to her mouth. Lord Robert lost what little remained of his color. "Do you mean . . . t-t-to call me out, sir?"

Christian gave a soft, bitter laugh. "Good God, no! I wouldn't trouble myself to swab out my pistol barrels over a whelp like you," he retorted. "But what I will do is take a horsewhip to your bare backside if I catch you pawing that girl again before you've the benefit of a parson."

Lucy wailed again. "Oh, Elise, no—!" Like a skittish colt, she shot a tremulous glance toward Christian. "He c-can't make me! Can he?"

Elise set her hands on her hips. "Make you *what*, Lucy?"

"M-Marry him—!" The withering gaze turned on Lord Robert.

Christian's cold, silvery eyes shot sudden sparks. "And have you some better solution, Miss Onslow?" he snapped. "Your reputation is now in tatters."

Lord Robert stepped forward, blinking nervously. "*Marriage?*" the lad choked, looking as if he'd vastly prefer the horse-whipping. "Why, I c-can't get married! I'm not of age!"

Christian leaned into him with barely tethered malevolence. "If you're bold enough to press your attentions on an innocent, sir, then you are old enough to be caught in the parson's mousetrap," he said grimly. "Your stepfather will, I have no doubt, sign the appropriate papers."

Lucy was crying in earnest now. Elise pressed one hand against Christian's chest and pushed him back onto his heels. "Now just stop, all of you!" she softly demanded. "What is this, Lucy? Have you no wish to marry?"

"Oh, Aunt Elise, not to *him!*" sniveled Lucy. "I've not even had a Season! I was only practicing my f-f-feminine wiles . . ."

At that, Lord Robert spun on his heel and gaped at Lucy. Lucy looked at her aunt and heaved another awful sob. Elise pressed her lips tightly together and cast Christian a somewhat desperate glance. His eyes were black and narrow, his fists balled up as if Lucy were his own daughter. Lamely, Elise sighed. "Christian, we've no choice," she said. "This must be hushed up. Even if Lucy were willing, and even if Lord Robert's parents permitted it, neither is mature enough for marriage."

"Yes, and they haven't a thimbleful of brains between them," he growled. But slowly, the tension left Christian's shoulders and an angry sigh escaped his lips. "Oh, bloody hell!" he grumbled, fixing his steely gaze on Lucy. "I cannot believe this! Miss Onslow, dry your eyes and go straight up the servants' stairs to your room. Then get on your knees and thank God for your aunt's restraint. And for pity's sake, child, save those feminine wiles for your husband, else you aren't apt to get one."

Lucy all but tripped over her skirts as she hastened from the room, bobbing and curtsying, and all the while clutching at the front of her dress. Christian turned his glower upon Robert as soon as the door clicked shut. "You, young man, will go out onto the veranda and await your stepfather's wrath. I mean to have a word with him. And I have little doubt as to how he will deal with you."

When Lord Robert looked as if he might protest, Christian grabbed him by his neckcloth and heaved him toward the door. "And should so much as a whisper of this pass your lips," Christian warned, "I'll drag your scrawny little arse to the nearest boxing salon, and beat all but the breath of life out of you. Then I'll take what little is left home to your mama, where she will, I suspect, exact a far worse punishment."

All his color gone, Lord Robert mumbled his gratitude, and more or less promised to cut out his tongue. Christian gave him one last nasty look. "Fine! Now get out before I lose what's left of my warmth and compassion!"

Lord Robert darted for the door and jerked it open. But at the last second, he spun about, his eyes suddenly narrowed. "A curious thing, though, Grayston," he said very quietly. "You never did mention what *you* were doing here."

"Out!" roared the marquis.

The door thumped shut. Dragging one hand through his hair, Christian turned to face Elise. "Well," he announced on a sigh. "I don't know how it came to this, Elise. I really don't. I have no experience—and even less business—in lecturing young men about their morals."

Elise leaned into him and rested her hands against his chest. "But it was admirably done, sir."

His eyes flashed with mild exasperation. Then swiftly, he kissed her and dragged her back into the library. "Wait for me here, Elise," he ordered, his voice grim. "It is time we had a serious talk, you and I. As soon as I'm done with Amherst."

Chapter Ten

❦

The course of true love never did run smooth.
—Shakespeare

In the void which existed in Christian's wake, Elise paced up and down the length of the library, hugging her arms to her body. Mere moments ago, the room had been infused with his masculine warmth, but now it felt cold and a bit desolate. Along the long row of windows, she paused to light more lamps in some hope of dispelling the sudden sense of emptiness. Fleetingly, she considered ordering a fire laid, then thought better of it. She was not at all sure that her untidy hair and slightly disheveled gown would go unnoticed by Ophelia's sharp-eyed servants. And so she strolled back along the row of reading tables which bisected the long room, rubbing her arms for warmth, and listening to the echo of her muted footsteps. Waiting. Just waiting. For Christian.

What a strange night it had been, she thought, skimming one fingertip over the surface of the table where they had done it. *Where they had made love.* At the memory of her wanton behavior, Elise felt heat flood her face.

She'd never done anything so risqué in her life. And oh, how she had enjoyed it! True to his word, the wicked marquis had seduced her well and proper, and Elise refused to make excuses for her behavior. She, who had always lived such a virtuous life, had finally yielded to one of the most blatant rakes in Christendom. Because she had learned the hard way that virtue would warm neither her heart nor her bed. But the memories of Christian's lovemaking—oh, that just might.

No, she would not make a total fool of herself over him, she vowed, kneeling to gather up the stack of magazines they'd scattered across the floor. She had Henriette to consider. But perhaps Christian was not quite the hell-bound scoundrel he wished people to think. She had been pondering it for days now. One had only to remember his reaction to Henriette's accident and his indignation over Lord Robert's ungentlemanly conduct to realize that Christian possessed just a little more honor than he wished to admit. Still, Elise could not allow herself to give words to that emotion which had blossomed against all hope and wisdom in her heart. Words sometimes gave rise to desperation, and desperation to recklessness.

Absently, Elise sat down and began to thumb through one of Ophelia's fashion periodicals. Really, why was she fretting over the future, when she so clearly did not have one? Not with the Marquis of Grayston. He would soon be on his way back to Paris, gone forever from her life. He had been quite clear on that point. He was the sort of rogue a woman took a night's pleasure from, he had said. Well, that was precisely what he'd given her—pure, blood-firing pleasure—brief though it had been. And that was all it could ever be.

But despite such high-minded resolve, when the library door swung open on near-silent hinges, hope leapt at once into Elise's heart. She sprang to her feet, and whirled about. But it was not Christian who entered. Denys stood on the threshold. Of late, his mood had grown increasingly black, and tonight he looked as if he had come with an unmistakable sense of purpose.

"Elise, my dear," he began, the censure in his voice subtle but unmistakable. "Why are you not in the ballroom? I have been searching the house for you."

Elise managed a wan smile and sat back down. "A touch of the headache," she murmured. It was not a lie, for suddenly, her head was pounding. "I thought I would not be missed."

Swiftly he closed the distance, and pulled out his own chair. He took her lightly by the hand, but there was little warmth in his touch. "Lord Grayston has also vanished," he said flatly. "I trust that arrogant dog has not been making a nuisance of himself?"

Elise cut her eyes toward the door. "No," she said quite truthfully. "He certainly has not. But really, Denys, you need not concern yourself."

Suddenly, he rose from his chair and strode across the room to the empty hearth. "Damn him!" he swore, pounding his fist on the chimney-piece. "Elise, what does he mean by coming here to Gotherington? *What—?*" His anger was almost palpable.

"I am sure, Denys, that I have no notion."

But it was as if he did not hear her. Instead, he set

one slipper on the fender, crossed his arms almost petulantly, and glared into the depths of the room. "All week he has thought himself such a clever fellow," Denys growled. "Such wit! Such charm! And in the field, always the first to shoulder his weapon. Always choosing the most difficult shot—just to see who he can impress! And his incessant flirtations! Elise, I find it appalling."

"Perhaps we should remember that he has been living on the Continent." Elise kept her tone cool and formal. "And I daresay his presence here is more Maynard's business than ours. After all, Lord Grayston is his friend."

Denys's fingers seemed to dig into the marble mantel. "Elise, do you really believe that?" he asked bitterly. "Mark me, men of his ilk do not trot off to the country in search of fresh air. And Maynard! What a joke! He turns white as a sheet whenever Grayston comes within ten paces."

Elise wanted to argue, but she could not quite find her voice. Denys had given words to something which had long troubled her. Indeed, Ophelia had never warmed toward Christian, and it was almost as if Maynard tolerated his presence rather than welcomed it. "Still," she said, "it is none of our business."

At last, he returned to his chair and sat down with a sigh. "No, perhaps not." To her shock, he leaned forward to gather both her hands into his own, and gave them a reassuring squeeze. "Oh, to hell with Grayston. We must talk about *us.*"

Elise began to shake her head, but Denys cut her off very firmly. "I know I have promised not to pressure you," he said quietly. "But really, Elise, it is time we made firm plans for our future. I know that Ophelia—Henry's own sister—favors my suit. And trust me, my dear, you need the guidance of a man, and the sooner the better."

Elise did not like his suddenly patronizing tone. "Do I?" She sat a little straighter in her chair. "How fortunate I am that you are willing to sacrifice yourself on the altar."

"My dear, it is no sacrifice whatsoever." He had not caught the sarcasm in her words.

Indeed, the more she studied him, the more on edge Denys appeared to be. What could have happened to rattle him so thoroughly? It was time to put an end to this charade once and for all. "Denys," she firmly began. "I am sorry to say this, but—"

To her shock, Denys interrupted again by lightly pressing one finger to her lips. "Please, my dear, let me finish." His tone was stern yet tender. "Elise, I could not but overhear your discussion with Amherst tonight. My dear, you are the very soul of generosity, but trust me when I say it would be best if you deferred such serious financial decisions. It is unseemly for a well-bred lady to worry her head with matters of money. Especially when someone else is willing to bear those burdens for her."

It took a moment to absorb his words. And then, for one awful moment, it was as if time were suspended by a thread. As if Elise's heart had thudded to a halt in her breast. Then suspicion struck her like a dash of cold water, and left her emotionally gasping. Words—no, *warnings*—began to swim in her head. *A man's character never alters, Elise,* he had whispered. *Unlike some men, I will never hide from you my true nature—or my motives.* She tried to catch her breath. *Surely, Elise, you cannot mean to marry that fortune hunter?*

But Denys did not look like a fortune hunter. Did he—? Good God, was she too naïve to know? He was smiling, and holding her hands quite gently. But his palms were cold and damp. His face was pale, his forehead beaded with sweat. And he was anxious; he'd been so since the moment he entered the room, she realized. No—since the moment he'd arrived at Gotherington. And suddenly, she was certain. Horribly certain. Oh, Denys was clever. Very, very clever.

But Elise could be clever, too. "You are referring to yourself, are you not?" she asked, forcing her voice to be light and uncertain. "You think that I have misjudged in giving half my fortune to Belinda and Lucy? I daresay you're right. Perhaps I ought to reconsider the amount?"

Denys smiled as if she were a confused child. "I am glad you understand," he answered, lightly patting her hand. "You will tell Amherst that your financial decisions must wait until we are wed, so that you need not be bothered with such matters."

The devil was in her then, and Elise did not know why. "Yes, Denys, as you wish," she conceded as she came gracefully to her feet. "And how very generous you are. I cannot wait to see Mr. Amherst's face when he learns the extent of your kindness."

"Kindness?" Denys rose from his chair uncertainly.

Brightly, Elise smiled. "Do you know, Denys, this almost obscene wealth Sir Henry bestowed upon me has in some ways been rather a burden. When you are rich, you can never be quite certain that you are loved unselfishly. But at last, you have lifted that weight from my shoulders."

She pretended to head toward the door. Just as she'd expected, Denys thrust out a staying hand, catching her hard by the shoulder. "Elise, my love, I'm afraid you have quite lost me." His words were gentle, but his fingers were digging into her flesh. "What, precisely, do you mean to tell Amherst?"

Her smile still plastered on her lips, Elise turned to face him. "Why, that you mean to support me, so that the girls might enjoy the whole of my fortune. Is that not what you meant?"

Denys's skin had drained of color, leaving his mouth tight and grim. "My God, have you totally lost your mind, Elise?" he hissed. "We cannot possibly live on my income."

Elise lifted her brows and let her gaze sweep down his length. "But you are always so well turned out," she murmured. "Such fine clothes and horses and guns. Dear me, Denys. Have you a great many debts which must be settled? Perhaps I shan't be able to afford that dowry after all."

Denys opened and closed his mouth soundlessly, clearly confused. "Well, of course I have debts, my love," he said, his face flushing lightly. "A gentleman has expenses."

"Oh, dear!" cooed Elise. "And are your creditors pressing you quite ruthlessly?"

His color deepened. At last, it seemed Denys was catching on to her sarcasm. "Elise, do you mean to speak to Amherst, or not?"

Elise let a bitter smile curve her mouth. "No, I do not,

and never did," she answered, turning again toward the door. "Really, Denys, what manner of fool have you taken me for?"

But he grabbed her shoulder again, his touch quite ruthless. "Damn you, Elise!" he growled. "You cannot do this! You have teased me and led me on for weeks now."

With deliberate slowness, she turned and lifted his trembling hand from her arm. "I have been nothing but honest with you, Denys," she murmured. "A courtesy which you have not deigned to return, it would now appear."

He shook her again, more harshly still. "By God, you'll not do this to me, Elise!" he whispered, his face a mask of rage. "I know what this is about! You have been listening to Grayston! He wants to see me ruined! That duplicitous bastard!"

Lightly, she lifted her brows. "Oh, I begin to see who the duplicitous bastard is in this little charade," she said quietly. "And I have been listening to nothing but my common sense. Now unhand me, Denys."

"No, damn you!" To her shock, he seized her quite viciously, shaking her until her teeth rattled. "Tell me! Tell me what he claims to know! What evidence does he have? How has he turned you against me?"

His grip was tightening, the muscle in his jaw working furiously. Elise felt a sudden spike of real fear. What a fool she had been to threaten him. The man was half-insane. How could she have failed to notice? "Take your hands off me, Mr. Roth," she ordered, struggling to turn away. "Or I shall scream the truth about you so loudly, everyone in the ballroom will hear."

In a flash, he seized her face in his hand, twisting it back into his. "Why, you goddamned slut!" he whispered malevolently. "I see the way of this! Grayston just wheedled his way between your legs, and—"

Roth did not complete his sentence. Instead, his shirt collar suddenly cut into his throat as Christian hauled him backward and slammed his skull into a row of encyclopedias. Stunned, Denys folded like a house of cards. For a moment, Christian simply stood there, his legs spread wide, his expression dark as Hades, glaring down as Denys staggered awkwardly to his feet. "That sounded perilously like an insult, Mr. Roth," he finally murmured. "And your language was appallingly foul. I believe an apology to the lady is order."

"Fuck off, Grayston," snarled Roth, shrugging his coat back into place.

For a heartbeat, Christian was silent. "Well," he said quietly. "It would appear that some things in life are simply preordained." Withdrawing an elaborate gold watch from his pocket, he snapped it open. "Mr. Roth, I fear we must meet. In about—oh, seven hours. Will that suit?"

"Christian, this is insane!" whispered Elise, starting forward.

Christian threw out an arm to stop her. Roth shot Elise a look of pure venom, then returned his glower to Christian. "This has been your plan all along, hasn't it, Grayston?" he sneered, jerking straight the knot of his neckcloth. "I'd wager you didn't know so much as Maynard Onslow's name until a fortnight past."

Christian looked at him in icy disdain. "I cannot think what you mean to imply, Roth," he answered. "Now if you would be so good as to name your second and your weapon?"

For a moment, Roth hesitated. "Onslow, then, damn you!" he finally spit out. "I somehow suspect he shall rather enjoy my putting a chunk of lead through your heart."

"Pistols it is," said Christian coldly. "I shall ask Treyhern to oblige me and make the appropriate arrangements. And now, Roth, take yourself off before I decide to kill you where you stand. I've already ruined enough of Onslow's carpets."

"Good God!" shrieked Elise as soon as the door slammed shut. "Have you lost your wits?"

But Christian's eyes had gone flat and cold. "Evil cannot go unpunished, Elise," he said, his voice as wintry as his gaze. "It simply cannot. Besides, Roth leaves me no choice now."

Elise reached out to touch him, but somehow, the gesture weakened and died. "Oh, no," she whispered. "No, no, no. Tell me you do not mean to risk a life over mere words—words spoken by a fool in the heat of anger?"

"Your pardon, Elise," said the marquis. "But for whom are you concerned?"

Mutely, Elise shook her head. "Dear Lord, how can you even ask?" she finally answered, her face twisting with anguish. "I am concerned for *you!* Should you miss—"

"Oh, I won't," he interjected, his certainty chilling. "I never do. It is but one of my many well-honed talents."

At once, Elise felt the hot well of tears threaten. "How dare you make a joke of it, Christian?" she cried. "What if you do kill him? What good will that do me? Is my honor to be salvaged at the cost of my heart? Must I watch you leave England forever and . . . *oh, my God."*

She looked at him in horror, but Christian made no answer. "Christian," she pleaded. "Tell me this is not what you came here to do. Tell me that Denys is wrong."

But he stood before her, silent and still, no longer the man she thought she knew. That handsome man with the laughing eyes and chagrined expression—the one who had just made love to her so recklessly and so passionately—yes, he had vanished. And before her stood a cold-eyed stranger. The Marquis of Grayston. A calculating gamester who could wager on life, death, or the turn of a card with the same equanimity. Or so it seemed to Elise. But was she even capable of separating the reality from a façade? After all, she had once thought Denys was as decent as Grayston was wicked.

Suddenly, Elise wanted a harsh, black line drawn between right and wrong. A code of conduct which was not subject to interpretation. Not this perplexing duality of purpose, this divergence of character. Could a man be both so ruthless and so kind? She did not know. And it seemed that Christian had grown weary of staring at her hand. The hand which no longer reached out to him. She watched as he turned and walked stiffly toward the door without another word. At once, Elise jerked into motion, following him. "Call this off, Christian," she begged. "Whatever your purpose—whatever wrong you hope to right— it serves no one's purpose. Stop it!"

He laid his hand flat against the door and bowed his head, refusing to look at her. "I cannot, Elise," he said quietly. "You know that honor precludes it."

Elise reached past him and seized the doorknob. "You used to brag that you were without honor, my lord," she answered hollowly. "For a time, I actually believed it. And I think I understood you better then."

He laughed a little cynically. "Perhaps you saw only what you wished to see."

Almost imperceptibly, Elise shook her head. "Then what a fool I was," she whispered. "For I had fallen half in love with him—that man who could so blithely claim to be one thing, and yet live his life quite honorably."

At last, the marquis turned from the door to face her, his expression shattered, his mouth twisted with what looked like bitter pain. Then just as swiftly, it was gone. "Remember, Elise," he said quietly. "There can be honor even amongst thieves. But that does not make them virtuous." And then, the door was open, and he had vanished into the shadows.

Chapter Eleven

Never make a defence or apology before you be accused.
—Charles I

*I*t took Christian but a few moments to slip back into the ballroom and make his request of Treyhern. As always, the earl was reticent, but he agreed to serve, and went at once in search of Roth to see if an apology could be elicited. Christian nodded tightly, and went off to find Amherst. He did not think Roth would apologize, for he feared too much what Christian might know. And Christian was not at all sure he wanted an apology. He had come here, he reminded himself, to kill Roth. Moreover, just when he had begun to doubt the righteousness of his intentions, fate had laid open a path. It was a sign. He must go forward. It was meant to be.

He found Amherst standing near the veranda doors, his expression almost as black as Christian's mood. "I have taken care of Robert," said the vicar grimly. "Another such trick, and he'll be sporting a blistered backside and a pair of colors. I thank you for handling the matter with such discretion."

Christian stared past him and into the darkness

beyond the veranda. "You may return the favor now, if you will?" His voice was without emotion. When Amherst lifted his brows, Christian turned and let his eyes run over the still-crowded ballroom. "There was a solicitor here from the village," he murmured. "Ah, yes— that balding fellow who is at present boring Lady Trey-hern to tears? Would you be so obliging as to fetch him up to my bedchamber in half an hour? There are some legal documents which I must execute. It must be discreetly done, and with a credible witness."

Without answering Amherst's look of surprise, Christian went at once to his room and laid out a sheaf of papers. Then after excusing Stallings for the night, he took out the banded rosewood box which was never far from his side. He snapped back the lock, then lifted his double-barreled dueling pistols and their various accoutrements from their blue baize casings. The monogrammed escutcheons winked in the lamplight as he turned each weapon this way and that, methodically inspecting them. It was a ritual he had performed more times than he allowed himself to remember. But this time, the precise preparations which he performed like some bizarre sort of sacrament brought him no peace.

Carefully, he gripped one. Cold and heavy in his hand, the weapon did not seem to balance properly tonight. He was almost relieved when he heard Amherst's knock. "You wished a document drawn, my lord?" said the rotund, meticulous-looking gentleman who followed the vicar into the room.

Christian motioned both men toward a small escritoire. "A conveyance for a piece of property," he said very quietly. "And I wish it done with the utmost care, so that there can be no question of my intent should some—er—misfortune befall me."

"Wise, very wise!" murmured the solicitor, seating himself and taking up a sheet of paper. "Now which property, and to whom?"

"This one," said Christian softly, his eyes catching and holding Amherst's. "Gotherington, and all its contents, acreage, and tenancies. To Major and Mrs. Maynard Onslow. And once that is done, sir, would you be good enough to draw me a will?"

It was late, long past midnight and far too close to dawn when Elise dredged up the nerve to go to him. The fact that she would be striding into a gentleman's bedchamber uninvited—and worse, that she scarcely knew what she meant to do once she got there—did not strike her as unusual. Nothing about this night had been usual, and Elise was almost beyond expecting that her life would ever be normal again.

Christian answered the door on her first knock, and she slipped inside. There was a lamp still lit by the bedside. He wore a sapphire silk dressing gown and little else, save a heavy shadow of beard. Both his bed linen and his hair were disheveled, as if he had attempted to sleep, and found that Morpheus eluded him. She looked up into his eyes, which were still cold and utterly without emotion. Again, he looked so very like the man she had seen sprawled by the tavern hearth, it took her breath for a moment.

He did not seem surprised to see her. Slowly, he let his gaze slide down her nightclothes, and when he saw her bare toes peeping from beneath her blue flannel wrapper, he gave that strange, rueful smile of his. "Are you some sort of angel, Elise, come to ease my final night on earth? If so, rest easy. Roth has not a prayer."

Elise pushed past him. "Do not bother to act the heartless gamester with me, Christian," she said grimly. "I know you for the fraud you are. And Denys probably hasn't fought a duel in his life. He's too craven."

Christian's brows arched at that. "Figured him out at last, have you?" he murmured, following her into the depths of his bedchamber.

She whirled about to face him, but he was lingering at his small dressing table, absently picking over his toiletries. "Oh, just stop it, Christian!" she demanded, her anger further fueled by his nonchalance. "Denys's fate is not what concerns me."

In the pier glass above the table, she saw him lift his chin and shoot her a blasé look. "Then what does, pray?" His voice was soft but impatient. "Elise, really, I need my rest."

She pointed a tremulous finger at the face in the mirror. "And I need the truth, Christian!" she insisted. "I think you owe me that, after . . . after what we have been to one another."

Lightly, he laughed. "Elise, my dear, do you imagine I make it a practice to be honest with the women I bed?" he asked, turning from the mirror. "Good Lord, I'd have been knifed in my sleep years ago."

Her eyes fell upon the rosewood box, laid open on a marquetry table by the window. Even in the lamplight, the barrels reflected a dull sheen. "You came prepared, I see."

"Always," he said dryly. "A man in my line of work finds it necessary."

She had begun to pace the room, but she jerked at once to a halt and walked purposefully toward him. "Damn you," she whispered, looking straight up into his silvery eyes. "Damn you for what you have done to me, Christian."

For the merest instant, he faltered. "To which of my sins do you refer, Elise?"

She resumed her pacing, the blue flannel whipping wildly about her ankles. "You let me see the merest glimpse of the man who hides beneath all that conceit and fury," she snapped. "A good man. A decent man. And that was what I fell in love with, Christian. Not your charm. Not your looks. And now you have the gall to stand there and insult my intelligence? Stop it! Just stop it right now!"

But he was looking at her incredulously, his face drained of all color. "Oh, you do not know me, Elise," he said quietly. "You really do not."

And then he surprised her by going to the bed and sitting down on the edge of the mattress. It was as if something inside him had crumpled inward. Christian let his head fall forward, pressing the heel of one hand against his eye socket. "What, then, Elise?" he asked hoarsely as he stared down into the carpet. "What the devil do you wish to know? I'll tell you. And then I want you to get the hell out of here, before one of us says or does something we will forever regret."

She had followed him through the room to the bed, and simply stood looking down at him. "I want to know if any of Denys's allegations are true." The emotion had left her voice now. "And I want to know why Maynard invited you here."

Until that moment, she had not noticed the sheaf of papers which lay atop his rumpled bed. He snatched it up, and thrust it at her. A little fearfully, Elise turned it toward the lamp. After a moment, she looked up at Christian, her expression blank.

"When I want something, Elise," he said grimly, "I get it. By hook or crook, it matters not one whit to me."

For a moment, Elise could not find her voice. "And so you took this from Maynard?" she finally asked, trying to make sense of what she'd just read. "At the card table? And then you—you forced . . ."

"*Blackmailed*, Elise," he interjected. "It is called blackmail. Are you too innocent to know what that is?"

Elise tossed the conveyance down beside the lamp. "I know what it is," she answered, sitting down beside him on the bed. "What I want to know is why. What is the score you wish to settle with Denys? Do you not owe me that much, Christian?"

At last, he looked up at her. His eyes were no longer cold. "I—yes, perhaps I do," he said quietly. "That, and a vast deal more, I do not doubt. But my quarrel with Denys has to do with my sister as much as it has to do with his unutterable discourtesy to you."

Elise looked at him in amazement. "With *Lenora?*"

Christian lifted his chin, and stared up into the bed hangings. "That bastard seduced her, and left her with child." He clasped his hands between his knees, an oddly boyish gesture. "She tried to reach me by letter, but as usual, I was flitting about Europe. She had no one else. No one. My father—he cared very little for her. I believe she thought he would make her life a living hell when he found out. I wish I could say that she was wrong."

"Oh, my God," whispered Elise.

Christian shook his head. "She was such easy prey for the likes of Roth. I do not doubt for one moment she thought herself loved, and in love. Had my father not been such an egregious snob—had he not hesitated to approve the marriage—perhaps she would have eventually seen the truth. Or perhaps not. But one thing is certain. She would not have taken her own life."

"Christian, why would Denys do such a thing?"

"Listen to me, Elise!" At last, Christian looked straight into her eyes, and gripped her shoulders hard, as if the pain would force her to absorb his words. "Roth's creditors have become merciless. He is ruined, and he is desperate. The man is a predator. Whatever happens, you *must* stay away from him. He tricked Lenora, and told her that if she were with child, nothing would stand in the way of their marriage. God only knows what ruse he might try with you."

"But Lenora did not marry him?" Elise's voice was weak.

"No," he bit out. "Somewhere between his sweet persuasions, he met someone else."

"Someone else? After he had . . . ?" Elise could not get the rest of the words out.

Christian laughed bitterly. "An American heiress with a dowry thrice Lenora's. Within the month, he set sail, following her family back to Boston without so much as writing Lenora to see if she carried his child. But his golden goose caught a chill, and lingered on her deathbed for weeks. She didn't live to see her wedding day."

Elise bent one knee and turned toward him on the bed. "Christian, I am so sorry." Gently, she cupped one hand on his stubbled cheek and turned his face into hers. "You must believe I did not realize the truth of Denys's character until tonight. But you must also know that killing him will not bring Lenora back. I beg you not to do this. For us, I beg you."

Again, he shook his head. "Elise, are you a fool? Don't you realize what I've done? And there is no us. Were those not your very words some three days past?"

Elise blinked back the tears which threatened. "Perhaps I must accept that," she said, her voice choking just a little. "But when tomorrow comes, what am I to tell Henriette? That you have killed Mr. Roth, and run away forever to France? Or worse, that he has put a ball through your heart? She is nine years old, Christian. And she believes that you hung the moon. So what, pray, am I to tell her?"

Christian shook his head. "Oh, no, Elise," he said grimly. "You will not do this to me. You are not going to make me feel responsible for a child's welfare and happiness."

For once, Elise let her posture sag. "Oh, Christian, I won't have to," she answered very softly. "I think you will do that yourself. Is that not the very thing which has brought you to this awful crossroads? Your infinite sense of responsibility? Your concern for Lenora? Your belief that had you stayed with her, you could have somehow kept her safe and happy?"

"Do not make me out some sort of saint, Elise."

"Oh, I don't!" Her tone was emphatic. "You are just a man, and one with more than a few shortcomings. But you have honor, and an almost infinite capacity to feel guilt. In short, you are very human. And that is why you will suffer for this, as you have suffered over Lenora.

Killing Roth will not expiate your sins, it will but add to them."

"You have asked me why, Elise." His face was again emotionless. "And I have entrusted to you my sister's secrets. She is buried in hallowed soil, and her name is unblemished, thank God. But this one last thing, I must do for her."

"Then I suppose we must add *loyal* to your list of virtues," she said quietly. "And it is just one more reason why I love you."

He surprised her then by taking both her hands in his, and leaning slowly forward to press his lips to her forehead. "Oh, you are such a fool, Elise," he whispered, brushing his mouth over her eyebrow. "You do not love me. What you feel is lust, pure and powerful."

Elise let her eyes drop shut and savored the feel of his lips feathering over her eyes, down her cheek, then over her jawbone. "Are you really going to do this, Christian?" she whispered. "Are you going through with this no matter what I say?"

"I am." Delicately, his tongue touched the swell of her bottom lip.

His merest touch was enough to make her pulse climb. "Then make love to me, Christian," she begged, her eyes still closed. "Make love to me just once more."

His hands went to her shoulders, and he gave her a little shake. "It won't change my mind," he whispered. "Open your eyes, Elise, and tell me that you know it will be just sex."

She shook her head and pressed her eyes tighter still. "Tomorrow you will leave," she said, apropos of nothing. And everything.

And then, he was on his knees beside her, the mattress creaking beneath his weight. She felt his hands run through her hair, from the temples and all the way down her back. "It is just for tonight, Elise," he whispered. "That is all it can be."

"Just for tonight," she echoed.

His hands went to the throat of her robe, and deftly undid it. "Let me see you, Elise," he demanded gruffly. "Take this off."

She swallowed hard and felt the rush of heat wash through her as Christian loomed over her, the breadth of his chest shutting out the lamplight. Quickly, a little desperately, he stripped away her clothing, and when her gown breezed up, baring her breasts and teasing her nipples, he made a little growling sound in his throat. "My God," he whispered. "Oh, my God, Elise."

Christian set his hands on the turn of her waist and slid his thumbs up and over her ribs, until her breasts were held captive in his fingers. Gently, he ran his thumbs around and around her nipples and then he leaned into her, kissing her. But Elise wanted more. Much more. She felt suddenly alive with her every fiber. He was dark seduction in the flesh, and his skill sent an urgency thrumming through her, a wish to be pressed down beneath the weight of his body. A wanton desire to be impaled on him, to feel the sweet pleasure and throbbing pain which only he could bring.

She shut her eyes again as his mouth closed over her left breast. His beard scraped harshly over the tender flesh as his teeth closed over her nipple, biting and sucking until her desire was drawn through her like a twisting silk ribbon. "Ah, I have to taste you, Elise," he rasped. "All over. Every sweet inch of your skin. And then I want you beneath me."

"Yes," she answered, and opened her eyes. He was staring at her, and there was something which looked like true tenderness in his gaze. "Christian . . ." she murmured, mystified. "I don't know when I came to love you. And I don't know why. I know only what is so."

She watched his throat work up and down. "Elise," he groaned. "Don't. Don't do this to me. It is not fair."

"Life is not fair, Christian, and we can rarely make it so," she whispered, reaching up to stroke his face with her fingertips. "If I do not tell you how I feel, I'm afraid I'll regret it for the rest of my life."

"God, Elise." His hands tightened on her shoulders. "When this day is done, don't ever think of me again. When I am gone, you will meet someone who deserves you. Someone who can be a good father to Henriette. Someone better than Roth, and better than me. Promise me that you will."

Weakly, she smiled. "And will you promise, Christian, that you will never think of me?" she softly returned. "Will this night not be, at the very least, a pleasant memory for you?"

The shattered expression was back. "Elise," he rasped, his eyes searching her face. "What do you want me to say? What do you want me to do?"

"Just make love to me, Christian. As if it were the last time. Because you have said that it is."

He cradled her face in his hands. "Then I will make it last for you, Elise. I will make it good enough to last for a very long time."

He opened his mouth over hers, and kissed her long

and deep, slowly molding his body to hers. She answered, sliding her hands up his chest and beneath the soft fabric of his robe, until she had eased it off his shoulders. As it parted down the center of his chest, the silk slithered off his arms and caught on his elbows, forming a pool of blue on the counterpane.

Elise drew a little away from him, and let her eyes drink in his body. Lamplight limned the breadth of his shoulders. Though she would not have believed it possible, he was more beautiful out of his clothes than in them. Gone was the sophisticated tailoring, the civilizing influence of well-starched linen, and in its place was pure, masculine splendor. His chest was smooth and layered with muscle, his arms taut with power. And there was a youthful vigor to his body that his ageless eyes belied.

She pushed away the robe, and let it slither onto the floor. Christian sat back on his heels, his erection pushing up between them. The flesh was taut and thickly veined, the tip crimson against the nest of black hair. Hesitantly, Elise reached out and took him between her palms. Christian's fingers dug at once into the flesh of her thighs, and he sucked in air between his teeth. "Ah, Elise."

A pearly drop of liquid seeped out, and curious, she touched it with the tip of one finger, smoothing around and around. He moaned again, and squeezed shut his eyes as his flesh throbbed insistently between her hands. "Ah, Elise," he said again. "So sweetly artless . . . my most dangerous fantasy come true."

"Am I?" she softly asked, stroking the full length of him.

He did not answer. Instead, he opened his eyes, seized her hands, and pushed her down onto the bed.

"Beautiful," he whispered, his eyes raking over her. "God, Elise, you are beautiful. So small and so . . . perfect." With his warm, long-fingered hands he shaped her shoulders, her waist, and the flare of her hips. His palms slid beneath the round fullness of her breasts and he massaged the tips with his thumbs. Elise arched against him, feeling wanton and desperate. He followed her down and brushed his mouth over hers, kissing her again lingeringly, as if they had a lifetime instead of an hour, his tongue circling and stroking hers as his hands stroked over her body.

He pulled away, and she looked up to see that Christian's eyes had softened again. With an impulsive gesture, he drew the weight of her hair over her shoulder. "Your crowning glory, Elise," he said, sliding his cheek over it in an almost feline adoration. "I want to make love to you, and I want it to be as beautiful as this. Tell me, Elise. Tell me how you would like it."

Elise was startled into silence. "I do not know," she admitted. "You must show me."

He lifted his cheek from her breast. "Shall I put out the lamp?"

Elise felt herself color. "No," she answered. "I want to see you, Christian. I want to remember every inch of you. I am not frightened."

He shifted his weight on top of her then, and bent his head to take her breast into his mouth. For long moments, he sucked her nipple while his hand played through her hair, which he'd spread across the opposite breast. And then with his open palm, he rubbed her nipple with a gently abrading rhythm which left her whimpering.

Elise moaned at the sensations which rippled through her. Soft, eager vibrations which left her aching for more. Her hands slid down his back, feeling the solid sleekness of his muscles there. She stroked the curve of his spine and shaped the firm muscles of his buttocks as the restless ache inside her built and built until she wanted to cry out. Perhaps she did, for through the haze of desire, she heard Christian gently shushing her.

He was kissing her, soothing her all over with his mouth. And then he rolled to one side and slid his hand down her belly, and lower, until his fingers found the damp place between her legs. With gentle but demanding pressure, he forced her thighs apart and let his thumb slide into the folds of her flesh until she gasped and arched upward with her breasts. His lips closed over hers as he shoved his fingers inside her body. He thrust his tongue deep into her mouth in rhythm with his fingers until Elise was left thrashing and whimpering.

And then he feathered kisses between her breasts and down her belly, pausing to probe her navel with the hot tip of his tongue. "Shall I?" His whisper was suggestive.

Elise let her head roll back into the pillow. "What?" she demanded, the words choking in her throat. "Oh, what . . . ?"

She sensed him lifting his head, felt the hot burn of his eyes on her face. "Tell me," he demanded. "Tell me what you want, Elise."

"I don't know. Just . . ."

She heard him chuckle softly in the darkness. "Mmm, this?" he murmured, sliding his tongue from her navel and into her thatch of curls. "Tell me, Elise."

She was drowning in sensation. "I—yes, I want, I want . . . oh, I don't *know.*"

And then, very gently, he stroked his tongue against the place his fingers had aroused, making her suck in her breath sharply.

"Oh. *Ohhh.*" She could find no other words.

"You like that?" His voice was rough and thick.

She could not answer, and he did not wait. He shoved her legs wider, shoved her knees up until his hands could slide beneath her thighs, until her most secret parts were fully exposed. And then he buried his tongue deep into her flesh. Her eyes flew wide at the incredible sensation. His tongue licked and teased, sliding through her warmth until her breathing became erratic. Her hands fisted in the sheet beneath them, and still he stroked. Her body was trembling now. Oh, she *yearned* for something. Yearned to arch her hips closer to his mouth. But when she tried, his strong hands forced her hips roughly against the mattress.

Every touch of his tongue sent a shuddering madness through her body, and Elise began to gasp and gasp for breath. He sucked the hard nub between his lips, and she gave a little scream. The pleasure was too much. Her hands came down to stay his. "No, Elise," he whispered. "Just let me. Just let me pleasure you in this way. Let it come, love, let it. I will make it good for you, I swear."

He touched her again, the pressure of his tongue a sweet, searching circle, and Elise lost control, her ordinary world splintering in a kaleidoscope of lamplight and colors. She reached out for him, and felt Christian drag her into his arms.

Long moments later, Elise came back to awareness, only to realize that she had dozed, but for how long, she did not know. She lay on her side, and he had nestled himself against her back. The remnants of a dream fell away, some gauzy memory of lying in a warm pool of water with the sun hot on her flesh. The warm, familiar smell of Christian's body enveloped her, and for a moment she felt secure and happy. And then the aching sense of grief was back, reminding her that loss was imminent. But on its heels came an almost feverish desire to celebrate what was left. To savor the moment and this man who had come so fleetingly into her life.

Christian was awake, too. Very much awake. She could feel the hard, warm length of his arousal pressed against her buttocks and the strength of his chest against her shoulder blades. "*Mmmm*," he said, his lips pressed to her neck. "You are back from Nirvana?"

She gave a sleepy laugh. "No," she mumbled into the pillow. "I am lost, Christian. Lost forever."

"Come back," he demanded, dragging her hips hard into his. "I have need of you." And then he was kissing her neck, suckling her earlobe. She could not see his face, and in her drowsy condition, it was like surrendering to some nocturnal fantasy. Fantasies she had always shut away and refused to acknowledge. But this one would not be refused. And she was not, apparently, quite sated. Instinctively, her hips arched backward.

His arm curled over her waist, and his hand slid down her stomach, his palm warm against her skin as he pressed her into him. "*Ahhh*," she heard herself moan. As the hardness rubbed her, a dark warmth began to flow through her, weighing down her limbs, rekindling that simmering urge until it became an almost tangible need. Suddenly, she felt his erection probing insistently between her buttocks.

"Christian?" The word was a thready whisper.

He answered with a low growl against the nape of her neck. "Open, love," he demanded. "Open for me. Lift your leg."

Obediently, she did as he commanded, and on another subtle move, the hard weight of his penis forced its way between her thighs. For long moments, he let himself slide back and forth through the slick, wet heat of her desire. "Ahh," he breathed. "Ah, Elise. Yes."

She reached down to touch him where he moved, but his hand slid from her belly to cover her fingers, dragging them away from his hardness. Firmly, he pressed her fingertips against her own flesh, encouraging her to rub and circle. It felt wicked. And good. Oh, so very, very good. Like a cat being stroked, she arched her back, her hips instinctively writhing against him.

It was, it seemed, just what he wanted. On a guttural sound, he shifted his pelvis and drove himself into her. Elise moaned from the shock of it, holding herself perfectly still as he pushed deeper and deeper into her still-wet sheath, stretching her almost beyond bearing.

"Ahhh, God almighty—!" she heard him grunt, his mouth pressed against her neck. "God. Elise. Are you all right?"

Very tentatively, she rolled her hips backward. Yes, she was very much all right. It felt strange but wonderful to have him buried so deeply inside her. And then, his hand slid beneath hers, his impatient fingers searching for the swollen nub of her sex, to do for her what she was not yet ready to do for herself. With a practiced hand, he touched her, and she gasped. Then, with a moan, Christian sank his teeth into the tender flesh of her neck and rocked his hips.

At once, Elise understood, and gave him what he demanded. For long moments, they moved in perfect harmony with one another, her hips rolling, taking him deep as he teased her with his fingers. The mounting urge possessed her. The rhythm moved through them, his into hers, building and building, until Elise was gasping in tempo with his thrusts. The soft sounds filled the darkness, and Christian began to drive harder and deeper.

His urgency was like a flame to tinder, and soon she was sobbing and struggling, whimpering his name as she fought for release. She could feel the heat of his sweat against her back, could hear the raw need in each breath as the air heaved in and out of his lungs. And then she was beyond waiting, beyond thinking. Her entire body went rigid, her every muscle pulsing as she came. It pushed Christian over the edge, and he shoved himself home on one final thrust. She could feel him throbbing deep inside her, could feel the warm flood of his seed pouring into her. Could feel herself falling deeper and deeper in love. With this man who was going to leave her.

Afterward, they drowsed, Christian still inside her. And then she felt his fingers playing through her hair, combing it across his pillow. "Elise," he said sadly. "It is time."

Elise pretended to be asleep, but he was not fooled. He eased his palm up and down the softness of her belly. "Tell me, Elise," he whispered. "When I am gone, and our lovemaking fades from your memory, do you think you will find it in your heart to forgive me?"

She came fully awake at that, stiffening in his embrace. "Forgive you?"

His lips brushed the nape of her neck. "For using you, I mean. To antagonize Roth."

She rolled a little away from him, and came up on her elbows, instinctively grasping the sheet and drawing it up to cover her breasts. "I was not—" she awkwardly began. "I never thought that . . ."

She could feel the blood draining from her face. Christian shoved back the pillow and sat up. "Elise?"

"Oh—!" She closed her eyes and shook her head, pressing her lips together for a moment. "Is that what you were doing, Christian?" she asked softly.

"Oh, God." His voice was weak.

Elise opened her eyes and forced a faint smile. "I suppose that I never considered myself Denys's possession," she admitted, her voice tight. "It never even occurred to me that I was being used. And if you were using me, I fell in love with you despite it. Are you laughing at me, Christian? That is how naïve I am."

Christian spun about to sit on the edge of the bed. "Naïve, Elise?" he asked, propping his elbows on his knees and staring once again into the carpet. "Yes, I suppose you are. And I took advantage of that. Now you have little cause to mourn my going. At least you can see me for what I am. I use people, Elise. And I do it very, very well."

"Yes," she answered. "You do."

His shoulders seemed to slump farther. "And so I will

consider your words of love undone, Elise," he said quietly. "I restore them to you, as if they were never spoken. That is my parting gift to you, precious little though it may be."

She laughed a little bitterly. "Then you are the naïve one, Christian, if you believe that love is a gift one can simply return," she answered. "Or worse, that it can be simply whisked away when it becomes emotionally inconvenient." Then Elise rose from the bed as soundless as a wraith, and began to pull on her nightclothes.

God, what a night it had been, Christian thought, as he watched her dress in the faint lamplight. He prayed he would never have another like it. And he prayed he would never forget it. Wordlessly, he drew the sight of her into him through his eyes and held it close to his heart with an invisible strength. It was another of those otherworldly moments, much like the one he'd experienced while warming her hands in that ramshackle inn. It was as if he watched her through a gossamer veil spun of almosts and maybes. A window onto what might have been; one which opened for him only in Elise's presence.

And then she secured the tie on her wrapper, and the moment was gone. "Elise," he said, scarcely recognizing his own voice. "You are not one of those foolish women who will turn up behind a tree or come charging into the midst of this mess, are you?"

"No, Christian." She smiled faintly. "I am not one of those foolish women."

"You will not come?" He jerked to his feet and clasped her tight against him. "Good God, promise me you will not."

"I promise," she said quietly. "Because I will not likely see you again, Christian. And so I would prefer to remember you as you are tonight; beautiful, naked, and strong in your convictions about right and wrong."

He pushed her away and let his eyes drift over her face for a long, uncertain moment. "Elise," he began abruptly. "You could, you know, come with me. To France, I mean. Both you and Henriette."

The smile came again, fainter still. "I cannot, Christian. I cannot do that to a child who so recently lost a parent. She needs familiar surroundings, and a sense of normalcy. And in your world—the sort of life you're going back to—you would soon grow weary of us."

He would not. He knew it, but his saying so would do neither of them any good now. And so he returned her faint smile, and lifted her hand to his lips, watching her carefully as he did so. He knew her well enough now to realize that Elise was on the verge of saying something. He could see her, carefully weighing her words, and he wanted desperately to know what was on her mind; yearned to hear some sliver of he knew not what in her voice.

He was still holding her hand when she spoke. "I have a proposal for you, Christian," she finally said. "Let us do this your way; coldly and calculatingly. We will cut a deal with the devil. If you will withdraw your challenge, I will become your mistress. Unless you have no further need of me now that your quarrel with Denys has been provoked—"

"It is not just that, Elise!" he growled, his fingers digging into her wrist. "If it ever was, it isn't now. You know that. Tell me you do."

Elise lifted her shoulders. "Does it matter?" she asked softly. "I am willing to be your lover. And I will not hide it, Christian. I will do it publicly."

"Elise," he said sadly. "You know you do not mean that. And even if you did, as you say, you must think of Henriette."

"Perhaps I am, Christian," she said quietly. "Perhaps I am."

Vehemently, he shook his head. "Society will not consider me the sort of man a child of tender years ought to be exposed to."

Elise turned slowly from the door to face him. "Would they not?" she answered a little sadly. "And yet I wonder, my lord, what your sister would say to that?"

He looked at her, unable to form a coherent answer. Unable to comprehend the strange mix of rage and longing which was beginning to roil up inside him. He felt the hot press of tears behind his eyes, and knew that if he spoke, it would be to curse her and to damn her and to plead with her to stay with him forever.

But it seemed that Elise did not expect him to answer. Within infinite weariness, she laid her hand on the brass doorknob, and gave him one last look over her shoulder. "I will be waiting, my lord," she said very quietly. "I will be waiting, should you change your mind." And then the door clicked softly shut behind her.

Chapter Twelve

✢

Hold then my sword, and turn away thy face, while I do run upon it.
—Dryden

The sun began its climb over the orchard in a band of crimson, burning off the morning's fog as it came. The day had dawned bitterly cold, bringing with it a sharp wind which skirled through the trees and stirred up the scents of damp earth and rotting apples. In a distant barnyard, a cock crowed just as a curricle spun through the orchard gate, churning up a wake of red and gold leaves. It was the surgeon, Christian guessed. A black leather valise sat at his feet, and his posture seemed rigid with disapproval, as if the fellow had no intention of climbing down unless blood was spilt.

Christian shrugged and turned his attention to Major Onslow and Lord Treyhern, who were seeing to the inspection and loading of the weapons. As he watched, Christian felt a familiar ice-cold calm settle over him. But this time, a heavy sense of hopelessness came with it, and he did not know why. Or perhaps he did. But no matter the cause, he told himself, he was doing what had to be done. Still, the apathy weighed down his mind and his limbs like a warm, wet blanket. Christian struggled to throw it off, just as he had done this morning while Stallings shaved him. Just as he had done while dressing. And when he took up his rosewood box to stride through the fields of Gotherington. But then, as now, the feeling simply would not go away.

Perhaps, as his valet had so sagely pointed out, what troubled him was simply the fact that this was his very first challenge. Oh, Christian had been slapped with a glove more times that he cared to count—cuckolded husbands and bested cardsharps were the rashest men alive—but never had he cared enough about anything to throw down the gauntlet himself. Not until now. And so this duel, the one which he had deliberately sought and meticulously plotted, should have mattered more than any which had gone before. This one was about honor and vengeance, not wounded pride.

He was recalled from his wanderings by Major Onslow, who sharply cleared his throat. Christian turned to look at him, and wished at once that he had not. He could have scarcely imagined that Onslow had any color left to lose, but today the major looked like the walking dead.

Too late, Christian realized that the poor devil no doubt feared that his home would be well and truly lost to him should Roth triumph. But Christian would not lose. And regardless of the outcome, Onslow would soon have nothing—not even his unwelcome houseguest—to fret over. The solicitor's tidy document lay signed and sealed upon Christian's escritoire, even as Stallings loaded their carriage. And as soon as Christian dispatched Denys Roth into the great beyond, he was bound for Southampton, and the first vessel leaving port. He would be relieved, Christian told himself, to have this business—*all* of it—over and done with. The familiarity of his empty mansion in the Rue de Berri, the tedium of his everyday life and its almost amazing vacuity—yes, the sheer normalcy of all that nothingness would at least be reassuring.

At last, Onslow gave the signal, and Christian stepped forward. The breeze picked up again, whipping at the folds of the major's cravat. They turned to watch Treyhern approach Roth.

"Sir, it is my duty to ask you again if you wish to apologize," Treyhern advised, his expression grim.

Fleetingly, Roth hesitated.

Suddenly, it seemed as if the wind died away to nothing. A protracted silence held sway over the orchard, as if even the gnarled trees were bowing over them in anticipation of their next breath. As if time had suddenly stopped. And then the cock crowed again, splintering the hush, forcing Christian to realize that his eyes were closed, and that he was fervently praying for Roth's capitulation.

He was instantly appalled. Damn such indecision! And damn Elise Middleton, too. This was at least half her fault. He had come here knowing what must be done and bloody eager for the doing of it. And now? Now his perfect moral certainty was riddled with doubts. His clear path forward had been half-obscured by her words—words which now began to echo in his head, sometimes even spoken in his dead sister's voice. It was beginning to seem to Christian that he had been half-bewitched since the day he'd met that virtuous vicar's daughter with her prim smile, her high-minded principles, and her naïve blue eyes.

"I shall not," Roth managed weakly. "I shall not apologize."

God. Oh, God. Christian blew out his breath sharply and, acting purely on instinct, stripped off his coat and hurled it aside. Then someone's hand was on his shoulder, turning him and pushing him back a pace. Christian blinked, and realized it was Lord Treyhern. The earl was drawing one barrel to full cock, and pressing the checkered butt of the weapon into Christian's hand. He grasped it, struggled to balance it levelly as his mind whirled.

Oh, God. Attention. Pay *attention.*

But something felt terribly wrong. Not fear. It was . . . *what—?*

Treyhern's faint shadow fell between them. "Two shots, gentlemen," intoned the earl solemnly. "On my mark."

And then Treyhern was counting, counting, counting. The rest of it happened as it always did, in flawlessly choreographed slow motion. Christian completed his turn a split second before Roth. He lifted his weapon. Drew an unwavering bead on Roth's heart. Watched Roth's arm come up. Watched him fumble with the trigger. Saw his face go ashen.

And still Christian did not fire.

Oh, God!

He could not. *He could not.*

So rare and unpredictable were his honorable intentions, Christian did not precisely comprehend them until the very instant the impotent *snap!* of Roth's cock spiked the silence. The hesitation should have cost him his life. But Christian saw . . . nothing. No flash. No spark. Good Lord, a *misfire—*?

But a misfire was as good as a shot. By rights, the next was Christian's. And at last, he knew the right thing. The only thing. With a swift, sudden conviction, he thrust his weapon heavenward and jerked the trigger home. The roar deafened him. The recoil rammed his wrist straight down, almost into his shoulder. A burst of smoke, hot and acrid, settled about his head. Then the ringing in his ears receded. And it was over.

Or perhaps not.

"Lower your bloody weapon!" Treyhern was bellowing. "He has deloped, you fool! He has yielded!"

And then, it was as if the hand of God had reached down and hurled Christian to the ground. The breath exploded from his lungs on a roar. A hot, sharp blade twisted in his shoulder, goring deep into his belly like some venomous snake. There was an awful warmth across his chest. Trickling into his armpit. Tumultuous voices and thundering footsteps came at him as if from a great distance.

"A pistol!" he heard Treyhern roar. "Give me a pistol! I mean to kill that goddamned cheating bastard!"

And then someone fell to his knees in the stiff orchard grass beside Christian. Fingers tugged at his waistcoat. Fabric ripped. Cold air. Colder hands. The metallic stench of fresh blood.

"Grayston," someone mumbled, but they were under water. Christian could see Major Onslow floating with him. Floating far, far away. "It is . . . clean wound," said the watery voice. "Breathe shallowly and . . . fine. Just fine."

* * *

Elise hovered at the parlor window, staring out into the broad expanse of Gotherington's front lawn as the surgeon's curricle spun down the carriageway at last. Fingertips pressed to the glass, she closed her eyes and let her forehead rest against one of the panes. It was cold against her skin, and it felt as though the chill helped to clear her jumbled thoughts. *He had come back. He had not killed Denys. He would be all right.* The words kept spinning in her head.

She had not seen him at all since leaving his bed last night. This morning, she had gone at once to the schoolroom to have breakfast with the children, in some faint hope that they would lift her spirits. And she had been there, lingering over another of Henriette's charcoals, when the commotion began. But no one had come to fetch her—indeed, why would they have thought to do so?—and so she had known nothing at all of what had happened until Ophelia's ear-splitting screams went ricocheting through the house.

Elise had flown down the stairs to the salon, where she had found Ophelia spread out in a near-faint on the red and gold divan, her dresser and her downstairs parlor maid madly fanning her face while Belinda and Lucinda argued over the hartshorn. "Oh, my God!" wailed Ophelia, one hand clamped over her eyes. "He'll surely die! Right here at Gotherington! Oh, Lud, the scandal! The scandal! We shall never survive it!"

And finally, Elise got it out of them. Christian. They had carried him in, still as death, his shirt soaked in blood. It had taken her the better part of ten minutes to wrench the details from Maynard. Between patting at his sweat-beaded forehead with his handkerchief and clutching Ophelia's clinging, white-knuckled hand, Maynard explained the full extent of Denys's treachery. The ball had gone through Christian's shoulder and out again. But he would live. *He would live.* Still, it was apparent even to Elise that only Maynard's experience in stanching battlefield injuries had stood between Christian and probable death.

When the major finished his story, Ophelia fell back onto the divan again, clasping both hands to her heart and heaving her impressive bosom as if hyperventilating. "Oh, Maynard, we shall never live down the notoriety!" she wailed between heaves. "A duel right here at Gotherington! A prominent member of the peerage—*a viscount!*—shot nearly dead at my ancestral home! And by a scoundrel! A scoundrel who played upon our trust and took us all in with his pretty face! It is too much to be borne!"

Maynard patted her hand yet again. "Oh, just relax and try to enjoy it, Ophelia," he murmured. "Grayston isn't apt to expire of his wound, but he has come close enough to put you on every guest list next Season."

Ophelia made a weak effort at lifting her head. "Oh, Maynard!" she said miserably. "I cannot think what you mean!"

But the major remained sanguine. "Oh, everyone will wish to hear this tale," he predicted. Then with a rueful smile, Maynard cut a knowing glance in Elise's direction. "Besides, my love, I'm not at all sure we have reached the dénouement. There may be even richer gossip yet to come, and there is nothing like firsthand tittle-tattle to spice up a dull London drawing—"

He was cut off by a racket on the stairs. A trunk and a bandbox were being hastily carried down, the first in a veritable downpour of baggage. Lord Treyhern's carriage was being brought around, and in short order, a bruised and limping Denys Roth was being shoved bodily inside it by the earl himself, whose usual stern expression had quite surpassed murderous. Treyhern returned to the salon to announce that Roth had been called—quite suddenly and most permanently—to India. He had gritted out the words, made a perfunctory bow to the ladies, then thundered back up the stairs.

Elise had gone at once to the quiet of the family parlor. She had needed to escape the inane racket of the salon. She had needed to think. But it now seemed as if she had been waiting hours for the doctor to leave, and for a hush to fall over the house. And then, just as his curricle vanished around the first turn, the squeak of a hinge brought her around.

Pratt, the butler, carried in a huge tea tray and gently set it down. "My lady," he said with mild reproach, "you missed your luncheon."

But Elise had no appetite. She thanked him warmly, and Pratt bowed his way out. Elise turned back to the window. She did not want tea. She wanted Christian. She needed to see him, needed to reassure herself that he really would recover. And she had to know how things stood between them. In that darkest hour just before dawn, she had wished a thousand times that she had agreed to run away with him to France. She had had to fight the urge to do what she had promised she would not—rush heedlessly into the fray in order to fling herself at his feet, and in the process, quite possibly make matters worse. But it now seemed matters could not get much worse. And if Christian did recover—if they truly were not lying to her—would he still want her? Had he ever really wanted her? He had begun his flirtation with her, or so he had said, simply to make Denys jealous. One part of her brain kept reminding her of that.

But the other part kept remembering that night in the inn, and many of the nights after. That first awful evening, Christian had not known her name, and yet he had invited her to share the bed with him. And she had been tempted. Oh, so tempted. Yes, there was a deep and undeniable attraction between them, despite the terrible thing that he had come here to do. He wanted her for his mistress, he had said. She hoped—oh, how she hoped—that he still did. Maynard's recitation of what had occurred in the orchard at dawn had proven what Elise had long suspected. Christian was a decent man. Far more so than he wished people—perhaps even himself—to believe. There was an honor in him which ran deep; not just the pretty façade of chivalry which so many men put on when it suited them to do so, but a truth which need never be spoken of.

And yet he was not the type of man one married. Was that not just what she had said to Henriette? At the time, she had wanted to believe it. And it really did not matter. It was enough that Christian found her desirable. It would have to be enough. He had said nothing to her of marriage, not even when he had invited her to run away with him to France. He did not want a wife.

But surely there was something left of last night's spark, something that they might kindle anew between them? She hoped so. And she was going to ask him. She was going to steel her nerve and plainly ask him. Because until she did so, until she heard the answer from his lips, she was not perfectly sure she could continue to breathe. And now the doctor had gone for the day, and Elise's questions could no longer wait. She had to go to him, at least to hold his hand while he slept, if nothing more. Of course, it would not be at all proper. And she was not at all sure she cared. She was in just the right mood to do something terribly improper. Her mind resolved, Elise pulled the draperies against the chilly air and turned resolutely from the window.

But then the door hinges squeaked again, and when she looked up, there he was, standing in his shirtsleeves with his injured shoulder propped weakly against the door frame, the other arm raised high, bracing his long, lean body against the lintel. He looked haggard and disreputable and dashing all at the same time. And almost frighteningly wan and weak.

"Have you enough tea for two?" he rasped, tilting his head toward the table.

Elise hastened forward to help him into a chair. "Really, my lord!" she said in a nervous rush. "One does not treat a gunshot wound with tea! I am quite sure they did not give you leave to be out of bed!"

He managed to cock one eyebrow arrogantly. "Lord, are you really going to scold me, Elise?" he murmured as he sat down. "I almost met my Maker this morning, in case you'd not heard. It will be a bit of a trick to further intimidate me today."

Elise sat down then, or perhaps it was more honest to say that her legs gave way. She landed on the settee gracelessly, crushing her skirts and petticoats. To cover her nervousness, she fell back on the training which had been instilled since girlhood. She threw her shoulders back and began to pour, keeping her eyes on the stream of steaming liquid, and well away from his silvery gaze, suddenly certain that if she looked at him, those enthralling eyes might compel her to say or do something unutterably foolish.

"I recall you take no milk or sugar," she managed to say, passing the cup with an unsteady hand. It teetered erratically over the table, but Christian did not move to take it. Not knowing what else to do, she simply held it there, the cup chattering perilously on the saucer.

And then she made the mistake. The mistake of looking into his eyes. "Elise," he said quietly. "Oh, Elise."

She set down the cup with an awful splash, and let her face fall forward into her hands. But it was too late. Her shoulders were shaking, and he had already seen the tears which were flooding forth. She did not hear him leave his chair, did not realize he'd sat down beside her. But she felt his good arm come around her, still secure and strong. "Oh, Elise," he said again. "Oh, my love, you do not want me. You really do not."

An awful sob shuddered through her. "I d-did not say I wanted you."

Bowing his head, Christian pressed his lips to her temple. "Remind me, my love, never to let you play at cards," he murmured. "You could not hide a good hand to save your very soul. But trust me, my dear, you do not want me. Throw me out, Elise, and be well rid of a bad bargain."

She refused to lift up her head. "I th-thought—by

now you—you'd be g-gone," she choked between snuffles. "Or worse—that you would be d-dead! So do not presume to t-tell me what I ought to do."

He slid his hand beneath her chin, and forced her head up. And then Christian was kissing her tears away and rubbing his cheek over hers. *"Shhh,* love, hush," he soothed. "I will not presume. I will wait for you to tell me."

Elise dashed one hand beneath her eye. "Well, I do w-want you, Christian," she admitted, struggling to sound brave.

He slid one finger around a loose lock of her hair and tucked it behind her ear. "Oh, Elise, I am nothing but trouble." His voice was tender as he searched her face with his eyes. "I am considered a rogue, a rake, and a rascal on at least two continents. And what's worse, I no longer seem able even to shoot straight. Someone will call me out, and you'll be a widow again before you're thirty."

Because her outrage suddenly overcame her fear, she did not fully absorb the last words. "Oh, stop it, Christian," she whispered. "Just stop it. *Your* opinion of *you* is the only one which concerns me."

He shook his head as if mystified. "Elise, you have always said you were naïve."

He bent to brush his lips over hers, but she pushed him away, unwilling to be quieted. "And besides that, you did not even try to kill Denys!" she said. "Maynard said that you deloped!"

He flashed her his wicked grin and bent his head closer. "What, did I misunderstand you, my love?" he whispered, brushing his lips over the turn of her ear.

"Did you wish the scoundrel dead after all? You need but say the word, and if Amherst will drive me, I can disembowel him with my good arm ere he reaches the coast."

"Oh, Christian, will you be serious!" She drew back with a chiding frown. "You *let* him live. You showed him more mercy than he deserved."

"Ah," said Christian, the wicked grin melting into something altogether different. "And for that single honorable act, you believe me to be redeemed? You think that I am worthy of you? But Elise, I am not. We are two entirely different sorts of people, you and I."

"You are worthy," she said certainly. "And I love you."

He smiled and shook his head. There was a new anguish in his eyes. "Perhaps you love how I make you feel in bed, Elise?" he said softly. "Perhaps that is new to you. But there are a thousand other fellows who can do—"

She cut him off with a shake of her head. "I do not want one of those thousand other fellows," she said softly. "I think I must have danced with every blasted one of them during the Season, and they never made me feel shivery or quivery all over."

"I beg your pardon," he said. "Did you say *shivery*—?"

"And so I want *you*," Elise interrupted. "You asked me what I wanted, and there it is, and you may tease me and call me a fool if you wish, which I daresay you will, because you always do. But I love you, and I do not care if you do not love me back in that precise way. You desire me, and you especially love the look on my face when I ring a peal over your head. And as you yourself said, *that* should count for *something*, shouldn't it?"

And then he was kissing her again. "Oh, Elise, Elise,

you goose," he murmured, sliding off the settee and onto his knees before her. "Elise, oh, how I love you! Will you do it, then? Will you be a fool for me at least once more? Will you and Henriette throw in your lot with mine, and come with me to Hollywell?"

She sat stiffly, still blinking as if tears threatened. "You . . . *what?*"

"To Hollywell, Elise," he repeated, giving her fingers a little squeeze. "It is my home. My seat. I must spend at least a part of the year there if I mean to take up the mantle of respectability and become a serious-minded English gentleman with sheep and corn and tenants and whatever other dull thing gentlemen seem required to worry their minds with. Do you think Treyhern would give me lessons?"

But Elise was still shaking her head and eyeing him narrowly. "Now that first part, Christian," she said slowly. "That is what I did not perfectly hear."

Despite the hindrance of the sling, Christian rose and gathered her against him. He looked down at her, his glittering gaze suddenly as soft as morning fog. "I love you, Elise. Will you marry me?"

"Yes!" she said, burying her face against his neck. "Yes, and yes. When, Christian? Let us not wait. Oh, I cannot wait."

That put an arch back in his eyebrow. "The banns will take a little time, love," he laughed. "But you will remember, my dear, what I said about putting a horse through all his paces before you bid?"

Elise lifted her head, her brows drawn together. "Yes—?"

"Perhaps this old stallion has a gait or two you've not

yet tried?" And then, completely forgetting his crippled state, Christian eased Elise back down onto the settee, knocking askew the tea tray in his haste. A hailstorm of silverware and saucers went clattering to the floor, but Elise, her ladylike poise already cast to the wind, just ignored it.

POCKET BOOKS
PROUDLY PRESENTS

No True Gentleman

Liz Carlyle

Available July 2002
from
Pocket Books

Turn the page for a preview of
No True Gentleman. . . .

Be easy, even forward, in making new acquaintances.

—Lord Chesterfield, 1776,
The Fine Gentleman's Etiquette

De Rohan approached Hyde Park via Constitution Hill, then took the footpath which ran west above the Serpentine. At this hour, the park was all but empty. A few moments of brisk walking took him well beyond the most public areas of the park, toward the paths more often frequented by those who wished to put their horses through their paces and by those who desired privacy. It was the latter who most interested de Rohan, and for the first time in a fortnight, it seemed he might be in luck. As he quietly approached the place where the path ran through a clump of rhododendron—the very one in which he'd seen the woman the previous day—he heard the low murmur of voices. Male voices—one almost imperceptibly edged with Cockney, the other a low, hard growl, followed by a cynical, familiar laugh.

At last! They had been working on this police corruption case for months. With a calm sense of certainty, de Rohan circled around so that he might approach at a point rather less obvious. By God, he'd nearly sell his soul to the devil if he could just get a good look at the both of them. Better still would be an opportunity to watch money change hands. It would be proof of his suspicions. And he would make a most credible witness.

The exhilaration thrummed through his blood. But halfway through the knot of high shrubs, he realized he was not alone. Farther along the path was a bench, tucked neatly into a roughly sculpted niche. On it sat a woman—damn it, *the* woman. She was reading a bloody book! De Rohan felt a moment of alarm. It worsened when the voices suddenly rose. Through a thinning veil of greenery, he saw the woman jerk to her feet. Had she heard him? Or the bribery which was occurring not a stone's throw past her shoulder?

His greater fear was confirmed when he rounded the corner. She was not looking at him. Instead, her head was cocked to one side, and she was staring in the direction of the murmurs. Murmurs which now seemed to be moving nearer . . .

Disconcerted, de Rohan set a foot wrong, and the gravel shifted noisily beneath his shoe.

With a soft, startled cry, the woman dropped her book and spun toward him, her dark red skirts whirling about her ankles. A broad-brimmed hat with a long red plume helped obscure her identity—but not from him.

"Wot the 'ell?" came the Cockney voice from the other side of the bushes.

Her hand flew to her lips, and she opened her mouth as if to speak. But heavy footsteps were striding toward them. So de Rohan did the quickest—and the stupidest—thing he could think of. What he'd burned to do for the last seven days. In one swift motion, he dragged the woman hard against his chest, spun toward the shadows, and covered her mouth with his.

Catherine had meant to scream. She really had. Right up until the instant that the square yard of rock-solid chest thudded against hers, sending her bonnet askew and melting her knees to jelly. But instead, she hesitated. This despite the fact that the dark stranger had jerked her into his arms and was forcing her deeper into the shrubbery. In that moment's hesitation, his mouth came down hard over hers, hot and demanding, urging her lips apart. With one arm banded tight about her waist and his fingers curled into her hair, the man drew her to him in a crush of red merino and cascading brown hair.

"For God's sake, kiss me," he hissed, barely lifting his mouth from hers.

Catherine gave a small, indignant gasp, but her good intentions exploded into flame when he seized the moment, sliding his insistent tongue inside her mouth. Desperate, it seemed. Quite inexplicably, she answered. He kissed her more deeply, with the expertise of a man who knew women well. Though his touch was gentle, he held her with a violent intensity. As if he were truly afraid to let her go. His male heat and extraordinary scent filled her nostrils. Her heart pounded in her ears. The men arguing in the bushes were but a vague memory. Dizzy with confusion, Catherine barely heard their footsteps on the graveled path behind her.

"Christ!" murmured a disgusted male voice. "A friggin' lovers' tryst!"

Catherine should have screamed for help, struggled harder in his arms, exploded with rage. Oh, yes—*should* have. But the man jerked his head up like a startled animal. His dark gaze held hers, commanding her silence. Over his shoulder, he spoke, his words harsh, angry barks. *"Go. Away. Now."*

The warning was meant, Catherine knew, for the men on the path. Clearly, he'd not realized that their footsteps were already retreating. For a long moment, the stranger's hard mouth lingered over hers, his eyes still black but no longer cold. He dipped his head again, an awkward, uncertain motion, and Catherine didn't make a sound. But slowly—quite reluctantly, it seemed—he stopped and stepped away, his gaze falling to a spot somewhere near her boots.

Absent the strength of his arms, Catherine's knees began to buckle. Unsteadily, she thrust out her hand to touch the edge of the bench, and his gaze flicked up in mild alarm. At once, a strong, steadying hand slid beneath her elbow.

"I daresay you'd like to backhand me for that," he

said, his voice low and thick, his unusual accent more pronounced.

"Sh-should I?" she managed to ask as he drew her just a little nearer.

"Slap me?" His mouth quirked into an uncertain smile. "Yes, soundly." But he was as shaken as she. Catherine could hear the merest hint of it in his deep, raspy voice. But his eyes were as steady as his grip.

Strangely, she had no wish to strike out at him. Instead, she forced a smile. "Did you enjoy it enough to make it worth a good wallop, then?" she asked, tilting her head to one side to study him. "I've a rather strong right arm, you know."

The man cut a quick glance away. "Oh, I enjoyed it," he admitted, his voice rueful. "Enough to be drawn and quartered, instead of merely knocked senseless."

Catherine started to laugh, but it faltered. Good heavens. This wasn't funny. It was . . . she didn't know what it was. But she knew his hand beneath her elbow was warm and strong.

"Tell me your name," she softly commanded, stepping slightly away from him. "Don't just tip your hat and walk off again."

As his fingers slid away, his expression seemed to harden, and he said nothing.

"You've taken some rather blatant liberties with me," she reminded him, thrusting out her right hand. "So perhaps we should be introduced? I'm Lady Catherine Wodeway."

Reluctantly, he took the proffered hand and, instead of shaking it, bowed elegantly over it. "De Rohan," he responded, his tone quite formal. "Maximilian de Rohan."

Catherine did not immediately draw her hand from his. "You were trying to hide me from those men, were you not?"

Surprise lit his eyes, then vanished so quickly she might have imagined it. He was, she thought, a man who was rarely surprised by anything. "They did sound as if they might be unsavory characters, didn't they?" he lightly agreed, bending down to pick up her book and his walking stick.

Catherine did laugh then. "Oh, come now, Mr. de Rohan!" she said as he pressed the book back into her hands. "Do I look such a fool as that? Why don't you tell me what you're up to?"

De Rohan felt himself bristle at the woman's persistence. She—*Lady Catherine Wodeway*—had no more business being involved in his affairs than he had in knowing her name. Still, he did know it. He'd learned a vast deal more than that, in fact. But she was right, damn it. He had taken liberties—abominable liberties—with her person. The fact that she had not strenuously objected did not obviate her right to an explanation.

"I am with the police," he finally answered. "And those were the sort of men who often discuss matters which they do not care to have overheard. By anyone."

"Oh." Lady Catherine's color drained. "I begin to comprehend."

For a moment, she stared down at the book she now held. It was, he noticed, a rather tattered copy of *The Female Speaker.* Unable to resist, and very much wishing to change the subject, he reached out and lightly touched it. "You are an admirer of Barbauld?" he asked, intrigued.

She looked up at him uncertainly. "Yes. No. I . . . oh, I don't know! I took it from my brother's library. I thought it might . . . oh, improve my mind—?"

"Why?" De Rohan lifted one brow and took her by the elbow again, as if to lead her from the shrubbery. "Does it need improving?"

Lady Catherine shook off his hand, her lips thinning in mild irritation. "Do not change the subject, sir. Tell me about those men. Do you know their names? You were waiting for them yesterday, were you not? That is why you warned me away. That is why you . . . you pulled me into the shadows and kissed me today, isn't it?"

Uncharacteristically, de Rohan hesitated. The woman was even more beautiful up close than at a distance. Her coloring was far warmer than that of most Englishwomen; her heavy hair and intelligent eyes were a perfectly matched shade of deep, rich mahogany. High cheekbones set off a jaw which was firm and elegant. A stubborn woman, he thought. But her mouth was wide and good-humored, and far too voluptuous to be considered beautiful. But then, de Rohan had never favored the delicate, bow-shaped look affected by most ladies of fashion.

"Yes," he finally responded. "Yes, that's why."

"The only reason—?"

De Rohan felt a spike of irritation. "The only reason what?"

"Why you kissed me," she persisted, her dark eyes relentless.

"I did not wish them to see your face," he gruffly explained. "Nor did I wish to be recognized, for that matter."

Lady Catherine cast him a skeptical glance. "Why do I wonder if you mightn't have managed it some other way?"

At that, he took her a little roughly by the elbow and hauled her away from the bench. He did not like being seen through so easily. "I have already apologized, madam, for my gauche, unconscionable behavior, so—"

"Actually, you haven't," she interjected, jerking to a halt again.

He released her arm, whirling about to stare at her incredulously.

"Apologized," she clarified, standing toe-to-toe to glare up at him. "You never did, you know."

"Then I *apologize!*" de Rohan growled. "Now, where, madam, is your mount?"

"Perhaps I walked?"

"You always ride." He snapped out the words without thinking.

"Do I?"

Lady Catherine ran a surprisingly steady gaze down his length, and de Rohan was shocked to realize that, despite his irritation, he rather liked her. She was a strong, capable sort of woman. And sensible, too, he thought. He had kissed her, and yet, instinctively, she'd known he meant her no harm. A more miss-ish sort would have flown up into the boughs just for the attention.

But now he had revealed a bit of his knowledge about her. What would she say if she knew how often he had waited for her? If she suspected for one moment the fanciful thoughts that went tripping through his head each time he watched her ride through the park? For a long moment, silence held sway in the shadows of the rhododendron.

Suddenly, she spoke, words tumbling from her mouth. "Mr. de Rohan, would you . . . or perhaps I should say that I . . . yes, strange as it sounds, I think that I should like to know you better. Would you care to—to perhaps become better acquainted? W-would you care to dine with me some evening?"

Dine with her?

De Rohan couldn't believe his ears. Couldn't believe his absurd reaction to her invitation. He would not allow himself to fall into that trap again. Of wanting what he was no longer destined to have. Of desiring, even briefly, someone who thought herself far above him. And whose values and motivations were undoubtedly quite different from his own. "I don't think you understood," he said harshly. "I am with the police."

Apparently, Lady Catherine did not take his point. "But surely that fact does not preclude you from accepting dinner invitations? From women who are grateful for having been rescued from—er—*unsavory* characters?"

De Rohan stared at her open countenance and bottomless brown eyes, hating the surge of renewed hope which coursed through him. Hating her for making him feel a moment of regret, an instant of doubt, about the choices he'd made. Perhaps, he abruptly decided, she was just a little too strong and capable. Most likely, she was just another bored society wife looking for some sycophant to ease her *ennui* between the sheets. There was a quick way to find out. "And is dinner all you require, Lady Catherine?" he asked, his voice seductively soft. "Or is there some other, more intimate sort of companionship you seek?"

"I beg your pardon?" Color flooded her face.

Ruthlessly, he pressed on. "In my experience, when a highborn lady asks a man like me to dine, she usually intends to indulge in something a little more decadent than a good meal and a fine bottle of wine."

The woman hadn't exaggerated about her strong right arm. But despite the warning, he failed to see it coming. The blow caught him square across the face, sending him reeling backward, one hand pressed to his mouth. Gracelessly, he stumbled, flailing backward with his walking stick and catching himself up against the edge of the bench. Good God, she hit like a man! More shoulder than wrist, more wrath than petulance. He looked down to see the smear of blood on the back of his hand, then he looked up to see the blazing visage of Lady

Catherine Wodeway staring at him across the narrow clearing.

"Here's some intimate companionship for you, Mr. de Rohan," she snapped, stalking off in a swish of red wool and hot temper. "Take that fancy stick of yours and go bugger yourself with it."

Return to
a time of romance...

**SONNET
BOOKS**

*Where today's
hottest romance authors
bring you vibrant
and vivid love stories
with a dash of history.*

PUBLISHED BY POCKET BOOKS